"Do you want to keep my pistol with you?"

"No, thanks, I have my own."

That surprised her. "Snakes in the big city, too?"

"The worst kind," Leif admitted. "The nutcases and grief-stricken family members who think I helped free a guilty defendant."

"I hadn't thought of that."

She stopped at her bedroom door, afraid she was a few heated breaths away from issuing the invitation to join her in her shower and in her bed. She needed a closed door between them, quick.

"Would you lock up once you get your gun?" she asked.

"You got it."

He leaned in close. One finger trailed a path from her forehead to her lips. Her defenses plummeted. Anticipation curled in her stomach, and wispy waves of heat knotted in her chest.

His mouth found hers and she melted.

UNREPENTANT COWBOY

BY
JOANNA WAYNE

MILLS & BOON

Joanna Wayne was born and raised in Shreveport, Louisiana, and received her undergraduate and graduate degrees from LSU Shreveport. She moved to New Orleans in 1984, and it was there that she attended her first writing class and joined her first professional writing organization. Her debut novel, *Deep in the Bayou,* was published in 1994.

Now, dozens of published books later, Joanna has made a name for herself as being on the cutting edge of romantic suspense in both series and single-title novels. She has been on the Waldenbooks bestseller list for romance and has won many industry awards. She is also a popular speaker at writing organizations and local community functions and has taught creative writing at the University of New Orleans Metropolitan College.

Joanna currently resides in a small community forty miles north of Houston, Texas, with her husband. Though she still has many family and emotional ties to Louisiana, she loves living in the Lone Star State. You may write Joanna at PO Box 852, Montgomery, Texas 77356, USA.

To my good friend Deedee, who always loves my
books, and to my own children and grandchildren,
who inspire me to write about loving families.
And a special thanks to my readers, who keep buying
my books year after year and still ask for more.
You keep my spirits up and make writing worthwhile
even when the going gets tough.

Chapter One

"We, the jury, find the defendant, Edward Blanco, not guilty on all counts in the murder of Evelyn Cox."

A synchronized gasp filled the courtroom accompanied by cries of horror and heartbreak from Evelyn's family. They knew that justice had not been served.

Members of the defense team pounded Leif Dalton on the back and reached for his hand. Edward Blanco flashed the same innocent smile he'd displayed for the jury through weeks of testimony. Only this time contempt for the trial and everyone connected with it burned in his ebony eyes.

Leif avoided eye contact as Blanco expressed his gratitude in gloating terms. Then Leif turned and managed a nod toward the judge and jury. The handshakes Leif exchanged with members of his defense team were forced and meaningless.

For the second time in his life, he was almost certain he'd helped a killer escape punishment and walk free to likely kill again—unless someone killed him first.

The prosecution hadn't had a chance. The evidence to convict Blanco simply hadn't been there. Everything their lead attorney fed the jury was strictly circumstantial, and that wasn't enough for jury members anymore.

They wanted the kind of proof they witnessed every week in countless TV police procedurals. They wanted a

DNA match. They wanted a killer who looked like a killer instead of the handsome, sophisticated man you'd choose for your own daughter to marry.

But he couldn't fault the jury for being fooled by Blanco. Leif had had his doubts about the man when the firm pressured him to take the case, but Blanco had quickly won him over. Throughout the trial Blanco had given an Oscarworthy performance.

Until two days ago when the final arguments had been made and the jury had gone into deliberation. Then, confident that he was going to walk from the courtroom a free man, Blanco had let one careless comment slip.

The comment was not an admission of guilt, but it was more than enough to convince Leif that not only was Blanco a psychopath capable of stalking and brutally murdering an innocent woman, but that he'd experienced no guilt afterward.

Leif had done his job. He'd argued his client's case honestly and effectively. He'd given Blanco what every citizen was guaranteed, the right to legal representation and a trial by jury.

Knowing that did nothing to alleviate the rumblings of guilt and remorse in the pit of his stomach.

"Let's go grab a drink," Chad encouraged. Chad was always the first one on his team ready to get down and party.

"Best whiskey in the house on me," another team member said. "Leif Dalton, still undefeated."

"I smell a promotion," Chad said as he offered another clap on the back.

Their enthusiasm failed to generate any gusto on Leif's part. "Sounds like fun, but I'm afraid you guys are going to have to celebrate without me."

"You're surely not going back to the office today. It's almost five o'clock."

"Plus, it's the Monday before Thanksgiving," Chad added. "Half the staff is on vacation."

"So am I, as of right now," Leif said. "But the trial was grueling. I'm beat."

"That sounds like code for you have a better offer," Morgan, one of the firms young law clerks, mocked.

A better offer. Damn. He was supposed to have dinner with Serena tonight.

"You caught me," he said, faking a grin and trying to think of a halfway decent excuse for getting out of his date with the ravishing runway star.

He should have ended his relationship with her weeks ago. It was going nowhere. Probably mostly his fault. Relationship problems usually were. But possessive women made him feel caged, and Serena was growing more possessive by the day.

They walked out of the courthouse and into the bruising gray of threatening thunderclouds. He ducked from the crowd to avoid the flash of media cameras and the reporters pushing microphones at him.

When he looked up he was face-to-face with Evelyn Cox's mother. She crucified him with her stare, then turned and stormed away without saying a word. He was tempted to run after her, but there wasn't one thing he could say that would make her feel any better or hate him any less. Her beloved thirty-two-year-old daughter, the mother of her two precious grandchildren, was dead and her killer was free.

When he reached his car, he called and left a message for Serena. She'd be pissed. He'd broken at least a dozen dates during the weeks he'd been working on the Blanco case.

Leif sat behind the wheel of his black Porsche, staring into space while the jagged shards of his life played havoc with his mind. He was only thirty-eight.

He'd accomplished every professional goal he'd set for

himself. His coworkers didn't know it yet, but the deal was already in the works. He'd be named partner in Dallas's most prestigious criminal defense law firm next month.

So why the hell was he fighting an overwhelming urge to start driving and not stop until Texas was so far behind him he couldn't even see it in his mind?

Finally, he started the engine and began the short drive to his downtown condominium. He flicked on the radio. A local talk show host was reporting on a woman's murder in a rural area just outside Dallas.

The victim's identity hadn't been released, but the body had been found by a hunter just after dawn this morning. The hunter had told reporters the body was covered in what looked like wounds from a hunting knife.

Sickening images crept into Leif's mind, remnants of crime-scene photos that had a way of lingering in the dark crevices of his consciousness long after the juries had made their decisions.

He frequently had to remind himself that the world was full of kind, loving, sane people. Psychos like Edward Blanco and whoever had committed this morning's murder were the exception. That didn't make it any easier on the victims' families.

Leif listened to the details—at least the details the police had given the media. He knew there were a few they'd keep secret—identifying facts that only they and the killer would know.

The body had been discovered in a rural area southwest of Dallas near the small town of Oak Grove.

Leif had been in that area a few months back when he'd made a wasted trip to Dry Gulch Ranch. For all he knew, he might have driven by the victim's house. She would have been alive then, planning her future, thinking she had a long life in front of her.

Or perhaps not. She might have been involved with drug addicts and dealers or a jealous boyfriend who'd kill rather than lose her.

A streak of lightning slashed through thick layers of dark clouds as Leif pulled into the parking garage. The crash of thunder that followed suggested the storm was imminent.

Leif flicked off the radio, left the car with the valet and took the key-secured elevator to the twenty-second floor.

Once inside his condo, he headed straight for the bar and poured himself two fingers of Glenmorangie. Glass in hand, he walked to the floor-to-ceiling windows, pulled back the drapes and stared out at the city just as huge raindrops began to pelt the glass.

His thoughts shifted to the Dry Gulch Ranch and the infamous reading of R. J. Dalton's will. Not that his biological father was dead, at least not yet. Or if he was Leif hadn't been notified. He wouldn't have made it to the funeral under any circumstances.

The old reprobate had had no use for Leif or his younger brother, Travis, when they'd desperately needed a father. Leif didn't need or want R.J. in his life now. He definitely wouldn't be letting R.J. manipulate his life as specified in his absurd will.

Leif took a slow sip of the whiskey and tried to clear his mind of troubling thoughts. Only along with everything else that was festering inside him tonight, the truth about his own failures forced its way to the forefront.

His failed marriage. The divorce. His relationship—or lack of one—with his teenage daughter, Effie.

His daughter had blamed the split between him and her mother totally on him. Leif had let it go at that, though the marriage had been a mistake from the beginning.

What they'd taken for love had probably been lust and their drives to succeed. In the end their shared workaholic, competitive tendencies had driven them apart. Marriage had become a stressful balancing act between two people who had nothing but their beloved daughter in common.

Celeste had suggested the divorce, but Leif had been the one who moved out. That was five years ago. Leif had been sure Effie would understand and come around with time. She hadn't, and she was fifteen now.

His career move from San Francisco to Dallas hadn't helped. What with his and Celeste's schedules and Effie's school and extracurricular activities, quality time with his daughter had become harder and harder to come by.

He saw Effie twice a year now, a week of summer vacation and the week between Christmas and New Year's. He made the trip to California. In spite of his coaxing, she'd never once visited him in Dallas.

He downed the last of his drink and then went back to the bar and refilled his glass. He'd just set the bottle down when he heard a timid tapping at his door. No doubt one of his neighbors since a visitor had to have a key to the building or else be buzzed inside by a tenant.

He ignored the would-be visitor and loosened his tie.

There was another knock, this one much louder than the first. Irritated, Leif walked to the door and peered through the keyhole to see who was so persistent.

Tattered jeans. A gray hoodie. Bright amber eyes shadowed by smeared mascara peering from beneath strands of dark, wet hair that had fallen over his forehead. A jolt rocked along his nerve endings.

His hands shook as he opened the door to greet the last person he'd expected to see tonight.

Chapter Two

Effie lowered her gaze to the toes of her wet boots, suddenly sure that coming here had been a miserable mistake.

"Hello, Dad."

"Effie. What are you doing here?"

Not the welcome most girls would expect from a father they hadn't seen in months. She went back to staring at her boots since she didn't have a great answer to his question.

He opened the door wider. "Come in. You're soaked."

"It's raining," she said, stating the obvious. She pushed her wet bangs to the side and leaned against the wall to wiggle out of her boots.

"There must have been some miscommunication," her dad said. "I had no idea you were coming."

"I meant to call first." She shrugged out of her wet hoodie.

Her father took the hoodie and placed it on an odd-shaped granite-topped table that took up most of the marble entryway. "Where's your mother?" he asked.

"She's in England on business. But it was her idea that I fly down and spend Thanksgiving with you."

"I'm glad she did." Finally, he pulled her into his arms for a hug.

Once the hug was out of the way, the reunion grew even more awkward. He looked past her, picked up her two suitcases and set them inside the condo.

She shifted her heavy computer bag from one shoulder to the other.

"Here, let me take that for you," he offered. Once the bag was on his shoulder, he closed and locked the door. "So you just flew from San Francisco to Dallas by yourself?" he asked, still looking puzzled.

"I'm fifteen."

"And no longer a kid, I know. Still, I can't imagine your mother letting you make the trip without checking with me first. What if I'd been out of town on business?"

"I was supposed to call, but then I forgot and…" She was never easy with lying. She'd actually hoped he'd be out of town. "If you have plans for the holiday, you don't have to change them on my account."

"I have no plans. If I did, I'd definitely change them. There's nowhere I'd rather be than with you."

His expression didn't mimic his words.

She turned away, aware of all the leather, glass and mirrors that surrounded her. The room felt more like an impersonal waiting room in a fancy office than a home.

"When did your mother go to England?" he asked.

"Two weeks ago."

"That's a long time to be away from home. Does that happen often?"

"It has this year. Mom's working on a big project." And a new life. Which meant a new life for Effie, as well. It definitely wouldn't be here in this condo. Not in London, either, if she got her way. Which was the real reason she was here.

"I didn't realize she's away so much."

"It's her job, Dad. And it's not like I need her around every second. I have school and my friends. And I've been helping out at a local horse stable in exchange for riding lessons."

"I heard about that. Your mother emailed a picture of you

in the saddle. She said you were becoming a full-fledged cowgirl."

"Not so much a cowgirl, but I like horseback riding."

"So do I, though I haven't done much of it lately. Who stays with you when your mother is away?"

"If she's on a short trip, you know, less than a week, then she usually lets me stay with my friend Betts—not that I need a babysitter." Try telling that to her mother.

"And when it's a long trip, like this one?" he questioned.

"Grandma and Granddad drive down from Portland. They dropped me off at the airport before they drove home today."

"How are your grandparents?"

"Grandma's doing fine. Granddad's having problems with his arthritis. He can't get around as well as he used to."

"I'm sorry to hear that."

She was tempted to bring up her other grandparent now, but she decided to wait. As her mother always said, timing was everything. And she couldn't risk any problems with her plan.

"Are you hungry?" he asked.

"I could eat. All they gave us on the plane was peanuts. They were selling sandwiches, but they looked as lousy as some of that stuff they pass off for food in the school cafeteria."

"I can order pizza. You do still like pizza, don't you?"

"Sure. As long as it doesn't have weird stuff on it like asparagus or pineapple."

"No way. I'm talking real pizza. Pepperoni, sausage, extra cheese, the works. But first we should probably call your mother and let her know you arrived safely."

"I texted her when the plane landed and told her I'd made it to Dallas."

"You should have called me from the airport. I would have picked you up myself or sent a car for you."

"I called your office. They said you were in court so I took a taxi."

"How did you get inside the building?"

"Easy. When the driver let me out, I dashed for the awning over the front door and just walked into the building with a woman who was fighting to close her umbrella in the wind. I figured if you weren't here, I'd try calling your cell phone."

"Thankfully, I came straight home from the courthouse. I got here a few minutes before you." He took a phone from his pocket and ordered the pizza.

Effie looked around a bit more. There were several framed photographs sitting around of her and her dad together. Guess that meant he didn't totally forget her when she was out of sight.

One of the photos was of him holding her in his arms when she was a baby. At least she guessed that was her. Another was of her holding his hand, a pair of Mickey Mouse ears propped on her head, the Disneyland sign in the background. Both of those had to have been taken long before the divorce.

The other photos included a shot of the two of them in the surf on Oahu and another with them zip-lining over a Puerto Rican rainforest. She remembered both of those trips well. Trips were okay, but she'd felt as if she were traveling with some big-shot stranger.

"You should slip into some dry clothes," he said. "I can throw those in the washer for you."

"Sure." Stupid washing machine was probably so fancy he didn't trust her to use it.

"I'll show you to the guest room. There are clean sheets on the bed and clean towels in the adjoining bathroom.

There's also a guest robe in the closet if you want to get comfortable."

Like they were going to spend a kick-back night together. He picked up her bags, and she followed him to a room that looked like it belonged in one of those Scottish castles they'd visited last Christmas. She couldn't imagine throwing her jeans across the pristine white love seat or kicking out of her shoes and flopping onto a bed covered in a silk coverlet and piled down with designer-coordinated pillows.

"Has anyone ever slept in here?" she asked.

"No," he admitted. "The room has never been used. Saving the christening for you."

"How long have you lived here?"

"A little over a year. I was hoping I could persuade you to come here for Christmas vacation, but this is even better. It will be my best Thanksgiving in years."

Her father set her bags down and opened the closet. "I can get more hangers if you need them."

"That's okay. I didn't bring any dresses. My jeans and T-shirts are just fine folded." And if things went as planned, she wouldn't be here long enough to unpack or to spill a soft drink all over his expensive coverlet.

He opened the top drawer in a tall chest. "When do you have to fly back to California?"

"I have a flight for Sunday afternoon."

"Great. That gives us almost a full week for me to show you Dallas—unless you'd rather go somewhere else for Thanksgiving. It's late to set up a long trip, but there are some great dude ranches within a few hours of here. We can go horseback riding and hiking and toast s'mores around a campfire."

Now they were getting somewhere. She hadn't planned on rocking the boat quite so soon, but she was never going to get a better opening than this. She took a deep breath and took the plunge.

"I've been to dude ranches in California. They're fun, but kinda corny. What I'd really like to do is visit a real working Texas ranch."

"I can probably work that out. One of the attorneys in our firm has a spread in the Hill Country and he's been trying to get me to come up for a long weekend. I'll give him a call while we're waiting on the pizza."

"No." The protest flew from her mouth before she could stop it. If she wasn't careful, this would get out of hand. She didn't want to go to just any ranch. "Why not visit the Dry Gulch Ranch?" she asked. "It's only an hour from Dallas."

From the look on her dad's face, you'd think she'd just suggested they visit the devil himself. Her mother had warned her it would be like this.

"How do you know about the Dry Gulch Ranch?"

"I got a letter from my grandfather."

Her father's face turned a fierce shade of red. "R.J. wrote to you?"

"It was just a note, Dad. No big deal."

"What did he write?"

"The basics. He said he was getting old and his health isn't so good. He's got a brain tumor. He said you knew about that. Anyway, he wants to meet me before he dies, so he invited me to his ranch."

"Oh, he did, did he? Did you show your mother that note?"

"I did. She said that was between me, you and my grand-father."

"It would have been nice if she'd prepared me for this."

"R. J. Dalton is my grandfather. I don't see why you're getting so freaked out about my wanting to meet him."

"I'll tell you why. R.J. has never been a part of my life. He's my father by blood only."

"Blood is thicker than water, they say."

Her dad was clearly not amused. "Did you answer R.J.'s note?"

"Yes," she said, seeing no reason to lie about it. "I've written him several times. We have a lot in common."

"Like what?"

"He's into horses. So am I, and I'd really like to visit the Dry Gulch Ranch and meet him and the horses."

Her dad looked as if he was ready to throw her back out into the storm. "That explains why you're here in Dallas."

She couldn't deny that. "I told him I'd spend Thanksgiving with him. I thought we could both go. I mean, if your father's dying, don't you want to at least go say goodbye?"

"We said our goodbyes years ago. *His* choice."

Kind of like he had when he'd moved out of the house and then across the country, ripping her life apart in the process. But she wasn't there to deal with that, not when she needed him to take her side against her well-meaning mother.

She crossed her arms. "I didn't mean to upset you, but I'd really like to meet my grandfather. It's important to me. Really important, Dad. It doesn't have to be Thanksgiving Day. We could drive out tomorrow."

"R. J. Dalton is not the man you think he is."

"Don't you think I should find that out for myself?"

"No, I don't."

"Well, I do. I'd like to meet him, and this might be my only chance."

Her father raked his fingers through his hair. He looked older than she remembered him, but he was still handsome. And she didn't just think that because he was her father. Betts thought he was handsome, too.

Now she just needed him to be reasonable. "Please, Dad," she pleaded. "Can't we just drive out to the Dry Gulch Ranch? We don't have to stay long. If nothing else, I could see the horses."

Her dad looked away and then exhaled slowly.

"Okay," he said. His agreement took her by surprise. "I'll drive you out to the ranch tomorrow, but don't expect too much in the way of R.J.'s becoming a grandfather to you. Family relationships are dispensable to him."

A trait her father had obviously inherited.

But R.J. had a ranch and horses and he wanted to know her better. He could be the answer to all her problems—if her father didn't ruin her plans and her life yet again.

Chapter Three

Joni Griffin leaned over the injured horse, gingerly applying the flexible vet wrap over the pillow wrap. Her hands moved with precision as she made sure the bandaging fit snugly enough to hold it in place but not so tight it caused undue pain.

R.J. watched the procedure over Joni's shoulder and muttered reassurances to the beautiful filly. "Poor girl. I should have been watching you more closely. Instead I let you get hurt."

"Horses get wounds just like people do," Joni said. "You can't prevent all of them. The good thing is you caught this one early and the cut's not all that deep."

"You think Miss Dazzler will be okay then?"

"I think she's going to be just fine, but you'll need to keep applying the hydrotherapy a few times a day until the swelling goes down, and the bandaging will have to be replaced each time. I also recommend one gram of phenylbutazone twice a day to help with the swelling."

"I can handle the bute and probably the treatment and bandaging if I have some help from Corky or Adam, but I don't wanna go trusting Miss Dazzler to anyone who's not a trained vet."

"I'm sure Adam can judge if the wound is healing right,"

Joni said. "Your son is amazing with horses. So is his wife, for that matter."

"Right on both counts. I notice you and my daughter-in-law have spent a lot of time together of late."

"Can't help but like Hadley. And your granddaughters are adorable."

"Yes, they are, but they're a handful. That's why I hate to ask Hadley to take on the full responsibility of Miss Dazzler, especially with Thanksgiving just two days away. She and Mattie Mae have been cooking up a storm."

"Sounds delicious."

"It will be. How about you join us for lunch that day?"

"I just may do that. Actually, Hadley has already invited me."

"Good. I s'pect we'll have enough food to feed half the citizens of Oak Grove."

"Then I'll definitely come and try to eat my share."

"Good. Now back to Miss Dazzler. I want somebody who knows what they're doing to take a good look at that wound every day, just to be sure it's healing right."

"I could show Adam what to look for."

"He's off at a cattle auction today."

"What about Corky?"

"He's a good enough cattle wrangler, but I don't trust him to take care of Miss Dazzler's injured fetlock. Not that he wouldn't like helping you do it. I think he's got a crush on you. Can't say that I blame him, mind you. If I were younger—"

"Okay, enough with the flattery. I'll see Miss Dazzler once a day until the fetlock is completely healed."

"I sure would appreciate that."

Joni smiled. It was hard to turn R.J. down, even though she already had a full plate this week. But R.J. loved his horses. That was always a plus in her book.

And she admired the way he hadn't given up on living even with the inoperable brain tumor slowly stealing his health and his life.

Miss Dazzler nuzzled Joni's neck as if she understood that she was to be treated like royalty.

"Hiring you to join his practice was the best decision Doc Benson made since he married that pretty little filly of his," R.J. said.

"Thank you. Be sure and tell him that."

"I do, every chance I get."

The decision had been great for her, as well. Blake Benson's practice offered the perfect opportunity for her to utilize her equine vet training. And he definitely had enough work to keep both of them busy.

Joni walked over to the freshwater spigot and washed her hands with a bar of soap hanging from rope attached to a large nail. "Will any of your other children be joining you for Thanksgiving?" she asked.

"Probably not."

"So, no takers except Adam on the terms of your will?"

"Nope. Haven't heard from nary a one of them except my oldest son, Jake. He's called a time or two to bombard me with questions."

"That shows he's concerned about you."

"Weren't none of those questions about my health. I guaran-damn-tee you that."

"Then what does he ask about?"

"The ranch. The will's provisions? My sanity, though he don't say that directly. I s'pect he wants to buy the ranch for himself—or find a way to beat me out of it."

"Ah, an apple that didn't fall far from the tree," she teased.

"Probably why the two of us don't gee-haw in harmony."

Joni didn't question R.J.'s sanity, but she could see why

his children might think he was sliding into senility. He'd invited them all to the reading of his will without letting them know he was still alive.

Then he'd insisted they move back to the ranch and take part in its operation for one full year if they wanted to inherit their share of the eight-million-dollar estate. So far only Adam had moved back, but he hadn't actually had to disrupt his life.

According to Hadley, Adam was just getting over injuries sustained while on active duty as a marine in Afghanistan and hadn't even had a job, much less a successful career, when he'd made the decision to move onto the ranch.

Besides, R.J. had jumped in to help when Adam's young daughters were abducted. That had given Adam a bit more incentive to get to know his father.

R.J. stepped away and spit a stream of tobacco into a spittoon near the back of the barn. "I don't blame my kids for having no use for me," he said once he'd wiped his mouth on the sleeve of his flannel shirt. "I was never a decent father to any of them. But it's my money and I'll do what I damn well please with it."

"The one with the gold makes the rules?"

He scratched his ruddy, whiskered jaw. "Call it what you please. Blood kin or not, I'm not leaving my ranch or my money to someone 'less I get to know them first and figure they're worthy."

"Did you define worthy in the will?"

"No, but I should have put it in there. Might have my attorney go back and take care of that."

Joni doubted he'd go that far. She was fairly certain that R.J. just wanted a chance to get to know all his children before the brain tumor claimed his life. And from what she knew of the crusty old rancher, he definitely wouldn't be beyond a little manipulation to get what he wanted.

"Did I tell you that I've been in contact with one of my granddaughters?" R.J. asked.

"No. How exciting for you."

"Yep. Effie Dalton. She lives in California, but she's going to be in Dallas visiting my son Leif this week. She wants to come out to the Dry Gulch and spend a few days."

Joni struggled to remember the basics of what R.J. had told her about his children in extensive detail over the past few weeks. "Is Leif the divorced defense attorney?"

"Yep. That's the one. Haven't heard a word from him since the reading of the will, but Effie thinks she can convince him to drive her out here."

"I know you'd love that."

"Doggone right, unless Leif's coming would just mean trouble. I told Effie if her dad wouldn't drive her out here to call me and I'd send a car to pick her up—anywhere, anytime."

"How old is she?"

"Fifteen. She lives with her mother. But get this. She loves horses and she's already talking about becoming an equine vet. I'd sure like for you to meet her while she's here. Maybe give her some encouragement."

"I'd love to. But now I'd best get to my next patient. You keep an eye on Miss Dazzler for me. And remember, she needs stall rest until the swelling is gone."

"No problem. I'll just come down and sit with her if she gets lonesome."

Joni suspected that if he'd taken as much interest in his children when they were growing up as he did his horses now, he wouldn't have to use bribes and manipulation to get them to visit him.

A horse at the far end of the elaborately renovated horse barn neighed.

"Old Bullet's calling my name," R.J. said. "Think I'll

have Corky saddle him up so I can take him for a short ride."

"Should you be riding alone?"

He gave her a wink and a click of his tongue. "Are you hinting you want to go along with me?"

No doubt he'd been as much a womanizer in his younger days as the locals claimed. His flirting was totally harmless now, though.

"I'd love to ride with you, Mr. Dalton, but I have three other calls to make this afternoon. I'll be lucky if I make it back here to check on Miss Dazzler by dark."

"You're too pretty to work all the time. You need a man to go home to. I've still got four unmarried sons, you know."

"I'll keep that in mind. Now you take care of yourself and I'll be back first thing in the morning to check on Miss Dazzler."

"You be careful and don't be out on these old deserted roads by yourself at night. I guess you heard about Evie Monsant getting murdered yesterday."

"I heard about a body being found yesterday morning. I didn't know it was Evie's until I saw the police tape all around her gate and house when I drove past last night on my way home."

"The media are already claiming it might be the work of The Hunter," R.J. said. "I don't put no stock in that myself, though. I'd put my money on her knowing the guy who killed her."

"Why?"

"She was a strange woman. Sticking to herself all the time. The way I heard it, she'd hardly say howdy if she met you face on. No telling what she was mixed up in."

Joni wasn't so sure. "The news reporters must know something if they're saying her death could be the work of a serial killer."

"Not necessarily. Those blowhards love putting the fear in everybody. Gets 'em higher ratings."

"I hope you're right. Not that it would make it any better for Evie, but the thought of a serial killer in Oak Grove is bloodcurdling," Joni admitted.

"You just be careful," R.J. said. "But I wouldn't worry about it too much. This is about as peaceful a place as you can find in all of Texas. I figure Evie Monsant brought her trouble with her."

"Maybe." But unexpected anxiety skidded along Joni's nerve endings as R.J. walked her to her aging pickup truck. She'd grown up in a rural area much like this one, where neighbors looked out for one another. She'd always felt safe, the same as she had since moving to Oak Grove nine months ago.

Still she might sleep with her shotgun in easy reach tonight.

She said her goodbyes to R.J., climbed behind the wheel and turned the key in the ignition. The motor made a grinding noise and then sputtered and died. It did the same on the second try. On the third try, there wasn't even a grind.

So much for getting through and getting home before dark.

EFFIE JUMPED OUT of Leif's black sports car and rushed to the metal gate. She unlatched it and hitched a ride on the bottom rung as it swung open, her ponytail bouncing behind her.

Her excitement over arriving at the Dry Gulch Ranch equaled Leif's displeasure. He'd done his best to talk her into a trip to anywhere but there. He'd even considered buying her a horse of her own when she got back to California, one she could keep at the stables where she worked.

That had felt too much like a bribe. Besides, his ex would

have killed him, a fate only slightly worse than playing nice with R.J. all afternoon. But Leif was also spending time with Effie, so there was a silver lining to his misery.

Once he'd driven across the cattle gap, Effie took her time getting back in the car; her gaze was focused on a young deer that had stepped out of a cluster of sycamore trees a few yards in front of them. She stood as still as a statue until the deer turned and ran back into the woods.

His daughter had obviously spent far too much time in the confines of the city.

She fastened her seat belt. "Grandpa didn't say he had deer on the ranch, too."

Grandpa. The word sounded irritatingly strange when used by Effie for a man he barely knew and Effie didn't know at all. "Who told you to call R.J. Grandpa?"

"I asked him what I should call him and he suggested Grandpa. That's what his twin granddaughters call him."

Leif seethed but went back to safer territory. "I suspect there are all kinds of creatures who call the Dry Gulch home."

"What kind of creatures?" Effie asked.

"Possums. Raccoons. Armadillos. Foxes. Skunks. Rattlesnakes."

"Rattlesnakes. Really?" She screwed her face into a repulsed scowl.

"Yes, but probably not out and about much this time of the year, though it's warm enough today you'd need to be careful if you were traipsing through high grass or walking along the riverbank."

"There's a river on the property?"

"More like a creek, but they call it a river."

"Can you swim in it? Not now, I know, but in the summer."

"I wouldn't recommend it."

"It doesn't matter. Grandpa says there's a spring-fed pool for swimming. There's also a small lake where he goes fishing. He said he'll teach me how. Do you remember the ranch at all?"

"Not from when I was a kid."

"When else were you here?"

"I paid a visit to the Dry Gulch a few months back along with your uncle Travis and R.J.'s four other *biological* children. We were given a tour of the ranch."

"You had a family reunion?"

"More like a reading of R.J.'s commandments."

"What does that mean?"

He knew he should let it go, but all Effie was getting from R.J. was propaganda. She should be exposed to a little of the truth.

"R.J. wants all his offspring to move back to the ranch and raise cattle. It's a requirement if we want to be included in his will."

"So if you move back here, part of the ranch will belong to you?"

That had backfired. Effie made it sound like manna from heaven instead of the bribe it was. "I'm not moving back here, so it's a moot point, but, yes, that's the gist of it."

"Why not move out here? I mean, who wouldn't want to own part of a ranch?"

"I'm not a rancher. I'm an attorney."

"What about Uncle Travis?"

"He's perfectly happy as a Dallas homicide detective. Believe me, he wants no part of R.J. or the Dry Gulch, either."

Effie exhaled sharply. "Well, I do. You could inherit it and give it to me."

He should have known not to get into this with Effie.

Horses were her current phase. Naturally, she'd think living on a ranch was a super idea.

Effie went back to staring out the window. "Did you move to Dallas to be closer to Uncle Travis?"

"No. He moved here after I did. He was a detective in Louisiana before taking a job in Dallas."

"So he moved to be closer to you?"

"No. He moved because he wanted a fresh start."

"Did he get divorced, too?"

"No. He was instrumental in getting a crooked police chief sent to jail. Why all the questions?"

"No reason." She went back to observing the passing scenery. The wooded area had given way to acres of pasture. A few head of cattle were off to the right, some grazing, most resting.

"Is this all part of the Dry Gulch?" Effie asked.

"So I was told."

"Where's Grandpa's house?"

"We're almost there. Keep watching and you'll make out the roof and chimneys when we round the next curve."

She stretched her neck for a better look and then started wiggling in her seat when the house came into view. The century-old structure in desperate need of a face-lift apparently excited her a lot more than his plush penthouse condo had.

A few minutes later, Leif pulled into the driveway that led to the separate three-car garage and stopped next to a beat-up pickup truck with a lifted hood. R.J. stood next to the right fender.

"Is that my grandfather?" Effie asked.

"That's R. J. Dalton."

She opened the door a crack and then hesitated, as if unsure of herself or of him. But when R.J. saw her and waved, she jumped from the car and ran to meet him much in the way she'd run to meet Leif when she was a little girl.

R.J. opened his arms, and Effie eagerly stepped into a giant bear hug. A pain so intense he nearly doubled over from it punched Leif in the chest. It had been years since Effie had hurled herself into his arms.

Reluctantly, Leif climbed from beneath the wheel and planted his feet on the concrete drive while R.J. and Effie exchanged greetings. He didn't see the woman until he'd walked to the other side of the stalled truck.

She was leaning over the engine with an expression on her face that suggested she'd like to plant a stick of dynamite under the hood and put the truck out of its misery.

"What's the problem?" Leif asked, thankful for any excuse to avoid dealing with R.J., even if only for a few seconds.

"Her battery conked out on her," R.J. answered for her.

"With misfortune's usual bad timing," she muttered.

"It could have been worse," R.J. said. "You could have been stranded on one of these back roads."

"Like I was yesterday," she said. "Fortunately, Tague Lambert happened by and gave me a start. He took a look at the battery and said I should get it replaced."

"So why didn't you?" Leif asked.

"I was planning to take it into Abe's Garage in Oak Grove tomorrow. Wednesday's my day off. Do you have a pair of jumper cables I can borrow, Mr. Dalton?"

"Sure as shootin'."

Leif stepped in closer for a better look at the dead battery before turning to the woman. She wasn't flagrantly sexy like Serena, but she had a natural girl-next-door kind of freshness about her. Impulsively, he checked her ring finger.

No golden band, but unless looks were deceiving she

was much too young to engage in a tryst with a jaded, approaching-forty attorney like himself.

Not that he was interested in a new relationship. He hadn't cleared the breakup hurdle of the one he was in yet.

"Even if you get the truck started, the battery is likely to give out on you again," Leif said. "I don't think you should try to drive it."

"I don't have a lot of choice. Sam Loden and his ailing mare are expecting me in about twenty minutes."

"Don't you go worrying," R.J. said. "I'll get you to Sam's, but first we need some introductions." He rested a thin, wrinkled hand on Effie's shoulder. "This is my granddaughter Effie Dalton, the one I told you about."

The woman wiped her hands on her jeans. "You must be the California granddaughter who loves horses?"

Effie smiled. "That's me."

"Then we have something in common. I love horses, too. And your grandfather has some of the most beautiful and spirited ones in the county."

"I can't wait to see them," Effie said.

"You won't have to wait long," R.J. assured her. He turned back to the woman. "This is Joni Griffin, the best vet in six counties—the prettiest, too."

A blush reddened Joni's cheeks. "There you go again. Flattery will not lower your bill."

"It's not flattery when it's true," R.J. said.

Leif extended a hand to the woman. "I'm Leif Dalton, Effie's father."

"And R.J.'s son," she acknowledged. "R.J.'s told me all about you."

He wouldn't begin to guess what that might include, since he figured R.J. knew very little about him except his name. And that he had a daughter who R.J. figured he could manipulate.

R.J. put out a hand to him. Leif had no choice but to take it or be seen as a total ass.

R.J.'s grip was much stronger than expected.

"Glad you and Effie are here?" R.J. said.

Leif only nodded. It was better than an outright lie. He turned back to the woman. "Can I give you a ride somewhere or take you to get a new battery?"

"You just got here," she said. "You've hardly had a chance to say hello to your dad."

An added benefit. "I'm sure he and Effie can find plenty to talk about until I get back."

"Actually, that's a dang good idea," R.J. said. "You drive the doc to Sam's place and I'll have my wrangler Corky take her truck into Oak Grove so that Abe can install a new battery."

Leif turned back to Joni. "I'm game if you are."

"Sam's ranch is off a dirt road. You'll get your sports car layered in mud from last night's rain."

"Mud I can handle. Not too keen on driving through whatever made all those scratches on your truck, though."

"You won't. Those are from a few of my more adventuresome trips."

"Through an Amazon jungle?"

"Close. Through Texas brush."

"So that's settled," R.J. said. "You two go heal animals and get to know each other. Corky will get a replacement battery, and Effie and me will check out the horses and try out the cookies Mattie Mae baked this morning."

Leif turned to his daughter. "Is that arrangement okay with you, Effie?"

"It's better than okay. I can't wait to see the horses."

"Call me if you need me for any reason," he said.

"Dad. I'm fifteen, not two."

"She'll be fine," R.J. assured him, as if he knew the first thing about parenting.

Leif was relieved for the chance to escape R.J.'s company, but as soon as they started walking toward his car, he had second thoughts about driving off and leaving his daughter alone with his so-called father.

"Be sure Effie meets the twins," Joni called back to R.J. as she stopped at the door to Leif's car.

"Absolutely," R.J. agreed. "I'll give Hadley a call now."

"The twins?" Leif questioned as he climbed behind the steering wheel.

"Lila and Lacy, your half brother Adam's daughters," Joni answered. "They're three and too adorable for words."

So Joni wasn't the only grandchild to be welcomed into the fold. Leif had received word from R.J.'s lawyer that Adam Dalton had been the first offspring to move onto the ranch. He hadn't realized Adam was married or had children, but then he hadn't really given it much thought.

His hand rested on the gearshift, but he made no move to shove it into Reverse.

"You don't have to do this if you'd rather stay here with Effie and R.J. I can find someone to give me a lift," Joni offered, obviously misreading his hesitation.

"Driving you to Sam's isn't a problem. I'm just not sure about leaving Effie here with my infamous father. Effie probably isn't as competent on a horse as she'd like everyone to believe. R.J. is liable to put her on some wild horse she can't control."

"R.J. would never do that."

"What makes you so sure?"

"I know him. He'll watch over her like a mother hen. Hadley fully trusts him with the twins, and they're only three years old."

"Okay, so I'm overreacting a bit, but you can't be too careful these days."

"Are you sure it's just that you're being careful? It sounds more like vindictive."

"Trust me—I have good reason for the way I feel about R.J."

"I know he wasn't much of a father to you or any of his children. He admits that. But people can change. You might even like R.J. if you gave him a chance."

"He had lots of chances. He blew them. Case closed."

She honored that request, and a few minutes later they were on a back road, his sleek sports car hugging the curves as they made their way to Joni's next four-legged patient.

Leif turned and studied Joni's profile. He'd always liked long hair on women, but Joni's short, shiny hair looked great on her. The bouncy locks hugged her cheeks and highlighted her long, dark eyelashes.

Even without makeup, her skin was flawless, so smooth it almost begged to be touched. Her lips were soft and inviting, her smile a killer. But it was the cute, slightly turned-up nose that added the final seductive touch.

Cute, casual, no apparent pretense, outspoken. She could definitely spell trouble.

But not for him.

The sooner he got out of Oak Grove, the better. He wanted no part of any attachment that would bring him back into R.J.'s world.

JONI GAVE LEIF directions to Sam Loden's ranch and then leaned back with her eyes straight ahead. The car, with its soft leather seats, had that invigorating new-car smell. She felt as though she were riding on a cloud. So why was she so uncomfortable?

Because R.J. had practically forced her on the man,

that's why. Driving a vet around who smelled of horse-flesh and antibiotic ointment was probably the last thing Leif wanted to be doing today.

Worse, he smelled of musky aftershave and was wearing a shirt that probably cost more than anything in her wardrobe. His jeans no doubt carried a designer label. Hers had a rip in the right leg and not the fake kind people paid extra for.

She raked her fingers through her short hair, tucking the right side behind her ear.

"You really didn't have to do this," she said, then was immediately sorry when she feared it made her sound ungrateful.

Leif turned toward her, a half smile playing on his lips. "I've heard all about Texas cowboy chivalry. I'm just trying to measure up."

"Is there no chivalry among attorneys?"

"Not a good day to ask me that."

"Why not?"

"I won a case yesterday that has me reconsidering my choice of professions."

"I've had days like that. But shouldn't winning have had the opposite effect?"

"One would think. But enough of my complaining. Let's talk about you."

"There's nothing much to tell. I'm an Oklahoma gal who wound up in Texas making barn calls and trying to convince the local ranchers that a female can be as capable as a man when it comes to dealing with sick horses."

"You've already won R.J.'s heart."

"I spent the night helping one of his favorite mares get through a difficult birth my first month here. That made me a golden girl in his mind."

"How do you fit in with the rest of Oak Grove?"

"So far, so good, except for the day of the UT/Oklahoma football game."

"Understandable. We Texans do take our college football seriously."

"Don't tell me you're a Longhorn alum?"

"No. I went to UCLA and then law school at Stanford. I'm barely a Texan except by birth. After Mother divorced R.J., she moved to San Francisco with my brother, Travis, and me. I only moved back to Dallas five years ago."

"Born a Texan, always a Texan," she said. "So say the natives."

"Is this the turn up ahead?" he asked.

"Yes, and then look for an old church that hasn't been used in years. It only has half a roof and seriously leans to the left. Just past that you'll come to the gate of Sleeping Dogs Ranch. That's the Loden spread."

Leif slowed and took the turn. "So what's it like dealing with cranky old ranchers all day?"

"I wouldn't know. Most of the time I deal with terrific guys who just want the best care for their horses. It's my dream job. However, there are times when I'm standing knee-deep in mud with my arms up to my elbows in horse while I try to coax a contrary foal into the world when I think I should have become a rock star."

"Do you sing?"

"Nothing that doesn't make the dogs howl. Hence the choice of becoming a vet was probably a wise one. What about you? What would you like to be on days you wish you weren't an attorney?"

"Independently wealthy or maybe a Walmart greeter. Those guys usually look pretty chipper and there's always junk food nearby."

She laughed, surprised to find that the tension she'd felt earlier was quickly dissolving.

Leif slowed as they approached the gate to the Sleeping Dogs Ranch.

"The gate has an automatic lock," she said. "The code is 6824. Enter it in that control box on your side, and I'll call and let Sam know we're here. That way he can meet me at the barn, tell me what needs attention and we can get right down to business."

"That sounds a little kinky," Leif said, his voice teasing.

A slow burn crept to her cheeks. The possibility of a kinky encounter in a barn definitely had potential.

But not with Sam Loden.

"Have you been in a lot of barns, Leif Dalton?"

"None in recent memory, but I'm always open to new experiences."

And new experiences usually sent her back into her shell. Maybe it was time she opened up to something besides work.

But not with Leif Dalton. He was a heartache waiting to happen. She didn't have time for that.

Still, there was no denying the buzz of awareness she felt just sitting next to him in a car.

Who knew what the day might bring?

Chapter Four

Leif had totally expected the afternoon to be a drag. As it turned out, the hours were flying by.

The doc was a pixie in jeans whose gentle persuasion with four-legged patients ten times her size was amazing. More impressive, not one of the seasoned ranchers had questioned her techniques or treatments. She undoubtedly knew her stuff.

This was their third stop, this one an emergency. Joni was tending a colicky horse that hadn't responded to the rancher's attempts to alleviate the pain.

The fretful horse was a two-year-old gelding. The panicky owner was a girl named Ruby, who appeared to be about Effie's age. Joni's stall-side manner was equally as reassuring to Ruby as it was to the horse.

His phone vibrated. Leif stepped away from his viewing spot just inside the barn door and checked the caller ID. Serena. He started to ignore the call. But if he didn't answer, she'd call again. Serena was a very persistent woman.

Besides, he felt a little guilty about ignoring her while he was pretty much mesmerized by a female vet.

"Hello."

"Leif, hi. It's Serena." All signs of the irritation she'd exhibited at his breaking their date had disappeared from her sultry voice.

"Hi, yourself. What's up?"

"I was just wondering how your day with your daughter is going?"

"Better than expected," he admitted without explaining that he wasn't actually with Effie.

"Does that mean you can escape that horrid ranch and return to civilization soon?"

"The ranch isn't horrid," he corrected her. He had nothing against fresh air, open spaces or even horses and cattle. "It's the ranch's owner I have a problem with."

"Then tell him that and head back to Dallas."

"It's not quite that simple. My schedule depends on Effie." And Joni's truck that he sure as hell wasn't about to mention.

"I have an offer neither you nor Effie can refuse," Serena crooned in her sexiest voice. "If you leave for Dallas now, you'll get home in time to show Effie how much more exciting Dallas society life is compared to hanging out with a bunch of smelly horses."

"That would be a hard sell with Effie."

"What if I throw in a fabulous outfit for her to wear? Just tell me her sizes and I can have one of the personal shoppers at Neiman's pick out a dress and shoes and have them delivered to your condo."

"What's the occasion?"

"Mallory George called a few minutes ago. Her daughter and son-in-law canceled for the opera tonight and Mallory's invited us and Effie to share their box."

He tried without total success to keep from laughing. "You have about as much chance of talking Effie into an opera as I do talking you into a hoedown."

"I'm not sure what a hoedown is but even the name sounds disgusting."

"Exactly."

"But I'm not just suggesting a musical performance," Serena persisted. "Afterward, there's a champagne reception for the world-famous soprano who has the starring role. It's black tie. Glitz and glamour equal to any D.C. event."

"I'm pretty sure Effie's not high on glitz and glamour."

"Nonsense. Any teenage girl alive would be thrilled with this opportunity. Your daughter will be so impressed, she'll forget all about horses and that Dry Goon Ranch."

"I wouldn't count on that, and it's the Dry Gulch Ranch."

"Whatever."

"Look, I appreciate the offer, Serena, but even if I wanted to give it a whirl, I can't make it back to Dallas in time."

"You could if you left now."

"Sorry. No can do. This is Effie's day, and she's determined to spend it in the saddle. You go to the opera and reception and have a marvelous time. I'll call you next week after Effie has flown back to California. We can get together then."

And when they did, he'd be honest with Serena and try to explain to her and himself why he had no enthusiasm for continuing a relationship with one of the continent's most beautiful women.

"After Thanksgiving I'll be in Miami for two weeks on a photo shoot," Serena said, sounding irritated. "And then I'll be flying to London for a *Vogue* shoot. I won't be back in Dallas until Christmas. I explained all of that to you last week. Did you forget?"

"Of course not," he lied. "I'll call you in Miami."

"If that's the best you can do, don't bother."

"I don't think this is the best time to discuss this."

"There's nothing to discuss. It's clear that I'm at the bottom of your list of priorities."

That was about the size of it. Still he hated breaking up

over the phone. It was kind of like leaving a note on the pillow the morning after. Zero class.

"We should talk, Serena, but now isn't the time."

"Save your breath, Leif. There's nothing left to talk about." She broke the connection.

He felt like a louse. A *relieved* louse. But to be fair, he'd warned her from the first he wouldn't be putting a ring on her finger or going furniture shopping. He was not a forever-type guy.

His phone vibrated again as he slipped it back in his pocket. Evidently, Serena had more to say.

He took the call. "I'm sorry if I pissed you off," he said, "but—"

"What?"

Damn. It was R.J. "I thought it was someone else on the phone."

"Must have been a woman."

"How'd you guess?"

"You started the conversation with an apology."

"Good point," Leif agreed. "Is the doc's truck ready to roll?"

"Nope. Turns out the battery's dying in my driveway might have been a blessing. That old jalopy has a slew of problems."

"Like what?"

"An oil leak. Hoses that need replacing. An engine in desperate need of a tune-up. It's a wonder the darn thing ran at all."

"Sounds like Joni needs to become bosom buddies with the local mechanic."

"Or else buy a new truck," R.J. said. "In the meantime, I told Abe to go ahead and take care of what needs fixing."

"Don't you think you should have talked to Joni first?"

"Nope. No use to jaw about it when something has to be

done. Can't have a sweet thing like Joni riding around in a vehicle that's likely to leave her stranded on some dark country road. When Abe's finished, the doc's ride should be as safe as a banker's wallet."

Leif had his doubts about that. He figured the only guarantee that truck would be safe was to replace it with a new one. "Did you get a cost estimate?"

"Don't matter. Abe's fair. He's not gonna rip off anybody. I told him to bill the repairs to me. Joni can pay me back whenever she has some spare cash lying around."

"That's mighty generous of you." And presumptuous. The same kind of controlling behavior that made R.J. think he could order his adult children around after ignoring them all their lives.

R.J. might convince Effie this sudden concern for family was genuine. Leif wasn't buying it.

"Where and when do we pick up the truck?" Leif asked.

"Abe says it won't be ready until late—maybe not until tomorrow. Just bring Joni back here with you and she can have dinner with us. After that one of us can drive her home if the truck's not ready."

There he went again. Making decisions for other people without consulting them. "Did it occur to you that Joni might have other plans for the evening?"

"Do you always go looking for complications, Leif? Sure you do," he muttered without waiting for a response. "You're a damned attorney."

"I suppose you have a problem with that."

"Don't go getting riled," R.J. said. "Didn't mean it as an insult."

Of course he had, but Leif didn't give a damn what R.J. thought of him. "I'll extend your invitation," Leif said. "Whether Joni accepts or not is up to her."

"Tell her Adam is grilling some Dry Gulch steaks. Hadley's cooking up her twice-baked potatoes and Mattie Mae made a couple of her famous pecan pies. If Joni has plans, she'll break 'em. Eatin' don't git no better than that."

So Adam and presumably his wife and daughters and a woman named Mattie Mae would all be there. A family dinner; only they weren't Leif's family and never would be. Hopefully, Effie had come to that same conclusion after half a day with her illustrious grandfather and was ready to put the whole family togetherness scene behind her.

"Can you put Effie on the phone?"

"I could if she was around."

"Where is she?"

"She and Hadley are riding the range. They're liable not to show up back here before dark."

"I thought Hadley had young children."

"She does. Lacy and Lila are here with me and Mattie Mae. We got a mean game of Chutes and Ladders going."

A doting grandfather—now that he was dying. "I'll give Effie a call on her cell phone."

"Capital idea. Let her tell you how much fun she's having. That girl loves horses. Knows a lot about them, too. Bright as a new-mint penny and more spunk than you can hang on a barbwire fence."

"Effie can do most anything she sets her mind to," Leif agreed. Her mother had made that claim about her many times over the past fifteen years, not always as a compliment.

"Tell Joni if she has any questions about her truck to call me or Abe," R.J. said. "Otherwise I'll catch her up to speed at dinner."

"I'll see she gets the message." Leif ended the call and punched in Effie's cell number. She didn't answer until the sixth ring. When she did, she sounded breathless.

"Dad. Guess what I'm doing?"

"You're out horseback riding with someone named Hadley."

"How did you know?"

"Your—" He barely caught himself before the word *grandfather* slid off his tongue. "R.J. told me. Sounds as if you're having fun."

"I am. We were galloping like the wind. I didn't hear the phone until we stopped to let the horses drink from a creek that just appeared like a mirage."

"I'm sure the horses appreciate that."

"They do. You should see Aunt Hadley's horse. She's a beautiful chestnut filly that Uncle Adam gave her for her birthday."

"What kind of horse are you riding?" he asked. Finally, Effie was communicating, and he wanted to encourage that—even if it was all about the horses at Dry Gulch Ranch.

"My mount's a black quarter horse named Dolly and she's perfect for me. She's spirited, but she stood real still until I was in the saddle. And she responded to my every pull on the reins as if she had no problem letting me be in control."

"That sounds like the perfect horse, all right."

"Aunt Hadley named her horse Kenda. It's an Indian name that means magical powers. Aunt Hadley says Kenda has the power to fill her heart with joy."

"Nice name." Aunts, uncles, a new grandfather. Effie was jumping on the family plan as if she was starving for relatives. Yet she'd all but closed him out since the divorce.

He'd tried everything he knew to get closer to her. It pissed him off royally that R.J. had gotten her to Texas with just a note and a promise of horses.

"We rode all the way to the gulch that the ranch is named

after," Effie continued. "It looks like a plain old gully to me, but it was dry as a bone."

"I think I missed that on my tour."

"We can go riding tomorrow and I'll show you the gully and the pool we're at now. Grandpa says he has the perfect horse for you."

Probably one that would buck Leif off the second he settled in the saddle. And now Effie was talking about tomorrow like it was a done deal.

"There's an old foreman's cabin nearby," Effie said. "No one lives inside, but I bet they could if they made a few repairs. I wanted to go inside and look around, but Aunt Hadley says it's full of spiders and scorpions. We're steering clear of it."

"Very smart of you and Hadley."

He'd like to stay clear of everything on the Dry Gulch Ranch, but if it took riding horses to connect with his daughter, then he'd have a sore butt and thighs by this time tomorrow.

That didn't make R.J. the winner. Once Effie went back to California, R.J. would hopefully fade back into the woodwork.

By the time Leif finished his conversation, Joni, Ruby and the young rancher—a man named Latham Watson—had stepped outside the barn and Joni was giving them instructions for follow-up care.

He waited until Joni turned his way, smiled and motioned him over.

"Does this mean the patient is on the mend?" he asked.

"Benjy is resting now," Ruby said. "I was afraid he was going to die, but Dr. Griffin knew exactly what to do."

"But you need to watch what he eats," Joni said. "No more leaving a bucket of apples where he can get to them."

"I won't," Ruby promised.

"I guess I better watch what goes on in my own barn a little closer, too," Latham said. "Got more on my plate some days than I can handle."

"I told him he needs to find a wife," Ruby said. "Mom's been dead for two years. That's long enough for him to get married again. Don't you think so, Dr. Griffin?"

Joni put up her hands and waved off the question. "Can't look to me for advice on that. I'm just the vet."

"I told Ruby I'd marry again when I found the right woman," Latham said. "You can't go rushing those things." They talked a minute more and then Joni was ready to move on.

The sun inched toward the horizon as Leif and Joni started back to his car, and the air started to grow cooler, though it was still warm for November. Leif had shed his lightweight denim jacket two hours ago.

The puddles from yesterday's storm had vanished, leaving the carpet of grass beneath their feet bouncy but dry. Even the oppressive humidity that had refused to acknowledge the arrival of fall had dissipated in the wake of last night's rain-producing front.

Leif took a deep breath, his lungs suddenly hungry for the fresh air. Somewhere along the way, without realizing it, he'd actually begun to relax. Thoughts of work and Edward Blanco had taken a backseat to watching Joni work.

He opened the passenger door for Joni and then walked around to his side and climbed behind the wheel. "Do you mind if I put the windows down?"

She laughed. "I understand completely. I get a little rank after a day in the stalls. You'll probably have to have your vehicle fumigated after chauffeuring me around all day."

"It's not that bad," he teased. "A half-dozen cans of deodorizing spray and it'll be good as new."

"Except for the odor of antibiotic ointment. That has a shelf life of forever."

"Now you tell me."

Leif started the car and headed back the way they'd come. "Actually, I was just thinking how nice and fresh the air smells out here."

"Spoken like a man who spends far too much time in a stuffy office."

"Everybody can't be a cowboy."

"Too bad. You'd look good in a Stetson and a pair of Western boots."

"I'll have you know, I own a pair of genuine, handmade ostrich-skin Western boots. When I wear them, I have to fight the urge to don a rhinestone jacket and break into a country ballad."

"Oh, no. Not another urban cowboy. You should take me shopping with you, and I'll point out when you look ridiculous."

"While you snicker behind my back?"

"Never. I'd snicker to your face."

"That's helpful. So where to next?"

"I'm through with my scheduled calls, but I do have one more stop to make. I promised my favorite cowboy I'd bring him a special feed mix for his steer."

"Your favorite, huh? Now you've gone and made me jealous."

"You should be. Jeffrey is too cute for words. Of course, he's also only eleven years old and the steer is one he's raising for his 4-H project."

"So where do Jeffrey and his steer live?"

"About a mile down the road we turned off on to get here. Unfortunately, I forgot to bring the feed with me, which means I have to go back home to pick it up."

"Where do you live?"

"About twelve miles from here, almost to the downtown area of Oak Grove, but near Abe's repair shop. You can drop me there if you don't mind. I have no idea what happened to Corky, but Abe surely has the new battery installed by now."

"Unfortunately, I have bad news. It seems the battery is only the beginning of your problems. Abe is making a few additional repairs."

"When did you hear that?"

"R.J. called while you were tending Benjy. The truck may not be ready until tomorrow."

She grimaced, took a deep breath and exhaled sharply. "What else have you heard and why do I suddenly see dollar signs dancing in front of my eyes?"

Leif explained the situation, including R.J.'s taking charge.

"That sounds just like R.J. Always ready to jump in and help."

Unless you happened to be a son he'd abandoned. Then you could live in hell and he wouldn't bother to send you a glass of cold water. "How many miles does your truck have on it?"

"Just over 150,000."

"Sounds as if it might be time to put it out to pasture."

"Easier said than done. I'm emotionally attached."

"To a truck?"

"Don't laugh. It got me through four years of undergrad work, four years of veterinary school and a one-year internship with a clinic in Oklahoma specializing in equine insemination and breeding. Getting rid of it would be like dumping an old friend."

Impressive. Joni was committed to a worn-out truck. Leif had never kept a vehicle long enough to need new tires. His record with relationships was worse.

But with that much schooling under her belt, apparently Joni Griffin was not as young as he'd assumed.

"Your old friend is not as dependable as he once was," Leif said. "Maybe you should start looking for a nice retirement home for lovable metal scrap."

"There's also a money issue," Joni admitted. "My school loans devour a huge chunk of my salary every month. I was hoping to make a dent in them before I had to purchase a new truck."

"I could help you get a low-interest vehicle loan."

The comment surprised him. He was not one to jump into women's financial issues. Not that he wasn't generous. He just didn't like ties that might bind.

"Thanks, but no thanks," Joni said, quickly letting him off the hook. "Blake has already offered to front me the money if I need a loan. I'll take him up on it if I have to— after I pay R.J. back for this round of repairs. Who knows? Abe and his mechanics may do such a good job that the truck will run for another fifty thousand miles."

"Good luck with that. So, moving on, I have a proposition you can't refuse," Leif said.

"I can if it involves loans or getting rid of my truck."

"Nope. It involves food, reputed to be as good as it gets."

"You've got my interest."

"Adam is grilling steaks, Hadley is making her specialty potatoes and Mattie Mae—whoever she is—is baking pecan pies."

"My mouth is watering already."

"Perfect since R.J. insists I bring you to dinner. And I'm sure I can use a little moral support around that table."

"Something tells me you can hold your own. Tell R.J. how much I appreciate the offer, but this should be Effie's special night with her newly found grandfather and a chance for you to connect with R.J., as well. I don't want to butt in."

"Trust me—you wouldn't be butting in. This is not going to be the return of the prodigal son. Besides, Effie will love talking veterinary work with you."

"I'd have to go home and shower first and then someone would have to take me home after dinner. That's a lot of extra driving."

"Not so much. I'll take you home to shower and pick up the special feed, go with you to deliver it and then we'll show up at the Dry Gulch just in time for dinner."

"That's really not necessary, Leif. I've already taken you away from your daughter too long."

"I don't appear to be missed. Effie's horseback riding with Hadley and may not make it back to the house until dark. And you have to eat."

"I have to admit it's hard to turn down Mattie Mae's pies," Joni admitted.

"Then it's settled. All I need are directions to your house and an explanation of how Mattie Mae fits into the Dry Gulch family."

"She's R.J.'s housekeeper, cook and longtime friend. She and her husband owned the neighboring ranch until he died a few years ago—or at least that's what I've been told. Now she lives in a small house in town, just across the street from the Oak Grove post office."

"The way R.J. talked I thought she lived at the ranch."

"No, she has her own home, but she spends some nights at the ranch. She has a bedroom suite on the second floor with her own bathroom."

"So she's not a romantic interest?"

"Not according to Hadley."

"It doesn't really matter," Leif said. "I was just curious

as to whether or not R.J. was still chasing skirts. So which way to your place?"

"Go back the way we came. Take a right at the first fork and then turn right again when we get to the highway. The last turnoff is just before we reach the downtown area.

"I'll tell you when to turn when we get there. But don't expect much from the house. It's old and furnished in what I lovingly call junk chic."

"Sounds fascinating. Do you live alone?"

"Yes, it's just me in a rambling old house that was meant for a large family. But after sharing an apartment with two other students for most of the past five years, all that space seems heavenly."

They settled into an easy silence as he drove. He couldn't remember the last time he'd felt this relaxed with a woman, especially one as attractive as Joni. Maybe it was because she lived in R.J.'s world, and that made the possibility of a romantic entanglement a total impossibility.

There was something about her that got to him, though. He wasn't sure if it was the perky personality, the cute nose with its spattering of freckles or her smile. But together, they were awesome.

There had to be a lot of cowboys fighting for her attentions.

"Take a left at Baxter Road," Joni said after they'd driven for about eight miles. "Then *mi casa* is two miles down on the right."

Once Leif made the turn, the scenery changed from fenced pastures to heavily wooded areas. An occasional driveway, some with multiple mailboxes, wandered into the thick clusters of trees. Now and then a house was partially visible through the pines and golden-hued oaks.

The isolation was a chilling reminder of the Oak Grove

murder. A woman alone in any of these houses would be an easy target.

"Is your house visible from the—" Leif stopped mid-sentence as streams of bright yellow police tape came into view. It wound around and through the links of a metal gate and a chain-link fence that edged the road. This time the drive sported only one rusted mailbox.

A pickup truck had pulled onto the shoulder and a man was leaning out the window snapping pictures of the house that would have gone unnoticed were it not for the bright-colored tape. As it was, Leif could barely make out a railed front porch and part of the roofline.

Two sheriff's patrol cars were parked in the driveway near the road. Leif pulled to the shoulder just past the pickup truck for a better look. No defense attorney could turn down a crime scene.

"I guess you heard about the Oak Grove woman who was murdered sometime yesterday," Joni said. She shuddered and pulled her arms tight around her chest. "That's where she lived."

"Did you know her?" Leif asked.

"I know her name was Evie Monsant and that she lived alone."

"That's more than they were reporting last night."

"She kept to herself. I've seen her at her mailbox, but she always looked away and pretended not to see me wave. She does the same with the other neighbors."

"She must have talked to someone."

"Not unless she had to. She'd only been in the area a few months. Gossip was that she was a recent widow and still grieving."

"Seems unlikely that a grieving widow would move to an area where she had no friends or family and then make it a point not to meet anyone."

Joni lowered her window a couple of inches. The slight breeze ruffled her short hair, sending dark wisps dancing about her face. "The news report I heard said she might be a victim of The Hunter. I would have never expected that in Oak Grove."

"That's merely speculation," Leif said. "I wouldn't put any trust in that at this point." Leif shifted into Drive, pushed down on the accelerator and sped away.

"But it does sound like his other murders," Joni argued. "An attractive woman living alone. An isolated setting. Leaving her in the woods after sexually assaulting her and then inflicting wounds with what appears to be a hunting knife."

"If the murder was the work of The Hunter, he's probably long gone from here by now," Leif said. "He's never killed in the same area twice in the past and his murders have always been months apart."

Still, Leif was getting bad vibes about Joni living so close to the victim.

A few minutes later they reached her drive. It was on the same side of the road as the victim's. The woods surrounding her house were just as thick.

He pulled into the dirt driveway leading to her house. Lengthening shadows crept across the gray clapboard porch, intensifying the feeling of isolation as Leif stopped a few yards from the front door.

Joni sat up straighter, her hands clasped tightly in her lap. When she turned toward him, her eyes mirrored the same dark thoughts that were eating at him.

He put an arm around her shoulders. She nestled against him, and a surge of protectiveness swept through him, stronger than any in recent memory. That was far too quickly followed by a kick of arousal, especially when

Joni snuggled closer in his arms, her head resting beneath his chin.

Joni pulled away quickly. He didn't know what she was feeling, but there was no denying the sensual jolt he'd experienced. He should run and run fast.

Instead he killed the engine and stepped out of his car.

Chapter Five

Joni unlocked the front door and pushed it open, her blood still thrumming from the rush of emotion she'd felt in Leif's arms. She'd always been too cautious to let a man get to her like that.

Mostly she'd been so busy with college and veterinary training that she hadn't had time for a boyfriend. But even if she could squeeze a relationship with Leif into her schedule, he was only passing through and in a big hurry to put his day in Oak Grove behind him.

"Sorry for that mini-meltdown," she said as he followed her inside.

"Don't be. That's what shoulders are for. And I wouldn't call that a meltdown. More like a reasonable reaction to a hideous neighborhood crime."

"Seeing the house did get to me. You don't expect that type of crime in Oak Grove. The worst they've had since I've been here is vandalism at the high school and a brawl after a rodeo where two guys got busted for fighting."

"No place is immune to crime these days. If you're nervous staying here alone, maybe you should spend a few nights with a friend or I'm sure R.J. would put you up at the Dry Gulch."

"I have two very good friends who are never far away. A Smith & Wesson pistol and a shotgun."

"And I guess you're an expert at using them, Annie Oakley."

"I am. Blake and the Lambert family made sure I learned to use both shortly after I moved here."

"Who are the Lamberts?"

"One of the nicest families you'll ever meet. Stick around Oak Grove awhile, and you'll find out for yourself."

Gee. Open her mouth, insert foot. Now he surely thought she was encouraging him to come back on her account.

"Have you ever killed anything?" Leif asked.

"Snakes. One a huge rattlesnake waiting on my front walk to welcome me home. But I like to ride and walk in the woods. You never know exactly what you'll run into."

"And you look so harmless," he teased.

"I wouldn't put me to the test if I were you."

"Not a chance."

Joni led him into the family room, a spacious area with lots of windows, an oversize sofa she'd bought at a second-hand store and two chairs she'd actually purchased new at a clearance sale. Next to the kitchen, it was her favorite room in the house.

Leif turned, giving the room a quick once-over. "So this is 'junk chic.'"

"Yes, a hodgepodge of mostly secondhand items I've picked up since moving into the house."

"You obviously have a way with putting bargains together. I don't even hang a picture without a decorator telling me where it should go." He smirked. "That sounded pretentious, didn't it?"

"Yes."

"I'm not actually a snob. I just have no taste."

"Of course you do. Everyone does. You go with what feels right. If it works for you, then it works. I mean, unless there's someone else you have to please."

"Just the cleaning lady, and she's not too particular as long as I don't explode over things getting broken from time to time."

So he lived alone. Interesting, but no reason she should go getting ideas. The hug was just a gesture of comfort, not a prelude to a date.

"I hate to admit it," Leif said, dropping into an easy chair and propping his feet on a leather footstool, "but I don't have anything in my house this comfortable."

"Which is good and bad," Joni said. "I fall asleep in that at least twice a week, usually during evening news."

"I can understand why if all your days are as busy as this one."

"Actually, this was a slow day." Joni bent to straighten a stack of magazines she'd left on the wooden coffee table. When she looked up, Leif's head was resting against the back of the chair, his eyes closed, loose locks of dark hair falling into his face.

Her heart did a crazy jump. She determined to ignore it. The guy was gorgeous. So what?

"How about some coffee while you wait for me to shower and change?"

"Is that the strongest beverage you have?"

"Almost. I'm not much of a drinker, but I have an open bottle of chardonnay in the fridge and an unopened bottle of whiskey in the pantry. The wine may have lost its pizzazz. I can't vouch for the whiskey, either. It was a gift from a thankful rancher."

"Time to check it out," Leif said.

"Then follow me."

He left his comfortable seat. The old pine-plank floor creaked as they walked to the kitchen.

Leif trailed his fingers along the edge of her dark harvest table. "This does not qualify as junk in anyone's book."

"You're right. It's a genuine antique and one of my best finds. I picked it up at an estate sale." Joni set the bottle of whiskey on the table and went back to the cupboard for a glass.

Leif picked up the bottle and studied the label. "This is good stuff. Your rancher buddy must have been quite impressed with you."

"I do good work." Now she was flirting—and enjoying it. Leif made that far too easy.

"Are you going to make me drink alone?" Leif asked.

"That depends on how big a hurry you're in to get back to the Dry Gulch."

"We can surely make time for a drink and a tour of the house."

"Okay." She got a second glass. "But don't expect much with the rest of the rooms. Most are empty except for cinderblock and four-by-four shelving laden with books of every description. And unpacked boxes of clothes I should have thrown away after undergrad school."

"So you're not only a bargain hunter. You're a hoarder, too."

"The preferred phrase is *collector*."

Leif poured two fingers of the amber liquid into each glass and handed one to her. He held up his glass for a toast. "To friendship, prize steers and truck repairs," he said.

Their eyes met as the glasses clinked. Her pulse quickened and a warm flush coated her insides like sweet honey. *Time to get the tour on the road.*

"We can start the tour with my office," she said. "I spend a lot more time there than I do in my kitchen."

"You mean you have to work at night after putting in a full day in the field?"

"Paperwork. Everything has to be documented. I only make brief notes on-site and then fill in the particulars later.

And I'm constantly reading the latest research. Veterinary medicine is ever changing."

"Unlike my work. Criminals keep repeating the same dumb crimes over and over for the same reasons. Greed, revenge and jealousy. Or some like The Hunter just kill for the thrill of it."

"If you don't mind, I'd just as soon not talk about crimes anymore tonight."

"Me and my big mouth. I promise to say nothing upsetting for the rest of the tour. Lead on."

Good. She definitely couldn't chance ending up in his arms again. After the office, she showed him the screened back porch that she'd made into a cozy outdoor living area and a hall bathroom that she'd redone from the floor up.

"I haven't seen one of those old claw-foot tubs in years—except in old movies. Is that a stray you rescued?"

"Yes, and I love it now. But there were days of tons of elbow grease and flesh-eating cleanser that I considered using the shotgun on it."

"And then the stains disappeared, you sank into a tub filled with bubbles, lit a few candles, put on some soft music...." He closed his eyes. "Ah, I can see it now."

And the thought of him visualizing that made her insides go mushy. She stepped away, chiding herself for reacting to him that way.

He was designer condos, big city, bright lights, Dallas. She was horses, jeans, scuffed boots, Oak Grove. He was a heartbreak waiting to happen. She liked her heart intact.

"End of tour," she said. "Help yourself to the whiskey and find a comfortable chair. I'll be ready in ten minutes."

"If you are, you'll break every record I've ever known for a woman getting dressed."

"I could make it in five." She rushed off without looking back.

LEIF DULY NOTED that the bedroom had been left off the tour. He had no idea if it was because Joni thought he was coming on too strong or if she just didn't consider it smart to share her personal space. Or maybe she'd left unmentionables lying around.

Whatever, it was for the best. So was getting out of earshot of the shower. No use encouraging stimulating visualizations.

He walked outside and settled in an inviting porch swing he hadn't noticed before. It didn't get much homier than this. Not that he knew about real homes. Another thing he could thank R.J. for. Even that didn't matter so much to Leif. It was Travis's heartbreak he'd never forgive the man for.

Leif had never given living outside the city a thought. When he was involved in a trial, the late hours at work would have meant staying in a hotel half the time.

But he had to admit it was peaceful out here. Chirping birds preparing to nest for the night. The autumn breeze whistling through the trees. A squirrel scurrying up the trunk of a gnarled oak.

This was probably the same peaceful feeling Evie Monsant had experienced before her world had turned deadly. The random victim of a serial killer? A carefully chosen victim of a copycat killer? Or had Evie Monsant's past just caught up with her?

He didn't know the local sheriff well enough to fish any information out of him. Most of the Dallas homicide department weren't too eager to answer his questions, either, considering he sat on the opposite side of the courtroom when a case went to trial.

But there was one homicide detective he could always depend on for an honest opinion, even though he was vacationing at Hilton Head this week. Leif punched in the number on his cell phone and waited for his brother to answer.

"Travis Dalton."

"Good. Glad I caught you."

"By the hair of your chinny, chin chin. I was just about to head out."

"Got a hot date?"

"Yes, I do. Eyes of blue, lips like cherry wine. And legs a mile long. Met her on the beach this morning. So what can I do for you in the next two minutes?"

"I was just wondering if you'd heard anything about the woman who was murdered in Oak Grove Monday morning. I figured the local sheriff department might have recruited some expertise from the Big D."

"Reluctantly. Sheriff Garcia likes to run his own show, but with The Hunter tag coming into play, the investigation outgrew him."

"So you have heard about it."

"Nothing official. I talked to one of my homicide buddies earlier and he mentioned it."

"Is he the lead detective on the case?"

"No, that honor has fallen to Josh Morgan, but that could change."

"Morgan. I don't think I've met him."

"You haven't. He's not a drinking buddy."

"Why is that?"

"He and I got off to a bad start when he got promoted to Homicide last year and we had to work a case together. Nothing serious, just different ways of getting the same job done. He's a strict by-the-book operator."

"So what did your buddy say when he called. Does he think this is the work of The Hunter?"

"Could be. It's his signature style, more or less. Certainly brutal enough. But each of the murders attributed to him have had small differences in execution."

"So it could be The Hunter's doing?"

"It could be. I haven't jumped on that theory yet."

"Why not?"

"Too much points to this not being a random killing."

"Like what?"

"Evie Monsant had a fake social security number and a fake name. No one's shown up to identify the body except for the local sheriff, who's only known her a few months."

"So you think she was hiding something or running from someone?"

"That would be my guess. So why your sudden interest in the case? Shouldn't you still be celebrating your big win in court yesterday?"

"Not sure that was a celebratory moment. And I passed by the scene of the crime a few minutes ago."

"What? You're in Oak Grove. Tell me you have a good reason for venturing into the realm of R.J."

"I do. Effie. She's in town to meet her grandfather."

Travis groaned repeatedly while Leif filled him in.

"So you've been at the Dry Gulch Ranch all day riding horses and getting chummy with R.J.?"

"Not exactly, but Effie has and I'm joining the family circus for dinner."

"Better you than me, but I understand your desire to keep Effie happy. I'll be home Thursday morning. Is she staying through Thanksgiving?"

"Yes. Care to join us for turkey?"

"Sure, if my plane's not delayed—unless lunch includes Serena."

"Nope. She's a thing of the past, or she will be once I get my condo key from her."

"Her decision or yours?"

"Hers," Leif admitted, "but it was inevitable. We're too different and she wanted more than I could give."

"More than anyone could give. About time you realized she's spoiled rotten and likes it that way."

"And she spoke so highly of you."

"Sure she did. Me, the lowly detective who didn't fit into her social circles. But what are your plans?"

"Thanksgiving at the Dry Gulch, unless I'm granted a last-minute reprieve."

"In that case, count me out, but I would like to see Effie while she's here."

"Then better buy a horse. That's the only thing that interests her these days."

They talked a few minutes more, and then Leif said goodbye without mentioning Joni. It seemed less complicated that way.

Not that he wouldn't love to see more of Joni. She not only got to him physically but she was fun to be with. They could have some good times. Maybe too good.

He might even start to think he could make it work with her. But then he'd become consumed in his work and end up disappointing her. She'd get hurt. They both would.

Besides, she was R.J.'s friend. She'd push a relationship between them and Leif had no intention of playing R.J.'s happy-family-game.

Better for everyone if he didn't get anything started with Joni. Now all he had to do was make sure he heeded that advice.

THE DINNER AT Dry Gulch Ranch was lively, lots of talk and laughter, much of the entertainment provided by two of the most adorable redheaded toddlers Leif had ever seen. Their mother, Hadley, was also a live wire and she and Adam looked and sounded like the perfect couple.

R.J. was quieter than he'd been that morning and he staggered once when got up from the table to get the second pie from the kitchen. The brain tumor was evidently taking its toll.

But that didn't stop R.J. from lavishing his attention on Effie. There was no consolidating the elderly man at the table with the father who'd let his sons grow up as orphans.

The others, especially Hadley and Adam, tried to include Leif in the night's conversation. Admittedly, he didn't make much of an effort. Even if he had, he would always be an outsider in the Dalton family.

But judging by the way Effie recounted the day's adventure in detail, there was no denying that she thought the visit to the Dry Gulch Ranch was a splendid success.

They were having pecan pie, ice cream and coffee when Effie hit him with her latest bombshell of an idea.

She turned to Hadley. "Tell Dad about the plans for tomorrow."

Hadley wiped her mouth with the floral-printed cotton napkin. "I teach a Sunday school class for eighth-grade girls. Since they're out of school this week for the holiday, I'm having them out to the ranch for a trail ride."

"Like a real cowboy trail ride," Effie broke in. "Uncle Adam is going to cook egg and chorizo tacos in a cast-iron skillet over an open fire."

Leif didn't have to wait to hear the rest. It was already settled in Effie's mind. He'd never have the heart to disappoint her.

"We'd love to have Effie join us," Hadley said. "Unless you have other plans."

"We don't have any plans," Effie said. "I don't have to go back to California until Sunday."

Irritation burned in Leif's chest. R.J. and even Adam and Hadley were teaming up against him. What chance

did he have of connecting with Effie when they were pit-
ting horses against him?

If Effie were the size of Lila and Lacy, he could just pick
her up and go home. But she wasn't and he was already
walking a thin line with her. He struggled to keep the irritation out of his voice.

"That would mean getting up long before daylight."

"Not if I spent the night here. Aunt Hadley says they
have a guest room that's never been used."

Good old Aunt Hadley. "You didn't bring any extra
clothes with you."

"I have something she can sleep in and an extra tooth-
brush," Hadley offered. "But of course the decision is up
to you."

If it were up to him they wouldn't even be here. Old
memories surfaced. He and Travis had both been years
younger than Effie when their mother had died. There had
been no invitation to stay at the Dry Gulch then. There
hadn't been so much as a phone call to see if they were
okay. No thought at all for what would happen to them.

But R.J. hadn't been a dying man then with all his sins
hanging over him like a death cloak.

"You can stay, too," R.J. said. "Help Adam with the
breakfast chores. Mattie Mae and me can drive over to the
cabin and stay with Lacy and Lila."

"I go help Daddy, too," Lila said.

Lacy slid off her chair and went over to stand by Adam.
"Me, too, Daddy. I'm a big girl."

Adam pulled her into his lap. "You are a big girl, but
you'd have to get up as early as cowboys do. You wouldn't
like that."

"Then Effie can stay with us."

"I can play with you when I get back from the trail ride,"
Effie said.

As if it were all decided. The food had been delicious going down. Now it was churning in Leif's stomach. He pushed back from the table. If he didn't get out of there soon, things were sure to come to a head.

And once he started telling R.J. how he felt, there would be no stopping until it was all out on the table. He couldn't put Effie or Joni through that.

"It's getting late," he said. "I still have a long drive in front of me."

"Then I can stay?" Effie asked.

"Why not?"

It hurt that she was as eager to escape him as he was to put distance between himself and R.J. He loved Effie more that he'd ever loved another human being in all his life. But he'd failed her. And if he didn't find a way to reach her soon, he'd lose her forever.

"I'll be back in the morning with your luggage, Effie. We'll talk more about the week's plans then."

"Sure. I'll see you tomorrow." She stacked some of the empty plates and carried them to the kitchen.

That was it. No hug. No thank-you for driving her out to the ranch. Being a stranger to his own daughter hurt most of all.

R.J. stood as the women and Adam cleared the rest of the table. "You're welcome to stay as long as you want, Leif. No strings. No demands."

"I think I've stayed long enough."

"If that's how you feel, but go easy on Effie. She's got a lot going on in her mind."

"You mean more than the Dry Gulch Ranch and horses?"

"Yeah. Hadley says she opened up to her a little when they were out this afternoon. She's worried about something but didn't want to talk about it. I'd say she needs her father."

Now R.J. was giving parenting advice. What a joke. Leif

went through the motions of politely thanking all of them for a great dinner and for making Effie feel so welcome.

"Can you give me a ride home?" Joni asked.

"That's the plan."

"If you'd rather not—"

"I want to take you home." That time when he said it he made sure it sounded sincere.

"Okay. I'll be with you in a minute."

The truth was he wanted to be alone with her more than he cared to admit. His time with her was the one thing that had gone right today.

Leif walked onto the porch to wait for her. Adam followed him. A new wave of tension clenched his muscles.

"I can imagine this was a tough night for you," Adam said. "You handled it well."

"I didn't have a lot of choice without upsetting Effie and making a scene in front of Joni."

"Effie's quite a kid. Hadley took to her immediately. Of course, they have this love of horses to build on."

"I noticed."

"I'm not an expert on horses or daughters, but it seems to me that you're pushing mighty hard to find some common ground with Effie."

"Is it that obvious?"

"Yeah. I know you've got no use for R.J. That's obvious, too."

"I have my reasons."

"Don't we all? R.J. wasn't the father any of us needed. But you can't undo the past."

"What's your point?"

"Maybe you should forget R.J. and concentrate on Effie this week. Go horseback riding with her. Show an interest in the animals. Just hang out together without trying to force her to see R.J. through your eyes. And if I'm out of line saying this, just tell me it's none of my damn business."

"I'll give your advice some thought," Leif said. "It can't get any more frustrating than the way things are now."

"If I can help with anything, let me know."

"Thanks. I will."

Leif decided it would be hard not to like Adam.

Joni joined him on the porch a few minutes later. Neither of them said anything until they were backing out of the driveway.

"You survived dinner," she said.

"Barely."

"Want to talk about it?"

"No. We've both dealt with enough trouble for one day."

"On the positive, Effie is a great kid. I know there's tension between you two, but time at the ranch might be exactly what both of you need. Out here you're not trying to fit into each other's world. You're just experiencing this new world together."

"That's pretty much what Adam said."

"Adam is a smart man, but his past was no picnic. Sometime you'll have to let him tell you his story."

"You sound as if you spend a lot of time at the Dry Gulch."

"Hadley and I were the new kids on the block together. She and Adam moved to the ranch a few months after I took the job with Blake Benson. We met when I came out to talk to R.J. about artificial insemination of his mares and almost instantly became friends."

"Poor mares. All the work, none of the fun."

"That's exactly what R.J. said."

"I'll wash my mouth out with soap." Leif flicked on the radio and they both sang along to a song by Blake Shelton. He was just starting to relax when they passed Evie Monsant's house.

Moonlight gave the police tape an eerie glow. Joni stopped singing and wrapped her arms tightly around her chest, just as she'd done that afternoon.

"I wonder if her killer's still in Oak Grove."

Fear. Dread. Anxiety. He heard shades of all of that in her voice. It wasn't paranoia. For all she knew, she could have been the one brutally attacked. And like Evie Monsant, no one would have heard her screams.

Everyone in Oak Grove seemed to count on Joni. She needed someone to count on tonight.

His hands tightened on the wheel. The rest of his life might be in a state of flux, but one thing was clear. In spite of any warning he might have given himself about getting involved with Joni, he would not be driving back to Dallas tonight.

Chapter Six

The beams from Leif's headlights cut through the layers of inky blackness and stalking shadows that mantled Joni's rented farmhouse. Before her neighbor's murder, coming home had always felt like reaching her haven—the welcoming space she'd created for herself.

Tonight, anxiety about Evie's murder edged her homecoming, along with the uneasiness of being with a man who got to her in too many ways to count.

It made no sense. She was around cute cowboys all the time, several who'd hit on her relentlessly. She noticed them. Occasionally, she even flirted back though most of the single guys around Oak Grove were too young for her. None had ever made her senses hum the way Leif did.

Not that the unexpected attraction mattered. When the intriguing attorney drove away tonight, she'd likely never see him again. Dallas was only an hour or two away, depending on traffic, but Leif wanted no part of Oak Grove or ranch life. This was the only life she wanted.

Leif stopped the car and killed the engine. "Don't you have any outside lighting?"

"I usually leave the porch light on when I know I'll return home after dark. Guess I forgot today."

"You should have solar spotlights along the drive and

the front of the house. I'll pick some up and install them for you tomorrow."

"It's not always this dark. Most nights the stars are so bright you can easily make your way up the walk without slipping on a loose rock or stumbling into a skunk."

"You would mention skunks. Talking from experience?"

"I see and smell them frequently. Only got sprayed directly once. Not an experience I'll forget."

"And not one I want to add to my repertoire."

Leif reached across her and into his glove compartment. His hand brushed her thigh. Casual. Meaningless. Pulse tingling.

He pulled a flashlight from the compartment. "Forewarned is forearmed."

"Or you could just leave your headlights on until I get in the house."

"But they don't illuminate all the grassy spots where a white-streaked creature might be planning an ambush."

Joni fished in her handbag for her keys. Leif opened his car door.

"No reason for you to get out," she said.

"A gentleman always walks his date to the door."

"A date is when a person asks another person out. This was more a matter of you being coerced into service."

He didn't argue the point. He just walked to her side of the car and opened her door.

Flashlight in his left hand, he fit his right hand to the curve of her back as they walked up the leaf-strewn stone path.

Her nerves began a slow, heated dance as possibilities surfaced. Would he ask to come in? Would he kiss her goodnight? Did she want him to?

Yes.... And no.

Once she'd fit the key into the lock, the flashlight beam

went dark, as did his headlights, which had evidently timed out. Once again, they were immersed in darkness.

Thoughts of Evie Monsant slunk back into her mind, dissolving the dizzying anticipation that had claimed her moments before. Weirdly, the merging of fear and her attraction to Leif made both more intense.

With her hand on the doorknob, she made a half turn and looked up at Leif. "Thanks for giving up your day for me."

"My pleasure."

"At least let me pay for your gas?"

He leaned in, planting a hand on the door frame. "Better yet, invite me in for an after-dinner drink?"

Her breath caught. Her senses reeled. "You have a long drive in front of you."

"There's nothing waiting for me in Dallas."

And nothing waiting for her when he drove away except disappointment, rattled nerves over Evie's murder and an empty house. She took a deep breath and then swallowed hard. "Sure. One drink can't hurt."

It was only a nightcap after a long day. No excuse at all for the warmth that flushed her body as she opened the door and Leif followed her inside.

A few minutes later they were settled in the cozy family room, both on the sofa, her on the end, pivoted so that she faced Leif.

She'd slipped out of her shoes and pulled her right knee onto the sofa between them. It kept him at a safe distance while she tried to figure out where he expected this to go and if this was moving too fast.

She sipped her whiskey, and the slow burn seared its way to the pit of her stomach. The mingling of titillation and alcohol was definitely not conducive to a clear mind.

"Tell me about you," Leif said. "How did you decide to become a veterinarian?"

"My parents bought me a puppy for my fifth birthday. It was a golden retriever, and we bonded at first lick—not sure which of us licked first."

"So you're a dog as well as a horse girl?"

"Dogs, cats, hamsters, bunnies—you name it. Mom said I got more excited over going to a pet store when I was young than a trip to the local water park. And I loved water parks. Still do, by the way."

"Ugh."

"Don't tell me you hate getting your hair wet and mussed," she teased.

"I hate standing in lines. Give me a good old Texas waterhole any day. Or a tubing trip, lazily drifting down a river in the Texas Hill Country."

"How long has it been since you've done that?"

"Too long." Leif's arm snaked across the back of the sofa until his fingertips brushed her shoulder. The touch was headier than the whiskey.

"When did your primary interest become horses?" he asked.

"I was probably a couple of years younger than Effie is now. My best friend's family bought a small horse farm near where we lived in southern Oklahoma. I was captivated the second I climbed into in the saddle."

"And from that, you made the decision to become an equine vet?"

"Not right away. But once I saw a newborn foal taking its first steps on those cute, spindly legs, I was a goner. From that point on, I knew I'd always want horses in my life. Becoming an equine vet was the natural choice for my life's work."

"I don't know if Effie's fascination will have the lasting fervor yours did, but she can't get enough of horses now. I have no doubt that R.J.'s promise of a stable full of beautiful animals is the only reason she flew to Texas for the Thanksgiving holidays."

"Does it really matter why she came, Leif? The important thing is she's here. Make the most of it. I'm sure she needs a father as much as you need her. Reach out to her every way that you can."

"Easier said than done when the only path to reaching her goes through R.J."

Bitterness hardened his words. His resentment of R.J. seemed to run soul deep. She hated to ask, dreaded hearing the worst about the dying rancher she liked so much, but she needed to know the truth. It was the only way she could take a stab at understanding the intensity of Leif's resentment.

"Did R.J. abuse you as a child?"

His brows arched. "Where did that come from?"

"I just know he must have done something horrible to you for you to resent him so much after all these years."

"I barely remember R.J., but I'm all but certain there was no physical abuse. Mom would have killed him had he laid an abusive hand on me or Travis. She was fiercely protective."

"What did cause their divorce?"

He looked away, and for a second she thought she'd pushed too far.

"The worst Mom ever said was that R.J. was not a fit father or husband. I only heard that years after the fact. I was only three and Travis was just nine months old when Mother left the Dry Gulch Ranch and moved to California."

"And you were never curious enough to look up R.J. when you were older?"

"Why would I be? He'd never been a father to me. Too bad he didn't leave it that way instead of coming up with that ludicrous will and then contacting Effie."

"Where is your mother now?"

"She died when I was eight."

Leif stood and walked to the window, staring into the darkness, his gaze intense and troubled. She doubted he was telling her the entire truth about his relationship with R.J. His scars went too deep for there not to be more.

She finished her whiskey and tried to stand. The room seemed to shift and she had to grip the arm of the sofa for balance.

Leif slid his arms around her waist. "Easy, baby. You really are a lightweight drinker."

"I'm not used to hard liquor." She steadied. "Guess that means it's time to call it a night."

"Definitely is for you." He took her hand. "But I'm thinking I shouldn't drive back to Dallas tonight."

Tension swelled. She liked Leif, liked him a lot. But she wasn't ready for this, not when she was too light-headed to think straight. "Not a good idea—"

He put a finger to her lips to shush her objections. "Don't worry, Joni. I've never gone into a woman's bedroom when I wasn't invited or taken advantage of a tipsy one. I just think you might sleep better tonight with a man in the house."

"Because of Evie Monsant? You think I could be in danger."

"I didn't say that. The truth is, I think Evie was targeted, not random. Her killer is probably long gone."

"What makes you think it wasn't random?"

"Because her real name was not Evie Monsant."

"How do you know that?"

"Personal source, but I'm sure it will be public knowledge by tomorrow or as soon as the police discover her true identity."

Joni mulled over the new bombshell. "That would explain why Evie was so mysterious and secretive. But it doesn't guarantee that she wasn't another random victim of The Hunter."

"No, but it opens up a keg of other more likely possibilities. Still, we'll both rest better if you're not out here alone tonight. Besides, like I said, there's no reason for me to rush back to Dallas. I can drive in tomorrow morning and pick up Effie's clothes."

Only there was one very good reason. "I don't have an extra bed, Leif."

"You have a sofa. I'm easy. Just toss me a pillow and I'll be fine."

"Are you sure?"

"Positive."

It sounded simple and straightforward. Leif on her sofa the entire night. Steps away.

Or in her bed, if she invited him. One night of torrid lovemaking when it had been two years since she'd been with a man. Put that way, she'd be a fool not to sleep with him.

But then Leif would be easy to fall in love with and probably impossible to forget. No sense wooing a broken heart. She had to keep this light and keep him out of her bed.

"I can offer you more than a pillow."

His brows arched expectantly.

"You can have a sheet and a blanket, too."

"You, Dr. Joni, are a tease."

He followed her to the hall linen closet. She handed him a spare pillow and a pillowcase. Her only extra sheets were a set of hot pink ones she'd gotten as a graduation gift from one of her eccentric great-aunts.

"Best I can do," she said, handing him the flat sheet.

"That should sufficiently emasculate my manhood."

Joni was sure a mere sheet could never lessen Leif's

virility or sex appeal, but she reached to the top shelf for an unfeminine blanket. "To keep you warm and hide the sheet from your psyche."

"Thank goodness."

"There are clean towels in the guest bathroom I showed you earlier if you want to shower."

"I think that's a necessity."

"Do you want to keep my pistol with you?"

"No, thanks. I have my own."

"On you?"

"In the car, but I'll get it."

That surprised her. "Snakes in the big city, too?"

"The worst kind," Leif admitted. "The nutcases and grief-stricken family members who think I helped free a guilty defendant."

"I hadn't thought of that."

They walked back toward the living area, side by side. The hall was narrow. Practically every step produced a brush of hands or arms or shoulders.

She stopped at her bedroom door, afraid she was a few heated breaths away from issuing the invitation to join her in her bed. She needed a closed door between them quick.

"Would you lock up once you get your gun?" she asked.

"You got it."

He leaned in close. One finger trailed a path down the side of her face, then across her lips. Her defenses plummeted. Anticipation curled in her stomach, and wispy waves of heat knotted in her chest.

His mouth found hers and she melted.

The kiss was bold, blowing her inhibitions away. She kissed him back, and the thrill of it hummed through every nerve. Drowning in desire, her body arched toward his, her breasts pushing hard against his chest.

Leif came to his senses first. His hands fell to her shoulders and he backed away. "Sorry, but I've wanted to do that ever since I met you. Now get some sleep. I'll be here when you wake up."

Speechless, she slipped into her room, closing the door with her foot and then pressing her back against it until she could regain her equilibrium.

If Leif's sole purpose in staying the night was for her to get a good night's sleep, his kiss had destroyed any chance of that.

LEIF WENT BACK to the car for his pistol, though he was practically certain the only danger either of them faced tonight was from his overactive libido. Once the front door was locked, he made his way to the bathroom for a very cold shower.

Had someone told him this morning he'd be spending the night in Oak Grove in the home of a sexy pixie, he'd have thought them nuts. Yet here he was and so turned on, he was nowhere near on top of his game.

Never had a first kiss affected him like that. Desire had hit so hard he'd had to fight Neanderthal instincts to throw her over his shoulder and carry her to the bed. He'd have scared her off forever. That was the last thing he wanted.

So what did he want? A lover practically in the shadow of Dry Gulch Ranch? A lustful shove into a world he hoped to never enter again after this week? A woman whose world was so different, it didn't even seem to spin on the same axis as his?

He dried off, picked up his dirty clothes and tiptoed back to the living room, wearing only the towel. The covers and pillow were waiting for him on the sofa, but like so many other nights, his mind wasn't even close to letting him sleep. He dropped into the overstuffed chair and propped his feet on the hassock.

Leaning back, he closed his eyes. With all that had happened today, strangley, it was Edward Blanco who skulked into his mind.

Edward Blanco, accused murderer. Innocent until proven guilty.

Leif had played a major role in seeing that Edward was not proven guilty. The end result was that another man capable of committing a brutal, senseless murder was back on the streets.

That was the job of a defense attorney. The responsibility of the prosecution was to prove beyond a reasonable doubt that the man was guilty. The duty of the jury was to vote their convictions.

Most of the time the system worked. Most of the time when Leif wrapped up a trial successfully, he was proud of the accomplishment. Watching Edward Blanco walk away a free man had made him feel like a traitor to the justice system and the human race.

If Edward was guilty and he killed again, it would be a repeat of the anguish Leif had felt when one of his first defendants had kidnapped and murdered a Texas coed within a year of his trial for a similar crime.

Call them sick, call them evil, call them clones of the devil. Whatever you labeled them, they were men with an addiction to committing the most heinous crimes over and over again.

Just like the infamous Hunter, Edward Blanco might well be one of them.

Leif forced the tormenting thoughts to the back of his mind, letting Effie take front and center. She'd been a Daddy's girl once. She had curled up in his arms at night for a bedtime story, had invited him to tea parties with her dolls and stuffed animals. He'd taught her how to ride a bicycle, had cheered her on during her first swim meet.

That Effie was gone to him forever. The Effie who'd replaced her was a young woman who didn't seem to want or need her father in her life.

But Joni was right. Effie was here, and it might be Leif's last chance to bridge the gulf that separated them. He'd let her get by with pushing him away for too long.

If it meant spending time at the Dry Gulch Ranch, so be it. He'd never think of R.J. as a father, never have any respect for the man. But he'd put up with him this week if that's what it took to reconnect with his daughter before it was too late.

Finally, he moved to the sofa and pulled the hot pink sheet over his naked body. The gray of dawn sent shadows dancing about the ceiling before he finally fell into a sound sleep. When he woke again, the sun had topped the horizon and the smell of coffee drifted from the kitchen.

Leif sat up and scanned the room for his clothes. He was certain he hadn't left them in the bathroom, but there was no sign of them, not even his boxer shorts. He did spy his watch on the coffee table.

He wrapped the sheet around his hips and headed to the kitchen. Joni was sitting at the table, her fingers wrapped around the curved handle of a pottery mug, her gaze fastened on an electronic tablet.

She looked up as he entered. Fully dressed, no makeup to mask her flawless skin, straight dark hair framing her heart-shaped face, she looked good enough to eat.

"What did you do with my clothes, woman?"

"Nothing. Did you misplace them?" Mischief made her dark eyes shine like morning dew.

"So you want fun and games, do you?" He pulled, loosening the knot so that the bright-hued sheet began a slow slide down his body.

Joni flew across the room and caught it just before it

sneaked past his hips. "Not that much fun." She tugged it back in place.

Her hair brushed his chest and the faint scent of lavender sent his senses reeling. His body sprung to life and he backed away before the bulge in his body gave the sheet a new shape.

"I woke up early and threw your clothes on to wash. After a day of following me from barn to barn, I thought clean clothes were in order. They're in the dryer now, but should be ready in—" she glanced at the kitchen clock "—ten minutes."

"Okay, but in the meantime, you may want to grab a pair of sunglasses or be blinded by my toga."

First time he'd ever had a woman jump up in the morning and wash clothes. "Is there more coffee in that pot?"

"There is. How do you take it?"

"Strong and black."

"That I can handle." She filled another pottery mug and handed it to him. Then she refilled her own.

"It's a beautiful morning, already in the high sixties," she said. "Shall we take our coffee to the back porch?"

"Why not?"

He followed her to the cozy, screened-in sitting area. They sat at a small bistro table in chairs that were more comfortable than they looked. The sun had fully cleared the horizon now and was filtering through the trees that sheltered the small backyard. The few leaves that remained were a mix of browns and golds. The ground was a carpet of dead leaves and pine needles.

Birds flitted from tree to tree and fought over the seeds in the scattered bird feeders. A dog barked in the distance. Sitting there, sipping coffee with Joni, the world of courts and trials, juries and prosecutors faded into a blur.

"I'm beginning to see what makes country life so appealing."

"Good, because I have a suggestion."

He knew from her tone he wouldn't like it. "I don't suppose it's to go back to bed and get it on."

"It's to go back to the Dry Gulch Ranch for breakfast."

He should have known the peace was too good to last. "Why on earth would I do that?"

"To spend some quality time with Effie. You could help Adam fix breakfast on the trail. Effie would be surprised to see you, but I really think she'd appreciate the effort on your part. You might even find it fun."

"I might, as long as R.J. isn't there."

"He won't be. And you said yourself that Effie won't visit you in your world. So join her in an activity that she's excited about. Let her see you in her world or at least a world she wants to be in."

"How do you know Adam would want me around?"

"If anyone will understand your need to reunite emotionally with your daughter, it's Adam. I'll call him for you, if you'd like, while you throw on your clothes."

"What will you do for transportation?"

"It's my day off. I thought I might go with you, saddle up one of R.J.'s horses and ride with Hadley and the girls."

He liked the idea, except for the thought they'd be on the Dry Gulch Ranch. But as much as he hated the thought of R.J. having anything to do with his life, he had to admit Joni was right.

"You're quite a persuader, Doc. Better than some attorneys I know."

"Then you'll do it?"

"It's worth a shot."

"After breakfast, you can drop me off at the garage to pick up my truck if that's not too much trouble."

"Good. Then I can blame you if the morning turns into a disaster."

"Spoken like a real man."

"Guess the sheet didn't totally rob me of my manhood."

He saw her quick glance in the direction of his manhood and had to fight even harder to keep it from busting loose. She blushed when she realized he'd noticed her eye movement. Then she hurriedly left to rescue his jeans from the dryer.

A few minutes later, Leif and Joni were on their way back to the Dry Gulch Ranch. Strangely, even the idea of running into R.J. didn't diminish his hopes for the morning's cowboy breakfast with Effie or his pleasure at spending time with Joni.

The attorney set of mind didn't resurface until he was pulling through the gate of the Dry Gulch Ranch. Then the bitterness and doubts took over again.

Anything involving R. J. Dalton was bound to turn out bad. Trouble was brewing. It was only a matter of time.

Chapter Seven

He knocked a wicked-looking spider from the sleeve of his camouflage hunting jacket and pushed a low-hanging branch out of his way. Taking a few steps to the right, he got the perfect view of the swaggering attorney as he walked from Joni's porch to his sleek black sports car.

Anger curdled inside him like fetid cream. Joni Griffin was pure and wholesome. She'd never take up with a slimy snake in the grass like Leif Dalton. Not if she really knew him.

Leif must have tricked her, twisted the truth and connived the way he did in the courtroom. Played her the way he did a jury with words and gestures and arrogant posturing to convince her he was trustworthy.

That was the only way she would have let him spend the night. In her house but not in her bed. He'd snuck up in the darkness and peered through Joni's living room window long after the lights in the house had been turned off.

He took out his binoculars and found a spot where he could peer into her bedroom. He dared not go closer. Not yet. But he'd make his move soon.

If Leif Dalton got in the way, he'd kill him. Another justified murder wouldn't matter in the scheme of things. Not when it meant that in the end, Joni Griffin would be his.

Then he could put the past behind him once and for all.

Chapter Eight

Leif flipped a tortilla in the cast-iron skillet and then moved to the right as the light breeze shifted the smoke from the open campfire. Adam added seasoning to the eggs. The bacon, sausage and potatoes were already cooked and warming in another covered skillet.

The odors were making his mouth water. "Do you eat like this every day on the ranch?"

"We have a big breakfast every morning," Adam admitted. "No trouble working off the calories on the ranch."

"I'm not a breakfast man myself," Leif said, "but I'm sure I would be if there was temptation like this around. At the most, I grab a bagel at the coffee shop where I stop off for my caffeine jump start. Once I get to the office, things get so hectic I sometimes miss lunch altogether."

"No doubt your life moves at a much faster pace than mine," Adam said. "Not that it's ever boring around here. But I like being near Hadley and the girls. And the ranch life suits me far better than I ever dreamed it would."

"What kind of work did you do before?"

"I was a marine until I was injured."

"How bad were you hurt?"

"Bad enough they thought I might never walk again."

"I'd have never guessed."

"Pain still flares up from time to time," Adam said. "And

if I get really tired, the right leg will start to lock up on me and the limp gets more noticeable. I was a lucky son of a bitch. Or bountifully blessed, as Hadley puts it."

"Obviously. Was that before or after you met Hadley?"

"After. That's a story for another time. Suffice it to say that the last place I planned to end up after my discharge was at the Dry Gulch Ranch or anywhere near R.J."

That Leif could identify with.

"The riders should be arriving any minute," Adam said as he slid the skillet full of scrambled eggs to the edge of the grate so that the eggs would stay hot. "Hadley tells me what time to have breakfast ready and she usually times it to perfection.

"By the way, she was thrilled when Joni called and said you two were joining us for the morning's adventure. She and Joni have become fast friends over the past few months. I should warn you, Hadley is also a zealous matchmaker."

Leif smiled at the thought of the sensual magnetism that already existed between him and Joni. Thankfully, he was smart enough to know that the physical attraction had no chance of growing into anything permanent. "I'm sure Hadley has someone much more suitable than a slightly jaded Big D defense attorney in mind for Joni."

As if on cue, the sound of voices, laughter and approaching horse hooves were added to the mix of crackling firewood, birdcalls and water dancing over a rocky creek bed.

The procession of riders was single file, with Hadley in the lead. He spotted Effie before she saw him. She was smiling and looking happier than he remembered seeing her in years.

She was older than the other girls by a couple of years, but with her sun-streaked dark hair pulled into a ponytail and her face fresh and clean as the morning itself, she looked incredibly young to him.

Her facial expression froze when she saw him, and then the smile slowly faded from her face. Following the lead of the others, she let the spirited black horse she was riding drink its fill from the pond. She didn't look back at Leif until she'd dismounted and looped the leash around a low-hanging branch of a scrawny pine tree.

She approached him warily as he served the tortillas. "What are you doing here?"

Evidently Joni hadn't mentioned he'd come back to the ranch with her. "I just decided to get in on the fun. Is that okay?"

"Sure." She looked relieved. "I'm just surprised to see you. I never thought you'd come back this early."

"It was worth it to see you riding up looking so competent and pleased in the saddle." He transferred a warm tortilla to her plate. "Besides, I didn't want to miss a chance at a cowboy breakfast."

"I know. It smells good. I'll find us a place to sit," she said.

"Is that your dad?" the girl in line behind her asked.

"Yes. He lives in Dallas. Dad, this is Mindy."

"Hi, Mindy. How about a tortilla?"

"I'll take two," she said.

"You got 'em."

This time the smile that Effie flashed him seemed genuine. And she'd asked him to sit with her. Maybe Joni was right. If he met Effie more than halfway in her world, maybe he could find a way to mend the broken bonds. Definitely worth a try.

Joni was last through the line. "What's the verdict?" she asked.

"Victory. She looked a little shocked to see me at first, but then she looked genuinely pleased that I'd made the effort to get here. She even invited me to sit with her for breakfast."

"Good. Looks like you'd best go shopping for some functional boots and a new Stetson."

"Let's not go that far yet."

He filled his plate and was on his way to sit down by Effie when his phone rang. He tried to ignore it, but then he stupidly checked the caller ID.

His ex, calling from London. Maybe he'd best take the call. But he'd keep it short, just let her know that Effie was safe and sound and smiling.

He stepped away from the others. "Good morning, Celeste."

"Hi. Hope I didn't wake you. I know it's early there, but I'm about to go into another meeting and not sure when I can get back to you."

"Actually, I'm having a cowboy breakfast on the trail."

Her laughter rang out over the phone. "I'd pay to see that. Sounds as if Effie talked you into visiting the Dry Gulch Ranch."

"You knew that was her plan?"

"It's all I've heard ever since she started corresponding with your father."

The word *father* used in any connection with R.J. grated on Leif's nerves. "A warning might have been useful."

"Surprising you was Effie's idea. But I have to admit, I thought it was a good one. Giving you time to contemplate and brood wouldn't have served her purpose or made the idea any more palatable to you."

"You might at least have told me she was coming to Dallas for the week. Suppose I hadn't been home?"

"What are you talking about? She cleared this with you weeks ago."

"I assure you, she didn't. That's not the type of thing

I'd forget. I didn't know she was coming until she rang the doorbell."

"Oh, dear. Knowing the mood she's been in of late, I should have followed up on that."

"Are you saying she lied to you?"

"Yes, but don't go getting all bent out of shape, Leif. With all the changes in her life right now, she's bound to be a little concerned. But it will all work out. It will just take a little time."

Major changes. Lies and conniving. Leif had never felt more out of the loop. He glanced back to where Effie was sitting. Joni had joined her, and the two appeared to be engrossed in their conversation.

"What changes?" Leif asked, knowing this wouldn't be good.

"I've been transferred to London permanently."

"What about Effie?"

"She'll move with me, of course. She's my daughter."

"She's *our* daughter. And the custody arrangement specifically states you can't take her anywhere that would interfere with my seeing her on a regular basis."

"You made the decision not to see Effie on a regular basis years ago, Leif."

The accusation struck to the quick. Worse, he couldn't deny it. He hadn't seen it like that at the time, but it had worked out that way. Years that he could never get back.

"You only see Effie twice a year now, Leif. Flying to London twice a year will not exactly cause you any hardship."

Celeste was right again. But the excitement he'd felt a few minutes ago dissolved into a hard knot in his stomach. Logical or not, he felt as if this was the beginning of the end. It was as if he were losing Effie forever.

Or maybe that had happened years ago, too, and he was only now coming to grips with the truth.

"Since Effie didn't tell you about the move, I don't suppose she told you about the rest of my news."

"There's more?"

"I'm getting married."

Leif waited for some kind of pang to hit. None did. The marriage had died so long ago that even the resentment that had resulted from the divorce had long since dissolved into nothingness.

"Congratulations. Who's the lucky guy?"

"No one you know. An Englishman. He works here in the London office. But he's a great guy. Effie likes him, and he adores her. The new situation will require some adjustment on Effie's part, but it will all work out. I'm sure of it."

Work out for everyone except Leif. "When's the wedding?"

"The Saturday before Christmas. But don't worry. Effie will be flying back to the States after the wedding. She'll finish her school year in her old school. Mom and Dad are coming down to live with her."

All the decisions about his daughter's life had been made with no input from him. It hurt, but it didn't surprise him. Celeste had always lived her life as she saw fit and others around her fell in line or got walked over.

Effie had been the exception. Celeste had always been a good mother. Leif had failed as a father. No wonder he hated R.J. so much. It reminded him of his own shortcomings.

Only he would never have done to Effie what R.J. had done to Leif and Travis. He wouldn't have treated a dog like that.

By the time Leif got off the phone with Celeste, Effie

had only a few bites left of her taco. He walked over and sat down beside her.

She stood as soon as he sat. "Time to hit the trail," she said without looking at him.

"I had to take the phone call," he said.

"I know. You're a very busy attorney." Resentment spilled from her voice.

"I've never been too busy for you, Effie. If you think I have, then I've given you the wrong impression."

"It doesn't matter. I have to go, Dad. The girls are already saddling up."

He had a lot more to say, but it wasn't the time or the place. But before the week was over he had to find a way to connect with her as a father. He was fast reaching the point of no return.

He felt it deep in his soul and it was scaring him to death.

"I'LL GET IT," R.J. called to Mattie Mae at the sound of the ringing doorbell.

"I'll get it, too," Lacy echoed.

R.J. got up slowly and stood for a second, his right hand on the arm of the sofa until he was certain he was steady on his feet. The times he wasn't were growing a bit more frequent. Still, he couldn't complain.

It had been a little over six months since the doc gave him his death sentence. Since then the growth of the brain tumor had slowed a bit. The outlook was no brighter, except that he might have gained a few more months of life. And he wanted all he could get.

Adam, Hadley, Lacy and Lila had changed his life. Too bad it had taken him so long to realize that he needed family and that they just might need him.

Lacy beat him to the door, but she couldn't reach the

latch that was used mostly to keep her and Lila in rather than to keep anyone out.

He opened the door and then felt a smile that came directly from the heart. And the eyes. Carolina Lambert was definitely nice to look at—proof positive that he wasn't dead yet. Carolina held her granddaughter Belle with one hand and a covered dish with the other.

"It's Belle," Lacy called. She grabbed the toddler visitor in a bear hug and tried to pick her up. Belle quickly wiggled her way to freedom.

Lila came running. "Come see our fort. Grandpa helped us make it out of sheets."

Next thing he knew, the three of them were running back toward the girls' playroom, all squealing like stuck pigs.

"Play nicely, Belle," Carolina called as they disappeared down the hallway.

R.J. stood back for Carolina to enter. "Whatever you're carrying there smells mighty good."

"It's a pumpkin roll. I made four of them this morning. Even with my whole crew coming for dinner, that's enough to share."

"Glad you thought of us. Mattie Mae will be glad, too. She's fretting over Thanksgiving dinner preparations like we were feeding the Pope instead of family."

"Will Hadley, Adam and the girls be here?"

"Yes, and Hadley's mom and my son Leif and his teenage daughter, Effie."

"Now that's a surprise. You told me about Effie's wanting to visit you, but you haven't said a thing about being in touch with Leif. Did you know they were coming?"

"Not for sure, not until yesterday. Leif might still back out. He barely speaks to me. The only thing that got him out to the ranch was Effie."

"So they are staying with you?"

"Effie slept over with Hadley and Adam last night so she could go on a trail ride this morning with a bunch of girls from church that Hadley had invited over. Leif drove back in to Dallas. Haven't seen him since."

"Still, he came yesterday. That's progress. Count your blessings, R.J. Even the small ones."

"I knew you were going to say that."

"Because it's true. Now, I should go say hello to Mattie and then tear Belle away from all the fun and get back to my kitchen."

"I know you're busy, but if you can spare me a minute, I could use some advice."

"About what?"

"Leif. I can't figure out why he's carrying such a grudge. It was his mom who divorced me and told me flat-out to stay out of their lives. I know I should have pressed to see him and his brother, but hell, considering my life back then, I figured they were better off without having me around."

"Maybe you should tell him that."

"He don't seem interested in anything I have to say. I'd let it go at that, except I really want to have a relationship with Effie."

"It sounds like that is going well so far."

"She loves horses. That gives us a bit of common ground. But Leif's so wrapped up in his bitterness and resentment that he won't even look me in the eye. And if he decides Effie can't see me anymore, then I lose her."

"Are they close?"

"There's a few briars in their relationship. I can't help but wonder if I'm not the cause of some of them. I don't know where to start trying to clear that up."

"I always start with prayer when faced with a problem that's too big for me."

"You do plenty of praying. I know that, Carolina. But

you do some talking, too, when you got something on your mind. God knows, you've lit into me a time or two over the years."

"Only when you needed it, and, frankly, it seldom did any good. You are as stubborn as an old scar."

"You'll get no argument from me on that score. But now I need advice. How do I approach Leif?"

"Just talk to him plain the way you're talking to me now. No B.S. or beating around the bush. Ask him how he feels about you."

"He hates me. That's evident."

"Ask him why."

"So I can listen to him rant about what a rotten father I was? I don't see how that's going to help me."

"But it's not all about you, R.J. Maybe Leif needs to say it out loud and confront you with his resentment before he can get past it. It won't be fun for you, but I'd say it's worth a shot."

"I don't know. I can't make amends at this point. Besides, Leif don't need a daddy at his age."

"But he just might need a father and some resolution."

He scratched his whiskered jaw. "I'll think on it."

"Good."

He watched her walk to the kitchen with the pumpkin roll. Carolina Lambert was far too pretty and too smart a woman to live the rest of her life alone. But she'd been truly in love with her husband, Hugh, before his death. It would take a hell of a man to replace him.

Someone who was nothing like R.J.

But that definitely didn't rule out one of his sons.

But likely not Leif. He just couldn't see Leif fitting into the ranching lifestyle, and Carolina, like Joni, would fit nowhere else.

Which meant that even if by some miracle he could patch

things up with Leif, his career would never permit him to comply with the provisions in R.J.'s will. He couldn't be expected to give up his success and all he'd worked for to move to the ranch and help operate it for a year.

Damn. Maybe R.J. should have thought the wording through a little better before he had the papers drawn up. The way it was now, he'd likely cut Effie right out of getting her fair share of his estate.

There was nothing right about that.

LEIF LIFTED THE ax over his head and brought it down hard, splitting the log in half. He bent, tossed that log out of the way and positioned the next one. Finally he developed a rhythm that made his stack of firewood grow almost as tall as Adam's.

He stopped and wiped his brow on his shirt sleeve. "And I thought the workouts I get at the gym were tough."

"They must be," Adam said. "You're in good shape for a desk jock."

"I can see why you would never need a gym," Leif said.

"Right," Adam said. "Just a lot of ointment for sore muscles. We've probably chopped enough wood for now, though. The women and Effie are likely back from their ride."

"And I still have to take Joni to pick up her car before I drive into Dallas for Effie's luggage."

"Are you planning to spend the night at the ranch tonight, as well?" Adam asked. "There are several spare bedrooms at the big house."

All cozied up with R.J. Leif shook his head. "I'm not up to that. I may stay at the motel in Oak Grove."

Adam only nodded. He'd likely guessed that Leif had stayed at Joni's last night since he'd showed up that morning with her in the same clothes he'd had on yesterday. Joni might have said as much to Hadley. Anyway Joni wanted to play it was up to her. He wouldn't push tonight. But if she invited him to stay, he wouldn't turn down the offer.

Once they'd tossed the firewood into the back of Adam's pickup truck, they drove to Adam's house. The structure was so new there was still work that needed to be done. The most obvious from the outside was finishing the side porch and adding the last two shutters.

There was no sign of Hadley or Effie, but Joni and Corky were in the front yard talking and laughing like old friends—or more. Leif felt a surprising jolt of jealousy. It certainly wasn't like he had a claim on her. They'd just met.

Leif scanned the area. There was no sign of his daughter.

"Effie went with Hadley up to the big house to pick up the girls," Joni said as Leif stepped out of the truck and approached the house. "They should be back any minute now."

"Did you deliver that load of hay over to Carmichael's place?" Adam asked Corky.

"I did, boss man. Now, if you don't need me for a few minutes, I'll drive Joni over to get her truck." He fingered his hat brim and gave Joni an aw-shucks smile.

"I'll drop her off to get her truck," Leif said, quickly aware he sounded far too possessive. He mellowed his tone. "Unless you'd rather Corky drive you."

"Not unless you want to stay at the ranch awhile longer," Joni said.

"No. As soon as I tell Effie goodbye, I'll be ready to cut out."

Adam settled the issue. "In that case, you can give me a hand unloading the firewood, Corky. Then you can give the horses a good brushing."

"You got it." Corky adjusted his sunglasses. "Guess I'll see you at lunch tomorrow then, Joni."

"I'll be here."

"Me, too." He smiled again before sauntering off to start unloading the firewood.

They waited around, but when Hadley returned, it was just her and her daughters in the car.

Irritation surged in Leif. "Where's Effie?"

"She stayed at the big house to help Mattie Mae roll out the crusts for fried peach pies. You can stop by there on your way out. I told R.J. you were here. He was surprised, so I guess he didn't see you drive past."

"That's not like him," Adam said.

"He was probably asleep," Hadley said. "His energy level is not what it was even a few weeks ago."

Leif had no intention of sitting around and discussing R.J.'s failing health. He refused to feel guilty for not playing the part of a loving son.

"I'm ready if you are, Joni. Hadley, just tell Effie I'll see her later today."

"I will."

Minutes later, they were heading to Abe's Garage. Leif's cell phone rang before he got there. It was Travis. Leif's thoughts immediately shifted to the Oak Grove murder case.

"Any news on the identity of the victim?" Leif asked after a quick hello.

"Yes, and be prepared to be shocked."

"Does this mean I know her?"

"You know her, all right. That's why I figured I better give you a quick heads-up. You'd best get prepared for a new surge of notoriety."

Leif cringed and waited for the rest of the story.

Chapter Nine

Joni watched as tension settled in Leif's face and pushed the muscles in his neck into tight cords. The most she could glean from listening to his end of the phone conversation was that the news involved a woman named Jill Trotter and that she was somehow connected to the Oak Grove murder.

When the phone conversation ended, Joni waited for Leif to broach the subject matter he'd found so distressful. Instead, he stared straight ahead, his troubled expression as stony as marble.

She endured the icy silence as long as she could. "Bad news?" she finally asked.

"Could have been better."

"I don't want to pry, but if you want to talk about it…"

"You're not prying. It will be all over the news in a matter of hours anyway. I was just trying to piece together what we know about the Oak Grove murder with what I remember of a trial from five years ago."

"One of your trials?"

"Yes. My first one after moving to Dallas, one that rocked Dallas like an earthquake."

"How are the two connected?"

"Jill Trotter, aka Evie Monsant, was accused of murdering her husband, Dr. Phillip Trotter. He'd been a much-loved professor before he'd left the education system to go into private practice as a psychiatrist. Jill, on the other hand, was a bit of a loner who had a history of chronic depression."

"Had she been one of his patients?"

"Yes, and one of his students before that. She was also a stunningly beautiful woman, which automatically made some women hate her. All in all, she made the perfect villain in the minds of the people."

"I don't remember the trial," Joni admitted. "But then, I didn't live in Texas at the time. I assume she was acquitted since she wasn't in jail."

"Yes, to the shock of the citizens of Dallas. The prosecution was sure they had an airtight case against her. I punched enough holes in their circumstantial evidence that after days of deliberation, the jury finally found Jill innocent."

"Did you believe she was innocent?"

"Yes. Still do. Unfortunately, the court of public opinion didn't. There were threats on her life and harassment on every front. Eventually she was forced to move out of Dallas just to get some peace and quiet."

"That explains why she changed her name and ended up a recluse in Oak Grove," Joni said. "But it seems so unfair that she'd be treated so cruelly after being found innocent."

"Justice and fairness don't always equate. And to be honest, guilty people are acquitted every day."

As far as Joni was concerned, this made the murder all the more disturbing. If she had it to do over again, Joni would have tried a lot harder to befriend Evie—or rather Jill. "Were there children involved?"

"Not between Jill and her husband, but he had children by a previous marriage. They were both in their twenties then and lived on the West Coast."

"Did they attend the trial?"

"No. I never met either of them. According to Jill, they'd cut off all contact with him after the divorce."

Joni leaned back in her seat and tried to put herself in Leif's place. He had to go up against the odds every day and defend men and women accused of committing horrible crimes. How he did his job could be the deciding factor between freedom or a life in prison or even death.

"I don't envy you your job, Leif Dalton. I'll take my horses and Oak Grove any day."

"There are days I'd like to shuck it all," Leif admitted. "But there are others when I wouldn't change places with anyone."

"So what happens next?" Joni asked. "Surely you won't be involved in the investigation."

"I might be questioned by the police to see what I know about people who might have threatened Jill, but the most invasive intrusion will come from the media. It was a high-profile case five years ago," Leif explained. "It will blow up all over again."

"Happy Thanksgiving."

"Exactly. I wouldn't mind so much if Effie wasn't here, but I hate that she has to hear all the talk of murder. As much as I hate to admit it, the ranch is probably the best place for her the rest of the week."

"I agree."

"You may want to avoid me, as well," Leif said.

She didn't. In fact, she'd like nothing better than to have him stay with her the rest of the week. She ached to feel his lips on hers again. Yearned for so much more.

"I'm not afraid of you, Leif Dalton." She tried to keep her tone light and teasing.

He reached across the seat, took her hand and squeezed it. "Maybe you should be."

But she'd been careful in relationships all her life. Had

put her career first. Had been wary of men with the potential to break her heart. Leif was miles out of the safe category.

But maybe it was time to take a chance on love.

LEIF GOT OUT of the car with Joni when they reached Abe's Garage. "I'll wait until you make sure it's ready."

"No need. I called while you and Adam were cutting wood. Abe assured me it was in top condition—for a truck with that many miles on it."

"I'll wait all the same and follow you home. I want to take a look around the property again and see how many outdoor lights I should pick up."

"That's really not necessary."

"Hey, I'm a man of my word."

"Okay. I'll only be a few minutes."

But it wasn't only the number of needed lights he wanted to check. It was also the locks on her doors and windows. He wanted to make sure they were as secure as possible.

What he hadn't told Joni in the car was that even after discovering Jill's identity, the police hadn't ruled out that she was a random victim. The original furor over her release had calmed down years ago. It was unlikely—though not impossible—that someone had waited five years for vengeance.

A random victim. Not necessarily of The Hunter, but quite possibly of a copycat killer.

If it was a copycat killer, he might live in the area. And once this murder went prime-time, he'd have more impetus to strike again. The world was full of dangerous kooks. Even a town like Oak Grove wasn't immune.

He made a quick call to Effie, hoping she hadn't heard the news. He'd prefer to tell her about the case in person, but hearing it from him over the phone was better than hearing the hype via a TV reporter.

The jubilant tone of her voice assured him that murder was the furthest thing from her mind. As soon as they'd exchanged hellos, she jumped into tales of her latest achievements.

"I made pie crust and the best peach pies in the world."

"Great. I can't wait to give them the taste test. I was sorry we didn't get to talk more this morning."

"You were on the phone. Business, no doubt. I'm used to that."

Accusation chipped the syllables in the last sentence.

"I was talking to your mother."

"Oh." Her voice dropped to a murmur.

No "sorry for lying." No mention that her mother was getting married and she was moving to London to live with her and the new husband. But Leif had no intentions of letting her skirt the issues forever. And now that he'd had a minute to think about it, he decided that he should wait and tell her in person about the victim being a former client of his.

"We'll talk about it later," he said

"Sure."

"I should be back early afternoon. Maybe the two of us can go horseback riding."

"Why? You don't even like horses."

"I like horses. I just don't have time to ride often."

"I know. You're busy."

At least she hadn't nixed the invitation. Once the connection was broken, he looked around the parking lot and spotted Joni standing next to her truck, talking to a young mechanic. He walked over and joined them.

The mechanic frowned at Leif and then quickly turned

his attention back to Joni. "If you have any trouble at all, give me a call. I'll take care of it."

"Thanks, Joey. I'm sure I'll be calling. My truck will see to that."

He grinned. "Anytime for any reason."

Another young man clearly enamored of Joni. Not that Leif blamed him. It wasn't just her looks or the fact that she could hold an intelligent conversation, though both fascinated him more by the minute. She was just so damn easy to be around.

He followed her back to her house and spent the next half hour checking out her locks. Like he'd suspected, they were old and flimsy and all needed replacing. He wasn't the handiest guy in the world with a hammer and screwdriver, but he could handle a job this simple.

"I wish you wouldn't bother with this, Leif. Your time would be much better spent with Effie. I can easily find someone else to change out the locks."

"One of your many admirers?" he teased.

"Sure. I have them by the hundreds."

"You gotta quit smiling at all the cowboys and mechanics in town. You're liable to have a riot on your hands."

"Jealous?"

"Yeah." Sadly, he wasn't altogether teasing. "So what are you doing the rest of the day?"

"I don't have anything planned."

"Then why not drive into Dallas with me? We'll make it a quick trip. Stop by my condo, pick up Effie's things, stop off at the hardware store and then head back to Oak Grove."

She hesitated.

"If you don't want to be seen with a notorious defense attorney, I'll understand."

"And miss a chance to see how the rich and famous live? I'll take my chances."

Only he was the one taking chances. The more time he spent with Joni, the more likely he was going to kiss her again. Who knew where that would lead?

Actually, he did. Nowhere but trouble. Falling for a woman who lived practically in R.J.'s backyard would be a disaster.

His phone vibrated on the way back to the car. This time it was Serena. So much for her promise that everything was over. But it was over. He'd deal with her and her mood swings later, when he had a dozen fewer emergencies claiming his attention.

JONI HADN'T REALIZED how appropriate her comment about Leif's living the life of the rich and famous was until they entered the building where his high-rise condo was located. The complex's spacious foyer was more luxurious and impressive than any five-star hotel she'd ever been in.

The carpet was a deep gray color and so thick and plush her feet sank in it as if it were quicksand. The furnishings included gleaming mahogany tables and overstuffed chairs in a muted plaid of magenta and black.

A bouquet of fresh flowers gracing a huge round table in the middle of the room was at least four feet tall, a mix of exotic flowers and shiny greenery. The fragrance was practically intoxicating. Original oil paintings added finishing touches to the pale gray walls.

"You should have told me we were visiting the Taj Mahal. I would have dressed for the occasion."

"It's Texas. Boots and jeans are always in fashion."

"Maybe if the jeans were made by Gucci."

"It's okay. They'll think you're with the cleaning crew."

She made a face.

He laughed and linked his arm with hers. "I realize the amenities are a bit over the top, but it's all about location. I don't have to face Dallas traffic twice a day or worry about being hounded by unhappy clients and nosy reporters."

"Nosy reporters," Joni repeated. "Isn't that redundant?"

"Right. Kind of like crooked politicians." He took out a card key and passed it in front of the security box at the elevator.

"No wonder you don't have to worry. Your condo is harder to get in than a bank vault," Joni said.

"Now you're exaggerating. All you need are the right keys. Effie didn't even need that."

He explained Effie surprising him Monday night as they took the elevator to his penthouse condo.

"Thankfully the local media sharks are apparently not as good at scooting by security as Effie was," he said. "Otherwise mikes and flashbulbs would have greeted us."

"Would it really be that bad?"

"Very likely. Anything they can twist into ammunition for their ratings war. Hopefully, they won't learn that I'll be spending Thanksgiving Day at the Dry Gulch."

"I don't know," Joni said. "That might make for some interesting fireworks. R.J. could probably give them a run for their money."

"You could be right."

By the time they reached the door to Leif's condo, her uneasiness with the surroundings had been replaced by a strange, titillating sensation in her stomach.

There was no rational explanation for her attraction to Leif. But they had clicked in some mysterious and sensual way that made just being with him a dizzying experience.

She didn't believe in love at first sight—or first kiss. But no man had ever affected her quite like this before. Perhaps because Leif's world was so far removed from hers that they might as well have come from alternate universes.

He opened the door, and she stepped inside. And Joni

came face-to-face with the most striking woman she'd ever seen. She was standing at a built-in mirrored bar, stirring a drink. Wearing nothing but black thong panties, a scrap of lacy bra and a pair of gold, nosebleed stilettos.

Their alternate universes had just collided with a heart-shattering crash.

Chapter Ten

Leif swallowed his shock along with a string of curses, mostly directed at himself. Would he never learn not to give out keys?

"Serena. What are you doing here? I thought—"

"I wanted to surprise you, of course," she interrupted.

"You did."

Clearly not deterred by her state of undress, she turned to Joni, who was standing with her back against the open door, looking as if she'd like to drop through the floor.

"I don't think we've met," Serena cooed in a voice as soft as silk.

"No, I don't think we have."

Joni was neither cooing nor smiling. He'd be lucky if she didn't bolt before he could explain—as if he could explain this.

"This is Dr. Griffin," Leif said. "And I'm sure we'd all be more comfortable if you'd put on your clothes."

"*Dr.* Griffin." Serena smiled. "You must be one of Leif's expert witnesses for an upcoming trial. I should have known he'd be taking care of business if he were able to escape his daughter. He's an absolute workaholic. Now, do excuse me while I grab a robe."

"Joni's not a witness," Leif corrected as Serena walked

away. "She's a friend. And I didn't escape Effie—she escaped me."

Leif could barely control his anger as he watched Serena strut away, her hips swaying. The thong enabled a full back view of her perfect body. For once the sight had zero effect on his libido.

Why in the hell had Serena assumed he'd be alone when she knew his daughter was in town? And what the devil was she doing there after yesterday's outburst and announcement that it was over between them?

"So much for security," Joni said.

"I'm sorry about this. Serena's a swimsuit model and not big into modesty. But, believe me, I had no idea she'd be here today."

"It's not a problem," Joni assured him, though he could have frozen from the icy chill her eyes and voice emoted.

"It's a problem," he said. "But if you'll excuse me a minute, I'll take care of it."

"There's nothing to take care of," Joni said, her back still against the door. "The two of you are obviously very close, and, like you said, we're just friends."

"I hope you know that I wouldn't have brought you into this situation if I'd had any idea Serena would be here and half-dressed."

"Which half exactly did you think was dressed?"

"Point made, but this isn't what it looks like."

"Whatever it is, it's none of my business, Leif. Thanks for the help yesterday and good luck with your daughter." She reached for the doorknob.

Leif grabbed her arm. "Would you just give me a minute and we'll both go back to Oak Grove as planned?"

"I'm sure I can find a way back to Oak Grove."

He was sure she could, too. Corky, Joey, Ruby's dad, Latham. They'd all be delighted to rush to her rescue.

"I'm not going to lie to you, Joni. Serena and I were dating, but we both knew it wasn't working. She called the relationship off yesterday. I thought that's where it stood."

"Apparently Serena had a change of heart. But for the record, you don't owe me any explanations about your love life."

"I realize that, but while we're setting the record straight, I'm not some kind of playboy who has women at my fingertips like hot and cold running water. I'm a workaholic, just like Serena said."

She pulled away from his grasp. "You still have complications here, Leif. My being here isn't helping."

"How about letting me be the judge of that? Give me five minutes to get things straight with Serena and pick up what I need to drive back to the ranch."

"There's really no reason for you to rush back."

"There is. There's Effie, and right now she's the most urgent problem in my life. I need your help reaching her, Joni. This is my last chance to have time with her. If you won't help me for my sake, do it for Effie's. Please."

Finally, Joni met his gaze. "Okay, but if I stay, it's for Effie. And for R.J. I know what it means for him to have time with his granddaughter."

For R.J. Great. As if Leif gave a damn what mattered to his sorry father. But he did need Joni's help with Effie. And he wasn't anywhere near ready to end things with Joni. "Five minutes," he said as he turned to walk away.

"Four now," Joni reminded him. "And counting."

Joni walked to Leif's well-stocked bar, took a highball glass from the hanging shelf and picked up a bottle of what was probably a much pricier whiskey than what she'd poured him last night.

Not that she'd liked the taste last night. And definitely not that she needed her judgment affected by alcohol. She sat the liquor bottle back down and opened a bottle of sparkling water.

What an idiot she'd been for daring to fantasize about a romantic relationship with Leif Dalton. Naturally, he hadn't pushed himself on her last night. He was used to cavorting with beautiful models who paraded around his house in the nude.

Flirting with Joni probably came as naturally to him as drinking her whiskey had. It meant nothing. Well, she'd learned her lesson. It was the last night he'd spend in her house and the last time she'd let her heart rate spiral out of control because of some incidental touch.

If he wanted advice on dealing with Effie, he'd better get it on the way home. After that, she had no intention of ever seeing him again.

R.J. and dear, sweet Mattie Mae would be upset that she canceled plans to have Thanksgiving dinner with them. Hadley would understand, but she'd have questions, especially since Joni had already confessed to her about Leif's spending the night at her house and the sparks of arousal that had ignited between them.

Hadley had told Joni to trust her gut feelings and go with them, but that was because Hadley had fallen head over heels for Adam the first time they'd met. Love at first sight had worked for them, but that was rare. From now on, Joni would rely strictly on her brain.

She downed the entire glass of water and poured another. She was taking her first sip when a string of words that would probably still get her mouth washed out with soap in her mother's house hammered the silence. The shrill female voice left no doubt who was slinging the curses.

A second later, Serena and the heavy scent of her perfume made an appearance. No sexy, runway walk this time. Serena darted through the room like an angry blue jay, her short black skirt and a cerulean silk blouse with a plunging neckline little more than a blur.

She didn't glance Joni's way as she jerked the door open and bolted through it, slamming it behind her.

Leif stepped into the living area a few seconds later. "Sorry to subject you to the vile language. Guess I didn't handle that too well."

"I'm just glad Effie wasn't here."

"Definitely, but in fairness to Serena, she had tried to call me earlier," Leif admitted. "I didn't want to get into a confrontation with her, so I didn't take the call. After that, she called the Dry Gulch and apparently talked to Mattie, who told her that Effie was at the ranch but that I had driven home."

"So she expected you to be alone?"

"Yes. Now, what do you say we drop the subject of Serena and start over as if she hadn't been here?"

Joni was as likely to do that as she was to stop wearing her faded jeans. But she did want to get things between her and Leif on firmer ground.

"Why did you ask me to ride into town with you?"

"I thought that was evident." He reached across the space between then and casually tucked a lock of hair behind her left ear. "I wanted to be with you."

The strumming of awareness swept through her again, riding each nerve and then settling in every erogenous zone in her body. But this time she would ignore the heated, traitorous passion if it took every ounce of determination she could muster.

"Would you like to see the rest of the house while you're here?" Leif asked.

The rest of the house—like his bedroom. No reason to put her resolve to that kind of test. She took her glass of water to the nearest chair. "I've seen enough. I'll wait here while you gather Effie's belongings."

"I won't be but a minute." He turned and left her alone.

Too restless to sit, she walked over and began to peruse the silver-framed photos on the intricately ornate metal-and-stone table behind the sofa.

There were several of Leif, Effie and a woman who must be Effie's mother, all likely taken before the divorce. They looked like a typical happy family.

Leif had been incredibly handsome even then, his dark hair untamed, his body lean. But then he'd lacked the rugged edges to his face that made him appear so virile and seductive now.

Effie's mother hadn't been as drop-dead gorgeous as Serena, but she was very attractive. Effie had her mouth and her heart-shaped face. But she had Leif's caramel-colored eyes and his mischievous smile.

In one photograph, Effie held Leif's hand and smiled up at him like he was a superhero. In another, she was perched on his shoulder as they watched a parade. In yet another, they were playing in the surf, both laughing.

From the pictures, one would think them a perfect family. But somehow Leif had ended up divorced and living thousands of miles away from his daughter. Now their relationship was tense and stressful. His little girl had not only grown up; she'd grown away from him.

Joni's mind was still on Effie when Leif returned with two pieces of luggage and two computer bags. He set them down by the front door.

"Looks like Effie was quite a daddy's girl when she was younger," Joni said as she returned a photograph to the table.

"That's what her mother used to say."

"What happened between you and her mother?"

"It's hard to pinpoint any one thing, but if I had to, I'd say we were both too set on pursuing our individual careers to foster the relationship."

"But you must have loved each other at one time."

"I guess so. I'm not much of an expert on love."

"How did you meet?"

"We were in graduate school together at Stanford. We shared a common dislike for one of our professors that resulted in our spending lots of late nights studying together. We hit it off, and once we'd graduated, marriage seemed the next logical step."

"How long had you been married before Effie was born?"

"Fourteen months. Celeste wanted to have a child before she started her career so that she didn't have to take a break and lose ground. She liked things to go according to plan."

"Is she also an attorney?"

"No, she's a very successful executive for an international banking corporation. But she was also a good mother. I'm the one who didn't measure up as a father. Not that I failed intentionally. I love Effie more than she'll ever know. But I made mistakes. I may be able to persuade a jury, but I can't force Effie to love me."

"It's not a matter of forcing her love, Leif. It's already there. I see it in the pictures when she was young. You just have to find a way to connect with her again, let her know how important she is to you."

"I tell her all the time."

"But do you always show her?"

"I try."

"She didn't see it that way this morning when you spent all your time on the phone instead of having breakfast with her."

"Did she tell you that?"

"Let's just say she didn't try to hide her disappointment that you'd surprised her with a visit and then spent all of your time working."

"I wasn't working. I was talking to her mother, who had plenty to tell me."

"You didn't explain that to Effie."

"She didn't give me a chance then."

"You have the rest of the week to spend quality time with her. Don't blow it. And don't make it about you but about her."

"I try, but if this week is anything like previous vacations with me, she balks or rolls her eyes at everything I suggest."

"Don't let her get by with that. Make her choose an activity. And listen when she talks."

"You make it sound easy."

"Then I'm not saying it right. None of this will be easy, but it is necessary if you want a close, loving relationship with Effie."

"I'll need your help with this."

"You can bounce ideas and issues off of me, but the real work is up to you and Effie."

Effie needed her father before she ended up as bitter about him as he was about R.J. So, as hard as it would be to spend time with Leif and not succumb to the attraction, she would do anything she could to help bring the two of them together.

Anything but fall in love with Leif.

A VAN FROM a local TV channel pulled up in front of the condominium complex just as Leif and Joni sped away. "Looks as if we split just in time," he said. "The vultures are circling."

Joni turned to look back at the action. "They didn't waste any time."

"Never do."

"But the public does have the right to know the facts about a murder," Joni said. "How else can they protect themselves?"

"There's a difference between reporting the facts and creating a story. If there are any facts to be had, they'll come from the police—not me. Pulling me into the limelight five years after a trial is creating a story."

A call came in over his cell phone, which was routed through the car's audio system. No name was listed with the number, so he let the call go unanswered.

The corner traffic light turned red. He stopped and then made a right turn. "The only good thing is that no one expects me to be at the Dry Gulch Ranch, so this shouldn't affect Effie."

"She's a smart girl," Joni said. "Once you explain the situation, she'll handle whatever happens."

"You're probably right again," Leif said. "I keep thinking I need to protect her."

"You do—from the evils in the world. Not from yourself and your life."

The calls continued. The third one was from Gerard Timberton, a senior partner in the law firm. That one he didn't ignore. He left it on speaker so that both his hands were free to drive.

"I guess you've heard by now that Jill Trotter was raped and murdered sometime in the wee hours of Monday morning," Gerard said, greeting him with the grisly news.

"I heard."

"I just got a call from Detective Josh Morgan with DPD homicide division."

"What did he want?" Leif asked. It was a rhetorical question. What he wanted was information that would lead to the identification and arrest of Jill's killer—information Leif didn't have.

"Basically, he wants to talk to you about the trial. I told him you were off until next Monday, but he says it's urgent."

"Did he leave a number where I can reach him?"

"He did."

Joni grabbed a pen from her purse and took down the number as Gerard dictated it.

"You're free to cooperate with him if you have any direct facts that might help," Gerard said, "but you don't have to share any information that you perceive as client privileged or that might in any way be damaging to the firm."

Naturally. The firm always came first. "My former client is dead," Leif said. "I'd like nothing better than to help the police find her killer, but it's not likely I can. If the murder was connected to Jill's not being convicted, someone waited a long time for vengeance."

"Then you'll call the detective?"

"Absolutely."

"Good. And then enjoy your holiday."

"I'll do my best. You have a good weekend, too."

They talked a minute more, but Leif's focus had switched to what he could remember about Jill's trial. There had been countless threats against Jill and Leif, but they had been the kind he usually got from kooks in the general population at large.

Not that those could be dismissed lightly, but they had stopped quickly once the trial was over and no longer in everyone's face.

As best he could remember, none of the threatening notes, letters or phone calls had come from family members or people directly affected by the murder of Jill's husband. If anything, he'd been surprised by the lack of involvement or concern from any of Phillip Trotter's family.

Phillip's two children were in California with their mother and hadn't come to the trial. His parents were dead. Leif remembered he had an older half brother who was a missionary or a teacher or a Peace Corps worker. Whatever, he had been in South America at the time.

There was also a younger brother. He was in prison. Or had been. At any rate, the prosecution for obvious reasons hadn't introduced him as a character witness.

No red flags—unless Leif was overlooking something.

He turned to Joni. "Would you mind if we made one quick stop at my office to pick up the files on the Trotter case?"

She frowned. "I'm still in the clothes I wore horseback riding this morning."

"So am I. We'll just dart in and dart out. Besides, it's not likely we'll run into anyone except the secretarial staff. Most of the attorneys have probably already started their holiday."

"All the same, I'll wait in the car. Are you going to call the detective first?"

"Yeah. May as well get that over with."

Leif made the call to the detective and for once things worked out in his favor, though it would mean persuading Joni to come inside with him. Josh Morgan agreed to meet him in his office for a quick question-and-answer session.

That was only after Leif mentioned that he was on his way back to Oak Grove to take a friend home who lived very near where Jill had been murdered. The rest of the weekend would belong to Effie and Joni, the two people most likely to avoid Leif if he gave them half a chance.

He planned to make sure they didn't get that chance.

THE PROSPECT OF being questioned by Detective Morgan made Joni nervous. She couldn't explain why except that this was the closest she'd ever come to a murder investigation. Even now, she couldn't imagine why the detective wanted her in on the conversation.

The three of them sat in Leif's impressive office, Leif in the power seat behind the curved desk made from a rich wood in a deep shade of pecan. His swivel chair was the same black leather as the sofa she shared with Detective Morgan.

Leif reeked of authority, but then so did the detective. Not that they were in a power play, but still she sensed suspicion in their every exchange.

The reasons for that might be a bit more obvious if she'd been part of their entire conversation, but for the previous half hour, she'd sat twiddling her thumbs in the firm's empty reception room.

Detective Morgan looked to be in his late forties; there was already graying at his temples. He was slightly shorter and a few pounds heavier than Leif, and his eyes were bracketed with significantly more wrinkles.

He crossed a leg over his opposite knee and turned to face Joni. "I understand that you were a neighbor of Jill Trotter's."

"I live on the same road, but my house is about a mile from hers. I've seen her at her mailbox but never actually met her."

"So Mr. Dalton told me. But you do drive by Mrs. Trotter's house every day?"

"Most days, only she was going by the name of Evie Monsant then."

"How long had she lived in the house?"

"I don't remember exactly, but I think she moved in about two months after I moved to Oak Grove. I've been there a little over nine months."

"But other than passing her house, the two of you never crossed paths?"

"No. I heard she shopped at the local grocery store from time to time, but that was about it. She didn't go to church in Oak Grove or eat at the diner or go to any community events. There was lots of speculation about why she was such a loner, but I don't think anyone thought she was in danger or that she was hiding her identity."

"There are still a lot of questions to be answered," the detective said. "That's why we're here."

"I wish I could be more helpful," Joni said. "I really don't know anything about the woman."

"Sometimes you may know more than you realize. Did you ever see cars at her house other than her own?"

Joni tapped her fingernails on the arm of the sofa while she gave that more thought. "Not on a regular basis, but there were workmen's vehicles from time to time, especially right after she moved in."

"What kind of workmen?"

"Repairmen, the cable guy, furniture delivery people, the telephone company truck. The type of people you'd expect to need when you move."

"What about lately?" the detective asked. "Have you noticed any vehicles around her house in the past week or so?"

"Last week there was a black pickup truck in her driveway and a man working on her roof."

"Can you remember what day that was?"

"Last Thursday, I think. Now that I think about it, there was a man in the area about two weeks ago looking for odd jobs," Joni added. "She may have hired him. I do remember that he was driving a black pickup truck, as well."

The detective leaned in closer. "You met this man?"

"Yes, he stopped by my house after work one day. Said

he'd lost his construction job in Dallas and was looking for any kind of work. I only talked to him a minute."

"So he wasn't from Oak Grove?"

"I don't think so. At least I'd never seen him before that day."

"Can you describe him?"

"Average height. He was heavier than you or Leif, but not fat. Kind of unkempt and rough-looking."

"What do you mean by unkempt?"

"He needed a haircut and his jeans were frayed around the hem. But what really put me off was a tattoo on his lower arm."

"Describe the tattoo."

"It was a pair of crossed hunting knives. One of the blades looked as if it were dripping blood. I'm not opposed to tattoos, but that one looked excessively gory. I thought it might be some kind of gang symbol."

"Sounds like it could be."

"Do you think he could be Jill Trotter's killer?"

"Right now everyone's a suspect, Dr. Griffin."

An icy shiver slithered up her spine. The killer might have stood on her front porch. She might have hired him or he might have overpowered her and dragged her into the woods behind her house and attacked her the way he had Jill. She could be the one in the morgue.

The tattoo became fixed in her mind. Hunting knives. A brutal murder. Her nerves rattled like dried bones. "Do you think he could be The Hunter?"

"I wouldn't go that far," the detective said. "But we can't rule out anything out at this point." He made a few notes on a small pad. "Do you think you could pick this guy out in a lineup or identify him from a mug shot?"

"Maybe. I'm not sure, but I'm willing to try. I could definitely pick out the tattoo."

"I may be calling on you. Right now, just keep your doors locked and call me if you see anything or anyone suspicious in the area." He took a business card from his pocket and placed it in her hand.

Her fingers shook as she closed them around the card. To think that a half hour ago, she'd been freaking out over facing one of Leif's model girlfriends. Now she might have to identify a serial killer.

She barely heard the rest of the conversation. Once she and Leif were back on the road, she was more than happy to have him stop at the hardware store for outdoor lighting and better locks for her house.

Funny how quickly priorities could change when a possible serial killer joined the game.

Leif was bent over the trunk of the car, retrieving packages. The trip into town had taken more time than he'd expected. He needed to get back to the ranch and spend some time with Effie.

He cared nothing about staying for dinner with R.J. If he dropped off the lights and locks now to install later, it would give him good reason to leave the ranch early and to return to Joni's place. Plus, he could borrow the tools he'd need from Adam.

He reached up to close the trunk. That's when he spotted a shadow, and then the man. He was crouched low, half-hidden in a clump of shrubbery and underbrush about ten yards from the house.

Adrenaline swept through Leif, triggering all his protective instincts. He dropped the packages, instinctively grabbed the lug wrench that was in plain sight and took off at a dead run.

Chapter Eleven

"Wait, I just want to talk to you," Leif called as the man made a run for it.

The man ignored his call and ran straight for the thickest wooded area, disappearing among the maze of evergreens, oaks, sycamores, ashes and honey mesquites. Proof enough for Leif that he was up to no good.

Leif darted around tree trunks and through thick underbrush, straining for glimpses of the escaping prowler and trying desperately to gain ground on him. He finally spotted him again, off to his left, but still too far away and moving too fast to get a good look at him.

Leif kept up the chase, maintaining his speed until he hit a low area, where his feet sank into the mush of dead leaves and mud. Even then, he pushed himself to keep up the pace.

Finally, he spotted the man again, this time near a towering pine that had been split by lightning. If he had a weapon, there was no sign of it. Definitely not a hunter. A shotgun or rifle would be easy to spot from this distance.

A few minutes and a little luck and he'd be able to tackle the man to the ground. Leif hurdled a downed limb. His breath burned in his lungs. But he was close enough now to hear the man's labored breathing as well, so he wasn't about to turn back.

He powered through an area of thick undergrowth, leaping over a low thorny shrub, clearing it without trouble. But then his right foot tangled with a clump of vines. Struggling to remain upright, Leif groped for a low-hanging branch.

He steadied himself without hitting the ground, but those few seconds of delay gave the intruder time to disappear again. Leif paused, hoping to hear footfalls or the scraping of limbs being pushed aside so he'd have a sense of the direction the man had taken.

But it was the sputter and knocking of an engine coming to life that split the silence. *Damn.* The man was getting away.

A second later, Leif spotted a four-wheeler topping a ravine and vanishing into the thick woods a good hundred and fifty yards from Joni's back door.

A hundred-and-fifty-yard trek to position himself so that he could spy on Joni. The man was a determined stalker.

A stream of unguarded curses flew from Leif's mouth, drawing a squawking protest from a murder of crows perched somewhere over his head. He started back to the house, angry at himself for letting the man get away without at least getting close enough to get a good look at him.

He spotted Joni as he reached the clearing near her house. She dashed toward him with a rifle that was almost as big as she was slung over her shoulder. She looked like an adolescent playing Annie Oakley in a school play. He smiled in spite of himself.

"Where are you going with that gun, Annie?"

"To rescue you."

"I appreciate the concern, but I'm not so much of a city slicker that I can't take care of myself."

"Really? What if that had been Evie's killer you were yelling at to stop and talk? Do you think that lug wrench would have saved you?"

"I was hoping not to have to use it, and we have no real reason to believe the trespasser was dangerous."

"Well, he wasn't making a friendly visit. He'd already broken into my house. He could have had a gun. You could have been shot."

She started to shake.

Leif pulled her into his arms. With all that was going on, she'd been worried about him.

For some crazy reason, that pleased him a lot. Unfortunately, the satisfaction only lasted a second.

In spite of his assurances to her, Joni might very well be in real danger. And Leif had just let the man who could be behind it get away.

DREAD CONSUMED JONI as she stepped back into the house. Her fear for Leif's safety had been so intense when she'd snatched the rifle from its rack, she hadn't even thought about why the intruder had broken into her home.

Now she felt violated and fearful of what she might discover. "If the man came here to rob me, he must have been very disappointed."

"He didn't appear to be carrying off loot," Leif said. "But you may have come home and interrupted him before he got started."

"You don't sound very convincing."

"Leaving all options open," Leif said as he stepped out of his soiled shoes. "At least the living room looks untouched, except for the mud he tracked in."

"And I hate scrubbing floors." But new and frightening possibilities lingered. What if she hadn't gone into Dallas with Leif? What if she'd been there alone when the man came calling? Why had he stayed around, waiting in the woods for her to return?

Clearly he wasn't just there to rob and plunder.

"Why would anyone be stalking me?" she said, voicing her fears aloud.

"Good question. If I'd gotten my hands on the son of a bitch, we might have some answers."

"Don't blame yourself. Had you not been here, who knows what he might have tried?"

Leif took her right hand in his and squeezed it. "I am here, and I'm not going anywhere without you until we get some answers."

That was only partly reassuring. Leif was the last person she needed to start depending on. No matter what he promised, he was only there for the rest of the weekend at best. Then he'd go back to his penthouse life in Dallas, a life she'd never fit into even had she wanted to. "You've already done enough, Leif. I can handle things from here. You should get back to the ranch."

"You make it hard for a man to play hero."

"Is that what you're doing?"

"My attempt at it. I'm not actually the hero type. But I am a man."

A fact of which she was most definitely aware.

"Now, let's explore the rest of the house," Leif said. "Then we'll call the local sheriff and apprise him of the break-in."

"Not Detective Morgan?" Joni asked, her anxiety still running high in spite of Leif's unruffled, businesslike method of handling the situation.

"We'll call him, too," Leif said. "But the local sheriff is right here on the scene."

"That makes sense, I guess. And then you will have definitely done enough. I can have someone else change the locks for me."

"You are determined to get rid of me," Leif said. "Have

you never dealt with an attorney before? We are as tenacious as a bulldog with his teeth in a steak."

"You may be stubborn, but I'm realistic. You have a daughter who needs you and whom you need."

"Exactly. So let's get moving—unless you'd rather wait here while I check out the house."

She'd rather fall asleep and wake up when the current nightmare was over. But avoidance wasn't her style.

Besides, Leif would only notice the obvious. She'd pick up on every nuance of change. She'd know if a rug was out of place, if her comforter was wrinkled from someone sitting on her bed. She'd be able to tell if her intimate belongings had been rifled through, as she imagined a pervert stalker might do.

Joni took a deep breath and exhaled slowly, determined to do what was necessary without sounding too dependent. "I want to look for myself, and I'd like to start in the bedroom."

"You got it." Leif put a reassuring hand on the small of her back.

It was easy to see why Serena had not wanted him to get away. But in the end, she hadn't had a choice any more than Joni would have. But Leif was here now, and she couldn't help but be thankful for that.

The bedroom door creaked as she eased it open. Slowly. With trepidation. Relief settled in quickly, along with embarrassment. Apparently she'd been reading too many suspense novels.

The bed was made as neatly as it had been when she'd hurried off with Leif that morning. No drawers appeared to have been rifled through. The only change was that the window was open, and she knew she'd left it shut.

"He opened the window," she said, walking over to close

it. "I guess he wanted to be sure he heard an approaching car. When he did, he must have escaped out the back door."

"Check to see if any of your jewelry is missing—or anything else he could convert to quick cash."

"If he took every piece of jewelry I own, it wouldn't get him enough money for a good high."

Still, she opened the top drawer of her chest, where she kept an extra watch, two pairs of silver earrings and some costume jewelry. "Jewelry all present and accounted for."

She opened the other drawers. Everything was still as neat as a pin. "Nothing seems to have been touched."

"You still need to report the break-in," Leif said, "but we should check the rest of the house first."

She turned to follow Leif out of the bedroom. When she did, she saw the sheet of paper on the floor near the edge of the tailored white bed skirt.

"Wait," she said as she bent to pick it up. The side facing her was blank. When she turned it over, she found a grainy image of Leif and another woman standing on some steep steps. A note was scribbled in red crayon beneath the picture.

A murderer and her corrupt attorney. Stay away
from Leif Dalton.

Leif stared at the note over her shoulder. "Son of a bitch."

"The prowler must have left it on the bed or the dresser and then the wind blew it to the floor," Joni said. "But why? Who's with you in the picture? Where was this taken?" The questions spilled over themselves as her muddled brain tried to make sense of the note.

"That's a picture of me and Jill Trotter right after she was acquitted," Leif said. "It was in half the newspapers in Texas the morning after the trial ended."

"It doesn't look like the woman I knew as Evie Monsant. She had dramatically changed her appearance."

"Trying to escape her past," Leif said.

"But who in Oak Grove would hate her enough to leave this note for me to find? Few people are even aware that you and I know each other"

"Someone who objects to your spending time with me knows and they apparently think you should be warned away from me."

She shook her head, still befuddled by the note. "Warning me about you would be one thing. Breaking into my house to do it is something a lunatic would do."

"Or someone who takes their grudge against me very seriously," Leif said.

"A grudge against you for doing your job? Everybody's entitled to legal representation. That's how the system works." She tossed the note onto the dresser.

"Careful how you handle evidence," Leif said. "You don't want to smudge fingerprints—if there are any. If you have a plastic bag, we can put it in that until we get it to Detective Morgan."

Evidence. The word made it sound so official and criminal. But still she didn't see the point in breaking in when the note could have been just slipped under the door or—

What was she thinking? Of course there was a point. The intruder had planned to wait for her and show her the picture. The note had probably been scribbled quickly when he realized that she hadn't returned alone.

Leif picked up the note carefully, touching only the tips of one corner.

"I'll get a bag," she said.

By the time she returned, Leif was on the phone. It was obvious he was talking to Detective Morgan. She pulled the window shut and locked it.

"The detective plans to return to Oak Grove early evening," Leif said once he'd finished the call. "He wants to come by here then."

"To pick up the note?"

"To talk to you. He's going to call Sheriff Garcia now and have him or one of his deputies stop by and pick up the note."

"So the local law enforcement agency and the DPD are working together on this case?"

Leif nodded. "That's usually the way when a high-profile crime takes place in a smaller community. The DPD will have a lot more manpower, expertise and equipment available to them."

"If the detective is coming out here tonight, he must suspect the break-in and Jill's murder are connected."

"If it is, he'll find out."

"And what am I supposed to do in the meantime? Twiddle my thumbs and wait for the lunatic who broke into my house to stop by for tea?"

"No tea and no shotgun receptions," Leif said. "I'll wait with you until the sheriff comes and then either you go with me to the ranch or I drop you off at the house of a friend until I can pick you up and bring you home."

He reached for her hand. His fingers wrapped around hers, and, like magic, his touch softened the jagged edges of the fear that had stitched itself around her heart.

But the cushion of protectiveness was only an illusion. She could not expect Leif to be at her side until Jill's killer was found. "You can stay until we've talked to the sheriff," Joni agreed. "In the meantime, I'm going to grab a quick shower. Help yourself to whiskey or coffee or whatever you see in the kitchen that you might like. I'll be out in a few minutes."

"Take as long as you need. I'll give my daughter a call

and tell her we'll be there soon, hopefully before she hears of my current notoriety."

"You should leave now, Leif. It's Effie you need to be taking care of, not me."

"Give it up, Joni. No way am I leaving here without you."

In spite of her protests, that was the best news she'd heard all day.

SHERIFF ANDY GARCIA arrived just as Leif was pouring himself a mug of fresh-brewed coffee. He escorted the lawman back to the kitchen and poured him a cup of the strong brew, hoping for a chance to talk to him before Joni joined them.

The sheriff took a seat at the kitchen table and then wasted no time in getting down to business. "Do you have the note that was left in the doc's bedroom?"

"I do." Leif handed it to him and then watched as the sheriff studied the scribbled writing though the plastic. His brows furrowed and he squinted as if he were deciphering a hidden code.

Garcia scratched his ruddy chin. "How long have you and Dr. Griffin been friends?"

"I met Joni yesterday at the Dry Gulch."

"Ah, the Dry Gulch. I guess that means you're kin to R.J."

"I'm his son," Leif admitted reluctantly.

"Here to cash in on your soon-to-be inheritance?"

Garcia did not mince words, but this time he had it all wrong. "I couldn't care less about the inheritance."

"So what brought you out to the ranch? I don't recall seeing you out this way before."

"My daughter flew in from California for the Thanksgiving holidays. She wanted to see her grandfather." Not that Leif could see how that was any of Garcia's business.

"So where's your daughter now?"

"At the Dry Gulch Ranch."

"Good. This is not the kind of situation you want to drag her into the way you did Dr. Griffin."

There was no missing the sarcasm now, and this was getting them nowhere. "For the record, I was as shocked as everyone else to find that the murder victim was a former client of mine."

"Jill Trotter, quite a famous case around these parts. Lots of people were convinced she was guilty. That would tend to make someone a few enemies. Any one of them might have tracked her down and took justice into their own hands."

"What they perceived as justice. Mrs. Trotter was acquitted," Leif reminded him.

"Right. Of course. That still leaves us with the problem of finding out who was upset enough about her getting off scot-free to want her dead."

"You're skipping a few steps there, aren't you, sheriff? There's no evidence that Jill's murder was related to the trial."

"Not yet, but this note here is pretty good evidence that she still has fervent enemies. Obviously, you do, too."

"That's one way of looking at it," Leif agreed.

"But not how you see things?" Sheriff Garcia said.

"Leif sipped his coffee. "The problem at hand, as I see it, is finding out if the man who left that note had anything to do with Jill Trotter's murder. If he did, Joni Griffin will need protection."

"So now you're telling me how to do my job?"

"I'm just stating the facts. The man broke into Joni's house and was still hanging around when we arrived. That's reason enough to think he might not have run at all if Joni had come home alone."

"I'll find out who left the note," the sheriff said. "Not much goes on around here I don't know about."

"Did Jill Trotter complain of being stalked or getting notes before she died?" Leif asked.

Garcia's mouth drew into tight lines. "I'm here to ask the questions."

Which likely meant the sheriff had either not received complaints from Jill Trotter or had ignored them.

"Can you describe the man you chased through the woods?" the sheriff asked.

"Only that he was about my height, muscled, moved like a younger man, maybe in his twenties or else in good physical shape."

"What was he wearing?"

"Jeans, a dark-colored pullover, not black but maybe wine-colored. Didn't see his hair. He wore a baseball cap, turned backward. It had a logo, but I didn't get close enough to identify it."

"Did you see a weapon?"

"No."

Joni joined them in the kitchen. Her short hair still damp from the shower, her freshly scrubbed skin glowing. The emerald sweater she wore with a pair of worn jeans made her dark eyes more bewitching than ever.

Garcia stood and introduced himself, his tone and demeanor becoming far more congenial the moment she entered the scene.

She poured herself a cup of coffee, refilled theirs and then joined them at the table.

Garcia dropped a few questions about the broken lock and finding the note. Finally the sheriff got down to the inevitable questions about romantic relationships.

Joni reached up and pushed a wet lock of bangs to the

side. "I haven't had a date with anyone since moving here nine months ago."

"But you must have been asked out a few times in the nine months you've lived in Oak Grove."

"A few," Joni admitted. "Unfortunately, I've been too busy working and getting familiarized with the job to have much of a social life."

"Yep. I've heard from some of the ranchers what a hard worker you are. They say Blake was smart to hire you."

"Thank you."

Garcia pulled a pen-size recorder from his shirt pocket. "If you would, just say the names of the men who've shown any type of romantic interest toward you into the recorder."

Joni looked up quickly and stared at the detective. "A romantic interest? What does that entail?"

"Anything that made you think they were interested in getting to know you on a more personal level."

"I'm not comfortable doing that."

"Don't worry, Doc. I'm not going to go around beating down doors and arresting guys without just cause."

"I can assure you every name I'll give you is a solid citizen."

"I know you believe that. But some guy who's keeping pretty close tabs on you is unhinged enough to break into your house."

Leif made mental notes of the names Joni supplied. Surprisingly, he recognized four of the five names. One was R.J.'s wrangler, Corky, who'd flirted openly yesterday at the ranch.

The second was Latham Watson, though Joni qualified his inclusion, insisting he'd only asked her to join him to attend a local rodeo his daughter, Ruby, was competing in and that it was merely a friendly gesture.

Both of those admirers knew she'd spent time with him

yesterday. If they'd stalked her house last night, they'd also know he spent the night with her.

The third name he recognized was Carl Adair, the son of a local, wealthy rancher known for his exploits with Dallas socialites. Leif had run into him at Dallas social events. Their history was a bit strained, since one of Carl's dates once had too much to drink and had flirted shamelessly with Leif at a fund-raising gala.

Naturally, Carl would have made it a priority to meet Oak Grove's new sexy veterinarian.

The fourth name was Joey Markham, a mechanic at Abe's Garage. No doubt that was the man who had practically drooled all over himself when they picked up Joni's truck.

The last name, Evan Singleton, the one he didn't recognize, was another young, single rancher in the area. He'd asked Joni out on several occasions, and she'd always turned him down. Just not her type, she said. Whatever that meant.

"A lot of suitor wannabes to collect in nine months," the sheriff noted.

"It's not the way it sounds," Joni assured him. "You asked for the name of anyone who's flirted. A lot of guys flirt with every available female they run into. It's just their way."

"Don't I know it? I wasn't inferring that you did anything to solicit their attention."

The number of interested men didn't surprise Leif in the least. Joni was smart, engaging, friendly and seemingly oblivious to the sensual effect she had on a man. It was an unbeatable combination.

The sheriff asked a few more questions that Joni couldn't answer. By the time he was through, they were still no closer to knowing the identity of the man who'd left the note.

Leif could sit still no longer. He stood and began to pace the small kitchen area. Garcia pushed his chair back from the table and stretched his legs under the table but didn't stand.

"Detective Morgan of the Dallas Police Department is sending out one of their crime-scene teams to check for fingerprints inside the house and to take a look around outside the house," Garcia said.

"Isn't that a little overkill?" Joni asked. "Considering nothing was taken and no harm was done except a broken lock that I'm changing out anyway."

"It could be," Garcia admitted. "Except that the note referred to a woman whose murder is currently under investigation."

"What time will the crime-scene team show up?"

"All they told me is sometime this afternoon. If you got somewhere you need to be, I can let them in and oversee the operation for you. "

"I can be here," Joni assured him.

"Suit yourself, but most find it upsetting to see their home treated as a crime scene. And most of the time, they make you wait outside anyway, sometimes for hours."

"Why don't we go to Dry Gulch Ranch?" Leif asked, grateful to the sheriff for pushing this his way. He couldn't leave Joni alone in the house but he did need to get back to Effie.

"Great idea," Garcia agreed. "Hang out with Hadley Dalton for a while. You two are friends, aren't you?"

"How did you know that?" Joni asked.

"I told you. I know what goes on in my county. Might be a good idea for you to go ahead and spend the night there, you having a broken lock and all. R.J. has plenty of room."

"I'm not sure what I'll do tonight," Joni said, "but I'll leave you to handle the crime scene. Just let me know when they finish up here."

"Sure thing. Leave me your cell number and I'll give you a call when they're done. But before you leave I'd appreciate your showing me around the house, especially the room where you found the note."

"Of course."

Garcia stood and she led the way on their tour.

Leif went back for another cup of coffee. It had been a long time since their breakfast on the trail, and hunger pangs were beginning to stab at his stomach. He started to look through the fridge for sandwich makings but decided against it.

He was eager to get back to the Dry Gulch. That was a feeling he'd never expected to have. But this was all about Effie.

Once he'd rinsed the empty cups and set them in the sink, he took out his phone and punched in her number. He got her voice mail again.

Hopefully, that wasn't because they were being harassed by news media or because she'd gotten the wrong idea about Jill's murder trial from the spin an irresponsible TV newscaster put on the story.

Jill Trotter wasn't the only thing he needed to discuss with Effie. She'd deliberately lied to him and her mother about getting in touch with him. He couldn't just ignore that, but he had a feeling that had as much to do with her mother getting remarried as it did with him.

Even if she liked her stepfather-to-be as much as Celeste said, sharing her mother with him would be a big adjustment. As would moving to London. Leaving her home. Leaving her school. Leaving her friends and Celeste's parents, the only grandparents Effie had known before R.J. insinuated himself into the picture.

Perhaps somewhere in the muddle of emotions, she might even be sorry about leaving him. So far she'd showed no sign of that. Nonetheless, Joni was right. If he was ever going to make a real connection with her again, it had to be now, when Effie was at her most vulnerable.

If he failed her now, she'd be lost to him forever.

EFFIE TOOK HER time currying Dolly. Working with the horses was more a treat for Effie than it was for the animals. She loved the scent of horses and fresh hay and the way the sun slanted through the open door, making everything the color of butterscotch.

The ranch and even her grandfather were all she'd hoped for and more. Before she'd arrived at the Dry Gulch she'd been afraid it would feel like a funeral since R.J. had an inoperable brain tumor. She'd expected him to be in bed all the time and so confused he might have forgotten inviting her.

The Dry Gulch was anything but gloomy. Lila and Lacy were partly responsible for that. The twins were so cute and funny. She'd always wished she had a little sister. Having twin cousins was the next best thing.

Both Hadley and Adam were super nice, as well. They made her feel like family.

But nothing was different with her dad. Even when he'd met her on the trial for breakfast, he'd spent more time on the phone than with her. Then he'd rushed off after the ride without even stopping by the big house to tell her he was cutting out.

Memories of the day her dad had packed his suitcase and marched out of the house crept back into her mind.

She'd be sure he wouldn't stay away long. Daddies always came back home.

Only hers hadn't.

Tears burned at the back of her eyes as Effie put the grooming brush away and walked to the back of the horse barn. She kicked out of her boots and dropped to a mini mountain of fresh hay.

Her cell phone rang. She checked the ID. Her dad again. Probably calling to say that he couldn't get back out to the ranch today. She tossed the phone, curled into a ball and cried until there were no more tears left inside her.

When the sobs subsided, she got up slowly, smoothing the worst of the wrinkles from her shirt. She splashed her tear-stained face with cool water from the nearest faucet and then stepped out the barn door and into the blinding afternoon sunlight.

She wiped her eyes on the hem of her T-shirt. Enough with crying, she decided. And enough with trying to find a way to get through to her father.

But that didn't mean she had to give up on her plans. Her grandfather wanted her on the Dry Gulch. She just had to use that to her favor.

Effie's pace was fast as she walked back to the big house. Now that she'd made up her mind what she had to do, she just wanted to get it over with. It would be easier if her dad was not around when she talked to R.J.

She was in luck. Not only was there no sign of her dad's car when she approached the house, but even Mattie's car was gone.

Effie took the back steps, vigorously wiping the bottoms of her boots on the black mat before entering. Only her grandfather wasn't alone. Her father's angry voice echoed through the house.

"The jury has made its decision. The least you can do is

have the decency to give Jill Trotter some peace and quiet so that she can go on with her life."

Effie hurried to the living room. Her grandfather was leaned back in his recliner, the toes of his striped socks stretched tightly across his big feet. The voices were coming from the TV. She looked up and saw her dad's face plastered on the screen. "What's going on?"

"Nothing new. They're just rehashing an old trial and trying to stir up trouble for Leif now that Jill Trotter's been murdered."

"Who's Jill Trotter?"

"A woman who was killed in Oak Grove a few nights ago. Your father was her lawyer several years back."

Her grandfather didn't have to say more. The images on the screen now said it all. A diverse group of people holding signs accusing her dad of helping to free a murderer crowded around her dad and an attractive blonde woman.

"Is the woman with him Jill Trotter?" she asked.

"Yep. They're standing on the courthouse steps right after she was acquitted. I don't know a lot about the case, but I'm sure your dad can explain it all when he gets here."

"Forget that. He never explains anything to me."

"Then I guess it's time I start."

This time the voice was live. She'd been so engrossed in the TV coverage, she hadn't heard her dad arrive.

"Let's take a walk, Effie. We need privacy for what I have to say."

Chapter Twelve

"What do you say we stop here?" Leif said.

Effie shrugged her agreement and dropped to the pine-straw carpet in the spotty shade provided by the needles of towering trees. She sat Indian-style, her elbows resting on her knees.

Leif pushed his sunglasses to the top of his head and joined her in the grass. He stretched his legs in front of him and leaned back against the decaying stump of an oak tree that had been chopped down years ago. At his suggestion they'd taken a walk to put some distance between them and the big house.

Joni had stayed with R.J., but she'd smiled her approval that he was keeping this personal with his daughter. As yet, he hadn't mentioned anything to Joni about the upcoming marriage of his ex and Effie's move to London.

What with the run-in with Serena and the break-in at Joni's house, there had been too much going on to get into that. But Joni was well aware that he needed to talk with his daughter about more than just the media hoopla surrounding the Jill Trotter trial.

They'd covered a good two hundred yards while he'd tried to go over exactly what he wanted to say. The fact that he still had no idea where to start evidenced how strained their relationship had become.

He breathed in the earthy, verdant scents that were so much a part of ranch life and so unfamiliar to him. The pastoral scene he found himself in was as foreign to his life as a trip to Madagascar or a boat ride down the Amazon. Yet, as bad as he hated to admit it, there was something soothing about the fresh air and open spaces.

He was a Texan by birth and now one by choice. But he wasn't a cowboy. His cowboy boots weren't scuffed. He'd packed and brought with him the only Western shirt he owned, one that had been bought for a company barbecue and worn only once. The cap on his head bore a Dallas Cowboys logo instead of the Stetson brand.

Yet sitting here with Effie, with a cool breeze at their backs and the mournful sound of mooing in the background, he could better understand how a man could get hooked on this lifestyle. He took a deep breath, soaking it all in.

A rabbit hopped past them, its back legs propelling it forward like metal springs. Blue jays squawked above them, and bullfrogs in the pond a few feet away answered in throaty, croaking calls.

Finally Effie looked at him. "So are you going to tell me why the newscasters are talking about you and some woman who got murdered or not?"

The irritation in her voice jerked him back to reality.

"For starters, you need to know that the media are making a story where one doesn't exist."

"You don't have to put a pink bow on the facts for me," Effie said. "I'm not a child."

"I realize that." *Too bad.* Back then, all he'd had to do was take her in his arms and spin her around and everything was giggles and hugs.

"Who murdered Jill Trotter?"

"That's under investigation," Leif answered.

"When we were leaving the house the newscaster said she might have been murdered by some serial killer they called The Hunter."

"As far as I know that's only speculation at this point." Leif described the Oak Grove murder as best he could without supplying any of the gorier details. He didn't want to frighten Effie unnecessarily, but he wouldn't lie to her, either.

"I don't understand what any of this has to do with you," Effie said.

"It doesn't, at least not directly. I represented Jill Trotter five years ago when she was accused of murdering her husband. In fact, that was my very first case after joining the Dallas firm."

He'd learned later that it was the case that had caused the firm to court him. They'd lost their last two high-profile murder cases. They were hoping some new blood would improve that record, and Leif was already making a name for himself in San Francisco as a tough defender in difficult cases.

In the end, their extremely lucrative offer along with the problems associated with the divorce had been too much to resist.

"You must have gotten her off," Effie said.

"The prosecution presented their evidence and I presented ours. Based on that evidence, the jury found Jill innocent."

"Was she?"

"I'm convinced that she was, and the evidence supported that."

"Then I don't get it. Why were the people they showed on TV holding up those signs and yelling at you and her?"

"A lot of people thought Jill was guilty, and they weren't happy with the outcome."

"Doesn't seem very fair."

"I agree," Leif said. "But it's just the nature of the job." To his surprise, Effie seemed not only to understand, but to be sympathizing with him.

Looked like Joni was right again. Effie was mature enough to handle the situation—at least for now.

Effie shuffled her feet, making trails with the toes of her boots in the pine straw. "Is being an attorney better here than in California?"

The hurt in her voice cut him to the quick. He laid a hand on her shoulder. "Nothing is better here, Effie. It's different but not better. How could it be when I'm so far away from you?"

Effie scooted away, avoiding his touch. Her back stiffened and she turned to stare at him accusingly. "So why did you move to Texas?"

Leif knew he had to level with her. She'd see right through his lies. Only he had no real explanation for the move except...

"The divorce hit me hard. It was affecting my work and my ability to focus. I couldn't seem to get things in perspective or move past the disillusionment."

"Are you saying the divorce was all Mother's fault?"

"Absolutely not." Though he'd seen it that way at the time. "My job was demanding. So was hers. We were both stressed and the pressure affected our relationship. We started arguing more and then not talking at all. I should have seen the divorce coming, but I just thought we'd work it out in time."

The words had come straight from the heart. He felt the pang of the heartbreak and sense of failure even now. But it was time for honesty.

"I must have added to the stress," Effie said.

"No. You were the bright spot in both our days. We

messed up our relationship, but we both loved you. Always have. Always will."

"But you didn't just leave Mother when you moved to Texas. You left me."

"I didn't foresee that, Effie. I planned for us to spend lots of quality time together. I envisioned you spending summers and holidays with me and we'd be just like we'd always been. I couldn't stand the way we were splitting up your life then, fighting over our time with you like you were property and not the daughter we both loved so much."

"How could you think it would be the same between us? You stopped being a real dad."

The indictment in her voice struck him like a punch to the gut. "I've never stopped being your dad, Effie. I never will."

"Those are just words. A real dad would have been there for my dance recitals. You'd have been there when I played soccer in summer league and for the school plays and all the special events the other fathers attended. A real father would have been there when I went to my first prom and to talk me through the heartache when I broke up with my first boyfriend."

Tears moistened Effie's eyes. She stood and walked away. "I prayed for two years that you'd move back to California. Instead you took me on expensive vacations, where we just rushed around from one activity to another. You never invited me into your real life. And you never bothered to come into mine."

"I was trying to find a place where we could relax and enjoy each other."

"It felt like you were just trying to impress me with all the money you were making in your great new life, the one you never made me a part of."

"I made mistakes, but it wasn't from lack of love, Effie. I never thought you wanted to be part of my life."

Not that there ever was much of a life. He'd worked to build his career and participated in social events that impressed the firm's senior partners but meant little to him. The women he'd dated had been little more than company and occasional sex. Even that had never been particularly great.

"I've failed you, Effie. It's the last thing I wanted to do, but I have. I know it's late in the game, but I'd like to start over. I want to be the father you want and deserve, but you'll have to help me."

He walked over and pulled her into his arms. She didn't pull away, but she didn't embrace him back.

"I'm going to give this my best shot, Effie, but you have to meet me halfway. Tell me how to start making up for lost years."

Effie pulled away again, but this time she didn't walk away. "If you really want to make my life different, talk to Mother for me. Convince her that I shouldn't be forced to move to London."

So this visit and the lies to him and her mother did stem from Celeste's upcoming marriage. Effie was clearly not as okay with it as her mother had claimed.

"I can understand you being upset that your mother is getting remarried, Effie. It's been just the two of you for so long and now there will be a husband in the picture."

"I'm not upset she's getting married," Effie protested with such passion that he had to believe her. "I'm thrilled Mother's found someone to share the rest of her life with. She deserves to be happy. I just don't want to finish high school in London."

"Having your grandparents leave their home in Napa

Valley to move in with you in San Francisco would be asking a lot of them."

"I don't have to stay in California. I'm willing to move to Texas."

Leif gulped in a breath of fresh air and tried to process this new and extremely unexpected announcement. Celeste wouldn't take that news well.

But Effie had lived with Celeste for the first fifteen years of her life. She shouldn't get upset if Effie lived with him for her junior and senior years of high school, not as long as Effie made frequent trips to London.

Only this new eagerness to live with him did not fit with the resentment she held on to so staunchly.

"Are you sure you'd be happy living with me? I mean, I'd love to have you, more than you can imagine. But I'd want you to be content and satisfied with the arrangement."

Effie stared at him, her mouth open, her eyes wide. "I wouldn't live with you, Dad. I could never live in that condo. It looks like something in a magazine. I'd be afraid to touch anything or have friends over."

"I could buy a house in the suburbs."

"You don't need to. That's why this is the perfect solution. I'd move onto the Dry Gulch Ranch. I know my grandfather is sick, but I can take care of myself and there's plenty of room. I could even be a help to Grandpa as his condition grows worse."

Leif fought his growing frustration. "R.J. can afford a nurse."

"But he'll need company and someone to talk to. And I would be here at night if he had an emergency. I could do the same chores here I do at the stables in California, plus I'd learn tons about horses from Hadley and Grandpa. There's plenty of room, and I wouldn't be a bother at all."

Anger seared through Leif like a wildfire in a Texas

draught. Effie had her new life in Texas all worked out. It included everything except him. But she couldn't have come up with this preposterous notion on her own.

"This is R.J.'s idea, isn't it?" Leif demanded. "He put you up to this. If he can't manipulate me, then he'll manipulate you."

Effie's eyes shot fire right back at him. "This is not his idea. He doesn't even know about it. I haven't asked him yet, but I'll bet he'll say yes. He likes having me here."

"You can move to Dallas, Effie. I'd love to have you live with me. But you are not moving in with R.J. He's not a parent, not even a true grandparent, in my mind."

Her hands flew to her hips. "Why do you hate him so much? Why won't you give him a chance?"

"Because he doesn't deserve one."

"Then maybe you should learn to forgive before you start preaching to me about it."

Tears filled her eyes and she stamped away without looking back.

Leif started to go after her, but there was nothing left to say. She'd never understand why he felt the way he did about R.J., not without him telling her the whole ugly truth. Even then she might not see things the way he did.

But even if he'd had a great relationship with R.J., he wouldn't have approved Effie's plans. She was only fifteen. She needed a parent watching over her to keep her safe and make sure she was cared for.

He didn't want to lose his daughter, but every move he made turned out to be the wrong one. Now he'd drawn his line in the sand and Effie had kicked the dirt in his face.

JONI SPOTTED LEIF sitting on a stump, his face buried in his hands, his shoulders drooped. She felt a tightening in her chest. He was a powerful man, smart, successful, charismatic. Extremely virile and ruggedly handsome.

But right now he looked like the defeated father of a teenage daughter. His vulnerability only increased the attraction she felt toward him.

He looked up as Joni joined him.

"Mind if I join you?"

"No, but I'll be lousy company. How did you know where to find me?"

"Effie told me when she came back to the house without you. I take it things didn't go well with her."

"You might say that. If you're here to give me a pep talk, it's a waste of time."

"I'm fresh out of pep talks. Actually I just wanted to let you know that I have to go back to my place. But don't worry—R.J. said he'd get Corky to drive me."

"What's your hurry?"

"I heard from Detective Morgan. He's on his way out to Oak Grove now and he needs to talk to me."

"Did he say why?"

Joni sat down on the ground, nearby but not so near that there would be the chance of an incidental touch. She needed to think clearly.

"The detective has a police artist's sketch of a suspect he wants me to look it."

"Does he think it might be the man who was working on Jill Trotter's ranch?"

"Apparently."

"I don't see why he'd have to meet you at your house. Why not just have him come here?" Leif asked.

"I'm not sure that's a good idea."

"Why not."

"I don't want to bring Effie into this."

"I'm sure you could find a private place to talk. Besides,

Effie knows about the murder now, so even if she realizes you're talking to a detective, it shouldn't come as a big surprise. You are a local resident."

"If you're sure."

"I am," he said.

"In that case, I'll check with Hadley and see if it's okay to use her house for the interview. If she agrees, I'll call the detective back and see if that works for him. That way I won't upset R.J."

"By all means, we want to protect R.J."

Leif's sarcasm set her on edge and forced her to go on the defensive. "R.J. is seventy-eight years old and he has a brain tumor. And he's my friend. So, yes, I want to protect him from unnecessary stress."

"Won't Morgan have to drive right by the big house to get to Hadley's cottage?"

"Yes, but with luck R.J. will be resting and not notice."

"Wherever you meet the detective, I'd like to sit in on the conversation."

"I didn't want to ask, but I'd hoped you would." She'd known Leif a mere twenty-four hours and yet she'd never felt this close to any man. Not just sensually, but in every way. He was easy to talk to, easy to be around, far too easy on the eyes.

"Want to talk about what happened with Effie?" she asked, needing to change the subject before she gave in to the need to kiss Leif that stirred deep inside her and threatened her control.

Joni listened while Leif told her what Effie had said about his not being a real father and never wanting her in his life.

"I know you're upset by her rejection, Leif. But she's talking about her feelings with you now. That's a big step forward."

"It didn't feel that way."

"At the risk of sounding like a street-corner philosopher, you have to work through the pain before you can get past it."

"Yeah, well, here's the kicker. Effie wants to move to Texas."

"That's wonderful, isn't it?"

"It would be if she wanted to move in with me, but she wants to move to the Dry Gulch Ranch."

That was a shocker. "Even if you were in favor, would her mother agree to that?"

"Who knows what she'd agree to now that she's leaving the country."

"I'm definitely not following you now."

Leif explained about Effie's mother getting married and moving to London. Once he did, Effie's choice made perfect sense to Joni.

It would give her mother a chance to adjust to married life and Effie a chance to finish high school in a system she was familiar with while spending her off time around R.J.'s magnificent horses.

But Joni was almost certain the desire to move to Texas went deeper than just living on the ranch. Even if Effie wasn't admitting it to herself, she was reaching out to her father in a way that still kept her heart protected. If she didn't care about him at all, there would be less tension and more just ignoring him.

Making Leif understand that wouldn't be easy.

"I think her moving to the Dry Gulch is an excellent idea, Leif. Hadley told me how much she likes Effie. I'm sure she and Adam would love having her around. So would R.J."

"So would I."

"Dallas is only an hour's drive from here in slow traffic

times. You could see Effie every weekend and perhaps a night or two doing the week if you wanted. You'd be with her for the big moments in her life yet to come. And you wouldn't have to worry about her spending so much time alone when you were involved in a big trial."

For a second, she thought she might be getting through to Leif. Then the muscles in his face tightened, and the strain drew his mouth into a scornful frown.

"Effie is not going to live with R.J. as long as I have anything to say about it. And I have everything to say about it."

He was impossible. "Do you honestly hate your father so much that you'd let it ruin your chance of having a relationship with Effie?"

"You don't know anything about my relationship with R.J., so don't go all judgmental on me."

"Then why don't you tell me what's really behind your anger, Leif, because right now you sound like a spoiled, petulant child."

She was so frustrated that she didn't sound much better herself.

Leif hooked his thumbs in the front pockets of his jeans. "Another time, when you're not already dealing with a nightmare. I've dragged you into enough misery for one day."

"If you're talking about the note, you had nothing to do with that."

"I'm the one he warned you to stay away from. Now the lead investigator in the murder case is coming here to talk to you."

"He's coming to talk about the handyman who stopped by my house," she reminded him. "Not the note."

"Unless the two are related."

"How could they be? For all we know the trespasser may have just been there to rob my house and left the note to throw off the sheriff. He may have only heard about you because your name is in the news.

"Whoever left the note knew we'd been together," Leif said. "And he's hanging around your house. At the very least he's stalking you."

Joni couldn't deny that. "I'll give Hadley and then the detective a call," she said, more anxious than ever to get it over with.

Leif slipped an arm around her waist. "I know you think I'm a major jerk where R.J. is concerned. I won't argue that point with you. But I want you to know how much I value your input regarding Effie."

"My input right now is that I think you're a father who's about to make a big mistake that will push your daughter even further away."

"Don't mince words to save my feelings."

"Would you prefer I lie and tell you what you want to hear?"

"No." He pulled her closer as his fingers tangled in the loose locks of hair at the back of her neck. "I like you just the way you are, to the point, gutsy as hell."

The wrath in his voice had dissolved into a raspy, seductive growl. Joni felt her control begin to unravel. She lit into Leif again about his nonrelationship with R.J., this time out of sheer frustration at the desire that rocked through her.

The next second Leif's lips were on hers and he was pressing his hard, muscular body against hers.

She had no argument for that.

Chapter Thirteen

Passion exploded inside Joni as Leif ravaged her lips with his kisses. Her heart raced and she felt as if she were floating with nothing to tether her to the earth.

She kissed him back, parting her lips, thrilled anew with every thrust of his tongue. When she pulled away for breath, his lips began a slow, burning journey down her neck to the swell of her cleavage.

Joni moaned in pleasure as emotions swirled inside her, obliterating any attempt at reason. Leif kissed her again and again, on her earlobes, her forehead and then back to her mouth. This time when he pulled away for air, she was so dizzy with desire that she had to lean against him to keep from losing her balance.

Leif trailed his fingers down her arms and took hold of both her hands. "If getting mad at me does that to you, we're going to have to argue a lot."

"Why, that was nothing, counselor. You should see me when I'm not mad." Her words were teasing, but she was certain her breathlessness gave her away.

"I take that as a challenge," Leif said.

"To be continued later," she pleaded. "Right now I should call the detective." As soon as the heated thrumming though her veins allowed her to think.

IF THERE HAD been any lingering doubt in Leif's mind that his attraction for Joni was growing out of hand, the kiss had finished it off. He was falling for her. It was frightening at best and dangerous at worst.

The timing couldn't have been worse. His relationship problems with Effie had just hit a new benchmark. The danger to Joni was accelerating with no clear indication whether or not her stalker was Jill's killer.

His cell phone vibrated. He pulled it from his pocket and checked the caller ID. When he saw that the call was from Travis, he walked away so that he wouldn't disturb Joni's conversation with the detective.

"What's up, bro?"

"I was just calling to congratulate you on your recent fame. Can't turn on the radio without hearing your name or catch the news on TV without seeing your ugly mug. Though I have to admit, you did look a bit more dashing at thirty-three than you do now."

"Thanks. You always know how to cheer up a guy."

"I do what I can. Actually, I was worried how the unwarranted notoriety and the murder were affecting Effie."

"She's more concerned with her own problems right now."

"What problems?"

Leif explained the situation with Celeste's upcoming marriage and Effie's bizarre plan for avoiding the move to London.

"That could work in your favor," Travis said. "Just tweak her plan a bit. Have her move in with you so that you could provide the proper supervision. Spend a couple of weekends a month at the ranch."

"Which would mean I'd have to deal with R.J. on a regular basis. You're the last person I'd expect to suggest that."

"He's dying, Leif. It's not like you're talking about years

of servitude or dancing to the terms of that manipulative will he engineered."

"No, he's manipulating my daughter. That's worse in my book."

"You got a point there, too. Hard to believe R.J. has developed a sense of family loyalty at this late date, but I guess staring your own mortality in the face can change a man's outlook."

"He can do what he wants—as long as it doesn't include me or Effie."

"I hear you. I would like to see Effie while she's in Dallas," Travis said.

"Good. Change your mind and come out to the Dry Gulch for Thanksgiving dinner tomorrow."

"Only if the turkey you're stuffing is R.J."

"What happened to the pep talk you were just giving me about his being a changed man?"

"That was for you, not me. Besides, I'll be working tomorrow. I'm at the airport now, flying back to Dallas a day early."

"Does this have anything to do with the Jill Trotter case?"

"You got it."

"Interesting. Do you know anything new that I don't?"

"Not yet, but the investigation is apparently heating up. The vet you were telling me about got a threatening note."

"I know, a note warning her to stay away from me."

"Is she?"

"No. She's here at the ranch now, a few steps away, on the phone with Detective Morgan."

"Sounds cozy. Do I detect a budding romance here?"

"With all the trouble I'm causing Joni, I'll be surprised if she even talks to me after this."

"Nice dodge of the question, attorney. Anyway, I've been

called in to do background checks on local admirers who may have delivered the note."

"I'd love to know if you learn anything useful."

"As long as the info doesn't become classified, I'll clue you in. In the meantime, Joni Griffin needs to stay safe."

Leif lowered his voice even more. "You sound like you think there's a connection between the note and Jill's murder."

"All I know is that Dr. Joni Griffin has become a significant part of the murder investigation. You figure it out from there."

But Leif couldn't figure it out. There were apparent gaps in his information, especially if Jill was killed for revenge by someone who believed she'd killed her husband. Nonetheless, Joni had become a key player in a murder investigation. That was reason enough to insist on spending the night at her place again tonight.

Unfortunately, the other reasons influencing his decision were not nearly as noble.

As it turned out, Adam was busy moving bales of hay to the northwest pasture, but Hadley seemed more than happy to give up her living room for the meeting with Detective Morgan. She'd taken the girls outside to climb, crawl, swing and slide on the wooden playground set Adam had built for them.

Joni and Leif took the two upholstered chairs that cuddled around a lamp table. Morgan took the sofa, an arrangement that permitted them all to make eye contact at will.

The detective had seemed congenial enough when he'd arrived, but his tone became deadly serious as he pulled a pencil drawing from a leather briefcase. He leaned forward and passed the sketch to Joni.

"Look closely at the facial features," the detective urged.

"Don't try to force a similarity between the picture and any-one you've ever seen before. Let the picture speak for itself."

Leif watched Joni as she examined the photo. She took her time, but Leif knew from the instantaneous tremble of her lips and the haunted glaze that darkened her eyes that something in the picture struck a chord with her.

"It's him," she whispered, lowering the picture and peering over it.

"You're sure?" the detective asked cautiously.

She nodded.

"Do you mind if I record this conversation?" the detective asked.

"No. Not if it will help you apprehend the killer."

Morgan set a pencil-size recorder on the coffee table that separated him from Joni. A red light blinked and then turned green.

"Will you state your full name for the record?"

Joni sat up straighter. "My name is Joni Marie Griffin."

"Can you tell me exactly where you've seen the man in the sketch before?"

"I can." Her voice was steady and strong with conviction. She clearly had no doubts. "The man in the sketch is the man who came to my house looking for work last week. He said he could do any kind of construction or handyman jobs that I had."

"But you didn't hire him?"

"No."

"Have you seen the man since then?"

"I saw him, or a man who resembled him, working on Jill Trotter's roof, though I knew her as Evie Monsant at the time."

"Were you able to get a good look at him when he was on her roof?"

"No," Joni admitted. "I was passing by her house in my

car, but I did notice that the pickup truck in her driveway was black."

"Was it the same pickup truck the man drove to your house?"

"I can't be certain of that, but they looked similar."

Leif leaned over for a better look at the sketch. He could easily see how Joni could be so sure. The facial features were exceptionally detailed, right down to the receding hairline, the shape of the eyes and a scar along the right jawline.

Whoever had given the description must have had a good look at the suspect.

When Joni finished describing the truck, Morgan had her hand him the sketch. He returned it to his briefcase and pulled out yet another sketch, this one a profile. He handed it to Joni.

"Does this man look familiar? Take your time. We're in no hurry here."

This time she answered in under a minute. "It's the same man."

"Thank you." Morgan reached over and turned off the recorder. "Great job, Dr. Griffin."

"Thank your sketch artist," Joni said. "The details made my job easy."

"The DPD is fortunate enough to have one of the most talented in the business," Morgan agreed. "When she gets accurate information, she's almost as definitive as a photo."

"Who gave the original description?" Leif asked.

"A rape victim who miraculously escaped meeting the same fate as Mrs. Trotter. She was a patient consultant for a cosmetic surgeon, so she was used to analyzing facial features so her description was more detailed than we normally get."

"Did he pose as a handyman with her, too?" Joni asked.

"I'm sorry," the detective said. "I'm not at liberty to say more. But you've been a tremendous help. With luck, we'll make an arrest before he can strike again."

"If you'll excuse me, I have to make a phone call," Morgan said. "I'll step outside."

"Are you finished with me?" Joni said.

"No. Please stay where you are. I'll be right back." The phone was in his hand and he was punching in a number before he'd cleared the front door.

Joni turned to Leif. "The man in that sketch stood on my front porch. I looked him right in the eye. In spite of his gory tattoo, I might have hired him to do some of the things my landlord doesn't take care of if I'd had the money." She trembled and wrapped her arms around her chest. "I might have been the woman attacked and murdered instead of Jill Trotter."

Leif reached for her hand. It was cold. Joni was spunky as hell, but she was only human. This was getting to her and with good reason. Which meant it might be the best time to tell her that there was no way he was leaving her alone in that house until the killer was in custody.

Morgan returned before he got the chance. This time he didn't sit, but stood between Joni's chair and the door.

"There are some developments you should know about, Joni. Listen, but don't get unduly upset. I can assure you that we have everything under control."

Words that struck fear in every citizen's heart, including Leif's.

Joni slipped her hand from Leif's. "What do you mean by under control? Is the suspect in custody?"

"Not yet, but we expect him to be soon. In the meantime, a pair of officers from the Dallas Police Department will stake out your house tonight and for the next twenty-four hours—perhaps longer."

"Why? Do you have some reason to suspect the handyman would come after me?"

"It's a precautionary measure. Someone broke into your house today and left a threatening note. If he comes back, we'll apprehend him."

"Because you think he could be Jill's killer?" Joni insisted.

"It's possible." The detective picked up his recorder and briefcase, clearly eager to head out now that he had what he needed from Joni.

"It's ludicrous," Joni protested. "A few hours ago Sheriff Garcia insinuated the man who broke into my house was a local admirer turned stalker who didn't want me hanging out with Leif. Now all of a sudden you think a killer I've only seen once would be stalking me instead of clearing out of Oak Grove as fast as he could."

"Like I said, staking out your house is just a precautionary measure."

Leif wasn't buying it, and he seriously doubted that Joni was, either. Something, perhaps the handwriting on the scribbled note he'd left her, had tied Joni to Jill's killer. And now the DPD was throwing everything they had into catching this man.

This had all the trappings of something big—like a dragnet to nab a serial killer. They wanted their man, even if it meant using Joni for bait.

"Your staking out the house is fine," Leif said. "As long as Joni isn't in it."

"Dr. Griffin will not be in danger at any time," the detective insisted. "The house will be watched every second. If the man who broke in today returns, he'll be arrested before he gets inside the house."

"If the officers are parked in front of my house, surely

the man would have better sense than to come barging in," Joni said.

"The officers will be out of sight but in position and with equipment that allows them to monitor the house at all times."

"But if he does get inside without their seeing him?" Joni asked. "What then?"

"That would be very unlikely, but if that happens, all you have to do is scream. Officers could reach you in a matter of seconds."

Leif became more certain of his conclusion by the second. They were hot on the trial of The Hunter and the trail ran right through Joni.

"Not good enough. You can have the house as long as it's okay with Joni, but Joni will not be in it," Leif reiterated.

The detective grimaced. "I can assure her safety."

"Not to my satisfaction," Leif said.

Joni placed a hand on Leif's arm. "I appreciate your concern, but this has to be my decision."

"What is your decision?" the detective asked.

"Will my staying in the house help you catch the killer?"

"It could."

"Then I'll stay."

The determination in her voice convinced Leif he'd never talk her out of it, not that he'd stop trying.

But he was just as determined. Officers hiding out in the woods wouldn't cut it. Joni might stay in her house tonight, but whether Morgan approved or not, she wouldn't be staying alone.

Chapter Fourteen

It was growing dark early now. The change suited him. Once the sun set, his blood seemed to run hotter and his energy level climbed.

His mother used to joke that he was like a vampire who came to life when the sun went down. She'd been partly right. Another side of him did awake fully at night, but it didn't fully disappear when the sun came up.

He settled in the chair, popped a small white pill and washed it down with a swig of cold beer. Alcohol and medication didn't mix. His psychiatrist had warned him of that all the time back when the shrink was still supplying the prescription.

Now he got a different kind of pill and a different kind of high without having to pretend to listen to the arrogant bastard who thought a couple of college degrees made him a god.

After reaching for the remote, he kicked back and turned on the evening news. It was a minute or two early, but coverage of Jill Trotter's murder might get top billing. He didn't want to miss a second of that.

A guy could get shot in a drug deal gone bad and the network anchors never gave that a mention. But let someone like Jill Trotter get what she had coming to her, and it got days of hype in the newspapers, on the radio and on the TV.

Of course they'd never say that, like her husband, Jill deserved to die. The Trotters were users. They took what they wanted from whomever they chose.

Jill had thought she was so smart. Changed her name. Changed her hair. Even had cosmetic surgery to change her appearance. No doubt she'd fooled lots of people. But not him.

He'd sat in that trial and watched her day after day—him and dozens of other trial junkies. He'd blended in perfectly, chatted with the others about Jill's guilt, joked about the stupid judge and cursed the sorry defense attorney. But all the while he'd been studying Jill, thinking about how he'd kill her, as well.

He'd memorized the little things about her. The sound of her voice. The way she walked. The way she tugged on a strand of her hair when thinking and then tucked it behind her right ear. The way her left eye squinted when she was irritated.

For five years he'd planned her death, perfecting how he'd torture and kill her. He'd almost given up on that dream, but then, when he'd least expected it, he'd stumbled across her.

The commercial ended and the female newscaster looked solemnly into the camera.

"Police report that they're looking for a person of interest in the Oak Grove murder of Jill Trotter. They have still not confirmed or denied that the brutal murder was the work of the serial killer who's been referred to as The Hunter."

He listened to the rest of the newscast as he finished off the beer. The police were a joke. They didn't have a clue. They might make an arrest but they'd have the wrong person, the same as they had when they'd arrested Jill Trotter for the murder of her husband.

But they might have another murder to solve soon.

He was tired of women who smiled and flirted and then dropped you for a rich attorney like Leif Dalton.

He'd warned Joni. And he never made threats he didn't mean to keep. If she let Leif back into her house tonight, his tolerance would come to an end.

Joni's fate was in her hands.

And in his. He'd have her one way or another.

Happy Thanksgiving to me.

Chapter Fifteen

For once the kitchen at the big house was quiet, though odors of cinnamon, pumpkin and spices wafted through every room. Tempting pies lined the counter. None had been cut as yet, so Leif took an apple from a wooden bowl overflowing with fruit and nuts.

He couldn't remember eating lunch—wasn't sure he had. Meals, like time, seemed to run together and had ever since Effie had arrived and Joni had been pulled into danger.

He felt like he was skidding across waxed glass with no way to stop or even to slow down enough to prepare for the upcoming crash.

Polishing the apple with his fingertips, he walked out the back door and sat down on the steps. The late-afternoon sun was already racing toward the horizon painting the sky in layers of gold.

It was the first time he'd been at the house alone. It felt eerily foreboding, as if the ranch had become too familiar and he was casting shadows that would pull him back here against his will.

Circumstances had already tilted his world at weird angles. In another hour or so, he'd be joining the Daltons for dinner again. Tonight they'd eat at Adam and Hadley's private oasis in the middle of Dry Gulch Ranch. Their house, but still so much a part of the ranch that there was no real separation from R.J.

Admittedly, they seemed happy with the arrangement— even Adam, who'd been the first to walk away the day they'd had the reading of the will. A few months seemed to have altered everything for him.

Adam was giving the women a break from the Thanksgiving Day meal preparations by making a pot of homemade chili.

Joni had left for Hadley's a few minutes ago after checking on one of R.J.'s injured horses. Leif had offered to drive her to the cottage, but she'd turned him down in favor of one of R.J.'s four-wheelers. He figured she needed some alone time what with all she'd been hit with today.

He wasn't sure where Effie and R.J. were. Wherever they were, hopefully Effie wasn't trying to persuade him to lobby for her ridiculous plan of moving in with him.

Leif took another bite of the apple and then pulled out his clean handkerchief to wipe the sweet juices from his lips and chin. The apple took the edge off Leif's hunger. Too bad it couldn't take the edge off his problems with Effie or the danger facing Joni.

Odd how that when the going got rough, a man's concentration always focused on the most cherished people in his life. Naturally, that would include Effie. She'd been the most important person in his life since the day she was born.

He'd been afraid to hold her at first, afraid his hands would be too rough for her porcelain-like skin or that he wouldn't support her head in just the right way. But once he'd taken her in his arms, he'd known he'd want to nourish and protect her for the rest of his life.

He loved his daughter so very much.

But his mind was also consumed by Joni. How could

she have reached such an exalted state of importance to him when he barely knew her? How could he feel so close to her and so protective of her?

How could he have grown dizzy with wanting her when they'd kissed? Leif knew infatuation, lust and pure physical excitement. The kiss had been far more than any of that.

The only thing he knew for certain was that he'd protect her with his life if it came to that.

R.J. LEANED AGAINST Miss Dazzler's stall. "You're looking down in the mouth tonight. Don't understand why you had to stay in the boring stall all day, do you, pretty lady?"

The injured filly pawed the straw at her feet and neighed softly as if she understood and appreciated the sympathy.

R.J. didn't spend nearly as much time with his horses as he had before the brain tumor had started causing problems for him, but he still came to the barn when he was especially troubled or needed to think.

This afternoon even the company of his horses wasn't doing a lot to clear his mind. There was just too damn much conflict floating around the ranch.

Joni was definitely not herself. She'd been quiet as a sleeping field mouse when she'd checked on Miss Dazzler. He hoped Leif wasn't the one causing her grief.

He kinda thought that might be the case, though. The two of them were spending an awful lot of time together for people who'd just met.

Joni was a good country girl. She'd be no match for someone as worldly and sophisticated as Leif, especially if Leif was anything like the womanizer R.J. had been at that age. Kind of like having his hens come home to roost for R.J.

And then there was the tension between Leif and Effie.

Thick enough you could use it for a mattress if you were looking to sleep with trouble.

The door to the horse barn creaked open. R.J. looked up. *Speak of the devil.*

Leif glanced around the barn. "Where's Effie?"

"At Adam's house."

"She didn't ride down there by herself, did she?"

"Nope. She caught a ride back to Adam's when he came down to bring a sweet potato casserole Hadley cooked up for tomorrow's lunch. She said she'd meet us there."

Leif nodded, but he didn't look pleased. R.J. figured the displeasure was more from being stuck there alone with him than with Effie not being there.

"Effie's really growing attached to Lila and Lacy," R.J. said.

"So it would seem."

Leif looked around the barn again, this time letting his gaze settle on the names of the horses displayed above the stalls. "You've got some nice animals. Miss Dazzler there is a real beauty."

"She's my favorite," R.J. admitted. "Got an injured fetlock now though. That's what brought the doc out yesterday." R.J. raked his thin fingers through his thinning hair. "You two seem to be hitting it off."

"Joni is easy to be around."

"She's a nice lady, Leif. Real nice. And honest. Don't go breaking her heart if you're just playing around."

Leif's brows arched and the muscles in his arms strained against his cotton shirtsleeves. "That, coming from you?"

"I never claimed to have set the best example in the world."

Amazingly, Leif didn't have a comeback. Instead, he walked through the barn, stopping at first one stall and then another. "Is there anything I can help you with while I'm here?"

"No," R.J. said, surprised at the offer. "They don't rely on me for any chores these days. Health is as undependable as Texas weather."

Leif stopped at Kenda's stall. "You seem to be getting around pretty good now."

"I'm having a good week. I suspect having Effie around is contributing to that. She's a very special young lady, Leif. Lots of heart."

"I know."

"So what's going on between you two? That angst runs too deep for me to be causing it."

"You're not helping," Leif said. "But you're right. Apparently the anger and resentment go back to the divorce and my moving to Dallas. She thinks I abandoned her."

"Did you?"

"Hell, no. Abandonment is when you don't even know where your kids are and couldn't care less. Abandonment is when you let your sons be raised as orphans after their mother dies. It's when you live your life with no worries about the price your children pay for your neglect."

Bitterness spewed from his mouth with the accusations. Only this had nothing to do with Effie and everything to do with R.J.

"I know I was a rotten father, Leif. I was a lousy husband, as well. I let my demons control my life. I failed everyone who ever meant anything to me. If I could change that, I would. But the past can't be undone."

"So you just decided to manipulate your children and grandchildren instead. You call the shots. We dance or get dropped from the will the way you dropped us from your life."

"I put out the olive branch. You gotta decide for yourself whether you want to take it or not."

"That's mighty big of you. But I don't need your money. I don't need anything from you and neither does Effie."

"You can spout your anger all you want, Leif. It's probably long past time you did. But I'm not your biggest worry. Effie is."

"Leave Effie out of this."

"All I'm saying is don't mess up your life the way I did. When you lose family and the people you love, you lose everything."

R.J. stepped back from the stall. He'd said enough. The rest was up to Leif. "We should get up to Adam's. Dinner should be ready about now."

He took a few steps toward the door. The barn began to spin, the animals' faces blurring so that he couldn't recognize them. He stumbled and fell to his knees.

Leif knelt beside him and steadied him with an arm around his shoulders. "Are you all right? Should I call for an ambulance?"

"No. This is how it is. The dizzy spells will get worse as time goes on, but for now I'm just lucky they come as seldom as they do."

Leif's gaze locked with his. The anger had turned to concern. It was progress, but R.J. knew it would be a long time before Leif could forgive him—if ever.

"Hate me if you want to, Leif. But do everything in your power to save your relationship with Effie. In the end, love and family are all that really matters."

IT WAS AFTER nine when Leif and Joni arrived back at her house. True to their word, there was no sign of law enforcement officers watching the house.

But they were there. The solar spotlights that Leif had

installed earlier in the day had been removed, leaving the outside of the house illuminated only by filtered moonlight.

"Still time to change your mind about staying here tonight," Leif said as she unlocked the front door.

"No. I just want the suspect apprehended so that I and the rest of Oak Grove can go back to our safe, comfortable lives. And if it does turn out that he's The Hunter, all of Texas will rest easier."

"Don't count on too much," Leif warned. "If The Hunter killed Jill and is still hanging around Oak Grove looking for victims, he's made a major change to his modus operandi."

"It could happen."

"It could, but I'm not convinced."

"You've seen me home safely," Joni said. "You don't have to stay. Really, I'm not afraid. I'm sure the stakeout officers have everything under control."

"You're not getting rid of me that easy."

She kicked out of her shoes. "Then we may as well get comfortable, roomie."

She was giving nonchalance a good shot, but Leif could tell by the way she'd been so quiet at dinner and driving home that she was anxious.

"Did you tell Hadley that you were being used as bait by the police?"

"No. I didn't mention the stakeout at all. Hadley would have spent the rest of the evening trying to talk me into staying at her place tonight."

"Hadley is a smart woman."

"So am I," Joni said. "And cautious. But Detective Morgan assured us both that I'm perfectly safe. I was surprised when he didn't hassle you about staying here tonight, though."

"He would have if he thought I was a hindrance."

Joni stopped at the kitchen door. "I'm not following you."

"The note made it clear what your stalker thinks of me. Morgan thinks I may be an added inducement to drawing him out in the open. That's the reason he told me to park my car in clear sight of anyone approaching the house."

"I hadn't thought of that."

"It doesn't change anything," Leif assured her.

"Except that you've become part of the bait, too. As you know, my kitchen is embarrassingly bare, but if you see anything you want, help yourself. We probably should have bought more whiskey."

"Better I keep my head clear tonight," Leif said.

"In that case, I'm going to excuse myself and take another shower and hope that will help me relax."

And he'd be left to listen to the water running and imagining her naked body beneath the spray. This was going to be a long night on every front.

Leif started a pot of coffee and then took out his trial notes from the Trotter case.

He was barely through the account of his first meeting with Jill when his phone rang.

Travis's name came up on the caller ID. Hopefully he was calling with good news—like maybe the suspect had already been apprehended.

"What's up?"

"Just calling to fill you in on the latest," Travis said.

"Hopefully, it's good news."

"It could be," Travis said. "I got a call from Morgan. He told me to hold up on the investigation of stalker suspects. They think they have their man. Now all they have to do is apprehend him."

"Did he insinuate that the suspect might be The Hunter?"

"As a matter of fact, he did, but that is off the record. He also mentioned that he ran into you again this afternoon while questioning Joni Griffin."

"Really? I didn't even think he knew you were my brother."

"Nothing much gets past Josh Morgan. He wouldn't have mentioned it to you during questioning. I told you he's a by-the-book guy."

"Just so he's good."

"I don't think you have any worries there. I did pick up some information about one of the names Joni had given the police that you might want to make her aware of."

"Which one?"

"Joey Markham, the mechanic."

"What about him?"

"He has a colorful rap sheet. Arrested on two different occasions for domestic violence."

"Is he married?"

"No. These were girlfriends. In both cases, he battered them so badly that they required hospital care."

"Did he do jail time?"

"The first honey dropped charges, but the second one testified against him. Joey did seven months for that crime."

"When was that?"

"Three years ago. The next arrest was for a case of road rage. He pulled a gun and actually shot it at a pregnant woman who'd almost sideswiped his car. She said she was just avoiding getting hit by an eighteen wheeler in another lane. Fortunately, the bullet missed its mark."

"What happened with that case?"

"He was sentenced to ten years. After a year, another judge cut his sentence and let him out of prison under the condition he see a psychiatrist for anger management on a regular basis."

"I can imagine how long that lasted."

"You got it. The psychiatrist told me that Joey came to three sessions and then just stopped going. He reported that to Joey's parole officer. He hasn't seen Joey or the parole officer since. The guy sounds like a powder keg about to explode."

"I guess the police will arrest him for parole violation?"

"Right, but that's no guarantee he'll stay in jail any longer than before. You should let Joni know in case he makes any more advances toward her before he's arrested."

The thought of Joni dating a lunatic like Joey Markham was sickening. The thought of her dating anyone was disturbing. Not that he had any say over who she dated. It wasn't as if they were lovers.

Not yet, anyway. When this was over…

He shook his head to clear the confusion. Once Joni was safe, he might have to rethink a lot of things about his life. Leif filled Travis in on the details concerning the sketch and the stakeout.

"Where is Effie staying tonight?" Travis asked.

"At the Dry Gulch Ranch."

"Are you there, too?"

"No, I'm with Joni at her place."

"I know the cops have you covered," Travis said. "The DPD is as good as it gets, but, still, be careful. A murderer who's cornered doesn't have a lot to lose and this one already hates you for some reason no one fully understands."

"Don't worry. I'm not crazy enough to do anything foolish." Not where Joni's safety was concerned.

Once the connection was broken, he went back to the trial notes.

"Is that fresh coffee I smell?"

"It is." Leif looked up as Joni joined him. One glimpse of her and every part of his body jumped to attention.

The shimmery silk nightshirt she was wearing skimmed her perky breasts and shapely hips and fell inches short of her knees. It was the color of a sparkling amethyst.

Her flawless complexion glowed. Her long-lashed dark eyes were like velvet. Locks of her ebony hair, still damp from the shower, danced about her face.

She smiled and he knew she must realize the effect she was having on him. He ached to take her in his arms and taste the luscious lips that had driven him wild earlier.

He didn't dare. Even with cops nearby on high alert, he and Joni were alone. He'd never be able to stop with a kiss. Not with every cell in his body hungering to make love to her.

But this was not the time or place. She was too vulnerable, and he didn't want to come on to her when her emotions were overwrought and her mind was on a serial killer.

When they made love for the first time, he wanted everything to be right. He wanted her to have no regrets. It had to be that way if they were to have any chance of building a real relationship.

And he did want that, more than he'd ever wanted anything in his life. It felt strange and a bit frightening to admit that even to himself, but he knew it was true.

She slid into a chair catty-corner from his and glanced at the file that lay open in front of him. "Are those the notes from Jill Trotter's trial?"

"They are."

"Why bother with them now? The DPD seems convinced they have their suspect."

"A good trial attorney never takes anything for granted."

"Which means you think the police may not be focusing their efforts on the right man."

"No one's in custody yet."

"I thought I heard you talking when I was getting ready for my shower. Did Detective Morgan call with any last-minute instructions?"

"No. I was talking to Travis. He had some interesting facts about your mechanic."

"Abe?"

"Joey Markham. He may be good at truck repairs, but he's tough on women."

"In what way?"

"He's been arrested at least twice for sending a girlfriend to the hospital and arrested once for shooting at a pregnant woman whose driving he didn't like."

"Geez, Louise. I would have never guessed he had such a violent streak. He's always so friendly when I take my truck to Abe's. Has he been in prison?"

"Twice, and he's likely going back."

"You don't think he's the man the police are expecting to appear tonight, do you?"

"Apparently not. Travis said they'd called off his investigation into the names you gave him even before he'd told them about Joey."

Leif filled Joni in on all the details he'd gotten from Travis.

"We have to tell Abe," she said. "He wouldn't want anyone like that working in his shop, not even for another day."

"I'll let Abe know first thing Friday morning unless the police tell him first. But I don't want you involved. You never know how a man like Joey will react."

"Then you shouldn't get involved, either, Leif Dalton. You're an attorney, not a cop. You shouldn't even be here tonight."

"Are you worried about me or just trying to get rid of me?"

Her cheeks turned red. The blush upped his arousal level. He was going to have one hell of a time making it through the night.

"I don't want you getting beat up. I may need a good attorney someday."

"Hopefully not a criminal defense attorney."

"Did you ever think of changing to some other type of practice?"

"Yes and no. But the truth is, I like what I do. If I could change anything, it would be to work for myself instead of a major firm."

"Then why don't you?"

"I wouldn't have nearly the perks or the salary I have now."

"Or your choice of supermodels," Joni added.

"No, I'd probably have to settle for a country vet."

She punched him playfully, picked up his empty mug and walked over to the coffeepot. "If you're pulling an all-nighter, I may as well join the party."

She rejoined him at the table. "So what are you looking for in that shaft of papers? Anything I can help you locate?"

"You can give it a shot," Leif said. "Problem is I don't have anything specific in mind. I'm hoping something might jump out at me."

"You mean like a reason for someone to come after Jill Trotter at this late date?"

"Something like that."

"You really aren't buying into The Hunter theory, are you?"

"I haven't ruled it out."

Leif would like to believe that the DPD was about to wrap everything up in a nice little package and deliver The Hunter to a jury that would put him away for life. But it just didn't make sense that a man who killed randomly would have had the picture of Leif and Jill Trotter that he'd left with the warning note. It made the crime seem much too personal.

"Start with these," he said, pushing a file of notes he'd taken in interviews with Jill Trotter in front of Joni.

"You got it, counselor."

Leif scanned a half-dozen pages before becoming so restless he couldn't sit any longer. He stood and paced the room, wondering what might be going on in the dark wooded area outside the house.

"Suzanne Markham," Joni announced like she was calling roll. "Does that name constitute a red flag?"

"Suzanne. Phillip's office manager for years before Jill insisted he fire her."

Leif had forgotten the fired office manager's last name was Markham until Joni triggered the memory. There had been so many names of people and places seared into his mind in the years since Jill's trial.

He scooted a chair next to Joni's and straddled it. "Exactly the kind of red flag I was looking for," he said.

"Do you think there could be a link between her and Joey the mechanic?"

"I think it's worth checking out."

"What's the rest of the story on Suzanne?" Joni asked.

"There's not much of one. She wasn't a major player in the trial since she died a year before Phillip was killed. When Phillip and Jill married, she decided he and Suzanne were having an affair. She hired a private eye to follow Phillip."

"What did the P.I. discover?"

"Nothing to support the idea of an affair, but Jill insisted Phillip fire her anyway. When I took over the case, I did my own investigation of Phillip's infidelity with the same results as her P.I., just to make certain the prosecutor didn't surprise me in the courtroom.

"I guess if there had been anything there, the prosecutor would have used it as motive for Jill to kill Phillip," Joni said.

"For a vet, you're certainly up-to-date on trial procedures."

"I got my education at the altar of *Law & Order*."

"And to think I went to law school and had to pass the bar."

"Was Suzanne married when she died?" Joni asked.

"Divorced and had been for years."

"Did she have a son?"

"Not that I'm aware of, but I suppose she could have."

"Shall I keep looking and see if I can find that info in the files?"

"Let me check with Travis first," Leif said. "He might have the name of Joey's mother."

Leif made the call. Travis answered on the first ring.

"Has there been an arrest?" Travis asked.

"If there has, no one's informed us. I called with a question."

"Shoot."

"Do you have the name of Joey Markham's mother?"

"I have it somewhere in the report. It's Suzy. Susan."

"Suzanne," Leif offered.

"Bingo. How did you know?"

"I think we may have just found a link between Joey Markham and Jill Trotter."

"Still doubting that the police have already identified the killer and that it's not Joey Markham?"

"Just keeping an open mind."

"My bet's still with the homicide department of the DPD," Travis said, "but you do make a good point."

By the time he'd finished the conversation, Joni had retrieved her laptop and had her search engine going.

Leif went back to the files to see if there were any notations on Suzanne's son.

Joni scored first. "Listen to this. Suzanne Markham had a son named Joseph Patrick Markham."

"Did you find an age for him?"

"I have a date of birth. He's twenty-six now. That definitely fits our Joey." She took her fingers from the keyboard. "I don't know why I'm getting excited about this information. It's could just be a coincidence that Joey Markham lives in the same town where Jill Trotter was murdered."

"An extremely bizarre coincidence."

"But that's all it can be, Leif. The police sketch of a murderous suspect is a definite match for the man who was working on Jill Trotter's roof. Besides, there's no motive for Suzanne's son to kill Jill."

"Unless he's the illegitimate son of Phillip Trotter and believes Jill killed his father."

Joni jumped from her chair. "Why didn't I think of that? That could be why Phillip hired her in the first place. She might have been pregnant with his child."

"But this is all speculation," Leif reminded her.

He looked at the clock on the oven and then pushed his empty mug away. "With luck, we'll know more tomorrow," he said. "And it will be a busy day. You should try to get some sleep."

"I'll try." She shut off her computer, rinsed both their mugs and walked to the kitchen door. "You know what I said earlier about not being afraid and not needing you to stay with me tonight?"

"I remember."

"I lied. Thanks for not taking me at my word."

With that she turned and was gone.

Letting her walk away without following her to her bedroom was quite possibly the hardest thing he'd ever done.

JONI WOKE TO a choking sensation and the feeling of cold fingers wrapped around her neck. She flung her arms and kicked her feet, desperately trying to fight off the attacker.

The fingers squeezed all the tighter.

She wasn't alone. She could hear angry voices coming from the far corner of the room. Fighting for breath, she tried to focus, but the faces were blurry. Only the biting words were clear.

"You are killing her, Leif. Your hate and your venom are choking the life out of Joni. You choke the life out of everything you touch, the same way you did Effie."

"Go to hell, R. J. Dalton. Burn for eternity. Only then can you pay for what you did."

Janie gave one last kick, freeing her feet from the sheets that had wrapped around her like snakes and her neck from the choking grip. Cold sweat ran down her face and between her breasts. She clawed at the silk nightshirt, tugging it away from her clammy skin.

Her breathing and pulse slowly returned to normal. Sliding off the bed, she padded to the window in her bare feet, tipped a slat in the blind and peered into the darkness.

The wind gusted, sending a new shower of dry leaves fluttering to the earth. The only sound was the creaking of the limbs in the oak tree that shaded her side yard. The night seemed calm, a placid hunting ground for the nocturnal animals that inhabited the woods.

Perhaps the hunting ground of a killer who'd already struck once this week.

And somewhere in the predawn darkness, police officers stood by while the killer might be waiting and watching for the first light of Thanksgiving morning to make his move.

She turned away from the window before her thoughts brought on a new flush of anxiety. But it hadn't been a killer who'd haunted her nightmare.

It had been Leif, a man who had touched her heart in ways it had never been touched before.

Leif, the smart, witty, protective attorney whom she was falling in love with.

Leif, who was losing his daughter because he couldn't let go of the bitterness he'd nursed for years. There had to be a way to get through to him.

But first she had to know the truth behind the destructive resentment. Joni glanced at the clock. It was four in the morning, yet she heard movement coming from the living room, where Leif was supposed to be sleeping on the sofa.

Obviously, he was awake, too. Maybe this was the perfect time for him to get his anger toward R.J. out in the open and then hopefully move past it.

The least she could do was offer to listen with an open mind. The worst he could do was refuse her proposal and continue to live with the burgeoning resentment.

Joni slipped out of her wet nightshirt and into a loose cotton robe. Then she opened her door and went in search of Leif and the secrets that were poisoning his life.

Chapter Sixteen

Leif looked up, put down the Trotter case files he'd been perusing for the past hour and rubbed his burning eyes. Joni was standing in the doorway, staring at him expectantly.

She had exchanged the nightshirt for a long, shapeless robe. Still, desire hit so quickly he had to struggle to keep from sporting a noticeable bulge. He quickly wiggled into his jeans, though he didn't bother with the top snap.

"Did I wake you?" he asked.

"No. I had a nightmare."

"That's the problem with going to bed with thoughts of killers dancing in your head."

"I didn't dream of killers. I dreamed of you and R.J."

"I can see where that would be a nightmare."

Joni walked over, settled on one end of the sofa and tugged the blanket from his makeshift bed around her legs. "Did you find anything else of interest in the files?"

"Not much." Leif closed the file binder and tossed it to the coffee table. "Enough about murder trials."

"I agree," Joni said. "In fact, that's why I'm here. I want to talk about you."

"Good topic. That should bore us both to sleep."

"I doubt that," Joni said.

"Where shall I start?"

"How about the point where you first started hating your father?"

"I don't think you really want to go there tonight, Joni."

"No, but I need to. I know that under ordinary circumstances, it would be too soon for us to get this personal. But nothing about our relationship has been normal."

"That was mostly dictated by a murder that we had no control over."

"I realize that. But the point is that so much has been packed into two days and nights that I feel as if I've known you for months—or longer."

Leif began to pace. He had no idea where this was going, but he didn't see how delving into the most painful part of his life was going to help things.

"I'm not trying to turn you off R.J., Joni. He's your friend. I get that. But you and I don't know the same man. Let's leave it at that."

"We could, if it wasn't for Effie. But you asked me to help you connect with her. I'm convinced she wants the same thing, but you've thrown R.J. up as a roadblock between you two."

"I didn't make him the enemy, Joni. He did that."

"But you're the one who's let the resentment turn venomous. I'm sure you have your reasons, but if I'm going to help you with Effie, I have to understand where you're coming from. I can't do that without knowing the truth."

The truth was that R.J. was ruining his life again and he wasn't sure anyone could help him mend things with his daughter. But if this relationship with Joni was going anywhere, he had to level with her.

And he definitely wasn't ready for Joni to drop out of his life.

"Okay, Joni. I'll give you the full version of life without father, but feel free to stop me once you've heard enough."

"I can handle it. I may be small, but I'm tougher than I look."

"You've already proven that."

Leif started to sit, but he decided he'd do better at staying in control of his emotions if he remained on his feet. He'd relived the worst of his past many times in his mind, but this would be the first time he'd ever shared it with anyone else. Even he and Travis hadn't talked about the heartbreaking details since becoming adults.

He leaned against the back of the sofa and forced himself back in time.

"You keep calling R.J. my father and Effie calls him Grandpa. But I don't remember his ever being a father to me. I was barely three years old when Mother left R.J. and moved with me and Travis to California."

"How old was Travis?"

"He's two years younger than me, so just a baby. I have a couple of vague recollections of living on the ranch, but I'm not sure I really remember the events or if Mother just told me about them."

"Good memories?"

"The one where I'm sitting on a pony and riding around in circles was nice. The other, not so great, but typical of a kid on a ranch. I'm crying because a rabbit I was chasing escaped under a barbwire fence. At any rate, it's a pony and a rabbit that I remember, not R.J."

"Then you didn't see him again after you moved to California?"

"I remember specifically *not* ever seeing him again. I knew I had a father back in Texas. I asked about him occasionally, mostly because other kids had fathers and I thought it might be nice to have one, too. But I don't remember ever asking to go see him or anything like that.

We were happy and I was a kid. Until Mother got breast cancer."

"How old were you then?"

"Eight. I was in the third grade and playing on my first soccer team. I remember Mother got so sick at one game she threw up all over the stands. Now I assume she was going through chemo and enduring a lot just to attend my games. Then I just thought she had a stomachache.

"Travis was in the first grade, small for his age. But nobody picked on him. They knew I'd sock them if they did."

"The tough big brother."

"But not near tough enough to protect him when he needed it most."

"When your mother died?"

"Right." The old pain pummeled Leif's heart and threatened his composure. "One of the last things she said to me before she died was that I was her little man and should look after Travis until our father came to get us. Go with your daddy, she said. He'll take care of you. And then she kissed me on the cheek and closed her eyes."

"I take it R.J. never came."

"You got it. He never even called. We stayed with the pastor of our church and his wife until after the funeral. They kept telling us our father would come for us, too. But it was the county that came."

"Did you go into foster care?"

"We went to a facility at first. I thought we were in a prison for kids, but then after about two weeks, they called us into the office and told us that a family wanted Travis, but that they couldn't take me."

"Oh, no. They split you up."

Leif put up a hand. "Don't start the pity party. If you do, I'll never get through this."

"I'm sorry, Leif. I'll just listen."

But the pity was there in her eyes. In a way that was good. At least she'd understand why he'd never have any use for R. J. Dalton.

"When Travis realized he was going away without me, he got hysterical. He grabbed hold of me and wouldn't let go. They had to pry his hands off me. As they dragged him out of the room, he was crying and begging them not to take him away. Begging me not to let them."

Moisture pooled in Leif's eyes. He wiped it away with the pads of his palms, took a deep breath and exhaled slowly. "I didn't see Travis again for three years."

"What happened to you during that time?"

"I was moved around from one foster home to another until I was eleven. Then I was lucky enough to land with a great family. They had three kids of their own, but they treated me like I was part of the family.

"When I told them about Travis, my foster mother went looking for him. Somehow she persuaded them to let him come to our house for my twelfth birthday."

"You must have both been thrilled."

"It was hell." Leif managed a smile for the first time since he'd started this trek through misery. "Travis would hardly speak to me. When it was time to go, he punched me in the stomach and asked me why we left him with those mean people and never came to get him. Seems he thought my foster dad was our father and that we'd deserted him."

"Then what happened?"

"My new mom took over. She hired a lawyer and fought the system until they moved Travis into her care. After that, things got back to normal. Travis took the knocks and came out of it a decent man, a great cop and the best brother a guy could have.

"None of it thanks to R. J. Dalton, who never once bothered to see if we were dead or alive until he found out he was dying. I'm not looking for retribution, but I won't be part of his penance, either."

Leif walked to the window and stared into the night. "R.J. is dead to me and I mean to keep it that way. If you can't understand that, then I guess it's over between us before it ever really started."

"I DO UNDERSTAND your feelings, Leif."

Joni not only understood, she hurt for Leif, the boy, who'd been forced to take on far too much before he'd even reached his teens. A boy whose heart had broken not for himself, but because he couldn't protect his little brother like his dying mother had asked of him.

The last thing she wanted to do was walk away from Leif, the man.

Joni crossed the room, put her arms around Leif's waist and rested her head on his broad shoulder.

"I doubt there's a man alive who'd feel any differently than you do, Leif, but—"

His muscles tensed and he turned to face her. "Don't tell me you're still going to stand there and defend the man."

"Not defend. I know his reputation. He's a drinker, a gambler, a womanizer, as they say in Texas—a rounder. He's the first to admit he's wasted his life."

"Is that the best you can say for him?"

"I don't know him that well, but lots of people around here do, Leif. They all claim that in spite of all his obnoxious behaviors, he's always been a fair man. And a generous one, when he had anything to be generous with."

"Generous now that he's dying and can't take it with him."

"You may be right, but talk to him before he does, Leif. There must be an explanation as to why he didn't come for you and Travis when your mother died."

"No explanation would satisfy me."

"If that turns out to be the case, then tell him exactly what you told me. Get the resentment and bitterness out of your system once and for all. Give yourself closure."

She stepped in closer and splayed her hands across his bare chest. "And then fight for your daughter, Leif. Fight for her the way you wish R.J. had fought to have a relationship with you. If you need my help, just ask. I'll be there if you need me for anything at all."

"A man can't ask for more than that."

Leif wrapped his arms around her and pulled her close. She rose to her tiptoes, hungry for his mouth to claim hers. When he did kiss her, she felt the thrill rush though her body, setting her on fire.

She held on tight, loving the hardness of him pressing into the contours of her. His hands slid down her back, cupping her buttocks while his mouth ravaged hers.

"Oh, Joni, I want—"

His words dissolved into the loud sound of someone's fists hammering at her front door. Joni's breath caught in her throat.

"That must be the police officers," Joni said as he stepped away from her. "They must have caught the killer."

"Let's hope you're right."

But he picked up his gun before he walked to the door.

Chapter Seventeen

"Who's there?" Leif called.

"Detective Josh Morgan."

Leif recognized the voice, though it was considerably more jubilant than it had been the last time they'd talked. He opened the door and Morgan and two uniformed officers stepped inside.

"I saw your light on and wanted you to know you can rest easy the remainder of the night. The Hunter has been apprehended."

"Are you sure?" Joni asked.

"I'm certain."

"Outside my house?"

"No," Morgan admitted. "He was apprehended in West Texas, near the Big Bend area. Apparently he'd decided to clear out of Oak Grove."

"How did they get him?" Leif asked.

"Stopped him on a speeding violation. Checked the license and found out the car had been stolen from San Antonio."

"How did the arresting officer know it was The Hunter?" Joni asked.

"You played a part in that. As soon as you matched the sketch with the suspect in Ms. Trotter's murder, we released it to every police department in Texas and the surrounding states. Couldn't have worked out better."

"You're right," Leif said. "It almost seems to wrap everything up too perfectly. Did he confess?"

"Confess? He bragged to the arresting officer about the number of young women he's raped and murdered. He gave names, dates, facts only he and the police would know. Weird thing was he wouldn't confess to Jill Trotter's murder even though we found her credit cards, a couple of prescriptions in her name and several pieces of expensive jewelry that we know belonged to her."

"If he obviously robbed Jill Trotter, why do you suppose he didn't admit to killing her like he did the others?" Joni asked.

"Apparently, she didn't meet his bragging right standards for age and beauty. You did. He's already admitted as much, said he'd already targeted you for his next victim. Then he decided he'd best clear out of the area and return when the police backed off."

Joni trembled, and Leif slipped his arm around her to steady her. Had he not talked her into going with him to the condo, she would have been home alone the day The Hunter left the note. Her raped and battered body would have been left in the wooded area for some hunter to find.

An acidic burn attacked the lining of his stomach.

"But you didn't know that before his confession. I still don't understand why you were so sure he was after me that you set a trap for him here," Joni said.

"We were counting on him following his established patterns. Leaving scribbled and confusing warning notes before he kills is something he's done in the last three murders before Jill Trotter, a fact we hadn't released to the press. But your worries are over. The Hunter is behind bars."

"Did he send a note to Jill?" Leif questioned.

"Not that we've found yet. But she could have destroyed it without reporting it. After all, before her death, Oak Grove was a quiet, almost crime-free oasis."

The officers thanked Joni again for her cooperation and then left. Joni held on to the back of the sofa, as if still in shock. "Can you believe it? Jill's killer really was The Hunter, and now he's behind bars. The worst is over. No one else will die at his hands."

Leif should be just as relieved, but he couldn't shed that last nagging fear that this wasn't completely wrapped up. But then he was always suspicious of things that seemed too good to be true.

Speaking of which...

"Now where were we when we were interrupted by the bearers of good news?"

"I think you were about to pick me up and carry me to bed," Joni said.

He was certain she was right.

JONI LAY AWAKE long after the passion was spent, drenched in the afterglow of their lovemaking. She wasn't a virgin, but making love with Leif was like nothing she'd ever experienced before.

Every touch, every kiss, every murmured word of endearment had been exquisitely delicious. And there had been a multitude of touches, kisses, thrusts, throbs and sexual exploration.

Leif had devoured her with his lips, his tongue, his fingers, his throbbing desire. Her primal hunger had never been so sated, her body so satisfied.

But that wouldn't last for long. Her need for him was already growing again.

She rolled to her side and slid her right leg over his. Her knee brushed the dampness where she'd pleasured him.

He moaned and turned and pulled her on top of him without opening his eyes. She could feel his growing erection beneath her.

"You're going to kill me, woman."

"But you'll die with a smile on your face."

And then his lips were on hers and the thrill of him was thrumming though every vein in her body again.

THERE WAS A chill to the air when Leif left the big house with R.J. He didn't expect anything to come of their morning walk, but if having this conversation with R.J. pleased Joni, it was worth it.

At that point if she'd urged Leif to climb in the saddle atop a bucking bull, he might have done that, as well. The ache in his thighs was a painful but sweet reminder of just how crazy about her he was.

Travis would never understand Leif's falling so fast. Hell, he didn't understand it himself. All he knew was that being with Joni made him happier than he'd ever been in his life.

Making a life together might be a little more difficult. Once he was a partner in the firm, he'd be expected to get involved in even more charitable and social events. It was part of the image they liked to portray.

"I've been thinking about that will of mine," R.J. said.

Here we go again with the manipulation, Leif thought. Still he slowed his pace so that R.J. could catch up with him.

"I guess I wasn't thinking it all through when I made the guidelines."

"It's your will," Leif said. "Your call."

"I know, and it works out great for Adam. He's taken to ranching like a fiddle player to a Texas roadhouse band. But you've got a career and you're awful damn good at what you do from what I hear."

"I like to think so."

"I guess I could make an exception with the requirement that states you have to actually work on the ranch to be included in the will."

"Don't do that on my account."

"I'm just saying, I could change it, if I decided to. That's all. Maybe I'd just expect someone like you with a full-time career to spend a certain number of weekends here a year. You could always build your own place the way Adam did."

"I'm not planning to build on the ranch."

"But if you did, you'd be close enough that Effie could enjoy the horses and see what it's like taking care of the animals. She's said she wants to be an equine vet."

"You don't have to live on a ranch to be a vet."

"No, but it helps. Besides, she could get a break from the city with all its pollution, traffic and crime. None of that can be good for a kid or a teenager."

"Effie definitely likes it out here." In fairness, he had to give R.J. that. But it wasn't the conversation he'd come out there to have. It was time for him to take control.

"You know what troubles me about this conversation, R.J.?"

"No, but judging from that tone I s'pect you're about to lay it on me."

"Where was all this worry about kids and teenagers back when Mother died? Do you have any idea what it was like for Travis and me when we had no living relatives to take us in?"

"I figure it was rough."

"*Rough?* Not getting a bike for Christmas is rough. Being torn away from the only family you know and carried off screaming to live with strangers who mistreat you, that's a living hell. Travis was just a little kid when he had to face that, only six years old.

"So don't talk to me now about how I should raise Effie on a ranch or how I'm depriving her of riding a horse every day. I've had pimples I treated better than you did us."

"Reckon you can't say it much plainer than that," R.J. said.

"Sometimes a little plain talk is called for."

"I agree. I don't expect anything I say to make much difference to you, Leif. You made up your mind a long time ago about me. Some, maybe most, of the anger and resentment you feel toward me is deserved.

"But I didn't know about your mother dying until you boys were both grown, and that's a fact. She told me to stay out of her life and I honored her wishes."

"You were notified of her death," Leif said. "Travis and I were told you were coming."

"I might have been notified, but I never got the message. I'm not proud of it, but I was drinking heavy at the time, really heavy. I got drunk as a skunk one night and like the fool I was, I got behind the wheel of my truck."

R.J. stopped, waited a moment and then started walking again, this time even slower than before. "Luckily I didn't kill nobody else, but I durn near killed myself. Might have been best if I had. Anyway, I ran the truck into a steel bridge guard. Totaled the truck, messed up my right knee and hit my head so hard I was in a coma for weeks."

Leif knew what was coming next, but he let R.J. finish his spiel about how all that had happened at the same time his mother was dying.

"I was a rotten father, Leif. I know that. But I can't change the past. All I can do is try to be a better man now. I can take care of the apologies. The forgiving is up to you."

When they reached the horse barn, they stepped inside to get out of the blustery wind.

"You can head back to the house whenever you want,"

R.J. said. "I'd like to spend some time with Miss Dazzler, but I figure Hadley and Joni will be getting back from the Hilbert's anytime now. They just went over to drop off some fried pies. Since Nora Hilbert had that heart attack, she don't do much baking and Leon loves sweets."

R.J. swayed and had to reach for a post to keep his balance. He stood there for at least a minute, head down, his flesh pasty. Then evidently the woozy spell passed and he walked over to his favorite filly.

"I'll stay and walk back with you," Leif said.

"Then you might as well grab a pitchfork and give the horses some fresh hay. They need a little Thanksgiving, too."

Leif went to work. The exercise felt good, far less stressful then preparing for a trial.

He could see how a man could get used to this.

JOEY PULLED THROUGH the gate at the Dry Gulch Ranch a few minutes after Joni and Leif.

He'd followed them to the ranch, keeping far enough away that they wouldn't notice. He kept the same slow pace now, giving them time to park and go inside before he drove up and surprised them.

Not that he'd be stupid enough to teach her some manners with the house full of people. He just wanted to see if Joni was drooling all over the attorney, lusting after his money. She hadn't taken her old truck out once since she'd hooked up with Leif Dalton and his expensive sports car.

She'd been just starting to notice Joey when Leif showed up in Oak Grove. Joey should have known that no matter how nice Joni seemed, she was just like every other bitch. One smell of money and they were gone.

She really pissed him off. He could feel the anger building, pushing against his skull. He pulled off to the side of the road and stopped the car. After opening the glove compartment quickly, he reached in for his pills.

They weren't there. He must have forgotten to put them in the car. It was too late to go back now. He'd just have to sit there a minute and try to cool off.

Once he lost his temper completely, it was too late.

Chapter Eighteen

Joni set the last plate on the table and stood back to admire her work. R.J. had told her to make herself at home and that was exactly what she'd done.

She'd arranged the flatware, plates, glasses and the only set of cotton napkins she could find in R.J.'s kitchen. She'd even made a centerpiece of holly, pinecones, nuts and the two scented pillar candles she'd picked up at the gift shop in Oak Grove last week.

She'd meant them to be a hostess gift, but adding them to the arrangement was an even better idea. Now it was time for a coffee break and to sit and think about what a fantastic Thanksgiving this was turning out to be.

The doorbell rang just as she filled her cup. Taking it with her, she hurried to the front door. Expecting Effie or a neighbor, she swung it open without checking to see who was there.

"Joey."

"Yeah. You're looking great," he said. "Am I interrupting dinner already?"

"No, I'm here early." That didn't explain why he was there. "Did R.J. invite you for dinner?"

"No, I was just driving around and thought I'd pop in and wish him a happy Thanksgiving. Is he here?"

"He and Leif walked down to the horse barn for a few minutes, but they'll be back soon."

"Then I'll just say hello to Mattie Mae and be on my way."

"I'm afraid she's not here, either. Her grandson picked her up yesterday and drove her to Austin to be with the rest of the family for a long weekend."

"Good for her. She needs to get out and go somewhere, but she's sure good company for R.J."

"I didn't realize you knew the Daltons so well," Joni said.

"Sure. I keep R.J.'s four-wheelers running for him. I even did some engine work on his tractor the other day. I'm a man of many talents."

Including a few that had sent him to jail. Before she'd known about that she was perfectly at ease with Joey. Now she was downright nervous around him. Once she told R.J. the truth about him, he wouldn't want him around, either.

"I was setting the table," she said. "There's still a lot to do and I'm the only one here, so I'd best get busy."

"Then what about taking a ride with me later? There's a real pretty stretch of back roads toward Austin. Lots of big-tooth maples. This time of the year, they look like they're on fire. Thanksgiving is always the best time for Texas foliage."

"I'm sorry, Joey. I can't today. I already have plans."

"With Leif Dalton?"

She didn't like the change in his tone when he said Leif's name. "I really have to go, Joey."

She started to close the door. Joey stopped it from closing with a heavy booted foot.

"You could invite me in."

She shook her head. "You need to go."

"And leave you here alone? I don't think so." He pushed his way inside. "You're going for that ride with me now,

Joni. You're going to walk to the truck with me and get in without making a scene. Do you understand me?"

Her heart pounded against her chest. "You don't want to do this, Joey. Leif will be back any second."

"You need a real man, Joni. Not that pansy attorney you're so infatuated with. Didn't you hear what they said about him on the news? He helps killers go free."

Joey tugged on her sweater, pinching her right nipple until the pain made her eyes water.

"Take your hands off of me, Joey Markham. You have no right to—"

He slapped her across the face with his left hand. "I have all the rights. *This* gives it to me." He waved a tiny black pistol at her. "Now walk out that door quietly and get in my truck."

"Put the gun away, Joey. You've been to prison before. You don't want to go back."

"I guess Mr. Pretty Boy Attorney told you all about my past. Well, here's something he didn't tell you, sweetheart. You won't be the first woman I've killed."

He ground the barrel of the pistol into her side as he shoved her toward the door. If she got in that truck with him, she might never come back alive. There was a lot less chance he'd kill her here, where people would hear the gunshot and come running to help her.

"I'm not going anywhere with you. I know who you are, Joey. I know you're Phillip Trotter's son. I know you killed him. Did you kill his wife, too?"

He leaned in so close, her skin crawled. "The Hunter killed her. Didn't you hear? Jill killed Phillip and The Hunter killed her. Now do you play nice or play dead?"

The back door opened and slammed shut again, almost as if the wind had caught it.

Joey jumped and turned to see who'd come in.

Joni broke away and made a run for the stairs. He pounced on her, jerking her to the floor before she reached the landing.

Only the man looking down at her now was not the friendly, flirty Joey she knew from Abe's Garage. The veins in his neck were so extended they looked as if they were about to burst through the skin. His face was bloodred, his nostrils flaring like an angry bull's.

Rage had turned him into a monster.

"Is anyone home?"

The voice was Effie's. Fear attacked with such force, Joni was afraid she might black out. She couldn't put Effie in danger.

"Either you walk to the truck quietly with me or I kill the girl," Joey said. "Decide quickly or I shoot you both."

"I'll do whatever you say, just please don't hurt Effie."

"Then start walking and smile as if you're excited to be with me. We're about to have some real fun."

Chapter Nineteen

Leif and R.J. were at the barn door, ready to start back toward the house when R.J.'s cell phone rang. He wiped his hands on his jeans and pulled the phone from his pocket.

"It's Hadley. Probably calling to say that she and Effie are back." He switched the phone to speaker so Leif could listen in on the conversation.

"Is anything wrong?" Hadley asked.

"Nothing a little turkey and dressing can't fix. Why do you ask?"

"I saw Joey Markham's truck parked at your house when I dropped Effie off. I thought…"

Leif didn't wait to hear the rest of the sentence. He took off for the house, running as fast as he could, his feet pounding the earth.

No reason to panic. Joey came around all the time.

Leif's mind might have believed him. His heart didn't. The nagging fear that had bothered him last night swelled into a frightening roar that consumed him.

There were too many ties between Joey and Jill Trotter to believe all of them were coincidence.

He reached the house in time to see Joni climb into the passenger seat of what must be Joey's truck. Joey waved at him as he closed Joni's door and headed to the driver's seat.

Leif reached the truck before Joey could yank it into gear

and speed away. He opened the truck door, grabbed Joey by the arm and tried to drag him from the truck.

Joey tried to kick him away, but Leif grabbed hold of the steering wheel and didn't let go. When Joey punched at him, Leif saw the pistol point at his head.

Joni screamed and started beating Joey with both her fists, distracting Joey just long enough for Leif to get in a couple of solid blows and drag Joey from the truck. Fists flying, Leif wrestled him to the ground.

"Don't kill my daddy."

Effie. She must have run out of the house. Leif yelled at her to get back inside.

Shots started firing randomly, ricocheting off the truck's door and front bumper. Someone screamed. Leif didn't know if it was Effie or Joni. He kept fighting, not even feeling the punches that pounded into him. He had to get his hands on that gun before Joey killed them all in a fit of blind rage.

"Run, Joni. Take Effie and run." Blood was dripping into his right eye now, blurring his vision to the point he couldn't see the pistol.

He got in a solid blow to Joey's stomach, but Joey came right back at him, hitting him in the head so hard that he blacked out for an instant.

"You should have stayed in Big D," Joey said, his words so thick with fury they were barely comprehensible. "You're not tough enough to make it on the ranch."

Joey might be right, but Leif had found what he wanted in Oak Grove. He loved Joni. He wanted a life with her. And he wouldn't be robbed of that happiness by some hot-headed punk. Fury darkened Joey's eyes to black sparks. The gun was in his hand. His fingers were on the trigger.

Leif exploded with equal fury. He knocked the gun

from Joey's hand. It skittered across the concrete drive like a rock.

Joey dived for it. A big cowboy boot came down on Joey's fingers and the gun.

"Fair fights are never what they're cracked up to be," R.J. said as he ground Joey's fingers until the sounds of cracking bones and Joey's cries filled the air.

R.J. stood over Joey, his own gun pointed at Joey's head as he kicked Joey's pistol so hard it bounced under the front steps.

"Don't make my day, boy," R.J. said. "I don't have that many of them left to waste, and I do love shootin' varmints. Now will someone call the sheriff or do I have to do everything myself?"

"Already made that call," Adam said, riding up on his horse. "Did it as soon as Hadley called and said R.J. explained Leif's reaction to hearing Joey was at the ranch."

A second later both Effie and Joni were in Leif's arms.

"I was so scared," Effie said. "I thought that man was going to kill you. I love you, Dad. I don't always act like it, but I do. I really do."

"Me, too," Joni said. "Me, too."

"And I love both of you. I plan to spend the rest of my life showing you how much."

Both his best girls in his arms. A father he might even grow to like to his rescue. And the promise of a life with Joni stretching out as far as his heart could see.

"I guess it's time I get some real cowboy boots," Leif said. "It looks like I'm home to stay."

* * * * *

Read on for a sneak peek of Joanna Wayne's next installment of her BIG "D" DADS: THE DALTONS *miniseries, only from Intrigue!*

Prologue

Faith Ashburn emphasized her deep-set brown eyes with a coat of thick black liner and then took a step away from the mirror to see the full effect of the makeup she'd caked onto her pale skin. The haunted eyes that stared back at her were the only part of the face she recognized.

Her irises mirrored the way she felt. Lost. Trapped in a nightmare. The anxiety was so intense the lining of her stomach seemed to be on fire.

But she'd go back out there tonight, into the smoke and groping, the stares that crawled across her skin like hairy spiders. She'd smile and endure the depravity—praying, always praying, for some crumb of information that would lead her to her son.

Cornell was eighteen. Physically, he was a man. Mentally and emotionally, he was a trusting, naive boy who needed his mother and his meds.

Faith's bare feet sank into the thick mauve carpet as she stepped back into her bedroom and tugged on her patterned panty hose. Then she pulled the low-cut, trampy black dress from the closet and stepped into it.

The fabric stretched over her bare breasts as she slid the spaghetti straps over her narrow shoulders. Her nipples were covered, but there was enough cleavage showing to suggest that she'd have no qualms about revealing everything if the offer appealed to her.

Reaching to the top shelf of her closet, she chose the bright red stiletto heels. They never failed to garner the instant attention of men high on booze, drugs and the stench of overripened sex.

Struck by a burst of vertigo, Faith held on to the bedpost until the dizziness passed. Then she tucked lipstick, her car keys and some mad money into the small sequined handbag that already carried her licensed pistol.

Stopping off in the kitchen, she poured two fingers of cheap whiskey into a glass. She swished the amber liquid around in her mouth, gargled and then spit it down the drain. Holding the glass over the sink, she ran one finger around the edges to collect the remaining liquor. She dotted it to her pulse points like expensive perfume.

Her muscles tightened. Her lungs felt clogged. She took a deep breath and walked out the door, carefully locking it behind her.

Six months of going unofficially undercover into the seediest areas of Dallas. Six months of questioning every drug addict and pervert who might have come in contact with Cornell, based on nothing but the one scrap of evidence the police had provided her.

Six months of crying herself to sleep when she came home as lost, confused and desperate as before.

God, please let tonight be different.

"ANOTHER BACKSTREET HOMICIDE, another trip to see Georgio. I'm beginning to think he gives a discount to killers. A lap dance from one of his girls when a body shows up at the morgue without identification."

"And the victims get younger and younger." Travis Dalton followed his partner, Reno, as they walked through a side door of the sleaziest strip joint in the most dangerous part of Dallas. Georgio reigned as king here, providing the local sex and drug addicts with everything they needed to feed their cravings.

Yet the rotten bastard always came out on top. His rule of threats and intimidation eliminated any chance of getting one of his patrons to testify against him. Not that they would have had a shred of credibility if they had.

A rap song blared from the sound system as a couple of seminude women with surgery-enhanced butts and breasts made love to skinny poles. Two others gyrated around the rim of the stage, collecting bills in their G-strings.

A familiar waitress whose name Travis couldn't remember sashayed up to him. "Business or pleasure, copper boy?"

"What do you think?"

"Business, but a girl can hope. Are you looking for Georgio?"

"For starters."

"Is it about that boy who got shot up in Oak Cliff last night?"

Now she had Tavis's full attention. "What do you know about that?"

"Nothing, I just figured that's what brought you here."

Travis had a hunch she knew more than she was admitting. He was about to question her further when he noticed a woman at the bar trying to peel a man's grip from her right wrist.

"Let go of me," she ordered, her voice rising above the din.

The man held tight while his free hand groped her breast. "I just want to be friends."

"You're hurting me."

Travis stormed to the bar. "You heard the woman. Move on, buddy."

"Why don't you mind your own business?"

"I am." He pulled the ID from the breast pocket of his blue pullover. "Dallas Police. Back off or I snap a nice metal bracelet on your wrist and haul you down to central lockup."

A thin stream of spittle made its way down the man's whiskered chin as his hands fell to his sides. Wiping it away with his shirtsleeve, he slid off the bar stool and stumbled backward.

"She's the one you should be arresting. She came on to me," he slurred.

Travis studied the woman and decided the drunk could be right. She was flaunting the trappings of a hooker, right down to a sexy pair of heels that made her shapely legs appear a mile long.

But one look into her haunted eyes, and Travis doubted she was looking to make a fast buck on her back. She had a delicate, fragile quality about her that suggested she'd be more at home in a convent than here shoving off drunks. Even the exaggerated makeup couldn't hide her innocence.

If he had to guess, he'd say she was here trying to get even with some jerk who had cheated on her. That didn't make it any less dangerous for her to be in this hellhole.

"Party's over, lady. I'm calling for a squad car to take you home."

"I have a car."

"Get behind the wheel and I'll have to arrest you for driving while intoxicated."

"I'm not drunk."

He couldn't argue that point. She smelled like a brewery, but she wasn't slurring her words and her eyes were clear, her pupils normal.

"I don't know what kind of game you're playing or who you're trying to get even with, but if you hang around here, you're going to run into more trouble than you can handle."

"I can take care of myself." She turned and started to walk away.

Travis moved quicker, setting himself in her path without realizing why he was bothering.

He looked around for Reno, but his partner wasn't in sight. He was probably already questioning Georgio, and Travis should be with him.

"Look, lady. You're in over your head here. I've got some urgent business, but sit tight for a few minutes and I'll be back to walk you to your car. In the meantime, don't make friends with any more perverts. That's an order."

She shrugged and nodded.

He stalked off to find Reno. He spotted him and Georgio a minute later near the door to the suite of private offices. When he looked back, the woman was gone.

Just as well, he told himself, especially if she'd gone home. He didn't need any more problems on his plate tonight. But even after he reached Reno and jumped into the murderous situation at hand, he couldn't fully shake her from his mind.

Whatever had brought her slumming could get her killed.

Chapter One

Four months later

Travis adjusted the leather-and-turquoise bolo tie; it was a close match to the one his brother was wearing with his Western-style tux. The irony of seeing his formerly Armani-faithful attorney brother dressed like this made it hard for Travis not to laugh.

"I never thought I'd see the day you got hitched to a cowgirl."

"I never thought I'd see the day you showed up at the Dry Gulch Ranch again," Leif answered.

"Couldn't miss the wedding of my favorite brother."

"Your *only* brother."

"Yeah, probably a good thing you don't have competition now that you're building a house on the Dry Gulch Ranch. On the bright side, I do like that I get to wear my cowboy boots with this rented Silverado monkey suit."

Travis rocked back on the heels of his new boots, bought for the conspicuous occasion of Leif's wedding to Joni Griffin. He'd never seen his brother happier. Not only was he so in love, he beamed when he looked at his veterinarian bride, but his daughter, Effie, would be living with him for her last two years of high school.

The Dry Gulch Ranch was spiffed up for the ceremony

and reception. Lights had been strung through the branches of giant oaks and stringy sycamores. A white tent had been set up with chairs leaving a makeshift aisle that led to a rose-covered altar, where the two lovers would take their vows.

Most of the chairs were taken. Leif's friends from the prestigious law firm from which he'd recently resigned to open his own office nearer the ranch mingled with what looked to be half the population of Oak Grove.

The women from both groups looked quite elegant. The male Big D lawyers were all in designer suits. The ranchers for the most part looked like they'd feel a lot more at home in their Wranglers than in their off-the-rack suits and choking ties.

In fact, a few of the younger cowboys were in jeans and sports coats. Travis figured they were the smart ones. Weekends he wasn't working a homicide case, he usually spent on a friend's ranch up in the Hill Country.

Riding, roping, baling hay, branding—he'd done it all and loved it. A weekend place on the Dry Gulch Ranch just a little over an hour from Dallas would have been the perfect solution for Travis. Except for one very large problem.

Rueben Jackson Dalton, his father by virtue of a healthy sperm.

"Time for us to join the preacher," Leif said, jerking Travis back into the moment.

He walked at his brother's side and felt a momentary sense of anxiety. He and Leif had been through hell together growing up, most of it caused by R.J.

It had been just the two of them against the world since their mother's death, and they'd always been as close as the horse to a saddle. Now Leif was marrying and moving onto R.J.'s spread.

Oh, hell, what was he worried about? R.J. would never

come between him and Leif. Besides, the old coot would be dead soon.

The music started.

Leif's fifteen-year-old daughter started down the make-shift aisle, looking so grown-up it made Travis's chest constrict. He could only imagine what it did to Leif. Travis winked at Effie as she took her place at the altar. She smiled so big it took over her face and lit up her eyes.

Travis looked up again and did a double take as he spotted the maid of honor gliding down the aisle. She damn sure didn't look the way she had the last time he'd seen her, but there was no doubt in his mind that the gorgeous lady was the same one he'd rescued in Georgio's four months ago.

He'd only spent a few minutes with her, but she'd preyed on his mind a lot since then, so much so that he'd found himself showing up at Georgio's palace of perversion even when his work didn't call for it.

All in the interest of talking to her and making sure she was safe. In spite of his efforts, he'd never caught sight of her again.

Travis studied the woman as she took her place a few feet away from him. She was absolutely stunning in a luscious creation the color of the amethyst ring his mother used to wear. She'd given it to him before she'd died.

It was the only prized possession Travis owned—well, that and the belt buckles he'd won in bull-riding competitions back when he had more guts than sense.

The wedding march sounded. The guests all stood. Travis's eyes remained fixed on the maid of honor. Finally, she looked at him, and when their eyes met, he saw the same tortured, haunting depths that had mesmerized him at their first meeting.

Travis forced his gaze away from the mystery woman and back to Effie and Leif. He wouldn't spoil the wedding, but before the night was over he'd have a little chat with the seductive maid of honor. Before he was through, he'd discover if she was as innocent as he'd first believed or if the demons who'd filled her eyes with anguish had actually driven her to the dark side of life.

If the latter were the case, he'd make damn sure she stayed away from his niece, Effie, even if it meant telling Leif the truth about his new wife's best friend.

The reception might have a lot more spectacular fireworks than originally planned. Travis was already itching for the first dance.

She looked at him with an unmistakable intent in her eyes.

"Marcie, this isn't—"

She uttered a sad, small laugh. "Of course it's not a good idea," she murmured, looking up at him. "Right now, I don't care. Do you?"

Joe looked down at her and knew exactly what she was doing.

She wrapped her arms around his neck. He knew her body as well as he knew his own, and he recognized her awakening desire in the suppleness of her muscles, in the softness of her skin and the sultriness in her eyes. He knew, as he always had, on a level much deeper than physical, how much she wanted him.

"No, I don't care," he said, and lowered his mouth to hers.

GONE

BY
MALLORY KANE

Published in Great Britain 2014
by Mills & Boon, an imprint of Harlequin (UK) Limited,
Eton House, 18-24 Paradise Road, Richmond, Surrey, TW9 1SR

© 2014 Rickey R. Mallory

ISBN: 978 0 263 91347 7

46-0114

Harlequin (UK) Limited's policy is to use papers that are natural, renewable and recyclable products and made from wood grown in sustainable forests. The logging and manufacturing processes conform to the legal environmental regulations of the country of origin.

Printed and bound in Spain
by Blackprint CPI, Barcelona

Mallory Kane has two very good reasons for loving reading and writing. Her mother was a librarian, and taught her to love and respect books as a precious resource. Her father could hold listeners spellbound for hours with his stories. He was always her biggest fan.

She loves romantic suspense with dangerous heroes and dauntless heroines, and enjoys tossing in a bit of her medical knowledge for an extra dose of intrigue. After twenty-five books published, Mallory is still amazed and thrilled that she actually gets to make up stories for a living.

Mallory lives in Tennessee with her computer-genius husband and three exceptionally intelligent cats. She enjoys hearing from readers. You can write her at mallory@mallorykane.com.

Michael, I love you more than anything.
Congratulations for making it through.
We are going to have so much fun!

Chapter One

There had been a time when just the sight of his wife had Joseph Powers panting with desire. From the blue eyes that sparked fire through his every nerve, to the tips of her pretty pink toes, he'd known, tasted and loved every inch of her. But that was a long time ago, back when they'd been a family, when they'd been happy, when they'd been three. Now, they were just two.

He hadn't seen her in a year, not since the last time she'd called him, crying and begging for his help, promising him that *this* time, unlike every time before, she was sure.

He'd expected her to call, if not today, then tomorrow. Knowing ahead of time didn't make it easier, though. It made it worse. Tomorrow was a big day for both of them. It was her birthday and the second anniversary of their child's disappearance.

He dreaded opening his front door and seeing her standing there, looking sad and lost. Although, she had sounded different this time. Not quite as desperate. Not quite as beaten down. The tone of her voice had given him a tiny scrap of hope. Maybe she'd finally agreed to take the antidepressants the doctor had prescribed. Maybe she wanted to see him, not to declare that *this* time she'd really found Joshua, but to let him know that she was doing better.

He laughed, a harsh sound that scratched his throat. *Yeah, and pigs can fly.*

He paced back and forth, wishing he could wipe away the memory that haunted him. That split second at the outdoor market when he'd reached down to pick up Joshua's baby carrier and encountered empty space. The helplessness, terror and anger of that horrifying instant had never faded. Nor had the guilt. They were as strong and all-consuming as they'd ever been. He'd taken out a lot of that anger on Marcie, just as she'd taken out her own sadness, rage and devastating grief on him.

There were some tragedies that were too awful to share, some burdens that could not be lifted.

The doorbell rang and Joe's heart skipped a beat. He opened the door and there she was, fresh and beautiful, her lovely face shiny and clean of makeup. Her beautiful dark hair was caught up in a ponytail and her wide blue eyes sparkled with unshed tears. No matter what had happened between them, no matter how impossible it was for them to live together with the specter of their missing child between them, he still loved her. He was still *in love* with her. That had never changed and he knew it never would.

Marcie looked pretty and sad and yet determined as she pushed past him into his apartment. He caught a faint scent of her melon-scented shampoo and his body responded. So much for not desiring her anymore.

"Marcie," he said with resignation, closing the door and turning to meet her gaze.

"Joe," she said as she glanced around his apartment. Her gaze stopped for an instant on the small framed photo on the kitchen counter. Joe's gaze followed hers automatically, although he knew the photo as well as he knew his own face in the mirror. It was a picture he'd taken of her and Joshua in the hospital, when Joshua was about four hours old. She walked over and picked up the frame, brushing her fingers across the glass, a wan smile on her face. "I saw him, Joe," she said without taking her eyes off the image.

"Marcie, don't—" he began as it occurred to him that she wasn't frantically excited, the way she'd been every other time she'd been *positive* that she'd spotted Joshua.

She touched the image of Joshua's round newborn face one more time, then set the frame down. She straightened, took a deep breath and clasped her shoulder bag more tightly. "I'm not hysterical," she said evenly. "I saw him. It was only a glimpse into the backseat of a car, but I know—" She stopped and pressed her lips together before continuing. "I'm almost positive it was Joshua."

Almost positive? Joe stared at her, trying to reconcile this new Marcie with the hysterical woman who, within the first six months after Joshua was gone, had been *absolutely positive* she'd spotted him at least four times. Who'd screamed and thrown things the first time he'd suggested that she go to a grief counselor. He ran a hand across the back of his neck. "Marcie, are you on medication?"

She rolled her eyes toward the ceiling and shook her head. "No," she said on a sigh, meeting his gaze again.

His wife's eyes were damp with tears, but she wasn't the broken and defeated fragile bird he'd watched her become as weeks stretched into months with no word about their missing child.

"You don't believe me," she said.

"About being on medication?"

"About Joshua."

He winced, the way he did whenever he heard his son's name. "We've gone through this so many times before. You can't keep doing this to yourself. You've got to try to get on with your life—"

"Like you did?" she retorted. "Just presto—" she snapped her fingers "—and it's oh, well, Joshua's gone. Guess I'll go help *other* parents find *their* lost children."

Six months after Joshua had disappeared, Joe had gone back to work, because he couldn't sit at home all day and watch Marcie turn into a depressed recluse. But his lucrative corporate attorney position had felt like a waste of time. So he'd quit and taken a job with the National Center for Missing and Exploited Children. The pay was so low it could almost have been considered volunteer work, but at least he felt he was doing something important. The job was both a blessing and a curse. He helped others search for their missing family members while holding out hope that one day, one of these trails would lead to his own son. Then maybe, no matter what the outcome, he and Marcie could finally get closure.

"Marcie, I've told you before, the fact that I went back to work didn't mean—"

"No," Marcie said, waving a hand dismissively. "I'm not letting myself get sucked into that argument. I came here for one reason and one reason only. I saw our son. I copied down the car's license plate and I need your help."

"You got the license plate number?"

"The woman has our child, Joe."

He steeled himself. So she'd written down a license plate this time. So she was calm—almost too calm, he thought—rather than hysterical. That didn't make her any less delusional. "Come on, Marcie. How good a look did you get? Was it a glance into the backseat at a red light? You can't possibly know for sure that a child you saw for a split second in a dark car is Joshua." He felt the empty hole inside him open up and start bleeding. A familiar stinging began behind his eyes. "Do I have to remind you what the police told us? How slim the chances are of finding him as time goes on?"

"I haven't forgotten a single word the police told us," Marcie said stiffly. "I can't be like you, Joe. I can't convince myself that he's dea-dead, so I can pretend I don't hurt anymore. I *saw* him and this time I have a way to find out who has him and I'm going to do it. If it's not him, then at least I'll *know*."

"What are you planning to do? Not go to the police," Joe said stonily, because he couldn't tell her that he didn't think Joshua was dead. Not all the time. "You burned your bridges there."

He was being unfair, blaming her for crying wolf

one too many times. During those first long weeks, his heart had jumped, too, every time he saw a woman with a baby. Time and again, he'd allowed her to call 911, hoping against all reason that she was right and the child she'd seen really was Joshua.

"I know that," she agreed. "But we don't need the police. You work for NCMEC now. You can run a license plate and find the woman."

"I can't do that. I can't use the center's resources for myself."

"Of course you can. It's what you do! Joshua is a missing child. He's on the register, just like the lost children of the parents you help every day. The only difference is, he's our child, Joe. He's my baby."

With those last three broken words, Marcie's face crumpled and she almost lost it. Almost. He wanted to reach out to her, to hold her and comfort her and, yes, take some comfort himself, but the two of them didn't do that anymore. It had been well over a year since they'd even touched.

As he gaped in stunned silence, she pulled herself together. The only sign of her near breakdown was the two tears that slid slowly down her cheeks.

He turned and headed to the kitchen, muttering something about a glass of water. But truthfully, he needed a moment to think about what she'd said and, yes, to get control of his own emotions.

She was right, of course. Joshua was listed in the National Center for Missing and Exploited Children database. There was no reason he couldn't run the plates. He was reviewing several cold cases in the New Orleans area. Joshua's disappearance could easily be classified as one of those. But as soon as he did, everyone from his staff here in New Orleans, to the employees at the center's headquarters in Virginia, would contact him and want to hear what he'd found out about Joshua that made him start searching again. He didn't want to tell them that once again, on the anniversary of their son's disappearance, his wife had started seeing their child everywhere she went.

He drew a glass of cold water from the refrigerator dispenser and took a long swallow, then wiped his face with a shaking hand. Scowling, he clenched his fist so hard his hand cramped.

He didn't have the strength or the will to get sucked into Marcie's fantasy world again, where Joshua was out there waiting for his mommy and daddy to find him. The sick emptiness inside him started aching and he imagined the taste of blood. After a second cooling swallow for himself, he took the water to Marcie. She refused it, so he set it down on the coffee table.

"Where did you see the car?" he asked.

"I drove up to Hammond yesterday to see my aunt, and when I pulled up to a red light, there was a woman in a Nissan hatchback with a child seat in the back. I eased forward until I could see him." She took a deep breath. "Joe—"

He closed his eyes.

"It was Joshua. I'm not saying I *know* it was him. But I'm almost positive. His face, Joe. That little widow's peak. The woman saw me looking and I swear she went white as a sheet. As soon as the light turned green she gunned her car and sped away. I couldn't keep up with her."

He picked up the water glass and took a sip because he couldn't meet her gaze. The hope in her expression would fuel his, and he knew that one of them had to remain rational. Being the unflappable, levelheaded one had been his job ever since that awful moment in the outdoor market. Yes, he was the rational one. The strong one. Trouble was, he was also the guilty one. It had been his fault that their baby was gone.

"What about the woman?" he asked. "Did you get a good look at her? Could you identify her if you saw her again?"

"Yes," she said, surprising him. "She was probably in her late forties. Her hair had that faded noncolor that blondes get before they go gray. I can't tell you how tall or how large she was, but behind the wheel of the Nissan she looked small and thin. Oh, and she had a scar on her upper lip."

Joe's surprise turned to amazement and worry. Previously when she'd insisted that she'd seen Joshua, her claims were vague and boundless. But today, not only did she have a description of the car and the license plate, but she also had a clear, concise description of the woman. The realization that she'd been thoughtful and careful about getting the information, combined with the mention of Joshua's widow's peak, had Joe's insides churning like an addict looking at a bag of heroin. For Joe, that bag held hope, and for him, hope was a drug that fed on his ability to function.

What could it hurt if he ran the plate at the center?

Maybe it would help Marcie—help them both—if he found out for sure that the child she saw was not Joshua. Even though his conscious mind was certain that this random sighting at a random red light could not possibly be the answer to their prayers, in another, deeper place, far below his conscious mind, a faint thought that was as much feelings as words arose, and it was anything but rational. He did his best to ignore its insidious, hopeful message.

"Maybe I could run that license plate." As soon as he said it he wanted to take it back. If he'd had any sense, he'd have waited until after he'd run it. Then he could have gone to her with a fait accompli. *It's not Joshua. Sorry, hon.*

"Joe? Really?" Her face brightened and her eyes welled with tears again. "Thank you," she whispered, stepping toward him.

It was the most natural thing in the world to open his arms and pull her in. But holding her sent conflicting emotions roiling through his insides. In one sense, it was like coming home. She was his beautiful princess. The girl he'd been in love with ever since they were in high school together. The woman he'd married and promised to love and cherish as long as they lived. The mother of his child.

But as wonderful as it was to hold her, it was even more painful. It reminded him of the countless nights they'd spent huddled together after Joshua had disappeared, clinging to each other as if each one feared the other would disappear. And the equally countless nights when they'd lain back-to-back, rigid and sleepless, but unwilling to offer or ask for help.

A shudder rippled through him as the struggle continued inside him between his need to hold this woman he'd loved as long as he could remember, and his need to protect himself from the painful, heartbreaking memories she'd brought with her.

Her body was lighter, less substantial than he remembered. She'd lost weight in the year since they'd split. He felt bones where before she'd been soft and curvy. He'd already noticed that her face was not just paler, but thinner, as well.

She pressed her temple against the hollow of his throat and he felt her tears dampening his skin. Carefully, he wrapped his arms around her and pressed his nose against her hair, breathing in the evocative scent of her shampoo.

Just a few seconds of comfort, he thought, trying not to notice that her body still fit with his, as though they were two parts of the same whole. "Happy birthday, Marcie," he said tentatively, wondering if mentioning it would cause her to pull away. But she didn't. After a few moments, she lifted her head slightly, causing Joe's nose to press more firmly against her hair. His arms tightened, and when they did, Marcie's fingers curled against his chest. She looked up at him, her eyes no longer wet with tears, but shimmering with something he'd thought was gone forever. His body recognized it, too. He almost groaned aloud as he felt the stirrings of arousal for the first time in a very long time. Gritting his teeth, he wrapped his fingers around her upper arms and set her away from him.

"Joe," she said, her voice low and sultry, a signal—an invitation—that he hadn't heard in two years, but that he'd never before ignored or denied. She looked at him with an unmistakable intent in her eyes.

"Marcie, this isn't—"

She uttered a sad, small laugh. "Of course it's not a good idea," she murmured, looking up at him. "Right now, I don't care. Do you?"

He looked down at her and knew exactly what she was doing. She was seeking a way to push aside the sadness and pain for a while. While it wasn't a good idea, it wasn't the worst thing they could do to each other.

She wrapped her arms around his neck. He knew her body as well as he knew his own and he recognized her awakening desire in the suppleness of her muscles, in the softness of her skin and the smokiness in her eyes. He knew as he always had, on a level much deeper than physical, how much she wanted him. "No, I don't care," he said and lowered his mouth to hers and kissed her.

Once he'd guided her to the bedroom, they came together on his unmade bed with a frenzy that echoed the need and excitement of their first time long ago. They stripped off their clothes without speaking, and Joe pulled her to him. As their bodies melded together like two parts of the same whole, he sighed and heard her quickening breaths echoing his. He was already hard and when Marcie felt him pressed against her, she whispered, "Now, Joe. Now."

"Not yet," he answered, moving his hand down to caress her. To his surprise, she was ready.

"Now," she whispered.

They made love quickly, greedily, like the long-lost lovers they were. It didn't take long for either of them to reach their climax. Once they were done and heaving with exertion and the delicious fatigue of satiation, they still clung to each other.

After their breaths and heartbeats finally returned to normal, she curled up against him, her head in the spot between his chest and shoulder where it fit perfectly. He kissed her languidly then lay beside her, trailing his fingers along her spine. He drifted then woke, then drifted again. Each time he came awake, he found that his fingertips were still lightly caressing her lusciously smooth, firm skin. They dozed.

A long time later, she touched his cheek. "Joe?"

He heard her voice through a pleasant, drowsy haze. "Mmm?" he whispered, not willing to leave his half-asleep world, where dreams and reality swirled, forming a strange, exotic fantasy.

She put her lips close to his ear. "How long will it take you to run the license plate?"

His fantasy world crashed as he jerked awake. "What?" he muttered automatically, although he'd heard her loud and clear. He sat up and reached for his pants, pulling them on without bothering to buckle the belt. Then he turned to her. She was still lying there on her side, but she'd pulled the sheet up to cover herself. "Is that what this was about?" he demanded.

Her eyes widened. Then they slid away from his gaze

to a point somewhere behind him as she sat up, pulling the sheet with her. "No, of course not," she said, sounding hurt. "I shouldn't have said anything. Sorry."

"Don't worry, Marcie. I'll get it, but I don't know what you're going to do with it. You can't take it to the police. This will be the fourth time you've cried wolf."

He pushed his fingers through his hair then wiped a hand down his face. "And when you've got the woman's name, what are you going to do? Scream at her, like you've done before? Try to grab her child?" He laughed, a harsh explosion that hurt his throat. "You're going to end up in prison—or the loony bin."

"Stop it!" Marcie cried. She tossed aside the covers and got out of bed, quickly donning her clothes. "That's not what I meant. I wouldn't do that. I'm sorry! I'm sorry, okay?" She grabbed her shoes and hurried from the bedroom into the living room.

Joe followed her. He didn't know what to say—what to think even. The sex had been mind-blowing, as it always was between them. But had she really done it just to convince him to help her with the license plate? He'd never thought of her as a calculating or manipulative person. But he hadn't seen her in a year.

During that time, she'd somehow managed to pull herself together, which seemed remarkable, given how sad and broken she'd been. What else had she learned in the past year? Was she transforming from grief-stricken mother to levelheaded supermom, resorting to anything, including sexual manipulation, to find her child?

When he stepped into the living room, she was fully dressed. Her hair, which had come out of its ponytail

during their lovemaking, was sleek and neat again, and
she regarded him with serene composure.

"I apologize, Joe. I didn't—" She stopped and started
again. "I'd better be going. When you run the tag, you
have my phone number."

"Yeah," he said. He crossed his arms and stood sto-
ically as she left, closing the door behind her. He didn't
move until he heard her car start and pull away from
the curb. Then he went into the bathroom and splashed
cold water on his face.

There for a moment, he'd thought that she'd finally
come to terms with their loss. To look at Joshua's disappearance, if not rationally, then at least with less de-
bilitating emotion. She'd finally conquered the frantic
desperation that had made her think every toddler she
saw was her child.

But now he wasn't so sure. She was a woman even
before she was a mother, so maybe she'd done what
women did. She'd used sex to get what she'd wanted. If
she'd never done it before, maybe it was for the simple
reason that in all the years they'd been together she'd
never needed to.

So she'd seduced him and, of course, as soon as she
beckoned, he'd followed her like a puppy starved for
attention. What a stupid jerk he was.

Chapter Two

That night, Marcie couldn't sleep. Every time she managed to drift off, her mind started playing tricks on her. One time she dreamed that she was running after the woman who had Joshua, but the police were chasing her like the Keystone Kops, laughing and pointing and popping up everywhere she turned. The next time she managed to relax, she dreamed of Joe, his strong arms and gentle words surrounding her. But too soon, the Keystone Kops were back and everyone was running in jerky circles like an ancient silent movie on fast-forward.

Finally she got up, exhausted by the disturbing and conflicting dreams, and went to the kitchen for a glass of water.

What had gotten into her, that she'd let herself get caught up in Joe again? Natural, she supposed, given that she'd known and loved him for almost half her life. But just because making love with him had felt natural and familiar and as wildly exciting as ever, it didn't make it a smart thing to do.

His harsh voice echoed in her head. *Is that what this*

was about? His words had sounded angry, but his tone also carried a note of hurt. Well, it had hurt her, too, that he would think that of her.

When he'd agreed to run the license plate, she'd been so grateful, so relieved. Stepping into his arms had felt like coming home. When he'd embraced her and kissed her, she'd been so consumed with desire and love that for those brief moments, the loneliness and grief of the past two years had flown out of her head.

Now, sitting in the big, lonely house they had bought together when they'd found out they were pregnant, she could see it all from Joe's point of view. His, to put it kindly, *unconventional* upbringing had instilled in him a distrust of women that had been a challenge for her from the moment they'd met. Over the years, she'd convinced him that she was nothing like his mother, and they'd had a happy marriage—or so she'd thought.

After Joshua was stolen, Joe's guilt had caused all his trust issues to resurface. Marcie knew that. She also knew that the unbearable pain of losing her baby had made her unfairly cruel and heartless toward him. She'd spent the first heartbreaking months blaming him for Joshua's disappearance. And the awful thing was that he'd accepted all the guilt and blame. He had taken everything she'd dished out.

They'd ended up so far apart that Marcie had been sure nothing could bring them back together. And nothing had. Until today.

She had gone to see him for one reason only. He was her last hope. He'd been right about the police. After she'd cried wolf so many times, they'd never listen to her again. And her friends had either given up on her, or had drifted away into the land of "call me if you need to talk."

Had she made love to him to secure his promise to run the license plate of that car? No, she told herself sternly. Not on any conscious level. It had truly been a sweet and poignant, if frenzied, reunion of long-estranged lovers. She shivered as her body tightened in memory of her explosive climax.

If Joe thought she'd manipulated him, wasn't that his problem, not hers? She'd gotten what she'd needed. His opinion of her was secondary. She'd been terrified that he would refuse to help her, but there had been no mistaking the excitement and hope in his eyes when she'd told him about the license plate and described the woman. He might act as if he were over Joshua, but she was still his wife and she knew him. He was as committed to following up on this crumb of hope as she was.

TUESDAY MORNING, JOE was in his office at the National Center for Missing and Exploited Children. After training and working at the headquarters in Alexandria, Virginia, for six months, he'd secured approval to open a satellite office in New Orleans. He had a small staff and an even smaller budget, but he believed in the center's mission and purpose, and he felt as though he were making up in a small way for the few seconds of inattention that had allowed someone to steal his son from him.

His purpose hadn't been entirely altruistic—maybe not at all. He'd checked the reports and descriptions of rescued children, as well as recovered remains, every

week, scarcely able to breathe until he'd finished reading each one.

He was staring at the computer screen, weighing the
pros and cons of entering his son's name and description
into the NCMEC database, when someone knocked on
the open door. He looked up. It was his mother. Kit Powers had on a short black skirt, a sleek red jacket and red
platform heels. She looked like a million dollars, as she
always did, and years younger than her real age, which
was probably early sixties. It occurred to him that he'd
never known for sure how old she was. "Kit," he said,
rising. "What are you doing here?"

She glanced over her shoulder at Jennie, the young
case-analysis intern who was standing behind her with
an openmouthed stare. "Thank you, sweetheart. I'm
going to tell my son to give you a raise." She looked at
Joe. "Give her a raise, darling. She's adorable."

Jennie blushed a bright pink and backed away.

"Interns don't make any money and *adorable* is not
a job requirement," he said. Why had she told the intern that he was her son? She'd always told him and
his younger brother, Teague, to call her Kit, and she'd
never introduced either of them in any other way than
"and this is Joe," or "this is Teague."

In her day, Kit Powers had been the most famous,
most recognizable exotic dancer in the French Quarter.
Joe knew a lot about his mother's life after he was born,
not so much from her as from the colorful characters
who had been her family, and therefore his. He'd been
babysat by transvestites in sequins and false eyelashes,
street mimes, jazz musicians who let him puff on a joint

when he was too young to fix his own breakfast. And he'd loved them almost as much as he loved Kit.

He knew that, no matter how much she needed money, his mother had never danced nude, but he'd seen photos of the costumes she'd worn. She'd appeared in some of the most beautiful and revealing costumes ever seen outside of Lady Gaga's closet. He also knew that she had a lot of money, probably from her famous lover Con Delancey, because she'd used it to set up very large trusts for Teague and him. Then, when Joshua was born, she'd done the same for him.

"What brings you out to Metairie?" he asked.

"Does a mother need a reason to come and see her son?" She stepped over and turned her cheek for a kiss, then looked around. "I've never seen your offices. Give me the tour."

He gestured around him. "Well, this is *the offices*. And that concludes the tour. Have a seat." He grabbed a stack of books from the only other chair in the room, but she waved a beautifully manicured hand.

"No. I really don't have time. I've got yoga this morning and I'm taking a cake-baking class in the afternoon."

Joe laughed. "You're going to yoga dressed like that?"

"Don't be silly. I have my yoga outfit in here." She indicated the large Coach leather tote over her shoulder.

"Okay. So, what's so important you had to take time out of your busy day to drive all the way out to Metairie?" he asked, smiling.

"It's actually not funny, Joseph. I had a very odd visitor a couple of days ago. Ethan Delancey."

"Delancey?" Joe frowned. He, like most people in New Orleans, knew that Kit Powers had had a long affair with the notorious Louisiana politician Con Delancey. The affair had lasted until Con decided to run for governor two years before his death. Up to that point, neither Con nor Kit had ever tried to hide it, although they'd never flaunted it, either.

Most older folks in the area figured Delancey was entitled, since rumors had flown for years that Lilibelle, Con's wife, had locked her bedroom door after the birth of their third child.

"What did he want?"

Kit glanced around, noticed Joe's diploma and some other framed documents on the wall next to the door and stepped over to examine them. She was stalling, and that wasn't like her.

"Kit, what's wrong?" he asked.

She turned and clasped her hands in front of her. "You read about the murder of Senator Darby Sills, I assume," she said.

"Sure." He frowned at her. She'd never made excuses for her lifestyle, never acted ashamed or guilty about the lovers she took. He and Teague knew men from every walk of life as friends of their mother, although few of them had been more famous or more notorious than Con Delancey. Was Senator Sills one of her conquests? "What about it?"

"Detective Delancey brought me something that was found in Darby Sills's house. He claimed he didn't know how Sills had come across it, but that it appeared to be the only copy."

A bad feeling began in Joe's chest, pressing down, making it hard to breathe. "The only copy of what?"

She dug into the tote and pulled out a thin manila folder that appeared to have only one sheet of paper in it. She handed him the folder and turned to gaze at the framed documents on the wall again.

Joe waited for a few seconds, thinking she'd explain, but she didn't. So he set the folder squarely in front of him on his desk and, after a bit of hesitation, made himself open it. The words he saw at the top of the form added a hundred-pound lead ingot to the weight on his chest.

"What is this?" he asked rhetorically, as his eyes swept down the form and back up. Of course, it was obvious what it was. The question he should have asked rose like a lump in his throat when his gaze landed on a small rectangle toward the top of the page. That tiny area contained a piece of information he had never known, never asked for, never thought he'd wanted.

The form was his birth certificate and in the space for Father was the name Robert Connor Delancey. He swallowed against a lump in his throat, started to speak, failed, cleared his throat and started again. "Is—is this true?" he croaked.

Kit turned around and met his gaze straight on for the first time since she'd come into his office. "Yes," she said. "That's a copy of your official birth certificate."

"Why didn't you—were you ashamed to tell me?"

Her eyes widened with surprise. "No," she said,

shaking her head. "No, darling. Of course not. I loved Con Delancey and he loved me. *And* he loved you."

"Then why didn't you ever tell me?"

"You may not believe me and I know you probably won't understand, but it was out of respect."

"Respect?" he said, cutting her off with a laugh. "For whom? Must be the Delanceys, because *your family* can hardly claim any respect."

His mother drew herself up to her full five feet five inches, tossed her head regally and glared at him. "Joseph, I loved your father. I never wanted to wave my status as *the other woman* in their faces. Con was Catholic and his church was important to him. He would never have gotten a divorce, even if Lilibelle had agreed to give him one, which she wouldn't have."

"How are you such an expert on the Delancey family?" he asked, then answered himself. "Never mind. You were shacking up with the patriarch. Of course you'd know all about them."

"I don't like your tone, young man," Kit snapped.

He had to fight to keep his mouth from turning up in a sneer. "Okay. I'll just have to live with that, because I don't like your lifestyle. Never have. Never will."

Kit Powers drew back her hand as if to slap her son, but he stopped her with a glare. "I'm sorry. I really am. But answer this for me, *Mom*. You made a special trip out here to tell me that Con Delancey is my father? Why now? Why today? I'm thirty years old. Did you not think it could wait another minute?"

His mother's face was pink with frustration and anger. "I'm not sure why you're so upset. I came out here to warn you. Detective Delancey told me that he couldn't guarantee who else saw the birth certificate. He's expecting the information to be leaked to the media, which is why he came to me as soon as he could."

"Wow," Joe said, feeling mean. "I'll be famous." He mimed a newspaper headline. "'Joseph Powers, bastard son of the infamous Con Delancey, let his own son be stolen at a local mall two years ago—'"

"Stop it!" Kit cried. "Stop that right now. You did not *let* him be taken."

"Forget it," he said, tired of the subject and tired of his mother. "I don't care who my father is or was. I never have. Now Teague—he'll get a kick out of being the bastard son of Con Delancey. What did he say?"

"Your brother is not Con Delancey's son," she said flatly.

"He's not?"

She shook her head. "Con left me when he decided to run for governor. I never saw him again. He moved back in with Lilibelle, three years before Teague was born. He was present in your life until you were almost three years old."

"So who *is*—"

"Don't even ask, because I'm not telling you. Either of you. Just let it go."

"So my brother—my *half brother*—doesn't get to know about his dad unless…I guess I should say *until* another Kit Powers scandal occurs? Great job of being a mother, *Kit*."

Her cheeks turned red as she looked at her watch. "I really should be going. My yoga class—"

"Right," Joe said, sitting back down behind his desk. "Well, thanks for the update," he said wryly.

Kit smoothed her skirt and her hair and started to turn toward the doorway.

"Mom?"

"What is it?" she asked, peering at him. "What's wrong?"

"Marcie thinks she saw Joshua."

Kit grimaced. "Oh, Joe." She thought for a couple of seconds. "Yesterday was her birthday, wasn't it? Goodness, has it really been two years? I'm sorry, sweetheart. She still thinks she sees him everywhere?"

Joe shook his head. "No. Until yesterday, I hadn't talked to her or seen her in nearly a year. When she showed up at my door, she seemed different. Not frantic. Not desperate. In fact she sounded pretty rational."

"Is she on medication? Maybe her doctor convinced her to take antidepressants."

He smiled wryly. "No, that's what I thought at first. But however she did it, she seems to have pulled herself together pretty well. She told me she saw a child in a car's backseat and thought it was Joshua. But, Mom, this time she got the car's license plate, and she provided a very good description of the woman driving."

Kit stared at him. "She did? Wow. That's a lot different than the last time."

"She's doing it right this time. She didn't jump out at the red light and scream at the woman to give her back her baby. She didn't scare anyone half to death by stalking them all over the outdoor marketplace. She followed the car, got the license tag and came to see me to see if I could run it for her."

"Joe, you're not buying in to this, are you? I don't think I can stand to see you disappointed again."

"It's a chance, and I can't afford not to take it. But no, I'm not buying in to it again. I'm waiting for the license plate to be run, then I'm going to do a background check on the woman, just like we do any suspected abductor. We check for arrest records, any complaints against them, friends, relatives, church, school, neighborhood. If I can't verify that the child is not Joshua, then we'll make a visit to the woman's house and request a DNA sample. Usually at that point, if the child is an abductee, the abductor's story breaks down. Those are the successful cases."

"And they're what percentage of your entire caseload?" Kit asked, her face suddenly pale and pinched.

"I'm not getting my hopes up, Kit, I promise." *Liar.* Of course he was getting his hopes up. Marcie was almost positive she'd seen their son.

"I have to go," his mother said, still looking as though she'd just heard awful news. She stepped forward and held out her arms for a hug. He got up, bent down and hugged her, accepting her tight, warm embrace in return. "I love you, Joe. You and Marcie. Please don't get yourselves hurt again. When you find out it's not Joshua, be careful. Let Marcie down easily."

"I love you, too, Kit."

She pulled back and looked him square in the eyes. "If you need anything—*anything*—you call me. Under-

stand? And, Joseph, it's about time you started calling
me Mom," she admonished.

Before he could think up an answer to that, she'd
slipped out the door.

THE PAST TWO YEARS had been the happiest that Rhoda
Sumner had ever had in her life. Her little boy was beautiful and perfect. That good-for-nothing mooch Howard,
who still claimed he was going to marry her one day
when his ship came in, spent most of his days over on
Bayou Picou, fishing. Rhoda cared about Howard. He
brought fish home and cleaned them himself, and he
handed over his disability check to her every month. He
was happy as a clam to have a woman, a place to live
and money for beer and bait. And he never said a word
about the kid who'd showed up two years ago. In fact,
his usual practice was to pretend the kid didn't exist.

Although Rhoda had never been blessed with a child,
she'd told everyone that Joshy was her grandson, and
she was rearing him because her daughter couldn't stay
off drugs. She took him to Sunday school, bought him
clothes at the Walmart in Hammond, and every morning from eight o'clock until ten, she sat him in a little
antique wooden school desk she'd found and played
educational games with him. He wasn't yet three and
he already knew how to count to twenty and identify
eight colors. He could get through *P* singing the alphabet song and she was starting to teach him that each
letter had a shape and a sound.

"Now which letter is this, Joshy?" she said, holding
up a flash card with a *B* on it.

"Bee!" he shouted.

"That's right. You are such a smart boy."

"I a smart boy," he replied and held up three fingers. "I'n three."

"Almost. Now, what letter—?" Before she could finish her sentence, she heard the front door slam. It was Howard. With a sniff of irritation, she got up from the low chair where she sat in front of Joshy.

"Oh, no!" Joshy said. "Howarr. Oh, no. He yells."

"I know, smart boy," Rhoda said to him. "Let's go into your room. I'll turn on the TV for you." She walked with Joshy into his room and turned the TV to a children's channel. "Watch TV while I talk to Howard, okay?"

"Okay, Gramma."

When Rhoda came out of Joshy's room and closed the door, Howard was staring into the open refrigerator door. "Rhoda!" he shouted as she walked into the kitchen.

"I'm right here," she snapped.

"Why isn't there ever anything to eat in here?"

"If I ever knew when you might show up, I could cook something for you."

"Whatcha got?" Howard asked, ignoring her admonishment.

"There's ham and I've got plenty of eggs."

"Got any Tabasco?"

Rhoda laughed. "When have I ever run out of Tabasco?"

Howard grunted. "Eggs and ham and lots of toast."

She sighed. "Want coffee?"

"What do you think?" he grumbled. "Where's the kid?"

That question surprised her. He'd seen her coming out of Joshy's room, so he had to know he was in there. And when had he started acknowledging that the boy even existed? "He's in his room," she said as she grabbed a plate of sliced ham and a carton of eggs out of the refrigerator. "Why?"

Howard just grunted as he sat down at the kitchen table and shook out the newspaper she'd carefully folded and set aside earlier, when she'd finished reading the headlines and the comics. It took her less than ten minutes to fix his breakfast. It took him less than five to wolf it down. He ate and drank his coffee without ever looking up from the paper.

"What are you doing here this time of the morning, Howard?"

"Hungry," he grunted.

"So your whoring ex-girlfriend don't cook?"

He looked at her flatly. "*If* I ever saw my whoring ex-girlfriend that lives over in Killian and has a sugar daddy, she'd probably treat me way better than my *boring* girlfriend."

Rhoda sniffed and nodded. "You're a real comedian, Howard. A real funny guy. I hope you're not planning on sticking around. I've got a lot to do today."

Howard ignored her and kept reading and sipping coffee. After a couple of minutes, he tapped the paper with his forefinger. "Here it is," he muttered, then folded the paper twice and pointed at an article.

"Here's what?" she asked, running water into the

sink and squirting dishwashing liquid into it. Steam rose, mixed with a few stray bubbles that escaped from the hot soapy water. "Is Kroger having a sale?"

"Look at this," he said, tapping the paper again.

"I'm busy."

"Look at it!" he shouted.

Rhoda slung water and soap off her fingers, dried them on her apron and took the paper. She saw an article about a new fishing camp being built near Killian. That was no news. The area was becoming more popular for fishing every year. "What?" she asked. "I don't see anything."

"I don't know how you find your glasses in the morning, woman. Right there in the middle. The column titled Delancey something-or-other."

Rhoda read the short article. Then she read it again, hoping that she'd misread it somehow. But she hadn't. She closed her eyes.

"You're such an idiot, Rho. How in the hell, out of all the kids in all the public places in a city as big as New Orleans, did you manage to grab a Delancey?"

"Wait a minute. We don't know for sure—"

"The hell we don't." Howard hauled his bulk up out of the kitchen chair and walked to the back door and looked out. "You don't think I missed the name and telephone number sewed into that little shirt and taped to the baby carrier, do you?"

Rhoda didn't say anything. She was still staring at the article, although after reading it six times, she could probably recite it by heart.

LOCAL ATTORNEY'S CONNECTION
WITH DELANCEYS SHOCKS
NEW ORLEANS

Papers confiscated during the investigation into
Senator Darby Sills's murder have revealed a star-
tling connection between a local attorney, Joseph
Robert Powers, and the powerful and influential
Delanceys of Chef Voleur and New Orleans, Lou-
isiana. Powers is the son of controversial French
Quarter celebrity Kit Powers, rumored to have
been politician Con Delancey's long-time lover.
A birth certificate confiscated from Sills's house
proves that Joseph Powers is in fact the son of Con
Delancey. The thirty-year-old Powers, who estab-
lished a satellite office of the National Center for
Missing and Exploited Children in New Orleans
after his own son, Joshua Joseph, disappeared in
March of 2012, could not be reached for comment.
A representative for the Delanceys informed us
that they are unaware of any connection and have
never met Powers or his mother.

She'd never talked about where Joshy had come
from, not even to Howard. Not surprisingly, he'd never
asked. Rhoda realized that she'd almost bought in to
her own lie. She'd almost told Howard that the article
couldn't be true because Joshy was her daughter's child.
Her daughter that didn't exist.

But no matter how much Rhoda wanted to deny it,
the fact was, little Joshy, who was her grandson in every

way but flesh and blood, was the son of Joseph Powers and the grandson of Con Delancey. She felt a sinking sensation in her stomach. Nothing good could come of this.

"What do you think of that, Rho?" Howard asked. When she looked at him he was sneering in the way he did when he knew he had the upper hand.

"I'm just going to have to be more careful. I won't take him to Sunday school anymore. After this article, everybody in the state is going to be staring at every child his age, asking themselves if that boy, or that one or that one, could be Con Delancey's grandson."

"You know what?" He thumped the paper. "This gives me an idea."

"What?" Rhoda didn't like the sound of Howard's voice or the look on his face. "What idea could you possibly have that would help anything?"

"Woman, if you'd listen to me for one minute, I'll tell you. That kid is a gold mine. All we gotta do is call the Delanceys and tell them we've got their grandkid and we'll be happy to give him back, for a price."

"No!" Rhoda said, backing toward the hallway to the bedrooms. She wanted to be between Howard and Joshy's room. Not that she could stop Howard if he decided to get to Joshy. "No. He is *not* a gold mine. He is my grandson. He's mine. He's nothing to do with you or them."

"If he's worth money, he's a *lot* to do with me. You know how bad I been wanting to build me a building near a dock where I could make a little money working on boat motors. We could build us a nice house out there on Bayou Picou."

"You listen to me, Howard Lelievre. I know things about you. I know your secrets. You start messing with my little Joshy and I'll get you in so much trouble they'll put you *under* the jail. Do you understand me?"

Howard gaped at her. "Oh, yeah? Are you really that stupid, woman? You know what I can do to you with one hand tied behind my back? You won't be able to tell nobody nothing once I get through with you."

Rhoda laughed. "Big talker. All I need is two seconds to grab my rifle. 'Cause I can put a slug through a rabbit's eye at thirty yards. Your big gigantic head'll be a piece of cake. Actually more like a bowl of pudding, and don't you forget it."

"Hell," he said. "What's the matter with you, woman? All I want to do is fish. And maybe have a little store or bait shop where I can fix motors and stuff. Don't you want enough money so you don't have to worry about anything?"

Not as much as I want that little boy. Rhoda shook her head. "You're an idiot, Howard," she said, pointing her finger at him. "Don't forget what I said. You touch one single hair on that child's head and you'll be answering to *me*."

To her relief, Howard actually looked worried. He shrugged, stuck his thumbs in the shoulder straps of his denim overalls and headed toward the front door. Rhoda heard him cursing under his breath.

"Watch what you say, you foul-mouthed good-for-nothing," she called after him. "Little pitchers have big ears."

His footsteps stopped. "Little pitchers can get *broken*, Rhoda."

looming. She called after him, "Marcie, pull over a moment," before he could whisper "on foot, they never out run Randall-anything ... now with no ... His strong voice ... a darker of the earlier ... His car on the ... He said ...

Chapter Three

Joe decided not to search for Marcie's license plate using NCMEC resources, if only because it was connected to the New Orleans Police Department's computer system. Now that his parentage was big news on page three of the *Times-Picayune,* he didn't want his name showing up there, especially since there were Delanceys on the police force. So he called up a friend whose mother was a police dispatcher in the Baton Rouge area.

"It's a Livingston Parish tag," Joe told his friend Terry. Within two hours he knew that the vehicle was a 2003 Nissan hatchback, registered to a Hardison Sumner, of Killian, Louisiana.

"Interesting note," Terry said. "Mom tells me that Hardison Sumner is deceased. Apparently it's his wife who's driving it."

"Did Sumner or his wife have a police record?"

"Nothing Mom could chase down. The car is clean, too. No outstanding parking tickets or citations. Say, Joe, I saw the papers the other day. Is everything okay with you—"

Joe cut him off, saying he had to be in court, thanked

him for the information and hung up. He'd decided about three seconds after his mother left yesterday that he wasn't going to answer any questions about his mother, his *alleged* father or himself. He wasn't going to mention it to Marcie, either, if she hadn't read it in the paper already. One personal crisis at a time was all he could handle. Who his father might be meant nothing to him compared to the possibility that following this lead might bring his son back to him.

He drove up to Metairie, to the house where he and Marcie had lived until he'd moved out. He'd needed to separate himself from her sadness and overwhelming grief. But he'd also wanted to save her from the added pain of facing him every day and knowing that his neglect had cost them their child.

As he walked up to the front door, he heard music playing from inside the house. It was Mozart, which surprised him. Marcie only listened to Mozart when she was painting. As far as he knew, she hadn't picked up a paintbrush since Joshua went missing. The fact that she was painting now shattered his heart, because he knew what it meant. She was pinning all her hopes on the license plate.

He knocked, and heard the sound echo through the house. The door's sidelights gave a distorted, beveled-glass view of the large foyer. After a moment, he saw her hurrying toward the door and he could tell by the way she moved that she was barefoot. Without warning, his body tightened and lust stabbed him. He'd always thought she had the prettiest feet he'd ever seen. Watching her skip through the house barefoot had always been a huge turn-on for him. He swallowed hard and took a deep breath as she threw the lock and opened the door.

"Yes?" she said, her ponytail still swinging. "Oh, Joe." Her face brightened and her cheeks turned pink. She smoothed stray hairs back from her face.

Facing her, he realized that despite the allure of her bare feet and the ponytail that revealed her beautiful face, he still resented her for using her body to persuade him.

"What are you doing here? Did you run the plate?"

"Yes," he said ungraciously.

"Well, come in and tell me," she said, standing aside and waving a hand. "I know it was a Livingston Parish plate. Where does the woman live? Did you find out anything about her? Does she have any children?"

Joe edged past her into the foyer of the home he was still paying for. He managed to avoid any physical contact. But he could still smell that damn melon-scented shampoo, mixed with the faint smell of oil paint. No, *resentment* was not the right word for what he felt toward her. He was *angry*.

"I've got the information and I'm going to go out there and speak with her, but, Marcie, this is going to be a bust. You know that, right?" Her face fell and he immediately felt like a heel. Still, confronting the issue now, before he came back to her with the disappointing truth, was better. The longer she lived with the idea that the child she'd seen might be Joshua, the harder it was going to be for her to accept that she was wrong again.

"I'm going with you," she said. "When—"

"Oh, hell, no, you're not," he snapped. "You'll wait right here until I get back."

Her cheeks flamed again but this time it wasn't a pretty little blush. It was the spotty red flare of anger. "I'm the one who saw him. I'm the one who got the plate number. I should get to be there when—"

"I said no!" he thundered.

She froze and stared at him.

"I came here to let you know that I'm going to talk to the woman, not to take you with me. I will come back and tell you what I find out, but you know what the odds are. We've heard the experts talk about that so many times. They've studied—"

"*They* didn't see him. *They* aren't his mother. *They* just compile statistics."

"Hon, it's been two years. Have you considered what the odds are that you would just happen to drive up right next to a car carrying our child?"

"No. I haven't considered the odds and I'm not going to. I don't care what the odds are. They don't matter. What matters is that I saw him and I didn't panic or go off half-cocked. I stayed calm and got the license number and gave it to you. I did everything right."

He felt bad for having yelled at her. "You did do everything right," he said gently. "Now you've asked me to help. I am. I'm going to handle this part of it. I'll come straight back here and tell you what happened."

"No, Joe. I can't just sit here and wait. I want to go. Please. I might be able to get a glimpse of Joshua. I might be able to call out to him—" She paused. "Joe?" she said, a tinge of apprehension in her voice. "Do you think he'll recognize my voice? Or was he too young? Oh, Joe, he's not going to remember us, is he?"

"Stop it, hon," Joe said, catching her arm. "You're getting upset. You can't think about that. If we—*when* we find him, we'll worry about that then. For now I'll take care of everything. I promise."

"Will you at least tell me where he is? Is he in Hammond? Are the people nice? Do they have any other children?"

"Absolutely not. I will not tell you anything else." He stepped toward the door. "I need to go. I have some work to do at the office," he said, but Marcie hadn't stopped staring at him.

"What's wrong?" he asked her.

"You're optimistic, aren't you?" she said as her lip started to quiver. "You're a little bit optimistic that she has Joshua."

He pushed past her without answering, grimacing when his arm brushed the firm softness of her breast. Once he was out the door and about to head down the sidewalk, he turned back. He cleared his throat and kicked a stone away with the toe of his shoe. Then he looked up at her. "Yeah, I guess I am. A little."

ON THE DRIVE out to the town of Killian, on the west side of Lake Maurepas, above New Orleans, Joe wished for companionship. He knew it would have been a disaster to bring Marcie, but her presence would have made the drive less boring and less nerve-wracking. Joe had never realized that something could be both boring and nerve-wracking at the same time. But the anticipation of seeing the woman and the child was torture, even though he didn't believe for one moment that the boy was his Joshua. At least he didn't think he did.

He spent most of the drive going over his plan in his head—once he had a plan. He would ask her if she'd noticed anyone suspicious lurking around her little boy. If she questioned him, he'd try to convince her that he was a government official.

Past Killian's tiny downtown area, the roads became little more than asphalt poured down over old shells and rocks. The asphalt dropped off to nothing at the shoulder, and when he met another vehicle, both of them ended up dangerously close to a small drop-off that was deep enough to bend the driveshaft.

When he found the Sumner house, it was set back off the road with what looked like three feet of crawl space under it. Much taller and it could almost be considered a stilt house. Although the ground around the house was dry and sported some fairly nice-looking grass, Joe knew that the area must flood, or the house wouldn't be built up like that.

He turned on a dirt road that was not more than a dirt path. He drove slowly and carefully, following the deep grooves that looked as though they were made by two vehicles that regularly traveled the area. Then he came upon a white plank house. There was an old green pickup and a Nissan hatchback in the front yard. The license plate of the Nissan matched exactly the number Marcie had given him.

So, this was the Sumner house and the vehicle was the same one that Marcie had seen. Although he knew the information he'd gotten was correct, the idea of being this close to the child who could be his son sent his pulse racing. Even being 99 percent sure that Marcie was wrong didn't stop a small sting of anticipation from pricking his chest and allowing hope to bloom.

The heavy, dreadful emptiness that had weighed on him since the moment he'd looked down to find the baby carrier, which he'd set at his feet, gone, came over him. It couldn't be Joshua. The odds were too high against it.

He eased past the Nissan until he had a good clear view of the front door. He pulled out his cell phone and turned it off. He didn't want anything to distract him.

Then he killed the engine and got out, remaining in the arc of the driver's side door, giving whoever was in the house plenty of time to look him over, check out his car and make up their mind that he was harmless.

He feigned looking around the yard and the house. Lying beside the concrete stoop, in the shade of the house, was a black-and-white spotted hound dog, resting. He wasn't asleep, because Joe had seen his head raise a couple of inches as his car approached. But he'd obviously decided neither the car nor the driver was worth getting up and barking at. Joe hoped the inhabitants of the house thought him as harmless as the hound did.

Still moving slowly, Joe closed the driver's door and walked slowly and deliberately toward the house. He saw a curtain flutter on the front window, then heard footsteps clattering on hardwood and the muffled sound of a female voice. He couldn't tell what she said.

About the time he stepped onto the sidewalk that started from nothing about forty feet from the stoop, the front door swung open and a small, slender woman in jeans and a T-shirt and a long gray braid came out, holding a twenty-two rifle in a way that told Joe she'd shot it before—lots of times before.

"What do you want?" she called out.

"My name is Joe Powers—" he began.

"I didn't ask you who you are. I asked you what do you want!" she yelled, lifting the barrel of the rifle about two inches.

"I'm a caseworker for the state," he said, using generic words that he hoped would sound unthreatening. "I want to talk to you about your child." Joe heard a voice from inside the house. It was a small voice—a child's voice, muffled by distance and the screen door. There was no way he could recognize it, or even tell if it were a little girl or a little boy. His heart began pounding so loudly that he wanted to muffle it with his palm.

"Hush, honey," the woman said, her tone kind and indulgent. "Go back to your room."

The child protested.

"No!" the woman said. "Go to your room." She lifted the rifle's barrel another two inches. "Now, you," she said to Joe. "Caseworker for what?"

"Ma'am. I wanted to ask you if you've seen anyone suspicious hanging around you or any friends of yours who have small children. It could happen close to home or when you're out shopping."

"Suspicious? The only suspicious person I see is you. What are you? A cop?"

Joe shook his head and spread his hands, palms out. "No, ma'am. I am not."

"Step out of the shade so I can get a look at you."

"May I just come inside for a minute?" Joe asked, not moving.

"Hell, no, you can't. Don't come any closer. Step sideways."

He stepped out of the shadow of a big pine tree that smelled like turpentine. "There," he said. "Ma'am, we're concerned about a man who has been reported at several malls and near some houses, watching women with small children."

"Shut up a minute," the woman commanded him. "Let me get a look at you."

Joe waited.

"Whereabouts?" she said as she lifted one hand to shade her eyes.

"Excuse me?" Joe asked. He'd heard what she said, but he needed a couple of seconds to sort out what she meant. He finally got that she was talking about where the suspicious character had been spotted. "In Hammond."

"What'd you say your name was?" she cried out, taking hold of the rifle with both hands again. "Where are you from?"

"I'll be happy to explain everything to you once we get inside. I'd like you to look at some pictures." Joe was afraid he was losing her. Was she more interested in him than in the safety of her child, or—?

Suddenly, with a pang in his stomach that felt like an ulcer, he knew why she was questioning him. A picture had been included with the article that had run in the *Times-Picayune*. It wasn't a good one, and it was a few years old, but still, he'd been recognizable.

Joe made a show of looking at his watch. "I'm afraid I've taken up too much of your time, ma'am. I probably ought to go. I've got other people to see. I appreciate you letting me talk to you."

"Gramma?"

There was the voice again. And unless he was horribly mistaken, the voice had said *Gramma*.

The woman's head snapped around toward the inside of the house. "What did I tell you, J—?" She cut herself off abruptly but Joe hadn't missed that she'd almost slipped and said the child's name. It started with a *J*.

His heart kicked into overdrive and his eyes began to sting.

"Gramma," the child called again, and Joe saw the screen door start to open. He strained to catch a glimpse of the child whose small fingers were reaching around the edge of the door, but Ms. Sumner glanced backward. "If you don't mind me right now, I will tan your hide! Now go to your room." She raised her rifle to her shoulder and sighted down the barrel. "And if you don't get out of here, I'm gonna shoot out your tires and then I'm going to shoot you. Coming around here making up stories to get inside my house. Now, you got to the count of three to get in that car and go! And don't you ever come back here!" She raised the gun to her shoulder. "One. Two—"

She fired. The bullet plowed a furrow in the dried

mud and bruised grass stems just to the right of Joe's feet. He jumped and ducked automatically.

"Hah! I aimed to miss that time, but I won't again!"

"Rhoda!" A booming voice came from somewhere to the left and behind the house. Joe heard heavy boots clomping and within seconds, a big, burly man appeared. He was dressed in denim overalls over a faded red T-shirt and he had a fishing rod in one hand and a tackle box in the other. When he saw Rhoda holding the rifle, he slowed down. "Are you all right, woman? What's going on?"

Rhoda whirled to look at the man and Joe took that as his cue to get out. He opened the driver's side door of his car.

"Look at him, Howard!" Rhoda shouted, turning the gun back toward Joe. "Don't he look familiar?"

Joe stood behind the open car door, using it as a shield in case the woman did decide to shoot again.

The burly fisherman spotted him and changed direction. "Hey! What the hell are you doing here? Ain't you got sense enough to get when a woman holding a gun tells you to get?" The man didn't move fast, but he lumbered along at a steady pace.

"Howard, don't scare him to death. *Look* at him!"

Joe glanced toward Ms. Sumner, who had angled her head and was sighting down the barrel again. He imagined he could see right down the inside of the barrel.

"Hey," Howard said. "I know you. You're that lawyer—"

Joe jumped into the driver's seat and cranked the engine. Rhoda fired again. And again, Joe's knee-jerk reaction was to duck. But this time he didn't hear the bullet. It must have passed just above or to the side of the car. He puffed his cheeks and blew out a breath of relief as he threw the transmission into Reverse and backed around in a semicircle, then took off, spinning his wheels and spraying mud and dirt everywhere. The deep tire grooves rocked him back and forth as he sped away, not taking the time to follow the trenches, just wanting to get out of there as fast as he could, hopefully without getting shot.

He heard two more rifle shots in quick succession. He winced and bunched his shoulders. When a beat passed and he didn't hear safety glass pop or feel anything slam into him, he relaxed a little. The base of his spine tingled at the imagined feel of a bullet striking him in the back. He gunned the accelerator and aimed the car for the curve up ahead that would put him out of sight and hopefully out of range of the woman's rifle.

Joe took the curve on two wheels and didn't slow down until he saw the city limits sign for Killian. He slowed to match the town's speed limit. After a couple of moments his brain calmed down enough to concentrate on something other than getting away from the gunfire.

He'd heard a child inside Rhoda Sumner's house. From the timbre of the voice, Joe figured it had to be about two or three years old. A toddler the age Joshua would be now. And she had almost said a name that started with a *J*.

Joe kept his fists white-knuckled on the steering wheel until he was several miles past Killian, then he pulled carefully onto the shoulder of the road and cut his engine. For a long time, he sat there, overwhelmed by all the emotions churning inside him. To his surprise and dismay, he felt a stinging in his eyes and a tightening in his throat. He hadn't cried since he was a kid—a little kid. He'd wanted to. There had been times as he'd held Marcie while she sobbed, that he'd wanted to bury his head in that soft, beautiful curve between her shoulder and neck and cry until the pain inside him subsided. But he never had. Not once.

Now, though, alone in his car, answerable to nobody, responsible for no one, he wept. The tears scalded his cheeks. The sobs made his chest and throat sore. The opposing forces of pain and hope nearly tore him apart.

The sun was going down when he finally wiped his face on his shirtsleeve and started the engine. At the first gas station he came to, he splashed cold water on his face and swore to himself that he would never cry again. He didn't know how women cried so much without it killing them.

As he drove back to Marcie's house, he thought about what he was going to tell her. He couldn't tell her that the man and woman had seen his photo and the scandalous article in the newspaper. If Rhoda and Howard had not already known whose child they'd stolen, they certainly knew now.

There was no way he could explain to her that because he'd driven out there, he'd confirmed for them that the child they had abducted two years ago was a Delancey.

And he sure couldn't tell her that he was convinced

that he'd found their son. After two years of not knowing whether his child was alive or dead, he'd found him.

Joe didn't know what Rhoda and Howard were going to do, but he did know one thing. In finding Joshua, he'd placed him in grave danger.

Chapter Four

Marcie looked at her watch. It was getting dark and she hadn't heard from Joe. She couldn't wait to hear what he'd found out. It still rankled that he'd refused to let her go with him. She was Joshua's mother. She had a perfect right to be there when he confronted the woman.

And she had a right to know where he was and how much longer it was going to take him to get home. Just as she started toward her purse to retrieve her cell phone, the landline rang. She picked it up on the second ring. Almost before she got the word *hello* out of her mouth, a deep, gruff voice said, "I know who you are, and I know who your husband is."

Disgusted, Marcie started to hang up.

"Mrs. Powers, do you want your kid back?"

Her hand froze in midair, stunned by what the awful voice was saying. She brought the phone back to her ear. "Wh-what did you say?" she asked through lips numb with shock.

"You heard me. Now you just listen and listen good. I'm going to call you back tomorrow and tell you what I want you to do. You got that?"

"Who is this?" Marcie demanded, putting all the steel she had into her voice.

He laughed. "Who am I? Why don't you ask your husband? Now you sit tight and don't tell nobody nothing. *Nobody!* Otherwise I'll have to send you a little present. How would you like to get one of your precious kid's fingers in a pretty box?"

Marcie gasped and her stomach turned over. "No! Please. I won't...say anything. Don't hurt him. I swear I won't tell. But where is he? How—"

"Shut! Up!" the man shouted. "Shut up! No questions. Don't talk or you'll get his finger in a pretty box."

She heard a click and the phone went dead.

Marcie stared at the words displayed on the tiny screen. *Out of area.* Her stomach cramped and her saliva turned acrid. She rushed to the sink and splashed cold water on her face, willing it to wash away the image of her precious baby's bloody finger in a box. She sucked in a mouthful of water, hoping the coolness would settle her stomach.

Was this her fault? Had the woman in the car known her? Known she was Joshua's real mother? That meant the little boy she'd seen really was hers. But it also meant she may have put his life in danger. Her baby! Her son! He was out there with a dangerous, violent man. Waiting for her to find him.

She didn't know how long she'd been sitting there at the kitchen counter when she finally heard a car pull up outside and cut its engine. When she straightened, she felt a twinge in her back. She hurried to the foyer and peered through the sidelights. It was Joe. Her knees literally went weak. She flung open the door and threw herself into his arms, almost knocking him over.

"Hey, Marcie, what—?"

"Joe! Somebody called!" she cried, pushing him away to look at him, then hugging him again. "I'm so scared. I don't know what to do!"

He gripped her upper arms and set her far enough away from him that he could see her face. "Tell me," he said. "Who was it?"

"It was a man. He said he had Joshua. He said not to tell anyone, that he'd—" Her breath hitched in a sob. She swallowed and went on. "He'd cut Joshua's finger off and send it to—"

"Marcie," Joe said sharply. "Calm down. I can't understand half of what you're saying. Who called? He said he had Joshua?"

Marcie took a deep breath, hearing it catch at the top like a sob. "I'm—I'm trying to tell you—"

"Marcie, breathe. Take deep, slow breaths. In and out. In and out."

He was talking to her like he had in the breathing classes while she was pregnant. His soothing voice acted on her like a tranquilizer. She breathed in and out, slowly, deeply.

"Now," he said, putting an arm around her and leading her to the couch. "Sit down and tell me exactly what the man said."

She nodded and took one more deep breath for good measure. "He said not to tell anyone or he'd—" She swallowed and took another long, slow breath. "He'd cut

off Joshua's finger and send it to me in a pretty…box."
She felt nauseated again, and out of breath. "Oh, Joe—"

"Shh," Joe said, pulling her to him and rubbing his
palm gently up and down her arm. "It's going to be
okay. That ugly bottom-feeder's not going to do that to
our son. He's a coward and a bully, hiding behind a little
boy. Don't worry. It's going to be all right."

Marcie closed her eyes and let herself be comforted
by him. She loved the feel of his strong chest against
her cheek, loved the soft caress of his hand on her arm.
She wished she could stay right where she was, not
thinking, not feeling anything except the comfort of
Joe's big, strong body surrounding her, protecting her.

But she'd seen the look on his face. The shock—
and the guilt. It was an expression she knew very well.
"Just a minute," she said, thinking of the man's terri-
fying words. "When I asked him who he was, he said
for me to ask you. What did he mean by that?" She
lifted her head from his chest. "Did you see him? Did
he have Joshua?"

Joe didn't answer.

"You *did!* That was him on the phone, wasn't it?" She
frowned. "You know who he is, don't you?"

Then suddenly, it all made sense. Joe had gone out to
that woman's home and questioned her about the child
and now a man was calling, wanting money for her little boy. "Oh, my God, it's not my fault. It's yours! You
saw Joshua, didn't you? I was right. The woman in the
Nissan has Joshua and now he's in danger because you
went out there. Is that man her husband?"

Joe knew exactly what had happened. Rhoda and

the man had recognized him as the bastard Delancey
son in the newspaper article. With a sigh, he realized
he had to tell Marcy everything.

"Okay, hon, I need you to calm down and listen to
me. I think Rhoda—the woman driving the Nissan,"
he added when he saw her puzzled expression, "took
Joshua because she wanted a child. But while I was trying to talk to her, a man showed up in a dirty T-shirt
and overalls, carrying a fishing rod. He figured out that
I was the father of Rhoda's child right away."

"How? How did he figure it out? What did you tell
him?"

He didn't answer her directly. "Listen to me, hon,
and stay strong, okay?"

Her eyes grew wide and haunted. "Stay—? What?
Oh, my God, what's wrong?"

Joe rubbed his palms up and down her arms. "I think
he's planning to try and get money from us."

"Money? Like—like a ransom?" Her expression
turned to horror. "They're holding my baby for *ransom*?
Why? Why now? That doesn't make sense. They've had
him for two years."

Joe shook his head. Suddenly, he couldn't go any
further. He couldn't tell her that Rhoda and Howard
had decided to hold their child for ransom because he
was a Delancey.

"What are we going to do? We don't have any
money."

"No, we don't," Joe said, *but the Delanceys do*.

"What are we going to do?"

"Right now, I'm afraid we're going to have to wait
for Howard to call back."

JOE WOKE UP, breathing in the faint, fresh air of the home where he and Marcie had been so happy for so long. Before he opened his eyes, he lay still, letting the scents of fresh linens, baby powder and a hint of vanilla wash over him. The poignant memories evoked by the mingled odors brought a lump to the back of his throat.

He shifted and opened his eyes. The first thing he saw was the black-button gaze of a stuffed panda bear. The bear sat in a tiny rocking chair next to the antique crib that had belonged to Marcie's grandmother. In his throat the lump grew, nearly cutting off his breath. He'd slept in the nursery. It hadn't been much of a problem last night. He'd turned out the light as he'd entered the room. Marcie had already converted the couch into a bed and made it up, so all he had to do was undress and climb under the covers. He'd deliberately avoided looking at anything in the room.

Now, in the bright light of morning, he couldn't ignore the baby toys, baby furniture, blue curtains and mobiles hanging over the crib. With the empty place inside him throbbing with grief for his son, he vaulted up off the hide-a-bed sofa, grabbed his slacks and slipped across the hall to the bathroom.

The hot shower eased the pain inside him and soothed the stinging in his eyes. When he stepped out of the stall and reached for a towel, he noticed a neatly folded pair of blue boxers and a white T-shirt. They hadn't been there when he'd started his shower. Gratefully, he donned the clean clothes, pulled on his jeans and headed downstairs to the kitchen.

Marcie was already there, making the coffee. As he

walked in, she finished pouring water into the coffeepot and turned it on. Her hair was damp and pulled back in a high ponytail that made her look like a college kid. But when she turned and looked at him, her eyes were rimmed with red and her nostrils and the corners of her mouth were pinched. She looked awful. Still beautiful, but awful nonetheless.

"Morning," he said.

She didn't answer him. She turned her attention back to the sink, rinsing glasses and placing them in the dishwasher. She dried her hands. Joe noticed that she'd been chewing on her fingernails.

"Marcie, don't you have some of the tranqs the doctor gave you? You ought to be taking them." He took her hand in his and rubbed his thumb across the ragged nails. "You're a nervous wreck."

She jerked her hand away and glared at him. "Thank you, *doctor*. But I don't want to be tranquilized. That man is going to call this morning. What good will I be if I'm drugged?"

He nodded. He understood. It just hurt him to see her hurting so badly. The coffeemaker grumbled and gurgled, announcing that the coffee was ready. She poured herself a cup and took it to the kitchen table and spooned sugar into it.

"Still like a little coffee with your sugar?" Joe said, hoping to make her smile, even if just a little.

He was rewarded with a wan upturn of her lips as she lifted the spoon and inspected it for lingering granules of sugar. She touched the spoon, wiping sugar onto her fingertip. "I'd let Joshua suck a little sugar off my fingertip. He loved—" She set the spoon down with a clatter and lifted the cup to her lips.

Joe poured himself a mugful and sat down beside her. He drank his black. He took a long swallow, regarding her over the rim of his mug as she sipped at hers.

"What happened to us?" she asked.

"What do you mean?" Joe asked, looking at the dark liquid in his mug, then picking it up and sipping.

"Just what I said. What happened?"

He set his mug down a little too hard. "You couldn't—or wouldn't—understand why I went back to work instead of sitting around here and moping, or going over to haunt the outdoor market in case someone showed up with a child, so you could get all excited for two minutes until you got a good look at them."

She shook her head, a pained expression on her face. When she set her cup down, a little bit of coffee sloshed out. "That's not what I'm talking about. I mean before—before Joshua. We weren't good for each other anymore. You were working ten- to twelve-hour days and I spent most of my time painting. I was usually in bed asleep by the time you got home. And you still managed to be jealous of me. You could never believe that I wasn't like your mother. I wasn't then and I'm not now."

He didn't say anything. He knew she was right about what their life had turned into before they got pregnant. But why in hell was she bringing all that up now? It was old news.

"What are you doing, Marcie? Do you really want to talk about that now? I think there are bigger issues here."

She shrugged. "I was so naive. I thought that having a baby would change things. I thought it would make you happy. Make you realize that I wasn't like your mother."

"Don't bring Kit into this," he snapped, a harsh, jagged panic ripping into his chest. He didn't want to talk about his mother. He didn't even want to think about her and the news she'd driven out to Metairie to tell him—was that just three days ago? He didn't want to have to explain to Marcie about the exposé in the newspaper that had prompted Howard to hold Joshua for ransom. He knew she'd have to know eventually, but he was in no hurry to spill this latest chapter in the story of his, as she always put it, *unconventional* upbringing.

"You never want to talk about her. It's like she's some kind of goddess on a pedestal, and you're her guardian." Marcie stood and grabbed her cup to take to the sink. It clattered noisily when she set it down. "What I never could understand is why you never thought about Joshua or me in the same way. Why couldn't you have appointed yourself *guardian* for your child? Maybe if you had—"

Joe stood so abruptly that he knocked the kitchen chair over. "Don't do this. Don't start with me now about letting him be taken."

Marcie turned on him, her electric blue eyes blazing. "But that's exactly what you did. You let him out of your sight. You set his carrier down on the ground. He was your baby and you let him—"

"Stop it!" Joe shouted, clenching his fists at his side.

"You don't have to keep hammering at me! I know! I know what I did! So shut—"

The harsh jangling of the phone made Joe swallow his words. He jumped and whirled toward the sound.

Marcie jumped, too, and let out a little screech of surprise. Then she pressed a hand against her chest. "Oh! It's him," she gasped. "It's him, isn't it? I don't—should I—"

Joe held up a hand that shook. "I'll get it," he said breathlessly. He was terrified. What would Howard demand in return for their child? Would he really hurt Joshua if they couldn't get the money he wanted? "I'll talk to him.

"Joe Powers," he said into the mouthpiece, noticing that the number was blocked.

"Ho-ho! It's you," the guttural voice said. "Did you get a look at your kid yesterday? I hope so because that just might be the last time you ever see him, if you don't do exactly what I say."

Joe glanced at Marcie, who was still standing by the sink. Her hands were clasped in front of her as if in prayer and she was watching him unblinkingly. Joe didn't like what he was about to do, and he knew Marcie wouldn't like it, but it was the only way he could keep the upper hand against this man who was at best a low-life opportunist, and at worst a psychopath. He hadn't worked any kidnappings with NCMEC, but he'd gotten some training from the FBI on handling abductions across state lines. The training plus common sense dictated that he couldn't let Howard get an advantage. Showing weakness could cause harm to the child.

"Hey," Howard said. "Are you listening to me? I said—"

"I heard what you said," Joe replied. "But I'm not interested." Out of the corner of his eye he saw Marcie start, then put her hands over her mouth. He held up his hand, palm out, hoping she understood the message. *Don't worry. I'm handling this. Stay calm.*

Before the other man could speak, Joe went on. "I don't even know if that's my kid. Can you prove that the child is even mine?"

"Joe!" Marcie gasped, starting toward him.

He held up his hand again, then turned his back on her and walked across the room.

"Wha—?" Howard exclaimed, apparently not prepared for that answer. "Of course he's yours, you stupid ass. The same day the newspaper said you lost your child, that's the day my girlfriend showed up with him."

"I'm going to need more than just your word on that, *Howard*. I need proof. Send me a picture of him and a picture of the clothes he was wearing when Rhoda took him." Joe felt Marcie's hand on his arm. He gave a quick shake of his head and touched his lips with his forefinger. "There was a label in his shirt. I want to see that before I talk to you any more."

"Wait!" Howard yelled. "Wait! How do I send it? You want that from me, you gotta give me your cell or your email."

Joe gave him his cell number. "Now you listen to me. If I don't see the pictures in one hour, don't even bother calling." And with that, he hung up. His hand shook as he cradled the phone. He closed his eyes. When he took a deep breath, it caught in his throat and he had to cough.

"Joe, what are you doing? What if they don't call back?" Tears were rolling down Marcie's cheeks. She squeezed the sleeve of his T-shirt in her fist. "Oh, my God! He was so close and now he may be gone again."

"Listen to me, Marcie," Joe said, turning and catching her by the arms. "We've got to keep the upper hand. That's the first thing they teach you at the center. If you show weakness, then they might hurt the child."

"But you just— What if they didn't save the shirt?"

"Then they'll tell us that. Trust me, hon. I know what I'm doing." He thought about his connection with the Delanceys. About how Rhoda and Howard had seen the newspaper article and were now angling for some of the Delancey money. He knew Howard would send the pictures.

What he didn't know was whether he and Marcie would recognize Joshua, who was now twenty months older than they'd last seen.

LOOKING SHELL-SHOCKED AND bewildered, Marcie went upstairs to dress and Joe called his office and talked to his senior caseworker, Valerie. "I won't be in today or Friday. I'll be doing some work from home," he told her.

"Good," she said, before he even finished the sentence. "There are reporters hanging around outside the office like vultures. I'll be thrilled to tell them that you aren't coming in."

"Reporters?" he said. "Are you kidding me?"

"I wish. They're stopping everybody, wanting to

know what we know about you and the Delanceys. Luckily, our staff and interns have enough sense not to answer. We're behind you all the way."

"Tell everybody I appreciate it," he said.

"Joe? Are you all right? You sound terrible."

"I'm fine, Val. Just trying to get everything sorted out. Don't answer any questions, and let everybody know that when all this settles down, we'll have a big celebration. We'll all go out to dinner, on me."

"I'll tell them."

"Thanks. I'm going to sign on from home and run some leads I've been working on for a couple of cold cases," he said. "What's the password for today?"

Valerie gave him the day's password and they hung up. He headed into the small room off the dining room that they'd set up as his home office.

Marcie came downstairs about the time the computer was booting up. "What are you doing?" she asked.

"I'm going to see what I can find out about Howard without having to go into the office," he said. "What about you?"

She shrugged. "Clean up the kitchen. I don't know. Maybe I'll try to read." She wrung her hands helplessly. "I don't know if I can stand this. How long do you think it's going to take for him to call back?"

"I don't know, hon. I'm thinking he'll call as soon as he can get the pictures. He's going to have a problem with Rhoda. She's not going to want to give the boy back. It's obvious that the reason she took him in the first place was to have a child of her own. When he comes to her wanting to take a picture and she finds out his harebrained scheme, she's liable to take—" He stopped, realizing where his thoughts were taking him, but he'd already said too much. Marcie's sharp eyes met his and he knew that she knew exactly where his thoughts were heading.

"She's going to take Joshua and run. Oh, my God, Joe, we've got to stop her."

He did his best to calm her down, but his careless words had started him thinking, too. She was right. The woman just might take the child and leave. She could have relatives anywhere. "This is her home. She's not likely to just pull up roots and head off to parts unknown."

"I would," Marcie said. "If it meant keeping my child safe. I'd do that—I'd travel to the ends of the earth."

Joe nodded. She was right. He'd do the same thing to protect his child, or Marcie.

"We've got to go out there. We've got to talk to her, reason with her, before that man gets his hands on our child." Marcie wrung her hands, then rubbed her temples. "We've got to go now."

Chapter Five

They forwarded the home phone to Joe's cell and headed northwest to Killian. They made it in just under an hour. As the car rounded a curve and the house came into sight, Joe muttered a curse under his breath.

"What is it?" Marcie asked. She'd held on to the grab bar the entire trip. When she let go, her fingers cramped. "What's wrong?"

Joe pulled up near the sidewalk that led up to the wooden front stoop of the house and stopped. He put the car into Park, and left it running. "Wait here," he said.

Marcie grabbed at his arm, latching on to his rolled-up shirtsleeve. "Tell me what's wrong. I'm tired of you ignoring me and refusing to answer my questions."

"When have I—?"

"Joe!"

He settled back down in the driver's seat and looked at her sidelong. "The Nissan was parked out here in front of the house yesterday beside a beat-up green truck."

"Oh," she said, then, *"Oh."* She squinted at the house and the yard, trying to see if there were any signs of the car being driven around to the back. But there were no tire tracks in the yard, or anywhere that she could see, except for the dirt road and the space where Joe had pulled in.

"So you think they're gone?" Her voice tried to quit on her, so great was her fear that they'd fled with her child.

Joe nodded grimly. "It looks like it." He shifted, preparing to climb out of the driver's seat.

Disappointment settled like a stone in her stomach. "I'm going with you," Marcie said, steeling herself for an argument, but to her surprise, Joe didn't say anything. He just reached back inside the car, cut the engine and removed the key.

"Watch your step," he said as they started up the sidewalk to the stoop.

"Did you go inside when you were here before?" she asked.

He shook his head with a wry smile. "Didn't get the chance."

"What did you do?"

"I parked there, just about exactly where the car is now, and I stood by the driver's side door. Rhoda was on the porch there, with a rifle."

Marcie gasped in surprise. "A rifle? Joe, she didn't shoot at you, did she?"

"Three times, I think. Maybe four."

Marcie felt like a bullet had just slammed into her own chest. She pressed a hand against her hammering heart. "Joe!"

"Once while I was standing there at the car door, and then at least twice more as I drove away."

"You could have been killed!"

He made a dismissive gesture. "I got the definite feeling that if Rhoda had wanted to wound or kill me, she'd have done it. Nah. She was making a point with those shots," he said as they reached the porch. He stopped her with a hand on her arm. "Wait here," he murmured.

"No—"

"Marcie, I don't think there's anybody here, but I want to make sure," he muttered sharply. "Here are the keys. If I yell, run back to the car and get out of here."

"I'm not going to leave you here alone," she said, refusing to take the keys.

He grabbed her hand and pressed the key ring into it. "Neither one of us is going another step until you promise me you'll do what I say. I can take care of myself, but Howard is a big man. If he grabs you, we're sunk."

She took the keys, glaring at him. "Fine. I'll just leave you to your fate."

He gave her a crooked smile and nodded. "Good. Now wait here."

She listened, not breathing, but didn't hear anything except his footsteps on hardwood. After about thirty seconds, he opened the screen door and came out onto the porch stoop.

"There's nobody in there. Let's go," he said, looking at his feet as he stepped onto the porch and cupped her elbow in his hand. "Come on."

"Wait a minute. I want to see inside. There might be a clue to where they went."

"I already looked. I didn't see anything."

"Joe, wait. Did you check to see if their luggage is gone? If their toothbrushes are still in the bathroom? They could have just gone shopping or to a movie. We could wait for them."

"What are you going to say?" he asked harshly. "'Hi there. Enjoy the movie? Great. Now give me my son.'"

Marcie glared at him. "What were you going to say?" she blustered back at him.

He winced. "To tell you the truth, I don't know. Now come on. All the more reason to get out of here in case they do come back."

"No," she said. "I want to go inside."

"I'm tired of arguing, Marcie. I told you there's nothing to see." He started down the two steps to the sidewalk, but she didn't move. He pointed to the west. "Howard came from that direction. He had a fishing pole. I doubt there's anything over there but docks and maybe a bait shop, but we could drive that way and see. Ask if anybody knows where they are."

She ignored him and turned toward the door.

He caught her shoulder and when she looked back, his expression was grim. "Marcie, don't."

"Why not? You said there was nobody in there. Is there…blood or something?" Her gaze widened and fear sharpened their blue depths.

"No, hon, nothing like that."

She shrugged, trying to remove his hand. "Then I don't see why I can't go in."

He sniffed, then let her go. "Okay. Go ahead."

Wondering at the defeated note in his voice, she opened the screen door and stepped into the cool, dim house. It took a moment for her eyes to adjust, after being in the bright sunlight. When they did, the first thing she saw was a small wooden table and two chairs. There were blocks and flash cards on the table and right beside it was a whiteboard with two words written on it in box letters. *JOSHY*. Underneath the name was the word *BOY*.

Marcie stared, uncomprehending for a few seconds. Then slowly, as if she were drugged or sick or had just landed on an alien planet, she began to make sense of the things she saw. A groan erupted from her throat and she sank to her knees next to the little table. This was what Joe hadn't wanted her to see. He'd known how much it would upset her. Tears welled in her eyes. She groped blindly on the table and her hand encountered a square, plastic building block. She held on to it as if it were a lifeline.

"He's two years old, almost two and a half," she murmured. "He's learning his *ABC*s—" She gestured vaguely toward the board. "Even words," she said, almost choking.

"I know, hon." She couldn't pinpoint where Joe's voice came from but his words were as hoarse and strained as hers. She felt his hand on her arm and she let him help her to her feet.

She turned to him, proffering the block, her lower lip trembling with the effort not to cry. He ignored the plastic cube and just pulled her close. But she didn't—

she couldn't—let him hold her right now. Hunching her shoulders, she stepped around him and went into the small kitchen. Beside the sink were several sippy cups turned upside down on a towel. An empty carton of juice was in the trash can.

Marcie felt as though she were choking and smothering. No matter how hard she tried, she couldn't get a full breath.

"Just breathe," Joe said softly in her ear. She hadn't heard him come up beside her. "Just breathe, slowly, evenly. You'll be okay."

She did what he told her to, because she had no choice. She was hyperventilating. She knew that. But she couldn't stop it without Joe's help. How many times had it happened since Joshua had disappeared? Five? Ten?

"Breathe evenly," he kept repeating. "Slowly."

Finally she could take a full breath without it hitching. "Okay," she said, a little breathlessly. "It's okay now."

"Come on, let's go outside." He took the block from her and bent to set it back down on the little table.

"No!" she cried, reaching for it. "I want to keep it."

"I don't see why—"

"Give it to me."

Joe gave her the block.

She held it in both hands, pressed against her chest. "She was teaching him, Joe. She was teaching my little boy. Look at the block. It has a *J* on it. Did you see the kitchen?"

He didn't speak. He just waited for her to finish.

"She took care of him. She gave him juice. Bought him little cups to drink out of." She tried to blink away the tears, but they kept filling her eyes and flowing down her cheeks. "She's had our son—known him—longer than we have."

Joe looked out the door, toward the sunlight. He clenched his jaw and tried to pretend that Marcie was someone else, one of the women he saw at the satellite office of NCMEC. But he knew that was a futile effort, for two reasons. First, she was his wife and she was talking about his son. But second, every time he met a mother or a father whose child had been taken from them, he felt the same way. The tarnished armor he tried to keep in place to protect himself from the pain of loss was barely more effective against strangers than it was against his and Marcie's personal anguish. He supposed his empathy for the heartbroken parents made him good at his job, but he was worried that his roiling emotions were going to cripple him in his search for his own child.

As he started to push the screen door open, Marcie shouted, "Joe!"

"What?" he asked distractedly.

"Your phone."

Then he heard it: his phone making a peculiar dinging sound. He froze.

"Is that—?"

He managed to nod. "A message."

"That's the picture," Marcie said breathlessly. "Oh, Joe, I'm afraid to look."

So was he. Reluctantly, he took the phone out of his

pocket and pressed the button to activate the screen. There, on top of a little icon that looked like a mailing envelope, was the number one, indicating that he had one new text message.

With Marcie hanging on to his arm with both hands, he tapped the envelope on the screen with a finger. For a second nothing happened, then a photo appeared.

It was a picture of a little boy, a toddler who could have been two or three years old. His hair was brown and had been dampened and combed back so that the slight widow's peak on his forehead was visible. His blue eyes, so much like his mother's, sparkled in the light from the camera's flash.

Marcie burst into tears and her nails dug into Joe's arm. "It's Joshua. Oh, my baby. My Joshua. Look at him. He's grown so big—" Her voice gave out and her entire body shook with her sobs. "Look at him, Joe. Look at him."

Joe was having trouble believing his eyes. He saw what Marcie saw, and his first reaction was that it was Joshua. But could he be 100 percent sure? Joshua at nine months had had chubby cheeks and a cute up-turned nose that didn't look like either his or Marcie's. This child's nose was straight and had a rounded tip. It still didn't look like his or Marcie's nose, but if he let himself, he could believe the boy's eyes were just like Marcie's. "Marcie, take it easy. We've got to be sure."

"You're not sure?" she exclaimed. "Well, I am. I carried him inside me for nine months. I watched him and held him and fed him and took care of him for another nine months." She jabbed her finger at the phone's screen. "That is my baby!"

At that instant, the phone dinged again and a second message appeared. When the picture came up, it was of the little T-shirt their baby had been wearing when he was stolen. The label said Joshua Joseph Powers. Below the name was his birth date.

Joe's throat closed up. He could barely breathe, much less talk. Marcie had clapped a hand over her mouth and now sobbed loudly. The phone rang, startling Joe as it vibrated. Marcie stood close as he answered, so he held the phone slightly away from his ear so she could hear, too.

"So now do you believe me?" Howard's slimy voice slithered through the receiver.

"Where are you?" Joe demanded. "Is Rhoda with you? Where is my son? Because I know you're not at Rhoda's house."

"Now you listen to me. All you need to know is I've got your kid. And if you want him back it's going to cost you half a million in cash."

Marcie gasped at the man's words.

"Half a million? You're crazy," Joe croaked. "I don't have that kind of money. Not in my wildest dreams. I might be able to scrape together a hundred thousand. Be reasonable. You can do a lot with a hundred thousand dollars."

"Now Mr. Joe Powers, even if you ain't got that money yourself, you and I both know where you can get it easy enough." Howard coughed harshly on his end of the line. "But I'm a reasonable man, Joey. I know it takes time. I'll give you plenty of time—twenty-four hours. When I call you back you'd better be ready to do exactly what I say. And don't forget. If you talk to the police, little Joshy's fingers start coming off and your wife starts getting presents."

The line went dead.

Marcie moaned. As Joe hung up, she stepped away from him. "What did he mean, he knows where you can get the money?"

Joe shrugged and shook his head, still looking at his cell phone.

"Why would he think we could get that kind of money? I wonder what he's talking about?"

"I don't know. We can't worry about that. Come on. I want to get home and look at this photo on the computer screen. I want to study it—see if there's anything in the background that might tell us where he's holding Joshua."

On the drive home, both of them were silent. Joe pulled up to the curb in front of the house and got out. Marcie followed him inside, not even commenting when he unlocked the door with the key he'd never given back to her.

While he headed to the study to transfer the picture to the desktop computer, she went upstairs to wash her face and hands, still carrying the plastic building block. She set it on the edge of the sink while she splashed water on her face. After patting her face dry with a towel, she glanced into the mirror, the towel still pressed against her nose and mouth. Her eyes were red and swollen from crying, but they sparkled with hope. A thrill fluttered through her chest like a butterfly. They'd found Joshua. Her baby. Now all they needed to do was pay the man and bring their little boy home.

She tossed the towel toward the drying rack, picked up the block and walked across the hall to the nursery. She turned on the light. Just like every time she went into Joshua's room, her heart squeezed and her eyes and throat stung with tears. She did her best to not view the room through the eyes of a grieving mother. It was different this time. She had to make everything ready for Joshua's homecoming.

Right now, the room was furnished for an infant. The baby bed would have to be converted to a toddler's bed. The changing table would have to go, as well. She could get a small table and chairs like the one at Rhoda's house, and a blackboard. A poignant smile lit Marcie's face as she imagined Joshua sitting at the table while she taught him letters and words. Her baby had grown into a little boy and she'd missed it, but now they had found him. She set the block on the dresser, turning it so that the *J* faced outward.

Her mood slightly brighter, she headed downstairs. Joe was at the computer, and Joshua's face filled the screen. Marcie gasped in surprise when she saw it. "Oh, Joe. Look at him. What's he holding?"

Joe zoomed in on Joshua's hands, so close Marcie could see the date on the newspaper he held.

"It's today's! It's Joshua and he's okay! Joe!"

Joe clicked the mouse to zoom the photo outward until the full photo was visible.

"He's crying. Do you think they hurt him?" Marcie said, her voice breaking. She reached out as if to wipe the tears off his cheeks. "Zoom in. I want to look at his face."

"I'm trying to see what kind of place they're holding him in. But it's dark."

"Do you think they're making him stay in the dark?"

"No, hon," Joe said. "See? I misspoke. It's not really that dark, just a little too dim to see much of the room. You're positive that's Joshua?"

"What? Of course it is. Why would you ask?"

"It's been two years. I just need to be absolutely sure."

Marcie put her hand on his shoulder and squeezed. "Go back up to his eyes. Remember that tiny mole just above his right eyelid?"

"Tiny mole?"

She chuckled. "It's just above the fold of his right eyelid. See? Right there?"

Joe looked more closely. "That's a mole? I never noticed it."

"You're just his father. I'm his mother," she said teasingly, leaning down and pressing her cheek against his hair.

He sighed deeply in relief. He looked up at her. "It's Joshua."

"Our child is alive. He's healthy. I don't think he's crying there because he's hurt. I think he's angry— probably because he has to hold the paper." She pointed at the screen. "See the little wrinkle in his forehead? He always looks like that when he doesn't get what he wants. Such a deep little frown."

She smiled and went on. "The woman took good care of him, and now we're going to get him back. I'm not sure I've ever been so happy in my life." She took a long breath. "I can't wait to have him back."

"I know," Joe said. "Me, too. I wish I could have gotten a glimpse of him at Rhoda's house, but I did hear her talking to him. She does love him. And he called her Gramma. I think you're absolutely right. I think he's just fine."

Joe switched screens and pulled up the second photo that Howard had sent. It was a close-up of the label inside the neck of the tiny shirt Joshua had been wearing the day he was abducted. Joe studied it, then zoomed in and studied it some more. "It's blurred," he muttered.

Marcie leaned in and looked at it more closely. "Yes, but you can make out the letters, colors and pattern. It's one of the labels your mother had monogrammed for us when he was born."

"You sewed all those in his clothes?"

"Yes," she said. "You mean you never noticed?"

He was still studying the label. "I knew there were labels with his name on them, but I couldn't tell you what they looked like. You're a hundred percent positive?"

"Yes. The font, the color and my awful, uneven stitching. I still have some, if you want to compare."

He shook his head. "Nope." He leaned back in his chair and rubbed his eyes, then got up and started pacing.

"What's wrong?" Marcie asked. "Is it the money?"

"Of course it's the money," he said. "In fact, I need

to go to the bank and get it. I have no idea what I'm going to tell them."

"You don't have to tell them anything, do you? How much do we...do you have anyway? Do you really have a hundred thousand dollars?"

Joe gave her a searching look. "Marcie, *we* have a little over a hundred thousand, plus Joshua's trust that Kit set up, which we can't touch." He frowned. "I guess I could borrow another hundred K from her, with Joshua's trust as collateral."

"Oh," Marcie said as a thought occurred to her. Kit Powers, Joe's mother, was rolling in money. "Maybe that's why they thought you could get half a million dollars. Because you're her son."

Joe didn't answer her. He'd stopped pacing and was staring toward the window with a pained expression on his face.

"Joe? What is it?"

"Hmm?" His gaze met hers. "Oh. Nothing. I was just thinking about Joshua. About how much of his life we've missed." He held out his arms to her and she stepped into the circle of his embrace, sighing as he enveloped her in the warm strength of his arms.

"I know. He's a big boy now. I need to change his room. Convert the baby bed into a toddler bed, get him a table and chairs where we can work on his letters and numbers."

Joe's arms tightened. "Hey, you're not going to cry again are you?"

"It's just that I'm afraid that man will hurt him."

"Hey." Joe pulled away to look down at her. He

touched her cheek. "Rhoda's there. You saw from her house how well she was caring for him. She'll keep him safe."

"Promise me," she said. "Promise me we'll have our baby back here wi—" She stopped before the words *with us* could escape her lips.

Joe bent his head and placed his mouth near her ear, his warm breath playing over her cheek and jaw. "We're going to get him back, Marcie. I swear." He pressed his lips to her ear, then scattered small kisses across the line of her jaw, up her cheek and temple to her forehead and down her nose. He drew in a deep breath and touched the corner of her mouth with his lips.

She parted her lips and sighed and Joe kissed her. It was soft yet firm, not deep or sexual. It was a reassuring kiss, a comforting kiss, and it brought tears to Marcie's eyes.

"Our son is coming home," he whispered, then pulled her close and tightened his embrace.

She hugged him back. "Thank you, Joe," she said softly. "Thank you.

"You look worried," she said, laying her head against his shoulder. "Are you afraid we don't have enough money?"

"Not really," he replied, pressing his cheek against her hair. But then he let go of her and backed away. "But it's going to take a while to get it all together. So I'd better get going."

"What should I do?"

"Stay by the phone, just in case. I'll unforward it

from my phone. I sure don't want to be talking to him while I'm trying to withdraw every dime we have."

"But, Joe, I don't want to talk to him, either. What if I say something wrong?"

"Just follow your instincts. I don't think he'll call back until tomorrow, like he said. But if he does, you just yell and scream at him like I know you want to, okay?" He kissed her forehead. "You'll do fine."

Marcie watched him walk out to the car, then she glanced around her. The kitchen was clean. She'd vacuumed the whole house just a couple of days before. There was nothing else she could think of that needed to be done. On the hall table, just inside the front door, she saw the pile of newspapers that she'd tossed there. That's what she could do. She'd have a cup of coffee and see if she could catch up on the past few days' news. She doubted she could concentrate enough to get through all the newspapers, but she could at least glance through them. She picked them up and headed to the kitchen. Maybe they would keep her occupied until Joe got back.

Chapter Six

"Joshy!" Rhoda said sternly. "I know you're tired of hot dogs, but that's all we've got, other than cereal and an apple." Thanks to that idiot Howard, who had no idea what three-year-olds ate. "Want some cereal?"

"Ceweal!" Joshy said. "Gramma has ceweal!" He toddled over to where his bouncy ball had rolled to a stop and picked it up. He threw it with all his might. It sailed about four feet and bounced against the metal wall and came back toward him. He giggled and tried to catch it.

"Get over here then. I have to hold the bowl, because stupid Howard didn't give us a table. He was probably afraid I'd take one of the legs off and hit him over the head with it." She poured milk from the cooler over the oat rings.

"Oh, no. Tupid Howarr," Joshy said, running over to the cot where Rhoda was sitting. "Me hold it."

"No. I'll hold it. Now be a good boy and eat." She let Joshy pick up the spoon and feed himself while she held the bowl close to him in case he spilled. While she waited for him to finish, she looked around the small wooden building. She knew what this place was. Howard slept here when he spent several nights on Bayou Picou, fishing. She didn't know whom it belonged to, but she'd been there on a couple of rare fishing trips with him. It had dark shutters on the windows, a portable chemical toilet and a gas generator. The lights were on right now, but she knew he couldn't run the generator 24/7, so she wondered what his plans were. If he had any. Knowing him, he hadn't thought past getting her and Joshy away from her house and making sure there was nothing in this place she could use as a weapon or a means of breaking out.

Joshy was finished with his cereal. He leaned down and slurped at the bowl, then peered up at her. "Gramma, look. I'n a good boy."

Rhoda smiled and kissed him on the forehead. "Yes, you are. Are you done now?"

He nodded as milk rolled down his chin.

A loud banging echoed through the building. Joshy jumped and started crying. "It's okay, darling," Rhoda said. "It's just stupid Howard."

Rhoda set Joshy's bowl on the counter while she listened to Howard undo the padlock that kept the cabin locked. Joshy clung to her side.

"Rhoda!" Howard called. "Get away from the door. I ain't about to have you trying to attack me and getting out the door." The door swung slowly open, revealing Howard standing on the balls of his feet, apparently ready to rush her if she tried anything.

Rhoda laughed at him. "You're such an idiot, Howard. I'm not going to try anything that might put Joshy in danger. You'll screw up soon enough and Joshy and I will just walk right out of here."

"Rho, I need help," Howard said. "I've gotta figure out a foolproof way to get the money and get us out of here without getting caught and hopefully without getting anybody hurt."

"Right," she said. "Good luck with that. I hope you brought us some water. I couldn't find any. And what are you going to do about that generator? I know you can't leave it on all the time, but we're going to need light, and if there comes a late cool spell we'll need heat."

"Aw, woman, quit your bitching. I'm going to take care of everything. I'll turn the generator off at night when you two are tucked in, and I'll turn it on in the morning, about the time you get up. We're supposed to have a thermostat and timer for it, but there's a couple of folks who haven't ponied up the money yet."

"We're going to need more blankets then. Howard, why'd you have to bring us out here? What do you think I'm gonna do? Call the police? It wouldn't take them ten minutes to figure out who he is," she whispered.

"No, I don't think you'll call the police. I think you'll take that kid and run. And I don't want that, Rho." He sat down on the cot. "I told 'em half a mil, Rho. Half a million dollars. I told Powers if he didn't have that kind of money he knew where he could get it. I was talking about the Delanceys," he finished with a sheepish grin.

"And now you need me to plan how you're going to get the money? Well, forget it. I've never been so mad at anyone in my life than I am at you right now. And

I promise you first chance I get, I'm going to *K-I-L-L* you. Now get up. Joshy needs to go to sleep."

Howard stood with a grunt.

"Come on, Joshy," she called. "Let's get in the bed. Time for you to go to sleep."

"But, Gramma, it's light out. Play ball?" Joshy said, peering around Rhoda's back at Howard. "Howarr, you go."

Howard laughed. "Hey, Rho, the kid's a smart-a—"

"Don't talk like that around him," Rhoda interrupted. "If you want any help from me, you'd better get us better accommodations."

"Good grief, woman, what else could you ask for? There's electricity, food, bottled water to drink—"

"I need water to clean with," she insisted.

"I got you a five-gallon jug of water. It's sitting right outside the door. You can come and get it."

"What? You get it."

"Aw, hell, no. You're liable to run out. Heck no."

"Me and Joshy are going to get into bed and read picture books, since there's nothing else to do here. We'll sit on the cot while you bring the water in. Then you can go start making arrangements for a better place for us to stay."

"You've already got food and water. I got toys for the kid and books for you. What else do you want? A big-screen TV?"

Rhoda scowled at him. "It doesn't have to be big-screen. And how about a microwave, and some more fruit. Yogurt, a couple of those microwavable complete meals that don't have to be refrigerated. *Coffee* would be nice."

Howard gaped at her. "Anything else, your highness? If I get you some of that, you'll help me?"

"If you get me *some* of that, I won't be waiting for you with an iron bar from that cot across your thick skull next time you come here. If you get me *all* of it, I might decide to help you, depending on what your plans are on the off chance this stupid scheme works."

From behind her, on the cot, Joshy murmured, "Tupid Howarr."

MARCIE PACED FROM the foyer to the kitchen and back, over and over again. Every time she walked into the kitchen, her eyes went straight to the section of newspaper that she'd folded and laid on the counter and her anger ramped up another few notches.

She picked up the paper, skimmed the article again, although by now she could quote it word for word, then slapped it back down on the table.

When she'd first spotted Joe's photo splashed across a double column, she'd stared in disbelief and shock. Then she'd read the headline—Local Attorney's Connection with Delanceys Shocks New Orleans—and skimmed the short piece.

Joe? Her Joe was the illegitimate son of Con Delancey? For a moment, the words floated around in her brain like letters in alphabet soup and all she could do was wait for them to settle down. She felt the numb tingling of shock all the way to her fingertips, although why, she wasn't sure. His mother was Kit Powers, Con

Delancey's long-time mistress. It made perfect sense that they'd had a child together.

Other things made sense now, too, like what Howard had said to Joe about getting the money. *If you ain't got that money yourself, you and I both know where you can get it easy enough.* Joe's kidnapped son was a Delancey. Joe could go to the Delanceys for the money.

Or could he? Everyone knew how the Delanceys felt about family. But they, like everyone else in the New Orleans metropolitan area, had seen the paper by now. How were they reacting to the news that Con Delancey had a bastard son?

She found herself back in the foyer, looking through the sidelights at the street, dimly lit with street lamps. Where was he? She looked at her watch. Anger bloomed in her chest, squeezing the air from her lungs. He'd known all this and hadn't told her. But when? When had he known? Just yesterday? Had he read the article with as much shock and trepidation as she had? Or had his mother told him years ago? It didn't matter. In either case, he'd kept it from her.

But why? Embarrassment? Shame? Some misguided notion of protecting her or Joshua? Whatever the reason and no matter how angry she was, her heart ached for him. Through all the years they'd been together, he'd never talked about his dad. Whenever she'd tried to bring it up, he'd changed the subject or shut down. She'd always figured, given his mother's lifestyle, that he didn't know who his father was. That maybe even Kit didn't know. Marcie had always resented Kit for that reason.

But whether Joe had known for hours or years, he should have told her. She was his wife. They had a child together. If anyone in the world deserved to know the truth about his parentage, it was her.

She thought about what he'd said as he'd left earlier. What if he had gone to the Delanceys to ask for the money without even consulting her?

She stalked back into the kitchen, picked up the paper and ripped the article out of it. She heard Joe's car pull into the driveway. She clenched her fist, crushing the newsprint.

JOE UNLOCKED THE front door and stepped inside. "Marcie?" He looked down the hall toward the kitchen, but didn't see her. He glanced into the living room and past it into the dining room as he walked across the tile foyer and into the kitchen. Marcie was standing at the French doors, looking out into the darkness.

"Where have you been?" she asked without turning around.

"I told you, to try and put together the money Howard is demanding. I also went by the office to see if I could find a Howard that lives in Killian or the surrounding area."

"It's late."

"Not really," he said. "It's just a little after seven."

She didn't comment on the time. "So how much money did you manage to get?"

He looked at her rigid back and slightly lifted head. "Marcie? What's wrong? Has something happened?

Did Howard call back?" He started toward her, but she whirled to face him and held up a hand.

"Don't," she said. She held out her other hand, which held a wrinkled, torn piece of a newspaper.

The paper was crushed almost into a wad, but that didn't matter. He recognized it. It was the article. She'd found it. His stomach felt like it had sunk to his knees.

"Did you drive over to Chef Voleur?"

"What?" he asked automatically, still staring at the article. "Chef Voleur? Why—? Oh. No, Marcie, I—" He stopped at the look in her eyes. If they were lasers his head would be exploding right now.

"Really? You didn't go to the Delanceys and ask them for five hundred thousand dollars to pay a kidnapper for their grandson?"

"No, I didn't. I have no reason to go to the Delanceys for money."

Her glare didn't cool one degree. "No? Do you think I can't read, Joe? That I wouldn't see this? That I can't figure out what's happening here? This—" she waved the wrinkled piece of newsprint "—is why our son has been kidnapped. That man read this article and figured he could get money from the Delanceys."

Joe closed his eyes and shook his head. "I only found out a few days ago."

"Really?" she said acidly. "You're almost thirty years old and your mother never told you who your father was?"

"That's right," he said. "She came to see me on her way to her yoga class the other day. She told me that a police detective, Ethan Delancey, had come to see her.

Said he had something she needed to see. And she, in turn, thought I needed to see it. Big of her, right? After all this time? I never asked about my father. I figured she didn't know." He shrugged. "I…never cared."

Marcie stared at him. "Well, maybe you care now. Because it's obvious that the reason these people have suddenly decided to demand a ransom for the child they *stole* and kept for two years as their own, is because they now know he's a Delancey."

Joe nodded. He didn't have an answer for her.

"So why didn't you go to them for the money?"

Her question shocked him. "Why—? Marcie, why do you *think* I didn't go to them? This is not their problem. They have no reason to give me anything. The Delanceys never knew Joshua existed. Hell, they didn't know *I* existed."

Marcie's cheeks flushed with anger and she held up the article again. "They know now, don't you think?"

He nodded, not looking at her. He knew she had a right to be angry. But he wished she'd get over it and help him figure out what to do. He was angry, too, and frightened for their son. "You aren't seriously suggesting I go walking up to their door and say, 'Hi, I'm Joe Powers, your long-lost brother/uncle/whatever, and I need half a million in cash, thank you very much.'"

Marcie's face began to crumple. "That's exactly what you should do. My baby is out there, possibly cold and scared. I don't even know if anyone is with him. They're holding him hostage somewhere. He could be all alone. And if the only way I can ever see my son again is by crawling to the Delanceys and begging them for help, then I will do that."

"No, you won't!" Joe thundered. "They are *not* my family! I may happen to have been born because one of Con Delancey's feisty little swimmers made it upstream to my mother's—" He stopped. "I'm not a Delancey and I'm not going to go to them begging for money. I'll take care of my son myself."

Marcie folded her arms across her middle, a sure sign that she knew she was losing the argument. "They would give it to you," she said stubbornly.

"Do you have any concept of how many people contact a family like the Delanceys every year, claiming they're a long-lost relative? They'd have been broke long ago."

"But you really are," she said, still hugging herself, her eyes sunken and sad.

Joe started to speak, stopped, then started again. "It's not going to happen." His voice was flat and hard. He hated to talk to her like that, but she was headed down a dangerous path.

"How—how much money were you able to get?"

Joe looked down at his feet. "I took out all our savings and cashed out every asset I could convert to cash. Then I went to Kit."

Marcie moaned. Joe knew why. She didn't like the idea of being in debt to Joe's mother. She thought of Kit as a cold, calculating businesswoman who neglected and endangered her son by the lifestyle she led.

"Joe? How much?"

He put his hands in his pants pockets. "I managed to get a hundred and seventy thousand."

"Now? You have it now?"

He nodded.

"Surely that will be enough. Maybe we convince him that if we go to the Delanceys the media and everybody will know something's up. That photographers and reporters are all following you looking for a story. If he holds out for half a million, he might end up with nothing, or in prison."

"Yeah. That makes sense, but I'm not sure Howard would agree."

"What else can we do? Can we borrow against the house or take a second mortgage?"

"That might yield us another hundred thousand, but it wouldn't be enough. Not if he insists on half a million."

"This is such a nightmare. I thought these past two years—not knowing if Joshua was alive—were the worst thing I'd ever had to live with. But now, knowing his life is in the hands of a man who only cares about money?" Marcie pressed her knuckles to her lips. "I'm terrified I'm never going to see my baby again."

Chapter Seven

Neither Joe nor Marcie were very hungry, so Joe fixed an omelet that they picked over, then by ten-thirty they were both in bed, Marcie in the master bedroom and Joe in the nursery on the sofa bed.

It was still dark when he turned over and opened his eyes, disturbed by a sound. His first sleepy instinct was that it was Joshua crying, but immediately, he realized his mistake. Joshua wasn't here. He picked up his phone and hit a button, checking the time. It wasn't even midnight.

The sound came again. This time he recognized it. It was Marcie, crying, like she'd done so many nights after Joshua's disappearance. He could hear her clearly, because he'd left the nursery door open, hoping it would help the air to circulate and dissipate the scent of baby powder that made him dream of his son.

He lay there for a couple of minutes, listening to her heartbreaking, muffled sobs, thinking maybe she was asleep and just dreaming about Joshua, and any moment now she'd wake up or turn over. But the sobs went on and on.

He got up and tiptoed over to her door, which was ajar, just like it had been for the nine months after Joshua had been born. They'd had baby monitors and even a baby cam, but she'd still insisted that the door be left open, in case the power went out or something else untoward happened.

Standing at the open door, Joe saw the outline of her body in the faint light from the window. She seemed so small in the king-sized bed. But the curve of her hip stirred memories of nights filled with lovemaking and laughter and a deep, sweet love that he realized would last forever, even if *they* did not.

Her body shook slightly as she cried, her shoulders hunched and her face buried in a pillow.

"Marcie?" he whispered.

The sobbing stopped suddenly.

"Hon, are you okay?"

Her breath caught, then she sniffled. After a few seconds, she said, "I'm…f-fine."

"Right," he countered gently. "You sound fine. Want some water or something?"

"No."

"Something else to drink?"

"No."

He pushed the door open farther and stepped inside. "Want to talk?" he asked, doubting seriously that she'd take him up on that offer.

She didn't speak right away. He heard more sniffles, then she cleared her throat. "Maybe," she whispered, surprising him. "Do you want to…sit…on the bed?"

He sat down on top of the covers. He had on boxer

shorts and a T-shirt, as much or more than he'd ever worn in bed with her, so he didn't feel uncomfortable. Not totally anyhow. His eyes were dilated, so he could see her dim outline as she sat up and pushed a pillow behind her back. He reached out and caught her hand.

"Tell me what's wrong," he said.

"What's wrong?" she began harshly, then stopped herself. She pulled in a deep breath and let it out slowly. "It's just everything, Joe. Finding Joshua, losing him again. You. The money—you know. How impossible it's going to be to get enough to satisfy that man."

He heard the desperation in her voice and recognized it. Squeezing her hand in an attempt at comfort, he nodded, as much to himself as to her. He'd felt overwhelmed and desperate every second of the past two years.

"Did you find Howard?" she asked.

"What?"

"Howard. You said earlier that you'd looked up all the Howards in Killian? Did you find him? I mean, how many could there be? Hopefully only a few."

"Yeah, there were four," he said. "One is in his eighties. One in his twenties, and two who could be our Howard's age. Of those two, one is a teacher at the grade school. There was almost no information about the last one, Howard Lelievre."

"Le-leave?" Marcie said, trying out the name. "That's the man who has Joshua?"

"Lelievre. It's a Cajun name and it's sure not spelled like it sounds." He spelled it for her.

"Do you think we can call the police now? Now that we know who he is? Oh, my God, we can't," she said, answering her own question before Joe could. "He said he'd hurt Joshua."

"I'm sorry, hon," Joe said. "I wish there were a way to bring the police in to help us."

Marcie clutched at his arm. "We've got to do something, Joe. What about some kind of an anonymous message? You know like, 'I have information that Howard Lelievre, of Killian, Louisiana, may be holding a child that belongs to someone else.'"

"What are the police going to do with that? With no names and no proof that he has the child, it's hardly probable cause."

"Probable—? Could you stop with all the legal mumbo jumbo? I am so sick of hearing it. If the police got a message like that about a child, aren't they required to investigate? Maybe the message could say 'child that belongs to Joe and Marcie Powers.' What about that, Joe? Would that be probable cause?" Her voice had gotten shrill.

"Even if they didn't decide it was a hoax spurred by the newspaper article, I'm not sure they could do anything more than drive out to Rhoda's house and ask a few questions of neighbors." He sighed. "No. We've got to do this ourselves, and we're going to have to think like Howard thinks. What if the police do go out there looking for him? What do you think he'll do? What will he think?"

She was silent.

"I mean it, Marcie. You know the answer to that. What's Howard going to think?"

After a moment, she said sheepishly, "He's going to

think that we called the police. But if he calls us, we could tell him we didn't." She held up her hands. "I know. I know. Why would he believe us? But, Joe, we've got to do something. I'll die if that man hurts Joshua."

Her voice was even and soft, but he heard and recognized the desperation behind her words. The feeling seethed inside him, too. "I know, hon. I think I might die, too, if we can't get him back safe and sound."

Marcie turned toward him and he held out his arm, just as he had so many nights as they settled in to sleep. It was a little awkward since she was under the covers and he was on top of them. Still, she sank into his side, resting her head on the curve of his shoulder. "I'm sorry, Joe."

"Sorry?" he said. "What for?"

"I don't mean to take everything out on you. You've always taken care of everything. I guess I'm used to you being able to fix any problem."

"If there were anything I could do—"

"I know," she said, putting her hand on his chest and spreading her fingers. "I know you would."

He tightened his arm around her shoulders and pulled her closer. Her head lay in the hollow between his shoulder and arm. It fit there perfectly. He pressed his face into her sweetly scented hair.

"Joe?"

"Hmm," he responded quietly.

"Could you sleep in here tonight? I think I'll sleep better with you here."

"Sure," he said. "I'll lie down in the recliner."

"No. Please, stay here." She patted the covers be-

side her. "I'll feel better with you here. Safe. Even…
hopeful."

Joe sighed. He wanted to warn her not to be too hopeful. It was an endlessly torturous feeling, he knew. It
meant waking up suddenly in the middle of the night,
with a new idea about how to go about searching for
their son. It meant not being able to concentrate on work
or anything else, because his mind was occupied with
trying to remember one more detail about those critical few seconds while he was taking his credit card out
of his wallet instead of watching his son. But he didn't
want to destroy the only frayed thread holding Marcie
together. That last fragile ray of hope. He knew exactly
how fragile it was because it was all that held him together, too.

After slipping under the covers, Joe pulled a pillow
under his head. "Try to get some sleep, hon. We need
to be rested, in case something happens."

"Like what?" she asked, stiffening beside him.
"What do you think is going to happen?"

He leaned over and kissed her on the top of her head,
then turned his back to her. "All I'm saying is, that while
we can, we need to rest. So close your eyes, sleepy-
head."

For a few moments, all was silent. Joe was drifting
off when he felt Marcie's hand on his back. She ran her
fingers up his spine to the nape of his neck, then he felt
her lift her head and kiss him there.

"Marcie?" he said, half convinced he was dreaming.
When she answered, "Hmm?" in his ear, he realized

that she was actually kissing his neck and the curve of his shoulder.

"What are you doing?" he asked.

"Saying good-night," she murmured. "This feels good." Kiss. "Right." Kiss. "Familiar." She planted the third kiss on the center of his back between his shoulder blades.

He turned onto his back and Marcie slipped beneath his arm, but she didn't lay her head on his shoulder. Instead she bent and kissed him on the side of the head, near his ear.

For some reason, her advances scared him. "Marcie?" he said, taking hold of her shoulders and studying her. "Are you all right?"

"Of course I am. Why? Do you think I'm asleep?" She smiled at him. "I can guarantee I'm not."

"Then what is this?"

"I thought you'd be happy to make love with me—" She paused. "I'm…sorry."

"Hey," he said, tightening his arm around her. "I have always been happy to make love to you. I just don't want you thinking you have to, or—"

Marcie bent her head and kissed him on the mouth. When she was done, she looked down at him. "Did that feel like I *had* to?" she asked, a small smile playing around her mouth. "I want to feel good, Joe. I want to hold you and be held by you. I want what we used to have."

Joe pulled Marcie to him and turned them both so that he was above her, then he pressed kisses along her cheek and jaw and down the column of her neck. Then he kissed her mouth, delving deeply, kissing her like a lover, like the lovers they'd been and still were. He moaned deep in his throat when she pressed herself more tightly against him and wrapped her arms around him. Desire grew into arousal and blossomed between them as it always had, quickening their pulses and driving sad thoughts out of their heads.

Marcie wanted Joe with a poignant, quiet desire that had built inside of her during the months they'd been apart. She had missed him so much. When he sank into her, he filled her the way she had longed for him to. It was like becoming whole. She exhaled in an exquisite sigh of desire, then soared quickly to a climax that seemed to go on forever. Finally drained, she collapsed against the bedclothes.

Joe groaned and found his own release in one last long thrust. Then he lay carefully atop Marcie, his weight suspended on his elbows and knees. "Hey," he whispered. "You okay?"

To his relief, she nodded. "I'm good, Joe. Really good." She yawned and stretched and he took the opportunity to kiss the soft underside of her chin.

"Yes, you are," he said. "In fact, I might go so far as to say you're spectacular."

Then he heard a beautiful, welcome sound, one he hadn't heard in a long time: Marcie chuckling.

THE NEXT MORNING when Joe came downstairs, he heard Marcie in the kitchen and smelled the delicious scent of freshly made coffee. He figured she'd be pacing back and forth with her mug, sipping nervously, wondering when Howard was going to call. He knew exactly how she felt. He wasn't prone to pacing, like she was, but he had woken up as nervous as a cat, wondering just exactly when the phone call would come, and what demands Howard would make.

As he descended the last stair he saw a car pull up to the curb through the sidelight of the front door. He watched as a tall, lean man in a sport coat and slacks got out of the car and walked up to ring the doorbell. He didn't recognize the man, but there seemed to be something familiar about him. Joe was pretty sure who he was, and if he were right, this morning house call was not going to be pleasant.

He opened the door before the doorbell rang.

"Hi," the man said, holding out a badge in a leather case. "I'm NOPD Detective Ethan Delancey. You're Joseph Powers?"

"That's right," Joe said. He kept his voice even, but he couldn't help glancing past the detective, wondering if Howard were smart enough or organized enough to have someone watching the house.

Delancey's eyes narrowed and Joe knew the detective had seen him checking the street for other cars.

"I wonder if I could come in for a minute," he said. "I'd like to ask you a couple of questions."

"About what?" Joe asked, carefully keeping his voice and his expression neutral. He didn't know what Delancey wanted, but none of the possibilities he could think of were palatable to him. And none of them boded good news.

The detective showed his first glint of emotion. For

a split second, Joe saw a hint of vague discomfort pass across his expression. "I spoke with your mother the other day."

"I'm aware of that," Joe said, still politely neutral.

"Mr. Powers, I can assure you, this won't take long."

Joe sighed. It was obvious that if he didn't let Detective Delancey in, the two of them could stand there all day, being eternally polite and quietly obstinate. He stepped back just far enough to allow the detective to ease past him into the foyer.

As they crossed into the living room, Marcie came through the dining room door. "Hello," she said to the visitor as she wiped her hands on a dish towel. She glanced nervously at Joe.

"Marcie, this is Detective Delancey." Before Joe could go any further, Delancey spoke up.

"Mrs. Powers," he said, nodding. "I just have a matter to discuss with your husband. It shouldn't take long." His voice was polite but dismissive.

A frown wrinkled Marcie's brow as she looked at the detective, then at Joe. She paused, as if making up her mind about something. "Would you like some coffee?" she said sweetly.

"No, ma'am. I've had too much today already."

"Joe? Coffee?"

"I'll wait," Joe said. "We should be done here in a few minutes."

Marcie's frown deepened. "Don't forget—"

He waved a hand. "Don't worry. But if necessary, you go ahead and handle it."

She opened her mouth, then closed it again. After a

second, she nodded. "I'll be upstairs then." She turned on her heel and left. He heard her footsteps on the stairs.

Joe turned to Delancey and gestured vaguely toward the sofa.

Delancey propped on the edge of the cushion, his elbows on his knees. "I won't take up much of your time, Mr. Powers, but I wanted to follow up with you on the matter I mentioned to your mother."

"Yes?" Joe didn't plan to give the detective anything. He wondered if Delancey had been dispatched by the family to issue the official Delancey welcome to the bastard son. If that's what he was doing here, Joe wanted no part of it. He didn't care if the gesture was genuine or for show.

"I assume she told you what I told her."

When Joe didn't react to the question, Delancey went on. "My partner came upon the copy of your birth certificate while doing a warrant search of Senator Darby Sills's personal financial records in his home, office and safety deposit box. I have no idea why Sills had the copy. You've probably seen in the news that he had been blackmailing a couple of people for several years. My best guess is that he'd either tried or planned to try to blackmail my—Con Delancey, regarding your birth."

Joe nodded. That was what he'd figured, too. He glanced at his watch, then sent a quick glance toward the stairs. It was almost nine o'clock. Howard was going to call soon, and he didn't want Delancey here when that phone call came in. "I'm aware of everything you told my mother, Detective. Was there some specific reason you wanted to speak with me about it?"

"May I ask when you first knew that Con Delancey was your father?"

"I suppose you may," Joe countered as he decided it was time for the detective to leave. He stood. "I found out that your grandfather was my father when my mother came to see me at my office after she talked to you."

Delancey stood, too. "You hadn't known before that?"

Joe shook his head. "If you'll excuse me, Detective, my wife and I are expecting an important phone call, so—"

Ethan Delancey gave Joe a hard look, then walked around him through the foyer and opened the front door. "Mr. Powers, I know about your child, as well. I'm really sorry about your loss."

Grimacing, Joe spoke through gritted teeth. "Thank you," he said, taking hold of the inside knob of the front door, thereby feeling as though he were taking control of the situation. But something in the other man's manner made him feel as though he weren't as in control as he'd like to be.

"You've spent a good deal of time searching in police databases within the past few days, as well as having others searching on your behalf."

"How—?" Joe bit his tongue.

"How do I know?" Delancey replied. "Because I've spent some time searching for you."

"Searching for me?"

"That's right." The detective shrugged. "Call it curiosity. When I first saw your birth certificate, I pretended it didn't bother me that my grandfather had fathered a son that was almost the same age as me. Our birthdays are about a month apart. But I finally had to admit I wanted to know more about you. So I looked up information about you in our database. That's where I read about your child's abduction. Then I found that you actually have access to our database."

"Through my job," Joe said.

Delancey nodded. "So I had one of our computer techs trace what you've looked at, and found out that within the past few days you'd accessed records of four people with the first name Howard in and around Killian. You almost immediately zeroed in on Howard Lelievre. I backtracked from his records and found that his disability check goes to Rhoda Sumner. Turns out that her records were flagged, because a dispatcher in Baton Rouge had run a license plate that turned out to be hers."

Joe looked at his watch. "That's fascinating, Detective, but could you get to the point? Are you here to arrest me for unauthorized use of protected information? I'm an attorney and as I told you, I'm authorized through the NCMEC to access those types of records."

"Not planning to arrest you," Detective Delancey said. "I think I know why you've been looking up everything you can find on Howard and Rhoda. A little digging told me that she has a child that appears to be around two years old."

Joe felt his face drain of color, but he did his best to maintain a neutral expression.

"You think Rhoda's child is your son, don't you?"

There it was. The thing Joe had dreaded since Marcie had given him Rhoda's license plate number. He should have predicted that the person who caught him poking around in the police database for information would be a Delancey. He wiped his face wearily. "I don't think. I know."

"That's what the phone call is, isn't it? It's Howard and Rhoda. They want money."

Joe didn't answer. He studied Ethan for a long time. It wasn't hard to convince himself that there was a resemblance between the two of them. Did his connection with the Delanceys go more than skin-deep? He paced back and forth for a moment, as Ethan stood quietly, watching him.

Finally he decided he had no choice but to confirm what the man already knew. He didn't have a clue what Delancey would do with the information, but it would be difficult for him to make the situation any worse.

"He's going to call this morning. Probably in a few minutes. But, Detective, he'll hurt my son if he knows we've gone to the police. He told Marcie he'd cut off one of Joshua's fingers and send it to her. I can't take that chance. I can't involve the police in any way." He stopped. "I don't know if you can possibly understand—"

Delancey nodded. "Let me explain something quickly. My brother Travis came back to New Orleans recently and found out in a single day that he had a son and that his son had been abducted. My brothers and cousins worked together with Travis to bring his son home safely." He gave Joe a small smile. "You have some things to learn about the Delanceys. We're a very large and very close family. There's nothing I wouldn't do for a brother or a cousin or…an uncle."

The way he said *uncle* hit Joe square in the solar plexus. For the first time, it occurred to him that in terms of genealogy, he *was* Ethan's uncle. An odd sensation fluttered in his chest, but he didn't have the time or the inclination to examine it. Right now his focus was on his son. "What are you saying?" Joe asked.

"I'm saying, you're not involving the police. You're involving your family."

Joe stared at the detective. "You're a police detective. How can you act on your own, outside the protection of your badge and authority?"

The detective shrugged. "It's worked before. You tell me what you need and—"

At that instant Marcie stalked into the room. Joe hadn't heard her footsteps on the stairs. "What's going on here?" she demanded in a shrill voice. "You." She turned to Delancey. "You get out of my house. I don't know why you came, but unless you're placing us under arrest, you have no right to be here."

"That's right, Mrs. Powers," Delancey said. "I don't have a right to be here. My reason for coming was to introduce myself to your husband, who, as it turns out, is my uncle." He gave her an innocent smile.

"Marcie—" Joe began, seeing the growing anger in her expression.

"No," she said, waving a hand at Joe without taking her eyes off Delancey. "Please leave my house, right now."

Joe gritted his teeth. Marcie was right, of course. They couldn't take even the slightest chance that Howard would find out that the detective had been here.

"Certainly, Mrs. Powers," Delancey said, then turned to Joe. "May we exchange phone numbers? Just to be safe?"

They agreed, then Joe walked him to the door.

As he stepped over the threshold, Delancey spoke one more time. "Please call me if you need anything. Our family will help in any way we can."

Chapter Eight

Joe watched until the detective got into his car and drove away. Then he walked into the kitchen where Marcie was just pouring him a cup of coffee. She set the cup on the counter and folded her arms.

Joe picked it up and muttered, "Thanks," as he blew on it.

"That man's name was Delancey?"

Joe nodded. "Detective Ethan Delancey."

"What was he doing here?"

"He's the one who told Kit they'd found my birth certificate."

Marcie stared at him. "So did he come here to tell you about it?"

"No. He assumed I already knew."

"Well, then, why was he here? And why was he talking about doing anything he could to help us. Joe, you told me you didn't go to the Delanceys. If you didn't, then what was that detective doing here and how did he know we need help?"

"Hon, I'm not lying to you. He's been looking up information about me. Curiosity about the bastard son,

I guess. So he saw in the police database where I ran Rhoda's license plate and searched for Howard. He figured out what was going on."

"He figured it out on his own?" she said doubtfully. "Joe, he's going to ruin everything. If Howard finds out that the police are—" A sob tore from her throat and she pressed her knuckles against her teeth. "Oh, my God, he'll hurt my baby. I can't stand it."

Joe reached for her but she backed away. "Marcie, stop it. Stop acting like I'm the enemy here. Now come on, hon. Calm down." He held out his arms. "Come on."

But she stood her ground. After a few seconds, though, she got her breathing under control. She looked up at him with accusing eyes. "What's going to happen now? Are the police going to take over? What's going to happen to Joshua?"

"Listen to me," Joe said, approaching her slowly. He brushed a finger across her cheek where a tear was falling. "Be still and let me tell you what he told me, okay?"

Just as he saw her relax a little and opened his mouth to explain how Detective Ethan Delancey had figured out what was going on, the phone rang.

Joe glanced at Marcie, brows raised, but she shook her head violently. She didn't want to talk to Howard. So he picked up the portable handset. "Hello?"

"Hey, Joe, whaddaya know? How'd you sleep last night?"

Howard's harsh voice grated across his nerves like fingernails on a blackboard. If the man were in the same room, Joe would gladly punch him right in his big, ugly nose.

Marcie stepped up close, so he held the handset so she could hear. The sweet scent of her hair tickled his nose as she leaned in to listen. Turning his head slightly away, he concentrated on dealing with Howard.

"I slept fine, Mr. Lelievre," he said coolly. "How about you? Did you sleep well knowing you're endangering the life of a child and breaking federal law?" He took a deep, fortifying breath and continued before Howard had a chance to speak. "Now you listen to me. I want to talk to my son. I want to ask him who he's with and what his name is and if he's hurt or sad."

Beside him, Marcie made a small, distressed sound.

He went on. "I need proof of life *and* proof that he's not being mistreated before I say another word to you."

"Oh, no, Joe, ol' buddy. You don't call the shots. I do."

"Not this one. If you don't put Joshua on the phone right now, I will hang up and you will get nothing, because I'll know that you don't really have my son."

Marcie's fingernails dug into the flesh of his forearm. He'd told Marcie before that they had to maintain control of the conversation. He knew that was what the FBI taught in their training on dealing with hostage situations. He hoped he was right in this case. He knew that Rhoda was a wild card. Everything he'd seen told him that she had stolen Joshua because she wanted a baby. He doubted that she had agreed to this plan to get money—unless Howard had promised her that they would never turn over the child. That they'd take the money and run.

He held his breath as he waited for Howard to answer.

"You hang up and you'll never see your kid. Now how much money have you got? I hope it's enough."

"Proof of life, Howard. Right now or I'm hanging up. Five. Four. Three—"

"Hey, woman," Howard yelled away from the phone. "Bring the kid over here. Now!"

Joe's pulse sped up. He heard voices in the background.

"Oh, just shut up and do it," Howard groused.

Then Joe heard Rhoda. "Joshy? Come out here, honey."

Joshy. His son. His pulse kicked up so high that he thought he might faint from lack of oxygen. He could barely breathe. Beside him, Marcie's nails dug deeper. Her breaths were short and sharp.

Rhoda said something unintelligible, then Joe heard a small, sweet voice. "Hello? Who's 'is?"

Marcie's breath whooshed out in a combination of sob and sigh. A tightness that hurt like hell squeezed Joe's chest. It felt like the broken shards of his heart were rubbing together, trying to find a fit. *Please,* he prayed. *Please be Joshua.*

"Hi," he said, and his voice cracked. "What's your name?"

"I'n Joshy. I'n a big boy."

Marcie sobbed.

Joe had to swallow the lump in his throat before he could speak. "I'll bet you are. Who's there with you?"

"Gramma and—oh-no Howarr," the toddler said.

It sounded as if Joshy thought that oh-no Howarr was his name. Joe almost laughed. Oh-no Howarr was a good name for the bully. "So, Joshy, do you know where you are right now?"

"Gramma said it's his fishy place."

"Whose fishy place, Joshy?"

"Oh-no Howarr."

"Is the fishy place fun? What are you doing there?"

"No," the child said. "I wan' go home. Dere's no TV here and I hafta eat ceweal. I's oh-no Howarr's fault."

"Gimme that phone, kid!" Howard yelled. "That's enough."

Joshy squealed and Joe heard small footsteps on an echoing hardwood floor. "Gramma! Howarr mean!"

"No!" Marcie cried. "Wait! Joshua, please?"

Marcie's terrified voice shattered Joe's already broken heart. He held his finger to his lips and shook his head.

"Awright, Joe, that's it. You've got your proof. Now—what about the money?"

"Where do you want it?" Joe asked harshly. "Tell me where and when and I'll be there."

"Not hardly," Howard said.

Joe's lungs seized. He grimaced, willing the man not to say the words he knew were coming.

"You don't bring the money. Your pretty wife does. And she comes alone."

"No!" Joe thundered. Marcie tugged on his arm. He didn't want to look at her, didn't want to give her a chance to agree with a dangerous scheme that he wasn't about to allow.

"Yes!" she cried, trying to grab the phone from Joe. "I'll do it. Name the time and place. When? Just tell me and I'll be there."

Howard laughed and the phone went dead.

The sudden dial tone shocked them both into frozen silence. Marcie was leaning on Joe, one hand on his arm and the other around his wrist, as if she could wrestle the phone from him. She let go as if his skin were on fire.

Joe set the phone down and Marcie grabbed it. She hit the code to redial the last number, but nothing happened. She cried out in frustration and slammed the phone down on the table.

"You made him angry!" she accused Joe. "You made him angry and he hung up. What are we going to do now?" She swiped at the tears on her cheeks as if she were swatting flies. But they kept falling. "Oh, dear God, we don't know anything. Why did he hang up?"

Joe picked up the handset and put it back on its cradle. "He thinks he's taken back the upper hand."

"He has," she retorted.

Joe didn't say anything. He picked up his mug, rinsed it, then ran cold water into it and took a long drink.

"Hasn't he?"

"No," he said, turning around. "Look at him. What's he dealing with? A kid that needs feeding, entertaining, maybe medication if he has a cold or an ear infection. And that's all."

Marcie glared at Joe in irritation. How could he be so rational? So smart? He was right, of course. Howard was sitting there with a toddler and no money. "He's going to have to call back," she said.

"Got it in one," Joe responded with a small smile.

No, she thought. You got it in one. You had to feed it to me. "But," she said as a thought occurred to her, "what's going to stop him from ignoring us and calling the Delanceys?" She gasped. "What if he's called them already? What if that's why that detective was here? To see if we'd heard from him? Howard could be playing us both."

"No. Ethan Delancey would have told me if they'd gotten a call. No, if Howard's not a complete idiot, he won't call the Delanceys as long as he thinks we might have gotten money from them. Besides, I never told him how much money I had. I just said we'd bring it to him."

"You've got it all figured out," Marcie said in awe, which earned her a suspicious glance until he apparently decided she wasn't being sarcastic.

"Not really," he said. "I'm playing the odds. If Howard is dumber or, God forbid, a lot smarter than he seems, I could be wrong. But based on the training I got on how to work with abductors, even though he's the one who hung up on us, he'll call back, because he hasn't gotten what he wants yet."

Marcie felt as though she were teetering on the edge of a cliff. She took a shaky breath and wiped her face with both hands, then shoved her fingers into her hair, pushing it back away from her face. "I don't know if I can just sit here until he does call back."

"We can forward the phone to my cell again and

go somewhere. You want to get some breakfast?" He glanced at his watch. "Or lunch?"

She shook her head. "I don't think I can eat," she said. "I'm going to switch from coffee to iced tea. Can I fix you a grilled cheese sandwich or some eggs?"

He sent her a look that she couldn't decipher. "You know I love your grilled cheese," he said. "Thanks."

Such a polite answer to her polite question. How did she and Joe go from midnight lovers to these sometimes hostile, sometimes carefully polite daytime enemies, she wondered. It was as if they were a real-life Psyche and Cupid. At night he came to her as her beautiful, sexy bridegroom, but during the day the lover disappeared almost as completely as Cupid had, and in the lover's place was this…this cold, rational attorney.

She got out three kinds of cheese and a loaf of sourdough bread and made him a grilled cheese sandwich, then retrieved the pitcher of sweetened iced tea from the refrigerator and poured them each a glass. Just about the time Joe had finished his sandwich and was drinking the last of his tea, the phone rang again.

Joe picked it up. He and Marcie stood, heads together as they listened.

"All right," Howard said. "Lemme talk to your pretty wife."

"She's here, standing right next to me."

"H-hello?" Marcie said.

"What's your name, woman? Marcella?"

"Marcie."

"Okay, *Marcie.* You listen close, because I ain't saying this but once. Old Joe found his way to Rhoda's house. He can show you how to get there. Once you're there at Rhoda's, I'll call you and tell you what to do next. You got that?"

Marcie looked at Joe, who nodded. "Yes. Yes, I've got it, but—"

"Joe, ol' buddy? You still there?"

"Yes," Joe said.

"You better stay home, if you know what's good for you and her and the kid. If you show up anywhere close I'll shoot you dead. I won't be shooting at yer feet or over your head like Rhoda likes to do. You got that?"

Marcie saw Joe's jaw tic. "Yes," he said gruffly.

"You sure?"

"I said yes."

"Okay. Miz Marcie, I need your cell phone. You and me, we're gonna handle this ourselves. Joe's out of it, you *capisce?* I'll call you, and when I do, I ain't gonna leave no message. Understand?"

"I've got it."

"Good. Now get this. You've got one hour and fifteen minutes to get to Rhoda's, once I hang up."

"Hang on," Joe said. "That's not enough time."

"It's gonna have to be, 'cause it's all you've got."

Joe shot Marcie a glance. "We need time to fill up the car."

"Aw, really? Well, in that case…" Howard said mockingly. "*What* did I tell you?" he yelled. "There ain't no *we,* Joe, ol' buddy, 'cause you ain't coming. Marcie? You'd better get going if you want to see the kid."

The line went dead.

Marcie looked at Joe, who stood there, the handset

clenched in his fist, his face stony. The muscle in his jaw quivered.

"Joe?"

He cut his gaze over at her. "I'm going with you."

"Oh, no, you're not," Marcie said firmly, fixing him with her sternest glare. "Did you not hear him? He will *shoot* you. If you don't believe him, I do, and I'll be damned if you're going to get yourself killed and not be here for Joshua and me."

He stared at her for a moment, as if she'd suddenly lapsed into an unknown language, then he blinked and looked down at the phone in his hand. He turned to put it into its cradle. When he turned back, his expression was harsh. "You listen to me. I'm not going to let you go out there by yourself. I'll be close by. So close that all you have to do is hit speed-dial one and I'll be there within two minutes. Understand?"

"You can't do that without him seeing you," she objected. "No. You can't, Joe. Listen to me. It's too dangerous."

"*You're* talking to *me* about dangerous?" He touched her cheek. "You are *not* doing this alone. I'll be close by. Call me. *Do you understand?*"

"Yes," she said, feeling the color drain from her face. "Don't you dare get yourself killed, Joe Powers. Don't you dare!"

Chapter Nine

Marcie ran upstairs to get a blanket and a coat to throw in the car just in case. When Marcie didn't come right back down, Joe went upstairs to check on her. She was standing in the hallway, a worried expression on her face. She had on jeans and was carrying her purse, a blanket and a coat.

"Got everything?" he asked.

"I don't know," she said, looking up at him. "I can't seem to get my thoughts together."

He gave her a little smile and held out his arms, not knowing whether she would be grateful or resentful that he wanted to comfort her. But she stepped forward and he pulled her into his embrace. "Do exactly what he says and remember, I'll be close." He lifted her chin with his finger. "Very close."

"What are you going to do?"

"Don't worry about that. You just concentrate on giving Howard the money and getting Joshua."

Her lip trembled at the mention of their son's name. She nodded.

Joe kissed her forehead, then handed her the satchel with the money in it. "Tell me which way you're going."

"We've been over that," she said.

"I know. Just tell me one more time, so we're both sure. My car needs gas, so I'm going to leave now and catch up with you on the road. You might not see me, but I'll be right behind you."

"Should I call you after he calls me?"

"No," he said quickly. "No. Don't call me. If Howard takes your phone away, he'll see that you called me and he'll assume you're telling me where you are. We can't take that chance. You just do what Howard tells you, and I'll keep up. I promise you I will."

She nodded, looking doubtful.

"Did you get that toy block you got from that house?"

"No. I forgot," she said, then gave him a small smile. "Thanks for reminding me. I know you think it's silly."

"I don't think it's silly at all. It's a connection to our child. Okay, then, you'd better grab that block. I've got to run. Marcie?" He looked into her eyes. She looked so frightened and so hopeful that it broke his heart. "Be careful." He turned to head down the stairs.

"Joe?"

He turned back.

"We will get him, won't we?"

He nodded and stepped close to her. He put his palms on both of her cheeks and kissed her lightly on the lips. "I swear to you we will." Then he turned and vaulted down the stairs. If his plan were going to work, he had only a couple of minutes to get ready.

WHEN ETHAN LEFT the Powerses' home, he didn't go far. He parked a block down the street, where he could watch the house without being seen. His cop's instincts and experience told him that he wouldn't have to wait long.

He thought about Joe Powers. From the moment his partner had shown him Joe's birth certificate, Ethan had felt a connection with the man who had been born within a month of Ethan himself. He figured he probably ought to be resentful of his grandfather for having a son and a grandson the same age. Instead, Ethan had been curious about Joe Powers, and now that curiosity was turned toward Powers's missing son.

Powers's front door opened and Joe emerged. He got into his car and drove away. That surprised Ethan. He'd figured the kidnapper would want Marcie to make the exchange. He debated following Joe, but the attorney hadn't looked as though he were headed for a ransom drop. He'd had nothing with him but his car keys. So Ethan continued to wait. Sure enough, within about one minute, Joe came walking through a neighbor's yard. After checking carefully to be sure no one was watching, he climbed into the trunk of the older vehicle.

Now *that* was interesting. Ethan perked up. He'd been right about the phone call. The exchange was this morning, and as he'd figured, the kidnapper had insisted that Marcie come alone to make the exchange. Joe had been warned not to go. Ethan understood Joe's need to be there to protect his wife and make sure the kidnapper hadn't harmed his son. It's what Ethan would have done. But those two facts didn't make Joe's plan any smarter or safer.

Ethan didn't have to wait five minutes before Marcie came out carrying a large purse and a large, obviously heavy tote. She passed by the trunk and opened the back right door and put the tote on the seat. Then she tossed her purse into the passenger seat. *Money.* The tote held money. There was a boxy shape to it that suggested stacks of bills. Ethan's heart raced. She was on her way to meet the kidnapper and, unbeknownst to her, her husband was hiding in the car's trunk, in the hopes of protecting her. Although Ethan understood Joe's motive, he couldn't even begin to fathom what Joe planned to do once Marcie got to the meeting place. He knew that climbing out of a car's trunk was a cumbersome process and he was dreadfully certain that if Joe tried to come to his wife's defense, he'd be dead or injured before he managed to get his feet on the ground.

That did it. Ethan had to follow them. Since he knew about the ransom call, he had an obligation to keep Marcie and Joe safe. As he pulled out behind her car, allowing enough room that she wouldn't notice that he was following her, his brain continued to process what he'd seen. They were going to need someone on their side to protect them against the kidnapper. He knew that it was possible to successfully exchange money for a kidnapped child or adult, but he had no idea what the percentages were. He certainly had no idea what the outcomes were when a family handled the exchange alone, without the help of the FBI or the police. All he knew was that he didn't want these new members of his family to be hurt or—worse—killed, because he didn't do his best to protect them.

Ethan dropped back a couple more car lengths from Marcie, which put him several blocks behind. He doubted seriously that she would notice him, but the kidnapper would be watching for a tail. And Ethan didn't want to be so close that the kidnapper could make him as a tail.

Before they even got as far as Kenner, Ethan's phone rang. He glanced at the dashboard, where the caller information was displayed on his car's Bluetooth. It was Dixon Lloyd, his partner.

"What's up, Dix. You know I took the day off, right?"

Dixon got straight to the point. "Our suspect in the household murder case just took a woman hostage," he said crisply.

"What?" Ethan wiped his face. "Damn it! Where?"

"Mercedes Boulevard."

"In Algiers? Listen, Dix, can you handle this by yourself? I'm—"

"No," Dixon said. "Even if I wanted to let you slide, the captain's demanding to know where you are. Said he didn't approve a day off."

Ethan muttered a few colorful words. "I left a message for him. He didn't call me back to tell me to come in."

"I'm just quoting him. He wants, and I quote, 'Delancey's butt out there at that house talking to that maniac *now!*'"

Ethan exited the interstate. "All right, I'm turning around. Where are you?"

"On my way there."

"Give me the address," he said.

Dixon recited it and Ethan tucked it into his memory. "Got it. I'm probably fifteen minutes away."

"Yeah, I'll be there in about nine minutes."

"See you," Ethan said, then punched the off button savagely, and cursed. He was abandoning Joe and Marcie, and he couldn't dispatch another officer in his stead. There would be too many questions. And talk about a blowup. If the captain found out that Ethan was planning to help with a kidnapping without reporting it first, he'd take possession of Ethan's badge by grabbing it through his butt.

He was still arguing with himself about whether he should reveal the kidnapping, when he got to the address Dixon had given him. Police cruisers and plain cars surrounded a pretty yellow house with blue shutters in the quiet neighborhood of Algiers. Two black vans were parked on the other side of the street and at least seven black-clad SWAT officers had rifles trained on the house.

Dixon saw him and waved him over.

"What's going on?" Ethan asked him in a whisper.

Dixon pointed to his phone. "Got him talking," he whispered, then turned his attention back to the phone. "No," he said patiently. "I've already told you, there's no way you're getting free passage out of here. Not a car and for damn sure not a plane. You're going to—" He winced and held the phone away from his ear and Ethan could hear a voice ranting and raving through the speaker.

"Sounds like you're doing great," he said to Dixon. "Why the hell did I have to bust my butt getting out here?"

Dixon raised his brow, shifted his gaze behind Ethan, then back as he continued talking to the killer who'd taken the woman hostage. "No, Donald, I haven't hung up on you and yes, I'm taking your demands *very* seriously," he said, just as the captain walked up next to Ethan.

"What the hell took you so long to get here, Delancey?"

BY THE TIME Marcie reached the road to Rhoda's house, it had started to rain. She turned on the windshield wipers and shivered, both from the damp chill in the air and from worry. She was already late. The rain was just going to make everything worse. The dirt-and-shell roads that wound through the swamps of south Louisiana could turn to gumbo within minutes in a rainstorm. Marcie had seen truck and ATV tires get so coated with the sticky stuff that their wheels would no longer turn.

Her phone rang, startling her. "Oh, no," she muttered. It was Howard. If he were watching the house, he knew she hadn't made it on time. She answered, her heart in her throat.

"Hey, Marcie," Howard said. "Where are you?"

She didn't want to lie, in case he could see her. "I'm close to Rhoda's house. I should be there in a few minutes."

"That means you're late. Well, I ain't got time to wait. Here's your instructions. Pay attention. You keep going on that same road until you come to a fork. There's a sign in the middle of the two roads. One side says Bayou DeChez. The other side don't say nothing. You take the fork without the sign. It's starting to rain, so watch your wheels. Don't run off the shoulder, else you'll get stuck. And trust me, woman, there ain't nobody gonna pull you out if you're that dumb. Keep going 'til you see a house on stilts. It's got a rusty metal roof and a blue door. You wait there."

"Wait?" Marcie cried, her heart sinking to her toes. "Why do I have to wait? How long? Will Joshua be there—?"

"Woman," Howard interrupted, "I told you, you don't get to ask questions. You better listen to me or you'll never get to see your kid. Now, you wait at that house and don't even think about going anywhere. I'll call you. Think you can handle that?"

Wait. She swallowed against the lump in her throat. "Yes," she said hoarsely. She knew that Joe was probably right and Howard was just a big coward and a bully who wanted people to pay attention to him. He liked running the show, so she needed to play up to him, because as far as her child was concerned, he *was* running the show.

The faint thread of hope that had kept her going for the past two years began to grow and strengthen. This was finally happening. If she did what Howard wanted her to, she would see Joshua soon. "Yes. I can handle it. When are you going to call back?"

Howard laughed. It was a gritty, ugly sound. "You

ask another question and this'll be the last time you ever hear my voice. Do you understand that?"

"Yes," she mumbled as despair warred with impatience inside her. "Yes. I understand," she said more loudly.

"It's started raining, so it'll get dark early. Don't slip off the road, 'cause if you get stuck in that swamp mud, it ain't going to be pretty. There a lot of gators."

"What if—?" Marcie cut off the question a split second before he hung up. She looked at her watch. It was almost two-thirty. His warnings ramped up the fear inside her to near panic. She was driving into the swamp alone in the rain in a car that didn't have four-wheel drive, carrying a bagful of cash and depending on the integrity of a man who was holding a two-year-old child for ransom.

She kept driving on down the road past Rhoda's house. The rain wasn't coming down hard, but that wasn't good news. It was one of those slow, steady rains that could last for days. The farther she drove, the longer the road in front of her seemed to stretch. The rain was creating a haze that hovered over the swamp on either side of the narrow road.

Finally, she came to the fork in the road. She had to park and get out to read the letters on the sign. Sure enough, the right-hand sign, block-printed with what looked like a Sharpie, was weathered and missing letters, but it was readable. BAYO_ DECHE_. The other sign might have had words on it at one time, but there was nothing recognizable there now.

Marcie got back into the car and took the left fork.

Her tires crunched on the broken oyster and mussel shells the highway department used in these parts to replace gravel on the narrow road. Just past the fork, she noticed a pile of broken electrical poles and wires on the side of the road.

Apprehension lodged in her chest. Obviously, they'd had electricity along this road at one time. But one of the hurricanes must have taken down the poles and nobody had ever replaced it. Thank God she'd brought a battery flashlight plus an emergency crank one.

Her tires slipped on the road that was getting muddier with every passing minute, and she crept along at a glacial speed. She prayed that it would stop raining and that no one else would try to drive out this way this afternoon. The road couldn't be more than fifteen feet wide and it dropped down at least a foot off each shoulder into murky water. She'd driven on some narrow roads in Louisiana, but never one this narrow. She had no idea what she would do if she met another vehicle. If the wheel of her car ever dropped off that edge, she'd be stuck.

Finally, she saw something dark looming over the right side of the road. The stilt house, maybe. She couldn't make out anything specific until she got much closer. When the structure began to take on shape and a little color, she saw how shabby it looked. There didn't appear to be anything underneath or behind it except murky swamp water. No boat and certainly no car, since there was obviously nowhere to pull off the road. The cabin itself was a crooked, wobbly thing that looked like it had been blown down during Katrina and set back upright by a careless, gigantic hand.

As she approached the house, Marcie carefully applied the brakes, but the tires slipped and the front of the car drifted slowly to the left. She compensated by turning the steering wheel, but it made no difference at all. A soft bump and the sudden dip in the front of the car told her that at least one wheel, possibly two, had gone over the shoulder. The car eased forward another inch, then stopped.

Marcie's throat was tight, her heart beating so hard and fast that she felt as though she couldn't breathe. She was frozen in place, afraid to move, worried that even the slightest shift of her body weight might send the car farther off the road until it nosedived into the muddy swamp.

For a long while she sat there, waiting to see if the car was going to slip any more. Finally, she decided that it either was or wasn't, but she would probably never know unless she moved. And she sure couldn't sit there all night…could she?

Marcie moved carefully, an inch or two at a time. Each time she moved an arm or leg, she stopped and held her breath, waiting to see if the car moved. She managed to slide out of the driver's seat and onto the center console without the car moving.

Now, all she had to do was get into the backseat and open the door and get out. She figured the hardest part was over, getting out from under the steering wheel and maneuvering over the gearshift on the console. She went into the backseat headfirst, rolling a bit so that she landed on her back. When she did, she felt an ominous shudder underneath her. The car was sliding.

Marcie froze, holding her breath until the steel frame quit moving. She took several deep breaths, then held her breath again, staying perfectly still. From what she could tell, the car seemed to have stabilized. So she eased the rear driver's side door open and climbed out. By the time she was standing on the muddy road, her legs felt like they were about to collapse and her whole body tingled from the adrenaline coursing through her veins. She looked up and down the road as far as she could see in the steady drizzle, which wasn't far, more than half afraid that Howard was watching, waiting to spring out and grab the money from her.

After squinting and staring in each direction, making sure she didn't detect any movement, she retrieved her purse from the passenger seat, then got the tote and the blanket from the backseat. Then she closed the doors as carefully as she could. But even for all her care, the car's frame groaned again.

She jumped backward. The vehicle gave another shudder, then slowly the front end dipped another several inches, placing the driver's side rear door right over a mud hole.

She stood there watching the back of the car for a few moments, fully expecting it to disappear, but it didn't move again. Looking up and down the muddy road, she crossed to the other side, walking as carefully as she could to avoid the deeper puddles. By the time she made it across the street and onto the narrow, rickety pier that led to the stairs, the soles of her tennis shoes were caked with sticky mud. She scraped the soles against the pier's rough wood until she'd gotten rid of most of it.

The stairs were wobbly, but much sturdier than the pier, although the soles of her shoes remained slippery. The weathered planks creaked in protest as she climbed, but nothing broke and she finally made it onto the small stoop. She'd estimated the height of the stilts with her eyes when she'd driven up. They looked to be about four feet above the level of the road. But now, looking down, it seemed as though the dark water was much farther below her. She carefully backed away from the edge of the porch and toward the door, almost tripping over a bucket that was about half-filled with rainwater. She shoved it out of the way with the toe of her shoe.

Her thoughts turned to Howard again. What if he were inside, waiting for her? What if he planned to ambush her inside the house, take the money and run? What if he didn't have Joshua and never intended to give her baby back to her. Marcie shivered and wiped rain out of her eyes. One thing was for certain—it was much too late to worry about whether Howard was inside the stilt house now. She was going inside because she had nowhere else to go.

When she pushed the door open and stepped inside, her hand automatically shot out to the right, patting the wall for a light switch, but there wasn't one. Her pulse began to race in the classic flight-or-fight adrenaline reaction. But still, she had to keep going. Otherwise she'd be out in the rain and probably catch hypothermia.

She remembered the pile of broken poles and wires

on the side of the road. Using the anemic sunlight that crept in through the open door, she examined the interior. It was a single room with two windows, one to the left of the door and a second directly across from it on the back wall.

Simple, thick curtains were pulled shut, shielding enough light that it would be almost impossible to see if she closed the door. She started toward the back window to open it, and something brushed across her face. With a little cry, she swiped at it, imagining a huge spider web or a bat. But her fingers touched a cool, small chain hanging from the ceiling. It felt like the type of ball chain that was used on lightbulbs and lamps.

She grabbed it and pulled, expecting nothing except a dry clicking sound. But a low-wattage lightbulb on the ceiling flared, surprising her. How could there be electricity? Then, just as the question formed in her mind, she heard the low growl of a gas-powered generator starting up. Relief made her jaw ache, although she hadn't realized she'd been clenching it.

The bulb was dim, but it helped a little as she surveyed the room. To her profound relief, it was empty. There was no one else here. Also, the little house felt much tighter and more secure from the inside than it had looked from the outside. Even so, she decided she would stay toward the middle of the room and not press her luck. While she was relatively sure that the one hundred and twenty-five—okay, thirty—pounds on her five-foot-eight-inch frame wouldn't tip the building over, she wasn't going to take any chances.

She did tiptoe over to the back window long enough

to push the curtains aside. What greeted her was a pane of streaked, dusty glass, through which she could see the pale pink beginnings of sunset seeping through the rain clouds and shadowed by cypress trees draped in Spanish moss. In the dimming light, the trees looked like ghostly figures with tattered shawls.

The swamps of Lakes Pontchartrain and Maurepas were beautiful in a rugged, primitive way. The water, dark as mud, stretched out as far as the horizon, its vastness blocked only by clusters of cypress or tupelo trees and marsh grass. As she watched, a white heron flapped its wings then rose from the murky water and flew above the treetops, stirring a flock of seagulls that followed him. Their calls harmonized with the low groans and squeals of alligators as they splashed water while climbing onto a fallen log to sun, or slid back into the water after prey.

As beautiful and primitively elegant as the swamp was, the idea that sunset was not that far away made Marcie pull the curtains closed again. When it got dark, she didn't want anything out there looking in at her.

She swung the tote and her purse off her shoulder and set them on the floor near the door. Arching her shoulder and neck, she wondered just how much the hundred and seventy thousand dollars in twenties and hundreds weighed. From the furrow the heavy tote had made in her shoulder and the ache in her arms from hauling it up the stairs, she'd say forty pounds. Her purse was heavy, too, with the extra things she'd thrown in—the two flashlights, a couple bottles of water, a small package of toiletries and several protein bars. She looked at the bars ruefully. They weren't really appropriate for Joshua. As she was throwing things into her purse, it had hit her that everything she had was for a nine-month-old and Joshua was almost two and a half now. But surely, he could eat a protein bar.

Setting down the heavy bag, she fished the flashlight out and began exploring the small cabin. The walls were covered with what looked like canvas—or maybe burlap—that had been given one coat of white paint. The effect was spotty and oddly interesting, with an abstract pattern of light and dark that played over the walls like strange graffiti.

On the south wall, barely visible in pink light from the back window, was a counter on which sat an old-fashioned bowl and pitcher. Marcie lifted the pitcher. It was full of fresh water. There was no refrigerator or icebox, no cabinets and no food. Good thing she'd brought the protein bars.

She turned toward the other side of the room, the north side, directing the flashlight's beam into the shadows. The first thing she saw was a metal folding cot, its squatty legs about twelve inches off the floor. On it was a threadbare blanket, rolled up. Pushed up against the wall behind it was a small space heater. She studied it briefly, thinking that it looked about as dangerous as any electrical appliance she'd ever seen.

The heater coils on the front were exposed. The three metal safety guards were broken. It was plugged into an extension cord that ran across the floor, up the wall and out through the back window.

This corner was where she was supposed to sleep?

She glanced toward the front door, thinking she'd rather sleep in her car with the blanket over her and the doors locked, than to be in here alone, sleeping essentially on the floor with nothing but that ragged, moth-eaten piece of wool touching her.

Looking back at the space heater and thinking that it was certainly thoughtful of Howard to provide warmth on this rainy day, she noticed a smaller, darker cube next to it with a cord that was plugged into the same extension cord. Walking over and crouching down, she shone the flashlight and saw that it was a radio of some kind, probably a walkie-talkie.

She picked it up. There was a small green light on its top. Her hand jerked and she almost dropped it. It was on. Did that mean someone—Howard—had been here? Did it mean he was listening to her right now?

Marcie wiped her hands down her jeans as if she'd touched something dirty. She had no idea what the range of the walkie-talkies was, or precisely how to operate them. Still staring at it, she thought back over the past few minutes. Had she said anything out loud? Anything Howard could use against her? She didn't think so.

Standing, she turned on her heel and did her best to pretend that the walkie-talkie wasn't on and that there was no one on the other end of it. Still, she shuddered. Nothing about her exploration of the cabin had made her feel any better about where she was or how long she was going to be forced to stay. Howard hadn't even hinted at when he would contact her. All he'd told her was to wait in the cabin.

He—or someone—had obviously left the water

and the cot and blanket for her because she would be here overnight. The meanness of his threats contrasted sharply with the thoughtfulness of the comfort items he'd provided. Marcie wondered if the latter were Rhoda's idea, and how she'd managed to convince Howard to provide them.

Well, if Marcie was going to have to be here overnight, it wasn't going to be on that cot, covered by that moth-eaten rag folded on top of it. Thank goodness she'd brought in her clean, fresh blanket. She could cover up with it, although she had little hope of sleeping a wink in this rickety cabin that only had one way in or out through a flimsy, hollow door.

Marcie wiped her face and did her best not to give in to the tears that were hovering just behind her eyes. Now that she was here alone in this grubby little hovel in this awful swamp that had practically devoured her car, it was getting harder and harder to believe that all this was going to lead her to her little boy. It felt like a wild-goose chase. All the horror stories she'd ever heard about kidnappings gone wrong swirled in her mind.

Despite her determination, her eyes stung and filled with tears. The tears spilled over her eyelids and ran down her cheeks. She knew what she needed. She needed Joe. If she could hear his low, reassuring voice pointing out all the odds that were in their favor, she'd calm down.

Then what he'd told her came rushing back to her memory. He'd promised her that he'd be close by, that all she had to do was call and he'd come to her rescue. But if that were true, why hadn't he rushed to her aid when the car slid into the swamp? Had he watched and decided that she wasn't in danger? Or had he been worried that Howard might be close by and didn't want to expose himself?

She wanted to call him, even though he'd told her not to. She knew it was a precaution to keep Howard from thinking she'd passed along her location. But she was terrified that if she didn't talk to him, she was going to have a full-blown panic attack. She hadn't had one of those since those first weeks after Joshua was taken, but she could feel the telltale symptoms starting. She could already feel her heart rate increasing.

She dug her phone out of her pocket and entered speed-dial one. Her fingers tightened around the phone as she heard the first ring. But it cut off in the middle. Pulling the phone away from her ear, she looked at the display. *No service.*

"No!" she cried. She shook the phone, as if that would help, then punched speed-dial one again. "Hello?" she cried into the speaker. "Hello!" Louder this time. "Joe? Hello? Please?" But the phone was dead. No sound. No service.

She held the phone high, then low, walked over to the back window and along the back wall, but no matter what she tried—checking voice mail, dialing a number, sending a text, even trying to access her email—it still indicated no service. Growling in frustration, she suppressed a sudden desire to fling the device at the wall. But, before she gave up, she wanted to try the phone outside in the open air. So she stepped outside onto the little stoop and tried her phone again. Still nothing. She looked around. Was she crazy to think that if she walked a few yards up or down the road, or got out from under the canopy of cypress branches, she might have more luck?

She started down the stairs, holding on to the rickety rail with one hand while continuing to check the phone with the other. Halfway down, she stopped, too frustrated and deflated to continue. Of course there was no cell service. Otherwise, why would Howard have left a walkie-talkie set up and charged and ready to use in the house?

She and Joe should have known that. What a stupid, dangerous game they were playing. They never should have bought in to Howard's threats. Never should have talked to him on their own. It was a mistake not to go to the police. No matter how many times she'd cried wolf in the past about seeing Joshua, the police were obligated to respond to a kidnapping or a child abduction. They'd have to help them. It was their job.

Marcie looked down at her car, submerged halfway up its front wheels. She had no idea where Joe was, if he'd managed to follow her at all. There was nothing she could do except wait. She thought for a moment about abandoning the money and heading back the way she'd come on foot. Eventually she'd find Joe or someone else.

But it was still raining, and the pink glow that had filtered through the clouds from the west was fading to a deep purple. It would be dark in no time. She had the flashlights, but how much good would they do if the rain increased. It terrified her to think that she might misstep and fall into the murky waters of the Maurepas swamp.

Feeling as old as Methuselah, she stood and climbed slowly back up the stairs. As she reached for the doorknob, a banshee's screech wailed from inside the shack.

Chapter Ten

Marcie let out a startled shriek a split second before her brain identified the screeching as the walkie-talkie. She approached the device with a level of dread and horror worthy of encountering an alien. When she picked it up, static made it vibrate in her hand.

"Marcie?" a scratchy, staticky voice said. It was Howard. It had to be.

She cleared her throat, took a deep breath and, trying to sound strong and confident, said, "H-Howard?" She grimaced. Her voice was as tentative and squeaky as a terrified little girl's.

"So you made it." Howard's slimy voice oozed through the speaker.

Marcie shuddered with dread. "Where…are you?"

He laughed. "You'll know soon enough. Point is, I know exactly where you are and what you've been doing."

Marcie glanced up and shone her flashlight into the corners and along the roofline. Did he have some kind of cameras set up? Was he watching her now? She didn't care, didn't have time to worry about his scare tactics. She wanted Joshua.

"Where do we meet?" she demanded, her voice more authoritative now. "And how soon? I want to get my child and get out of here."

"Now you know you can't do that, Marcie. Not with your car like it is."

"You know— Where are you? Is Joshua with you?" Marcie's anger ignited like the fuse on a stick of dynamite. "I have your damned money. Give me my baby!" She stalked over to the door and looked out. "Where. Are. You?"

"You sure are bossy, considering." He laughed.

"Just tell me where he is. That's all I want to know."

"Don't you worry. Rhoda's taking good care of him. She's all smitten with him for some strange reason. Poopy diapers and runny nose and all."

"Howard!" Marcie growled through clenched teeth. "I want my child—now."

"Soon enough. Soon enough. First, I'm going to have some fun."

Terror flashed through her like a lightning bolt, sending tingling fear all the way to her fingers and toes. "Fun?" she repeated weakly.

He didn't answer. Marcie looked out the door again, and saw an old, dirty green pickup approaching from the same direction she'd come from.

"Howard?"

"There you are," Howard said. He stuck an arm out the window and waved at her. "Wave back. Say hi."

The truck was loud. She couldn't believe she hadn't

heard it, but there it was, lumbering up the muddy road, with Howard at the wheel. He waved again, then honked his horn. The earsplitting sound made her nearly jump out of her skin.

Then it hit her. The truck. The exchange. Maybe he had Joshua! She ran out the door and started down the stairs, her terror forgotten. She could deal with whatever Howard had planned for her, as long as she got her little boy back.

Her foot slipped on a step and she almost fell, but she caught herself on the flimsy rail. Suddenly out of breath, she stopped and regrouped. She had to be careful. She had to stay safe and sound for her baby. Before she got halfway down the stairs, the horn honked again. She stopped and looked over the rail. Howard gunned the engine and he rammed the pickup into the rear fender of her car. The car's back end twisted until it was almost perpendicular to the road. As she watched, stunned, he backed up, shifted gears with a metallic groan, then rammed her car again. The impact didn't do much damage to the bumper, but it forced the car a little farther off the road. From Marcie's vantage point it looked as though it would nosedive into the swampy water any second.

She shook herself. *Joshua!* What if he was in the truck? Was he safe? Was he in a safety seat? Dear God, what if he wasn't? He could be hurt by the collisions.

"Joshua!" she cried. "Howard! Where's Joshua?" She rushed down the stairs, trying to see inside the truck, but couldn't see anyone else. "Howard! Do you have Joshua?"

But Howard was gunning the engine and didn't hear her. She remembered she was still holding the walkie-talkie, so she pressed the button.

"Where's Joshua?" she cried. "Where is my son?" She ran down a few more steps, just as her car groaned and moved slowly forward. Howard gunned the truck's engine again.

"No, wait!" she cried, reaching the bottom step and running across the pier to the road.

The truck's gears ground loudly as Howard shifted into first. Marcie was almost across the road when he pulled forward, spraying mud. She kept running as he eased past her car without so much as tapping the fender and sped up. She was parallel with the passenger door, but still an arm's length away, when he passed her.

"Hey, Marcie!" Howard yelled into the walkie-talkie and waved out the window at her again. She stopped pumping her arms and legs and struggled to breathe as she whispered to herself over and over again, "He doesn't have Joshua. He doesn't have him. Rhoda wouldn't let him take the child without her." She swallowed. "He doesn't have him."

She stood in the middle of the muddy road, her chest heaving with its efforts to get enough oxygen as the truck headed deeper into the bayou, away from civilization. As he disappeared from view, Howard waved one last time.

She watched the truck's tail until it disappeared around a bend and the sound of its motor faded. He would come back. She knew it. But the minutes passed, the sun went down and the sky began to darken, and all she heard were the calls of birds as they settled down, the occasional moan of an alligator and the whispers of the evening breeze rustling the leaves.

As dusk stole color from the world and turned everything gray, she turned around and trudged back to the house. She looked at her car. Now the car was facing the opposite direction and the wheels were totally submerged in the murky water. She couldn't see the right front tire at all.

She'd already decided that there was no way of getting the car back on the road, but now, after watching Howard ram it again and again, and knowing that he could have stopped the truck at any moment and confronted her, panic crawled up the back of her throat. Maybe she hadn't abandoned all hope of getting her car back on the road. But now, she knew it was hopeless. She was stuck in this death trap of a cabin, on this deserted road, stranded and helpless. The promise that Joe had made to her, that he would be close by in case anything happened, was fading as fast as her belief that she would ever see her child again.

It was truly dark now, and the relaxing, tranquil sounds of the swamp during the day were turning ominous. The quiet groans of the alligators now echoed through the darkness like moaning ghosts. The bird calls that were interesting and beautiful during the daytime now sounded predatory.

Marcie wasn't sure she had the strength to climb back up the stairs to the house. She finally made it, though. When she slammed the door, she examined it for a lock. There was a laughably ineffective push lock in the knob. She tested it to see if it worked. It did, but Marcie knew that even she, as tired as she was, could kick it in with scarcely any effort.

She looked down at herself. She was soaked and the bottoms of her jeans and her tennis shoes were covered with mud. To her surprise, she still held the walkie-talkie in her hand and the little green light was still on. She was tempted to press the talk button and vent all her fear and frustration and anger at Howard by screaming and cursing at him. But all that would do was make her sick, and if Howard was anywhere near Joshua, he'd hear her. She didn't want that to be his first introduction to her. She put the walkie-talkie back on its charger and stood there staring at it, not really thinking of anything, for a long time.

Wet droplets drizzling down her back and numbness in her toes reminded her that she was wet and getting colder by the moment. If she were going to be able to rest at all, she had to dry off somehow. She hadn't brought a change of clothes, because she hadn't thought about being stranded or caught in the rain.

After taking off the mud-caked shoes, she stripped off her wet jeans and set them aside. With all the rain, the bucket that was sitting on the stoop might be three-quarters full by now. She went outside, shivering in her wet wool peacoat and underwear, and quickly rinsed out the jeans and cleaned as much mud as she could off her tennis shoes. It was no longer raining, although at this point that didn't mean much. The road was impassible, her car was out of commission and she was already soaked.

Back inside, she tested the space heater to see if it
worked. It did. She twisted the knob until it clicked
twice. Sure enough, the wires began to turn orange
and she heard a fan kick on, blowing warm air her way.
Turning the cot onto its side, she used it as a drying
rack, hanging her coat and jeans on it and setting her
tennis shoes in front of it. For a moment, she stood in
front of the heater, shivering as the warm air drifted
across her chilled skin. She chafed her arms and held
out one foot and then the other to the heat, until her toes
began to tingle as the numbness faded.

Looking at the pink wool blanket she'd brought with
her, she considered whether she had the nerve to strip
completely. She was already barefoot, with nothing
on her lower half but her panties. If anyone—and by
anyone she meant Howard—forced their way into the
house, she'd hardly be any more vulnerable wrapped
in a blanket than she was right now. She still had nothing to use as a weapon.

Weapon. "Oh, my God," she whispered. She'd completely forgotten that after Joe had moved out, she'd
bought a small can of pepper spray to keep in her purse,
for those times when she came home late at night. Or
when being alone in that big house, without him or
Joshua, made her feel exposed and helpless. She went
over to her purse and dug down in it until her fingers
closed around the cylindrical shape of the pepper spray.
Pulling it out, she examined it with the flashlight. It was
a narrow spray can about four inches long. The spray
button was on the top and it had a wristband for easy
carrying. She slipped it over her wrist. At least now she

wasn't totally helpless. If Howard tried to attack or hurt her, an eyeful of the spray might stop him.

Letting the spray can dangle by her wrist, she grabbed a protein bar and one of the water bottles she'd stowed in her purse, and sat over by the space heater. Then she peeled off her damp sweater and her silk undershirt and draped them over the upturned cot.

Soon she was warm and cozy in her pink wool blanket and sitting in front of the fire. She drank half the water in one long swallow, then chewed a couple of bites of the protein bar. It wasn't the tastiest supper she'd ever had by a long shot, but she could feel the bar hit her stomach and figured that by morning she'd be glad she'd eaten it.

By the time she finished, she could barely keep her eyes open and her muscles and joints were aching. At least her feet had finally warmed up. Not wanting to take down her makeshift drying rack, she left the cot where it was and lay down on the floor. She eyed the ratty wool blanket that had been provided for her, but immediately rejected it.

She dragged her purse and the tote bag full of money over near her, and then wrapped up in the blanket like a mummy, using her purse for a pillow. She closed her tired eyes, but after a few minutes, she had to give up. She couldn't go to sleep. Her mind was racing too fast. The events of the past few days ran amok in her head.

Joe, looking irritated and grim when he'd opened the door of his apartment to her—had that been a few days ago? The detective standing next to Joe in their living room, both of them acting as if they had no idea how much they looked alike. The little wooden table and chairs in Rhoda's house, and the small blackboard with the name *Joshy* written on it. The blue-and-white plastic block she'd picked up, with the *J* in red on one side and an image of a little boy on the other. Her child, her little Joshua, with his wide dark eyes and the little widow's peak in the center of his forehead, in the child seat in the back of the Nissan.

Sighing, she turned over and scooted just a little closer to the heater, then closed her eyes again. She started singing "Danny Boy" in her head, her usual lullaby that worked better than anything else to help her fall asleep. But soon, her back, facing away from the heater, was getting chilly. She wondered if it would hurt to turn the thermostat up to high. Maybe she'd do that. She pulled her knees up to her chest and stuck her hands inside the folds of the blanket. After a while, if she were still cold. She shrugged her shoulders and tried to relax, then tucked her chin into the blanket and began humming "Danny Boy" again.

She heard a noise.

She didn't realize she'd been asleep until she jerked awake. What was that? She lifted her head and felt the heater on her face.

She heard it again. It sounded like someone—or something—was scratching around the foot of the stairs. *Howard!* Her pulse hammered in her temples. She grabbed her cell phone and started punching in 911 before she remembered that there was no service out here. Still, she looked at the display optimistically.

It still said *no service*. She tried speed-dial one, tried texting, even tried 911 again. But nothing happened.

In a few seconds, she heard the noise a third time. It was fainter, as if the creature making it were moving away. Or had realized they were making noise and were trying to be quiet. No animal would do that, would they? She could almost hear Joe's rational voice in her head. *Sure, if they were being chased by a predator.*

Somehow she didn't think the creature down there would be classified as prey. As soon as that thought crossed her mind, she deliberately dismissed it.

And surely it wasn't Howard. Why would he bother to sneak? He hadn't been cautious this afternoon. No, he would probably walk right up the stairs, clomping in heavy shoes on every step, and push the door in, because that tiny lock on the doorknob wouldn't keep out a raccoon, much less a man who looked like he topped two hundred pounds easily. With that thought in her head, she began imagining that the scratching and rustling were actually the creaking of the stairs as someone crept up them.

As quietly as she could, she pushed herself to her feet and reached for her undershirt and sweater. She pulled them over her head, breathing as carefully and steadily as she could so she could keep listening. She slipped on her tennis shoes and her coat, leaving the jeans, because they'd be much too hard to put on, especially quietly.

Still aware of the rustling and scratching, she moved silently around the cabin, watching the display on her phone. She wasn't even sure why she was still trying. It was obviously a waste of time. Still, what did it hurt? Maybe somewhere, in an awkward corner or arm's length out a window, she might conceivably pick up one bar and manage to dial 911, or Joe. Staring at the display, she wandered close to the door and once again stood still, barely breathing. Listening.

Had the noise stopped? She didn't hear it anymore. Maybe whatever it was had given up and gone away. Holding her breath, she stood like a statue. She heard what sounded like the click of claws on wood, getting fainter with each second that passed. She forced a small, quiet laugh. It probably *was* a raccoon. Luckily it hadn't climbed the stairs and somehow pushed the door open using its little prehensile fingers. She'd have probably fainted.

After another minute of waiting and listening, Marcie still didn't hear anything. She should go back to bed and try to sleep as much as possible, or she would be exhausted in the morning. But she was too hyper now. There was no way she could get to sleep.

She looked at her phone. It was ridiculous that she couldn't pick up a signal somewhere. She was worried about Joe. About what had happened that kept him from showing up. He'd told her he'd be there within minutes, if she called him. Maybe he was just far back enough toward town that he could pick up a signal on his phone and therefore he didn't realize that she couldn't. Maybe he was still waiting for her to call.

Hadn't he told her once that phone signals might be stronger at night than during the day? Or was that radio signals? She couldn't remember, but if he were out there waiting for her call, she had to try and see if she could find at least one bar. It made sense that there might be a better chance at night, didn't it? There probably were fewer phone calls being made, fewer internet connections being used.

She started to unlock the door but she paused, thinking of the noise she'd heard. "Come on, Marcie," she whispered to herself. She hadn't been afraid of the swamp in the daytime. There shouldn't be anything to fear at night. It was the same swamp with the same wildlife. And all she wanted to do was step out onto the stoop and check her phone. It wasn't as if she were going down the stairs.

She took a deep breath, then turned the lock and stepped out onto the porch, a little surprised at how dark it was. The moon wasn't up yet and although the sky was clear and the stars were bright, the cypress trees and Spanish moss draped the bayou with shadows. The night was quiet, nothing but rainwater dripping and the breeze stirring the leaves. Was it a sleepy, all-the-animals-are-happy silence? She didn't think so. It seemed to her that the air was laden with caution, as if the wildlife were holding their breaths.

Marcie glanced at the phone's display. Still no signal. With a frustrated sigh and a stinging of her eyelids, she stuck the phone into the pocket of her coat. Maybe she'd go back inside and wrestle on her jeans, then go down to the pier, or maybe all the way to the road, and check the phone again. As she felt behind her for the doorknob, she heard the same rustling sound.

She froze. Her first thought was Howard. Shock burned through her nerve endings as her body tensed.

Was she scaring herself? After all, the stairs creaked whenever a slight breeze stirred. Nothing could climb up here without making a lot more noise than she'd heard.

Still, she put her finger on the pepper spray can button, then whirled, prepared to drench whatever was behind her. But before she'd stopped spinning, powerful arms grabbed her and shoved her against the rough board wall of the cabin.

Chapter Eleven

With a yelp, Marcie tried to throw herself sideways, hoping her momentum didn't send her plummeting over the railing or down the stairs. She managed to hit the button on the pepper spray can, but the shot of spray was deflected by the shadowy figure's arm. He clamped an ironlike hand over her mouth. She gasped and tried to scream, but the hand was too strong. Tried to bite him but her lips were pressed too tightly against her teeth.

"No!" she tried to cry. Nothing but a muffled groan came from her throat. *No!* He would not overpower her. She'd throw herself over the rail first. She struggled with all her strength, pushing, kicking, trying to bite. She sucked in air to try one more time to scream and caught a whiff of a familiar scent. A pleasant, poignant mixture of soap, citrus and clean cotton. At the same time she heard a low voice urging her to stop struggling. The combination stopped her cold.

Joe? Her fingertips tingled even as her limbs went limp with relief.

"Marcie," he whispered urgently. "Stop wiggling. You're going to send us right over the edge."

She gasped again, but the only noise she made through his hand was a mumble.

"Shh! Marcie. It's Joe."

"Mm-mmmph," she groaned, which sounded nothing like *I know*.

Joe pulled her inside and kicked the door closed. "Are you going to be quiet?" he muttered.

"Mmm-hmm, mmm mmm," she said. *Of course I am*. She nodded again.

He let go of her and took his hand away from her mouth.

"Joe? Wh-what are you—?" she cried, her hand over her heart. "You scared me almost totally to death!"

"Sorry," he muttered. "Are you okay?"

She licked her lips and tasted blood. "Ow." When she touched her finger to the sore place, it came away red. "I bit my lip."

"Yeah," he said. "Trying to bite me."

"What are you doing here—?" But before she finished speaking the full realization of what it meant to have Joe right here, right in front of her, hit her and she flung herself into his arms. "Oh, my God, oh, my God, Joe! You're here!" She wrapped her arms around his waist and hugged him as tightly as she could.

"Please, don't let this be a dream," she said as her eyes filled with tears and her voice turned thick with emotion.

"Hey," he said, pulling her tightly into his embrace. "It's no dream. I'm here. I'm right here."

For a moment, she just held on to him and relished the feel of his strong arms around her. She buried her nose in his shirt, seeking that little hollow just under his collarbone. He smelled so good. Like soap and clean shirts. Like Joe.

Then reality pushed its way into the middle of her joy and relief. "Joe, no! You can't be here. You have to leave. Howard said he'd— If he finds out you're here, he'll hurt Joshua. We can't—" She tried to swallow around a sudden lump in her throat. "We can't let him cut our baby's finger off. You've got to get out of here!"

"Hey, shh." Joe held on to her, wrapping his arms around her and holding her so close she could feel his heart beating. "It's going to be okay."

"Wait! Wait a minute." She lifted her head and felt cool air on her cheeks. She realized they were wet with tears. "We've been so stupid. We can't stay here and wait for that horrible man. We've got to get out of here and call the police. I don't care what they said about me. They have to help us. It's their job, right? They've got to. We can't do this on our own. Joe, I'm so scared."

"I know," he whispered, his voice muffled because he was pressing his nose into her hair. "I'm scared, too." His embrace tightened and she heard him take a shaky breath.

"What's the matter?" she asked, peering at him in the darkness.

She felt his spine go rigid.

"Joe? What is it?"

"We can't leave, Marcie."

"What do you mean? Why not? Where did you park your car?"

He let go of her and his gaze met hers. His expression was grim. "I don't have a car. I hid in your trunk."

"You hid—?" She laughed uneasily. "In the trunk of my car? I can't believe I didn't know you were in there."

He nodded. "Hah. There could be cats fighting in the trunk and you wouldn't open it. I knew I'd be safe there."

"I don't like trying to open the trunk with an armload of stuff. It's much easier to throw the bags in the backseat." She smiled at him. "I can't believe you're here."

"I wasn't going to let you come out here alone, no matter what Howard said."

"You said you had to get gas. That you'd catch up with me."

He shrugged, then winced. "I'm sorry for not telling you the truth. I considered following you in the other car, but I decided that would be too obvious. Howard would be sure to spot it. I doubt many strangers drive out this far."

"I couldn't believe I was on a road. It's so narrow. I was afraid the car was going to go over the edge any second. And then it did."

"So I figured the only thing I could do was hide in the trunk and wait until it got dark to get out." He rubbed his shoulder. "I didn't expect to be rammed by a truck."

"Oh, Joe. You were in the trunk when Howard rammed the car. Are you all right?"

"A little sore from being knocked around, but nothing serious. There's actually a lot of buffer in your bumper."

"That's good to know," she said wryly. "How did you do it? I didn't see your car when I left the house."

"I put it into the garage and closed the door manually."

She couldn't decide if she was more thrilled to see him, or more angry that he hadn't told her what he was going to do. "But why didn't you tell me? You didn't have to ride in the trunk the whole way. We could have stopped along the way to let you get into the car."

Joe shook his head. "Nope. I didn't want to put that kind of pressure on you. If you knew I was in the trunk and Howard confronted you or started asking you questions, I didn't want you to have to lie to him. If you didn't know I was there, you wouldn't have to worry about anything but the truth as you knew it."

Marcie looked at her husband, the man she'd accused of not caring for their son as much as she did. The man she'd resented for moving on with his life, instead of wallowing in the loss of the child they'd made together. She'd never thought of him as particularly courageous, never really thought about that at all. He was just a man, a man she'd fallen in love with. A man who had been scarred by an unstable childhood and a mother who was most kindly described as a stripper. But now, looking at him with his hair tousled and his shirt wrinkled, she thought she was beginning to see the kind of man he really was.

She doubted he'd ever forgive her for the things she'd said to him when she was hurting so badly that nothing he or anyone did could ease her grief and pain. He'd put up with more from her than any husband, much less a husband who had lost a child, should have to.

Every time she'd gone to him with a crazy story of having seen Joshua, he'd supported her. Even this last time. And he hadn't done it to placate her, she knew, but because, even after she'd cried wolf so many times, he still believed she might have actually seen Joshua.

If—no, when—they got Joshua back, what then? Joe wouldn't come back to her, she was sure about that. She'd destroyed any hope that he could look past the way she'd treated him. But he'd be there for his son. She didn't doubt that for one instant. Maybe not every day, but he'd be there.

Of all the things she didn't know about her husband, she did know one thing for sure. He loved his son more than anything in the world. He would do anything, even sacrifice his life, for their son. Maybe someday, far enough in the future that the wounds she'd inflicted on him had healed, he would be willing to try again to be a family. To be three once more.

Joe watched Marcie, becoming more worried about her by the second. She'd been staring at nothing for several moments. "Hon? Are you okay?" he asked. Was she angry at him for lying to her?

"What?" Marcie blinked several times then looked at him. "I can't believe you did that. It was a brave thing to do. And—" she took a breath "—you could have been hurt really badly if Howard had rammed the car any harder."

"So Howard drove by, banged into the car a few times to be sure you couldn't drive it, then just drove away? Did he talk to you at all? Did he give you any information about the swap?"

"No," she said. "When I saw his pickup, the only thing I could think about was Joshua. At first I was sure Howard had him with him, that he was there to make the exchange. But then he rammed into the car, and all I could think about was that Joshua might be in that truck. I was terrified. Was he in there, not in a child seat? Was Howard just letting my baby bounce around in there? I ran down there, but he just took off, spraying mud everywhere."

"I could hear you yelling, and I figured the other voice I heard was Howard's, but I couldn't make out what you were saying. So he didn't give you any information about when we could make the swap?"

She crossed her arms. "He never got out of the pickup, and I'm glad he didn't. He's awfully creepy." She shivered. "Oh, Joe, I've been so scared."

"I know, hon," he said. He held out his arms for her. He expected her to hesitate but she didn't. She stepped right into his embrace. As he pulled her close and breathed in the familiar scent of her hair, he asked himself what kind of idiot had he been to leave her? He should have had enough patience, enough love in him, to stay with her through the worst of her grief. Instead, he'd told himself that she was better off without him. That she'd heal faster without him around to remind her that *he* had let their child be stolen.

He'd been so wrong. He'd convinced himself that he'd done it for her. That moving out and going to work for NCMEC were for her. Now he knew better. He'd been running away.

And now, if he couldn't get their little boy back, he'd be a coward and a failure. Even if they got Joshua back, Marcie would never trust him around their son again. Not that she'd refuse to let him see him. She wasn't cruel. But trust—no. It would take more than a lifetime to earn her trust again.

He pressed his nose into her sweet-smelling hair and tried to blink away the stinging behind his eyes.

"What do we do now?" she asked.

He took a deep breath, then lifted his head. "I think we try to sleep. It's been a very long day and tomorrow is going to be longer. You need to try to get some sleep." He glanced around and saw the cot upturned with her clothes on it. Then he set her away from him and looked her up and down. "I take it your clothes got wet? That's why you have no pants on?"

She looked down at herself. "Oh. I forgot." She shivered and glanced at the cot. "I doubt my jeans are dry yet. Can you believe this place has electricity—and a heater? Howard has provided us with all the comforts of home."

"I can't believe it hasn't burned down. That heater is dangerous. The safety guard is gone. I'm not so sure it's a good idea to leave it on."

Marcie shivered. "But it's getting colder," she said. "What do you think the temperature is outside? Like thirty?"

Joe laughed. "No. More like fifty. Maybe a little lower."

"Really? I'm freezing."

"I'm going to get the clothes off the cot so you can sleep on it. I'll lie beside you. Then if Howard or an alligator shows up, I'll be between you and the door."

"An alligator? Really?" A tiny smile lit her face and his heart began to pound. Her smile was so beautiful.

Shrugging, he smiled back at her. Then she surprised him by hugging him again.

"Thank you for hiding in the trunk," she whispered.

"No problem," he said, still trying to keep it light. He figured she'd push away from him any minute now. That was probably a good thing because holding her was becoming one of his favorite things—again. But she didn't. Instead, her arms tightened around his waist, sending a surge of desire through him that was both pleasant and painful. He gritted his teeth, trying to quell the inevitable reaction of his body. It worked—kind of.

Finally, she stirred and stepped backward. Joe let her go.

"I'm not sure why they have electricity anyhow. There's only one light—one bulb—and that space heater. Nothing else. Not a coffeepot or a toaster or anything."

"This is obviously a fishing camp. Maybe they bring that stuff with them."

Just then there was a buzzing, then a click that sounded like it came from the generator outside. The heater clicked, too, then the coils began to fade to black.

Marcie gasped and clutched his arm. "Somebody cut off the generator," she said, worried. "Do you think it's Howard?"

"No," he said, stepping over to the window.

"But what if it *is* him?"

Joe parted the curtains slightly and looked down. "Nobody out there. I think it sounded like a timer, cutting off. Looks like that's all the warmth we're going to get tonight. Let's get you tucked into that cot before the little bit of heat we've got totally dissipates."

"I don't think sleeping in that cot off the floor is going to be very warm. What if we both slept on the floor?"

He glanced at her but she wasn't looking directly at him.

"Would that work?" she asked. "Could we keep warm if we snuggled together?"

Joe didn't even have to think about it. He'd be warm all right. Too warm. And with his wife's exquisitely sexy body pressed tightly against him, he wouldn't sleep a wink.

JOE HAD MANAGED to maneuver so that Marcie was spooned against his back, but the fact that his front wasn't pressed against her hadn't made as much difference as he'd hoped it would. Maybe his arousal wasn't pressed up against her, but her breasts were against his back and her upper thighs were pressed against his butt. He found it as hard to get to sleep lying like this as he'd figured it would be facing the other direction.

Finally he'd started to drift off, only to hear Marcie's quiet murmur close to his ears.

"Joe? What's going to happen tomorrow?"

"Hmm?" he said, still half-asleep.

"Tomorrow. What are we going to do? Hand over the money and hope that Howard keeps his word?"

"I don't see how we can do anything else. We came here in good faith, with as much money as we could get together." He yawned. "I suppose we've got to believe that Howard will be acting in good faith, too."

"That's what bothers me. You told me that you think Rhoda really loves Joshua. I think so, too. Look at everything she was doing for him—teaching him, taking care of him. I'll bet there's no way he can convince her to give him up."

Joe didn't know how to answer Marcie. She'd echoed his very thoughts. He tried to think of something to say to reassure her but he was acutely aware of the silence stretching out.

"You don't think we're going to get him back, do y—?" Her voice broke. "Oh, Joe, I don't know if I can live if we don't get our baby back."

Joe turned over and sat up, leaning back against the rough plank wall of the house. "I don't know, Marcie. I wish I did. I wish I could say that I'm sure everything will go just as we planned tomorrow. My fear is that, while Howard may have thought up the blackmail scheme, Rhoda's really the brains of that outfit. But if Rhoda is behind this, she may have a plan to take the money and run."

Marcie sat up, too, and pulled her knees up to her chin and wrapped her arms around them. "I'm so scared," she said, starting to cry. "My little boy. What will I do if I never see him again? What will I do?"

Joe put his arm around her but she remained stiff

and unyielding. Her shoulders shook as she cried silently. He wished he could do something to make her feel better. Wished he could reassure her, but whether it was Howard or Rhoda running the show, he didn't believe for one minute that they were planning to give Joshua back to them.

He kept his arm around her, kept patting her arm and murmuring to her. He didn't know how to make her feel better. He never had. He'd failed at comforting her after Joshua was taken. He'd been too consumed with guilt then. The job with the NCMEC had helped, but he still carried around plenty of guilt and it still weighed him down, keeping him from being able to lift up Marcie.

He had to do something, but what? He had no idea. All he knew was that he'd give anything, even his life, to put their child back into her arms. To that end, he had to come up with a plan to counter Howard's.

After a long time, Marcie's sobs quieted, her shoulders stopped shaking and she laid her head against his chest. He figured she was asleep, and he pressed his cheek against her hair and closed his eyes.

After a few minutes, she spoke. "Joe?"

"Hmm?"

"Thank you for hiding in the trunk."

"You already thanked me for that," Joe said.

"Well, it's worth two. It was a very brave thing to do."

"No, it wasn't," he said. "You're the brave one. You drove out here to confront Howard all by yourself."

"But that's just it. I wasn't by myself. You promised me you'd be here when I needed you, and you were."

He pressed a kiss to her temple, wishing he were as brave as she made him sound.

They sat in silence for a while, watching the orange coils on the space heater. After several minutes, Marcie spoke. "Tomorrow, if everything goes well, we'll have our baby back." She sighed. "What then?" she asked in a trembling voice. "When we get Joshua back? What then?"

"What do you mean?" he asked.

"How…will we handle that?"

"You mean Joshua? We'll just have to do everything we can to help him. He'll grieve for Rhoda, of course. And it will take a while for him to learn to trust us. We've got the resources of the center that we can use. There are a couple of really good child psychologists we refer reunited families to, and—"

"Joe," she interrupted, sitting up straight. "I know you have the knowledge and the resources to do all the right things for Joshua. I'm talking about us—the three of us."

He had no idea what she wanted him to say. What he'd like to say was, *We'll all be together and we can get on with being a family, like we were before. We can be three again.* But that wasn't his call. It was hers. She'd never had a problem expressing her opinion, so if that was what she wanted, she'd tell him.

No, this was a deeper question. They both knew that they'd been drifting apart since before Joshua was born. Trouble was, he wasn't sure why. "The most important thing is to be there for him. Once we make sure we can do that, then we'll see."

Marcie heard the hesitation in Joe's voice and understood exactly what was bothering him. She'd said horrible things, unforgiveable things, to him. She'd even
told him that she never wanted to see him again because
seeing him reminded her of what he'd done. Right after
that he'd moved out. She wanted to tell him she was
sorry for the hurtful, unforgiveable things she'd said.
But when she opened her mouth to say the words, they
wouldn't come out. There was a big gap between wanting to make peace for the sake of their son, and forgiving him for letting Joshua be stolen.

Marcie's eyes welled with tears again, but this time
she was crying, not only for Joshua, but also for herself. She pulled away from Joe and lay down on the hard
floor, turning her back on him and closing her eyes. She
didn't sleep for a long time. Her brain swirled with all
the things she'd never said to him. All the times she
hadn't reached out to soothe his pain.

The last thing she remembered before falling asleep
was that Joe was still sitting up, his back propped
against the wall.

Chapter Twelve

The screeching and static of the walkie-talkie split the air, shocking Marcie awake. She shot upright, her heart hammering against her chest. Walkie-talkie. *Howard.*

She glanced around. Where was it? Then she remembered it was next to the heater, plugged into the same extension cord. As she threw off the blanket so she could crawl toward the walkie-talkie, she looked for Joe.

She didn't see him. "Joe?" she said softly, just as Howard's awful voice came through the walkie-talkie.

"Marcie! Time to rise and shine," Howard said on a rough laugh. "Hope it's not too early for you."

Joe appeared from out of the shadows on the other side of the cabin as she was picking up the walkie-talkie. He offered her a tin cup of water but she shook her head and held out the radio.

"Answer him but don't tell him anything. Just see what he wants," Joe whispered. "I've got an idea."

She frowned. Joe seemed different this morning from last night. Today he had an air of confidence that she hadn't seen before. "What? What's your idea?" she asked, then realized that she was whispering, too. Howard couldn't hear her unless she pressed the talk button on her device, but like Joe, she was still afraid to speak loudly, even if the button wasn't pushed.

Static sounded. "Marcie! Hey, woman, wake up! Don't you want your kid?"

Joe nodded at the radio.

She pressed the talk button. "I'm here," she said. "Where's my son? I want him *now!*" Releasing the button, she looked directly at Joe. "What idea? Tell me."

He shook his head. "You don't need to know that right now. Just listen to Howard."

"What? I don't need—?"

Howard's voice interrupted her. "Yeah, yeah. You're awfully demanding for somebody who's not controlling things. Hold your horses and listen to me."

"What do you mean I don't need to know?" she said shortly to Joe. "How am I supposed to—?"

"Hey! Are you listening?" Howard asked.

Glaring at Joe, she pushed the button just long enough to say, "Yes, Howard. I'm listening." Then to Joe, she said, "Now tell me what your idea is, so I'll know what I'm talking about."

"All you need to do is agree with whatever he says. Just do that, would you?" Joe said impatiently.

"In exactly twenty minutes," Howard continued, "I want you out of that house and down the stairs. Got it? So here's what you do. You bring the bag of money and nothing else down the stairs and out to the road."

"What's wrong with you?" Marcie asked Joe, who was frowning.

Joe nodded toward the walkie-talkie. "Talk to him."

She stood there, her thumb poised over the button, so furious at Joe her ears burned. "I don't know what to tell him, now do I?"

"Marcie, just answer him."

Just answer him, she mocked in her mind as she pressed the button. "Okay," she said into the speaker. "Down to the road. Nothing but the money."

"Dammit, woman!" Howard growled. "What are you doing over there? You'd better answer me when I talk to you or I can stop this right now and you'll never see your kid again."

"I was—I was getting the bag of money," she said, trying to sound afraid, although she figured it came across as more angry than scared.

"You've got twenty minutes to do that. Right now you pay attention to me."

"O-okay."

"Now you listen good. Bring the money and the walkie-talkie with you. Wait at the foot of the stairs until I call you and tell you what to do next."

Marcie pressed the button. "Howard? Why all this spy stuff? I'm here, right where you told me to be. I have the money with me. Just bring me my son!"

"Don't make me mad, Marcie. I'm getting tired of this. Have you forgotten what'll happen if you don't do exactly what I tell you?"

"No," she said quickly, Howard's threat to cut off Joshua's finger blossoming in her mind in full color. "No, no, I haven't. Okay. Twenty minutes. Bottom of the stairs. I swear, Howard, if you—"

Joe raised his hand. Marcie gave him a look that

should have dropped him where he stood, but she let go of the button. "What?"

"Watch what you say. And remember, he doesn't know I'm here. That's our ace in the hole."

She rolled her eyes. "Thanks. I couldn't possibly have figured that out by myself."

Howard started talking again. "And, woman? You better hope you've got enough money there, or you won't have your money or your kid."

"I want to talk to Joshua," she said.

Joe scowled and held up his hand.

She sliced her hand through the air in the universal gesture for *shut up*.

Increased static announced Howard opening his mic again. "Someone needs to teach you how to do what you're told." As he spoke, Marcie could hear something in the background. Something that sounded a lot like a child crying.

"Oh, I hear him. Please. Let me talk to my baby. I'll do anything you want."

"I swear, woman, the kid's gonna be the one that suffers if you don't stop yammering."

"I'm—I'm sorry. I'm just so afraid. How do I know I can trust you to bring my child to me?" She let go of the talk button.

"I told you not to say anything. Just to agree to what he says," Joe said.

"You haven't been here. I've begged him to let me talk to Joshua every single time he calls. I need to keep that up."

Howard's voice broke in. "Well, I reckon you're just

going to have to decide—do you want your kid back
or not?"

Joe held her gaze for a few seconds, then nodded.
"Do what you think is best."

Marcie wondered if he were being sarcastic, but his
gaze was clear and earnest and his tone was respectful.
"Thanks," she said.

Joe nodded his approval of what she was saying.

She pressed the talk button. "I want him back, Howard. I want him *now!*"

"I've had enough of you."

"Howard?" she said. "Howard! When are you coming?" She sniffed in frustration and released the button. "It sounds completely dead now. Do you think he
turned the walkie-talkie off?"

"Maybe."

She stomped over to set the walkie-talkie in the charger. Then she confronted Joe with her hands propped on
her hips. "What was all that? I have handled this alone
up to now. Why couldn't you trust me?"

"I didn't want you to make him too angry. Like I said
before, it's good, in fact it's essential to keep the upper
hand, but it's a fine line—"

"Stop it!" she cried. "Just stop with the damn closing remarks. I hate it when you sound like a lawyer."

He raised his brows.

She drew a long breath. "Okay," she said, raising her
hands, palm out, in a gesture of surrender. "Okay. I'm
sorry. Can you tell me now what your big idea is? Now
that there's no chance of me spilling it to Howard?"

"That's not why I didn't want to tell you."

"Then why?" she demanded.

"I'd wanted to talk to you before he called. I wanted to tell you what I was thinking, see if you thought it was a good idea, and I didn't want to be telling you while you were trying to talk to him."

"Oh." Joe's explanation made sense. The irritation and frustration burning inside her eased. "Okay," she said. "Tell me about it."

"I was hoping that Howard would want you out of the house for the exchange. Out in the open is much safer for him. You can't surprise him with a weapon or have an accomplice sneak up on him. That way he can control the swap."

"That makes sense—for him."

"Right. That's why you're going to refuse to come out of the house. Here's what we're going to do."

MARCIE CLUTCHED THE walkie-talkie to her chest as she stared out the window. Behind her Joe had his elbows on the counter and was scribbling something with a pen on the back of an envelope Marcie had found in her purse.

"What time is it?" Marcie asked.

"About three minutes later than the last time you asked," Joe muttered.

"Seriously. What time?" she insisted.

"Eight-thirty."

"It's been at least twenty-five minutes. Why doesn't he come on?" she said. "I'm going to be a nervous wreck by the time he gets here." She turned around and looked at Joe. She hadn't asked him what he wanted the pen and paper for. At first she'd thought he might be working out how he was going to overpower Howard, since his lawyer's brain worked better from an outline, no matter what he was planning. But he'd been writing too long and too consistently. "What are you writing?"

He didn't answer. The pen continued to scratch on the paper. Marcie didn't ask again. She had the sense that whatever he was writing was extremely important to him. She turned back to the window to watch for Howard's green pickup truck.

"A will," Joe said.

Her breath caught in her throat. "A w-will?" she stammered. "What do you think is going to happen?"

"Nothing, but I've never done a will. You'd think I of all people would have already taken care of that, but I guess even attorneys are subject to the arrogance of youth. Besides…" he began, then stopped.

Marcie filled in what he didn't say. People thought about wills when they had someone they wanted to make sure would be cared for. Joe had lost his son and his wife. So why would he make a will? Her eyes filled with tears for about the two hundredth time since she'd seen her baby in the backseat of Rhoda's Nissan. She'd have thought she would have been empty of tears and sadness by now. But apparently those wells were bottomless. Now Joe had hope again. Hope that he once again might have a wife and son to care for. And… he thought he might die before the day was over. Her heart wrenched so suddenly and tightly in her chest that she gasped.

"Marcie?" he said, glancing at her in concern.

"Joe, you're not thinking that Howard is capable of

killing, are you?" She heard the click of the ballpoint pen and the paper being folded.

"I think everybody is capable of killing."

"Don't philosophize, please. Just answer the question."

"I'm not philosophizing," he said. "I really do think everybody could kill if they had to. You'd kill for Joshua, wouldn't you?"

She nodded without hesitation. *And to save you.*

"There. See. And I certainly would. For Joshua or you."

Marcie realized that she believed him, and believing him gave her a depth of courage and determination that she'd never felt before. "What would Howard kill for, I wonder?"

"I think he'd kill for Rhoda. I believe he loves her. And I think that's what makes him dangerous. The fact that he'd do anything for her."

The implications of his words stabbed into her with the force of a knife. She realized that she'd never thought about Howard as a person. She'd never considered that he might love someone, or that he was doing this for any other reason than greed. But now that she thought about him in this new light, the implications were horrific. He would kill Joe and her if it meant that Rhoda could keep Joshua.

She turned to face Joe. In his gaze, she saw the answer to her next question. But she asked it anyway. "You think he'd kill to keep Rhoda from losing Joshua, don't you?"

He dropped his gaze as he nodded.

"That's why you don't want me to go out there."

"All he has to do is shoot you, then he's got the money and Rhoda's got the child she always wanted."

"Oh, my God," she said. "I didn't think about that at all." She turned back to the window. "Joe? You've told me what I'm supposed to do, but what about you? What are you planning to do once he comes inside?"

"Don't worry about that. Your biggest job is to forget that I'm even here. You *have* to stay focused on Howard. Don't even think about me. If you do, you might give me away."

"I can handle it, Joe. I know I can."

"Just remember. Everything we're doing is for Joshua." He held out the folded envelope. "Put this in your purse."

"Joe—you don't need this," she began, but the determination in his expression stopped her. She meekly tucked the envelope down into her bag. Just as she did, the walkie-talkie screeched. Marcie jumped and almost dropped it. As she was scrabbling to catch it, Howard's voice crackled through the static.

"Where the hell are you, woman? You're supposed to be down here in the middle of the road."

Marcie glanced at Joe and saw his slight nod, then pressed the talk button. "I'm here, Howard. In the house."

"Well get your butt down here like I told you. I've got the kid and I've got a sharp knife. If you ain't down here in the next ten seconds, I'll cut off a finger. I swear I will."

"Oh, no, you won't," Marcie growled. "If you touch

one hair on his head, I'll burn this money. I swear I will."

"You won't do that," Howard said. "That house'll go up like a box of matches, with you in it. Now get down here."

Joe watched his wife. He'd told her she needed to be totally focused on her job, which was to get Howard up the stairs and into the house. Well, she was focused all right. He was pretty sure if Howard were in the same room with her, she'd have his eyes clawed out inside of a minute.

She was like a mother lion, protecting her cub. Joe hadn't imagined how good she would be at her part of their plan. As for his role, he had no idea if it would work. He just had to react to what Howard did. He hoped he could manage to keep Howard busy long enough to allow Marcie to run to the pickup. He hadn't told her what she'd have to do yet because he wanted her full of adrenaline and ready for anything. Then when he yelled at her to make a run for it, he was counting on her reacting on instinct rather than stopping to think about what she was doing.

"I've tested some of the money to see if it burns fast. It does, Howard. It does."

Through the walkie-talkie, Howard cursed.

"I'm not coming down there. You come up here. *And you bring my son.* Do you understand?"

The other end of the walkie-talkie stayed silent, so Marcie pushed the talk button again. "Howard? I want to talk to him. Hold the walkie-talkie so he can talk into it. I want to hear him now!"

After a pause, she heard the mic click on. "You bitch. You can't order me around. I'll shoot the house down. I've got my rifle."

Joe put his hand on Marcie's arm, but she shrugged it off. "My child, Howard. I want to hear my child talk. Otherwise you go ahead and shoot. I'll be burning money."

"All right, all right. Hang on," Howard said, then cut off his mic for another few moments. "I can't let him talk to you. He's tied up and got duct tape on his mouth."

"Take it off!"

"Nope." The static stopped.

Marcie frowned at her walkie-talkie. "What's he—?"

Then amidst static, Howard said, "Nope. I can't—I can't watch him and you at the same time."

"Do it now! Take that tape off his mouth now. He's probably scared to death!"

As Joe listened to the two of them he came to a stunning realization. It surprised him that he hadn't thought about it before. Howard didn't have Joshua. He'd driven to the house in his pickup, maybe with a rifle, maybe not. But he'd come here expecting Marcie to be waiting in the middle of the road with a sack of money. He'd tell her to leave the money in the middle of the road and go back to the house. She'd demand to see her child, but Howard would tell her that the only way she'd get Joshua back was to obey him. Then, when she'd done what he'd told her to, he'd pick up the money and speed away, back to Rhoda and Joshua, and the three of them would be miles and miles from Louisiana by nightfall. Joe nodded to himself in satisfaction. Knowing that

Joshua wasn't in the pickup made his plan a lot easier. He touched Marcie on the arm.

"What?" she asked shortly. "You told me to focus. I'm focused. Don't interrupt."

"What you said about the money—that's really smart. Tell him to bring Joshua up here now or you'll start lighting bills on fire and dropping them over the rail."

"Now you want me out there? I thought you didn't want me to get shot."

"All you have to do is go to the railing and drop the burning bills over the edge. You'll be shielded somewhat by the corner of the house."

Marcie gazed at him with narrowed eyes. "Okay. I'll try it. All we're doing now is arguing back and forth." She pressed the talk button. "Howard, bring Joshua up here right now. I've got your money, but I'm not coming down there. I don't trust you for one second."

"I'll shoot the stilts and that house'll fall flat with you in it. I'm telling you for the last time. Get down here with that money!"

"Oh, I'll send your money down," she said mockingly. "One bill at a time. Watch for it. You can't miss it." She let go of the talk button and set the walkie-talkie down.

"Take the walkie-talkie with you," Joe said.

"I'm going to need both hands to light the bills on fire and throw them over the rail. I'll just yell at him."

"You've got to stay in the shadow of the house, as close to the door as you can."

She picked up a stack of hundreds from the bag, tore

the wrapper off, then peeled off about a dozen. "Have you seen any matches?" she asked.

Joe searched for a moment. "Here's a candle lighter in the drawer, if it works." He clicked it and a small yellow flame sprang up from its tip.

"Drawer?" Marcie said. "There's a drawer?"

Joe nodded. "Two of them. They're pretty shallow, though."

"I didn't see them," she said, reaching for the lighter, but Joe held on to it.

"Marcie, remember. Stay close to the door. If you see him raise his rifle, duck back inside."

She nodded and opened the door.

"Wait!" Joe whispered. "I'm putting the walkie-talkie right here on the floor next to the door." His pulse began to race as she stepped out onto the stoop. He was dying to look out and see if he could see Howard's pickup, but he didn't dare. Everything, even their lives, depended on Howard not knowing he was there.

"Here you go, Howard," Marcie called. "In case you can't see them from there, these are hundreds. Benjamins."

The walkie-talkie crackled. "…burning that money… regret it." Joe couldn't hear everything Howard said, but he got the gist of it.

"Where is he?" he asked.

"Still in the truck," she answered. Then she yelled, "Two hundred at a time, Howard!"

"Be careful," Joe warned her. "If he opens the door and starts to get out, he could be going for his rifle."

"I'm watching him," she said as Howard's voice interrupted her.

"Okay, okay. You win! I'm bringing the kid up."

"Now it's three hundred at a time!" she shouted.

The walkie-talkie crackled again. "Stop it! I'm coming up."

"Good job," Joe said. "Now get inside."

"No, wait. I want to see Joshua."

"Marcie!"

"I am not moving until I can see my baby." She heard Joe muttering curses but her attention was on Howard. He got out of the pickup, then opened the rear door and leaned inside. She held her breath as she waited for him to lift her little boy out of the rear seat.

"Joe, he's doing it. He's getting Joshua. Look through the window. He won't be able to see a tiny space in the curtains. Look, Joe."

The curtains fluttered as Joe parted them slightly. "What do you see?" he asked her.

"Nothing yet. He's doing something—maybe unhooking the child seat. Wait. He's straightening up."

The walkie-talkie crackled with Howard's yell. "Marcie!"

"I'm here." She waved.

"Careful," Joe whispered.

"Get inside," Howard demanded. "Or I'm not coming up."

"What?" she called out. "Howard, please. He's my baby."

"Because I said so." Howard's voice nearly drowned out Joe's. "Get inside and wait there. I'm coming up the stairs with the kid, but I swear I'll drop him right back down them. Now get in there and stay there. You got me?"

"What's he doing?" she asked Joe.

"I don't know," Joe said. "Maybe he's afraid you have a weapon."

She clicked the talk button. "Okay, okay. But you'd better not hurt my baby."

When Marcie closed the door, Joe was still at the window, watching Howard. "He's pulling something out of the backseat," he said.

She went over to the window. Joe held out his arm and made room for her to stand in front of him. That way both of them could look out through the same tiny crack in the curtains. "See him?" Joe asked.

"Oh, yes," Marcie breathed. "Look. He's got him. Oh, no, he's got Joshua wrapped in a blanket. Do you think he's all right? You don't think he's sick, do you?"

Joe saw the same thing Marcie did, but he immediately drew a different conclusion. Howard was lifting a bundle into his arms, holding it as if he were holding a sleeping child, but Joe knew better. Howard didn't have Joshua.

Chapter Thirteen

Joe sighed in frustration and a bit of relief. Howard didn't have Joshua. He'd been right about the guy. He really did love Rhoda too much to take the child away from her, or maybe she wouldn't let him. Joe craved a glimpse of his son, but he was glad that he didn't have to worry about making sure his child was all right while trying to take Howard down.

Whatever Howard's reason, his plan all along had been to overpower Marcie, then take the money and run. Rhoda was probably waiting with Joshua for Howard to pick them up. The three of them would be out of the state and headed for parts unknown hours before Marcie could find help on this bayou road.

But Howard hadn't counted on Joe being there. And Joe was counting on that. He intended for this day to end with Howard and Rhoda in custody for kidnapping, and his son back in his wife's arms.

"Oh," Marcie said, pressing her hand to her throat. "I feel faint. I'd almost given up ever seeing him again. He's here, Joe." Her voice sounded choked. "I had no idea how I would react if I ever got the chance to see my baby again, to hold him, to have him come home with us." She wrapped her other arm around Joe's waist and hugged him. "I don't think I've ever been this happy in my entire life."

Her lilting tone and happy words ripped through Joe's heart like a knife through rotten cloth, leaving ugly jagged edges. How was he going to tell her? He was afraid that she'd break down completely, and he needed her to be strong, because without her, Joe's plan would fail. He swallowed. "Listen to me, hon," Joe said. "Don't let your emotions overwhelm you. We've still got to overpower Howard and restrain him, remember?"

He felt her head move as she nodded. "I know. I know. And we've got to do it without hurting or endangering Joshua. I can do it, Joe. I'm ready."

"Okay," he said. "Then we've got to get away from the window and get set up."

"I want to watch for a little while longer. Just until he—"

"Marcie, listen." Joe took her arm from around his waist and stepped away from her. "We've got to be ready. We can't make even one mistake. If we do, we may lose—everything." Joe gritted his teeth. He hated what he was doing. He was in effect lying to her. He had to pretend that he believed it was Joshua in that bundle. Otherwise Marcie would know something was wrong. If he slipped up and gave her any hint that Howard didn't have Joshua, at best he could ruin everything. At worst, he could get them both hurt or killed.

She stepped away from the window and squared her

shoulders. "Okay. You want me here, right beside the door?"

"Yes. There. When he pushes or kicks the door open, you'll be arm's length from him. I'll be behind the door." He gestured vaguely in that direction. He hadn't told her much about what he was planning to do. "Now, do you have the spray?"

She nodded. "What are you going to use as a weapon?" she asked.

"Shh." He held his finger to his mouth as heavy footsteps sounded on the pier. Howard was almost here, and just in time to save Joe from answering. He'd inventoried and assessed everything he could find in the house, everything in Marcie's purse and everything in their car. Marcie would use her pepper spray to initially disable Howard, but stinging eyes was not enough of a deterrent. He needed something that would render Howard unconscious or at least incapable of fighting back.

The weapon he'd settled on was unconventional at best, but it was probably the one that could do the most damage in the shortest amount of time, and last long enough for Joe to tie him up. But he couldn't allow Marcie to even catch a glimpse of what he'd chosen. She wouldn't let him within a hundred yards of Joshua if she knew what he was planning to use.

Marcie stood right next to the closed door, the can of pepper spray at the ready in her right hand and several bungee cords tucked into the waistband of her jeans. She was so nervous that her hands wouldn't stop shaking, and she had to clamp her jaw to stop her teeth from chattering. She was dying to see what Joe was doing, but he had insisted on keeping the curtains closed, which put them in near total darkness. He wanted to catch Howard off guard when he stepped into the dark house. Also, Joe had commanded her not to take her eyes off the door.

"You've got to focus on nothing but making sure the pepper spray goes directly into his eyes," he told her. "He's probably going to be talking, maybe even threatening you. But you can't listen to him, because if you miss, then it won't matter what I've planned to do, because if he's not hurting and if he doesn't let go of the blanket, I can't take him down. It won't matter that he doesn't know I'm here. At full strength, he's a lot stronger than me."

She could hear the rustling of his clothing and an occasional metallic click as he worked on whatever he was doing. Then the generator kicked on and drowned out his quiet movements.

At that moment, Howard's boots clomped up the stairs to the house. Marcie thought his footsteps sounded unusually heavy, even for a man of his size. Her heart leapt. That had to be because he was carrying Joshua. She heard him grunt with effort as he reached the top step and set his boot onto the stoop. The floor shuddered. Marcie swallowed, drew in a fortifying breath and raised the can of spray. She placed her finger on the nozzle and concentrated on the door.

With a grunt louder than his first one, Howard kicked the door with his boot. The noise echoed off the walls. Marcie tensed.

"I'm coming in, Marcie," he said loudly. "I've got the

kid. You stand away from the door. Try anything and I'll turn around and throw him over the rail. Got that? I'll throw. Him. Over."

"Yes," she said, not having to fake the quaver in her voice. She gritted her teeth and tried not to think about Joshua or about what Joe was doing. She had to concentrate. She only had one chance to do this right.

She watched the doorknob as Howard turned it and the door began to ease open. As the door swung open, Marcie's heart screamed at her to look at the bundle in his arms. Just one glimpse wouldn't hurt, would it?

Focus. She fought her mother's instinct to care for her child and it was the hardest thing she'd ever had to do in her life.

Focus! Her entire world seemed to be moving in slow motion, including her own movements. Raising her arm, she fixed her gaze on his head, which was turning in her direction. When she saw the side of his face as he turned his head toward her, she pressed the nozzle, aiming it directly at his eyes. The sound of the aerosol was muffled by Howard's agonized roar. He threw up an arm to ward off the spray and when he did the bundle dropped to the floor. Then he lunged at her. She dove beneath his arm toward the bundle, screaming, "Joshua!" over and over. Somewhere along the way she dropped the spray can.

Joe timed his movement to the sound of the aerosol spray. He propelled himself at Howard at the same instant that Howard lunged at Marcie. Joe had no idea how much—if any—spray had gone into Howard's eyes. But some had, judging by the man's bellows.

Clutching the fiery hot space heater by the handle on the top, he held it in front of him like a shield as he propelled himself forward. He'd cushioned the uninsulated back with a torn piece of the ratty blanket, but as he landed on top of the bigger man with the heater between them, the metal seared his hands and chest.

Howard screamed like a woman as Joe growled out loud and pressed the coils into the back of Howard's head with all the strength he had. He knew he had only a split second to inflict as much damage as possible, and he'd underestimated the pain of the burning metal against his own skin, even through the blanket. But the longer he could hold on, the better chance he'd have of disabling Howard. The smell of burning hair filled the air as Howard flailed and bucked. Joe bore down on him with all his might. He felt a tug against his hands, as the electrical cord stretched to its limit. Then the tug suddenly relaxed and he knew the heater had come unplugged.

"Marcie!" he yelled. "Bungee cords—now! *Come on, Marcie!*" He registered her sobs in the part of his brain that was always aware of her, so he knew she'd found out that the bundle of blankets was not her child.

Joe felt himself being drawn to her, but he tamped down that urge with all his will. If he let her grief and shock distract him, he might lose this fight. He'd known she'd be upset. He'd planned around it, but damn it he needed those cords. Grimacing with pain and effort, he leaned every bit of his weight on the still blazing hot heater.

"Marcie!" he yelled again as Howard tried to buck

him off. He had to get ready to tie up Howard. He only hoped Howard was hurting enough that he wouldn't be able to throw him off. Joe rose up, still pressing the coils against Howard's cheek, and grabbed the man's left hand. With an effort, he swung his left knee forward and pinned the hand. Then he finally let go of the heater and drew his right knee forward to pin Howard's right hand. The heater tumbled onto the floor.

Howard lifted his head, roaring like a wounded lion. His neck and the side of his face bore a red-and-black pattern of the exposed heater coils. It was an ugly sight. Joe swallowed hard and looked at the man's hands. He took a breath to yell for Marcie one last time, but, miraculously, she was there with the cords.

Resisting the urge to double his fist and coldcock Howard on the side of the head, Joe instead grabbed a bungee cord and slipped one end like a lasso over Howard's left wrist. Then, with a twist, he yanked Howard's right wrist up and wrapped the elastic cord back and forth around both wrists. As he worked, heaving with the effort and doing his best to ignore the pain in his burned hands, Howard's hefty body gave up the fight and collapsed. He lay limp. His roar deflated into a low moaning. His entire torso trembled. Probably shock from the pain. After a few seconds of struggle, Joe finally managed to hook the bungee cord tightly onto itself.

Only then did he dare to get off the man and stand up. His head spun dizzily and he had trouble catching his breath. For a few seconds he bent at the waist and propped his hands on his knees like a basketball player, easing the pressure on his lungs.

"Marcie, can you…wrap his ankles?" he gasped. "If he kicks, stop. I'll…get it."

He hadn't realized how tense he'd been. Or how focused. But obviously his body had pumped massive quantities of adrenaline to his muscles and nerves, because now that he'd stopped, his limbs tingled and trembled with the aftereffects. It took a few seconds for him to be able to breathe normally.

When he finally straightened, his palms felt lit on fire. He turned them up and saw that they were bright red and he could see blisters beginning to form. That was going to be a problem very soon, so he needed to make sure Howard was sufficiently trussed now.

Howard was still moaning when Joe checked Marcie's work with the bungee cord on Howard's ankles. She'd done a good job. He felt the tension in both cords and adjusted Marcie's a little and his own a lot. He'd wound the elastic way too tight in his haste to put Howard out of commission.

As soon as he was sure the cords were tight enough to keep Howard from getting loose, but not so tight that they cut off his circulation, he turned to Marcie.

Behind him, Howard was beginning to stir. "You burned me," he muttered. "I'll sue."

Marcie was crouched on the floor, holding two more bungee cords. When she raised her gaze to his, her face looked haunted and her normally lovely, sparkly eyes were dull.

"He didn't bring Joshua," she said flatly. "But you

knew that he wouldn't, didn't you? It was your plan all along, wasn't it? You knew he didn't have my baby."

Joe held out a hand to help her to her feet, but she ignored it and rose on her own. She tossed the cords onto the floor and stood there, staring at Howard, who had quit struggling so much, but was still moaning and muttering an occasional curse, presumably aimed at them. "You wouldn't have used the heater if you'd thought he'd be holding Joshua."

"Marcie, hon, come here."

She ignored that, too.

"I'm sure Joshua is with Rhoda," he said. "Howard wanted the money. But Rhoda loves Joshua. You know that. You said it yourself. So she wasn't about to risk Howard doing something to him, either accidentally or on purpose."

She nodded, then looked up at him. "She's going to run," she said. "I'll never see my baby again."

Joe held out his arms, but Marcie shrank away from him and wrapped her arms around herself. "Hon," he said. "We don't know that she's running. She and Joshua are probably back at her house."

But Marcie was shaking her head. "No. No. No. She wouldn't sit there and wait for the police. I don't even think she'd wait for Howard. If he did this once he'd do it again. She's taken my baby and run—some place where we'll never find them."

"You can't know that," he protested.

Marcie straightened and fixed him with a gaze. "Oh, yes, I can."

"But how? Why are you so sure?" he asked, bewildered.

"Because it's what I would do."

Joe stared at Marcie. Of course. As soon as she'd said those words—words only a mother could say with confidence—he knew that was what was happening. If Rhoda hadn't already taken Joshua and left, she was probably preparing to go right now.

Joe stalked over to where Howard was lying on his stomach, with his hands tied behind his back. He was moaning and cursing. Joe nudged him in the side with the toe of his shoe.

"Ahh, you son of a bitch, you burned me. Need a doctor," Howard gasped.

"Where's Rhoda?" he asked him.

"Go to hell," Howard muttered.

"Where is she, Howard? I can burn the other side of your face, you know."

"Went back to the house."

Joe turned back to Marcie. "Come on, Marcie. Let's go. We need to get to Rhoda's house. She's probably waiting there for Howard to pick them up. We need to get there before she decides Howard isn't coming and takes off on her own."

"But the car's stuck." Then, for the first time since Howard came into the house, Marcie perked up. She went to the door and looked outside. "Howard's truck! We can take his truck and then if Rhoda does see us, she'll think it's Howard."

"That's right, hon." Joe crouched down beside Howard and shook his shoulder. "Howard. Where are your keys?"

"Need doctor," Howard whispered. "Hurting bad."

"Come on, Howard. Do I need to pat you down? I'll do it."

The only sound from Howard was a long groan.

Joe patted Howard's pockets and came up with a set of keys. "Here we go," he said, holding up the keys. "Marcie, think you can drive?"

"I guess so, if I have to. Why?"

Joe held out his hands, which were about half-covered in clear blisters now. She looked at them, made a small, low sound in distress, then took the keys. "Are we ready to go?" she asked.

"Yeah," he replied. "We can come back and get this stuff later. Our first priority is to find Rhoda and call the police."

Marcie drove the pickup. Despite its creakiness and filth, the engine was surprisingly peppy. The starter groaned, as did the transmission when she shifted gears, but she didn't have any trouble driving it. She didn't speak on the drive and neither did Joe. Her head was filled with worry about Joshua and anger at Joe for not warning her that Howard didn't have her baby.

But then, a question wormed its way into her consciousness. If she'd known Joshua wasn't there, could she have been as convincing as a mother desperate to see and hold her child? She pushed away the argument that Joe had done the best thing for the situation. She wanted to wallow in her grief and anger a little while longer.

As they approached Rhoda's house, Marcie said shortly, "I was about here when Howard called me yesterday."

Joe looked at his phone. "I've got two bars," he said. He dialed the number Ethan Delancey had given him.

"Detective Delancey?" he asked when someone answered.

"Joe Powers," Ethan said on an audible sigh. "I'm glad to hear from you. Are you and your wife all right?"

"Yeah, we're fine." There was a lot unsaid in that terse comment, and Joe knew that eventually both he and Marcie would have to go through it all in excruciating detail, but for now— "Fine," he repeated. "We're in Howard's truck, almost to Rhoda's house."

"I know you don't have your son," Ethan said without preamble. "I've been trying to call you, but your phone kept going to voice mail."

"That's right. There's no cell service in the middle of Bayou DeChez," Joe said wryly. "We're hoping Rhoda's at her house with Joshua."

"I ordered surveillance on Rhoda Sumner's house yesterday morning, as soon as I left your house. There was no activity at all at the house until this morning, when one of my officers reported that she and a toddler were brought to the house in an old green pickup that I'm assuming is Howard Lelievre's. Just about twenty minutes ago, she put two suitcases in her car, then she and the toddler got into the car and headed north on I-55. My officer stopped her and took her into custody."

Joe breathed a sigh of relief. "That's great. Where are they now?"

"They're at the Hammond Police Department, right off I-55. You know how to get there?"

"Thomas Street, right? I can get there. Who should we ask for?"

"I tell you what. I'll be at the front desk. If something comes up and I'm not there, call me on my cell."

"Detective," Joe said, "thank you for stopping Rhoda. I can't tell you how grateful we are. We'll be there in about twenty minutes." He started to wipe a hand across his face, then saw the tissues wrapped around his palms. "I know where Howard is. He's in a stilt house on Bayou DeChez, a few miles west of Rhoda's house. He's tied up with bungee cords and his face and neck and upper back have been burned. He's the kidnapper who was demanding a ransom for Joshua. I'm sure the police are going to have a lot of questions for me. Please tell them I'm available anytime. I'm willing to do whatever I need to. I'm the one who burned him and left him there, tied up."

"I see," Ethan said. "I'll call the Killian P.D. and have them get somebody out there. They'll be calling you for a statement."

"Thanks, Detective."

"How's your wife?"

Joe glanced at Marcie, who hadn't taken her eyes off the road. Her hands were white-knuckled on the steering wheel. "We're both hanging in there, I guess."

"I need to let you know that the police chief in Hammond has ordered that the Department of Protective Child Services be brought in to take care of the boy."

"What? Why?" Joe blurted before he was able to control himself.

Marcie glanced over at him, disturbed by his tone. "What is it?" she asked.

"I'm sure you know why. You must have had experience with this type of situation at your job. Your son was nine months old when he was taken. He's thirty-three months old now. Obviously he's not going to remember you."

This time Joe was successful at controlling his outburst. He swallowed the anguished protest he wanted to make. "I don't think I agree with that," he said carefully.

Marcie sent him a sidelong glance. "Joe!" she said. "What's wrong?"

He just shook his head.

"I'm sorry. I wanted to give you a heads-up so you could prepare Marcie." Ethan sighed.

"Yeah," Joe said wryly. "Thanks."

"What's the matter?" Marcie said as soon as he hung up. "What did he say?"

Joe pocketed the phone, trying to figure out if there was any way to tell her about Child Services without sending her over the edge. He could feel her brittle control and he knew from past experience just how fragile that control was.

Chapter Fourteen

"Joe? What did Detective Delancey say? Is it something about Joshua?" Marcie asked, tugging at Joe's arm.

Joe grimaced. "Why don't we get some coffee? There's a diner in Killian and we're almost there. Maybe even some breakfast?"

"No! I don't want anything except my baby. What. Did. He. Tell. You?"

Joe saw Marcie's fingers tighten even more on the steering wheel. "They did find Rhoda," he said, choosing his words very carefully, "and she had Joshua with her."

Marcie threw her head back. "Ahh." She sighed. "Thank God. He's all right? He's good?"

"Apparently he's fine. They've taken them to Hammond, to the police station."

"We have to go. We have to get there now! How far is it to Hammond?"

"Marcie," Joe said, laying his hand lightly on her arm. "Pull over. You're nervous as a cat and you shouldn't be driving."

"No, Joe. That'll just waste time. We've got to get there. It's our son. My baby!"

"Pull over!" Joe shouted. "Now!"

Marcie jumped and shot him an alarmed look, but she stopped the truck and folded her arms. "Okay, Joe," she said, biting off each word. "I've stopped. What are you going to do? You can't drive. Your palms are covered with blisters. I don't know why you're being so mean. I'm perfectly capable of driving. I'm fine. I'm—" Her voice cracked.

Tears formed in her eyes and slipped down her cheeks. Joe wanted to apologize to her for yelling. He'd never raised his voice to her. Never needed to. But right now he was just as anxious as she was to see Joshua. He wanted to hold him, to kiss and hug his son. He wanted to be able to hand Marcie their child, to see her face when she got to hold her little boy for the first time in almost two years. And he knew that's what Marcie wanted, too.

But he knew it was going to be a long, painful time before either one of them could touch their child, or kiss him or hold him. It was going to be a long time— if ever—before the three of them were a family again.

What kind of coward was he that he couldn't tell her what Detective Delancey had told him? He couldn't bear to be the one to tell her that she couldn't talk to or touch her child. He was that much of a coward.

"Change seats," he growled, opening the passenger door. His hand burned and he felt blisters pop. "I'm going to drive."

"This ought to be good," she snapped. "Look at you.

Your hands are covered with blisters. How do you think you're going to drive?"

"Pretty damn carefully," he stormed at her.

With a sniff of frustration, she put the pickup in Neutral and engaged the emergency brake. Climbing out of the driver's seat, she walked around the front of the pickup as Joe walked around the back and got behind the wheel. He carefully released the brake, then shifted into first. He gritted his teeth as more blisters popped on his palms.

It took about twenty minutes to get to the Hammond Police Department. By the time they were parked, Marcie had handed Joe about a dozen tissues to wrap his hands in. He parked the truck and stepped on the emergency brake, and for a moment, he just sat, staring at his tissue-wrapped hands on the steering wheel.

"Joe?"

He clenched his teeth, took a long breath, then turned to Marcie. "I have to tell you something before we go in there."

She turned pale. "No, Joe. You said he was all right."

"He is all right, hon. Just listen to me. You need to know that...there are procedures for this kind of thing."

"No, Joe. No procedures. I need my baby. I need to hold him."

Joe swallowed hard. "I know, hon. I understand. But like I said, there are procedures for dealing with a child who's been stolen from his parents. Joshua was so young, and he's been gone for a long time."

"No," Marcie whispered brokenly. "No, Joe, please."

Her eyes were red, her cheeks chapped from the tears and the rain and the cool air. "Please. I need my baby."

Joe's heart ripped in two as he spoke the next few words. "Child Services is going to take him."

"No!" Marcie cried. "I won't let them. Child Services can't take my baby." She fumbled for the door latch and threw herself out of the truck. As soon as her feet hit the ground she was running toward the big front door of the station.

Joe jumped out and ran after her. He caught up with her about three steps from the door. He caught her arm and turned her around to face him. "Marcie, don't. You've got to handle this rationally. You have *got* to calm down. If you act irrationally, the Child Services people will wonder if you're capable of taking care of Joshua. You know they'll have access to the police's records of complaints against you for those previous incidents."

"Capable of taking—?" She choked and had to cough. "I am his *mother.* There is no one more capable."

"Hon, I know that," he said, feeling tears sting his own eyes. "But we have to convince them."

"Why, Joe?" The question sounded as if it were ripped from her throat. "Why would they keep him from me?" She almost collapsed in his arms. *Almost.*

But from somewhere, she drew on a reservoir of strength that he didn't realize she had left in her. She drew herself up to her full height, wiped her eyes, then pinned him with a glare.

"This is your fault," she whispered. "All of it. I have

been through hell these past two years, and so has my child. I would be happy if I never had to see you again."

Joe's eyes stung. "Marcie, come on. You're upset."

"You're damned right I'm upset. But I need to appear calm and collected. I'm going in there and I'm going to make sure those people know that I can take care of my child. You can go in there with me if you want, but—" She lifted a finger and pointed it at him. "Do not talk. Do not contradict me. Do not touch my child. I will do this on my own. Joshua and I don't need you." The whole time she talked, tears streamed down her face. She pulled a tissue from her purse and dried them, then straightened her back and walked into the station as if she were the police chief.

Joe wiped his wet cheeks with the cuff of his shirt. She was right. It all was his fault. All she'd ever done was try to deal with the devastation and grief he'd caused. For one ridiculous moment, he considered leaving the station. But he knew, even if she didn't, that both of them were in for hours and hours of questions, explanations and interrogations. He had to be here. Besides, he wasn't sure he'd be able to draw breath if they didn't allow him a glimpse of his son—and soon.

MARCIE STOPPED AT the door to the Hammond Police Department. She blotted the last of the tears from her cheeks, smoothed back her hair, then pushed the door open and stepped into the air-conditioned station.

Standing at the desk was the detective who'd come to see Joe the other day. Her brain registered again how much he and Joe looked alike, as he held out his hand to her.

"Mrs. Powers," he said. "I'm so glad to see you. Are you injured at all? We can have emergency medical technicians here within a few minutes."

She shook her head.

"What about some coffee or a glass of water?"

She shook her head again. "I'm ready to see my child," she said evenly.

Detective Delancey looked toward the door. "Where's your husband?"

She shrugged as the door pushed inward and Joe came in. Marcie tried not to look at him, but she couldn't help it. She hadn't really taken in his appearance once Howard was immobilized. In the sunlight that poured in through the glass doors, she saw that his hair was full of dust and dirt, his shirt was wrinkled and stained and his hands dripped with ragged facial tissues that were dotted with blood.

"Joe!" Delancey said. "What happened to your hands?"

"They're burned," Joe said, looking at them as if they didn't belong to him. "I guess I need to clean them up and bandage them."

Ethan was already turning to the desk sergeant. "Call for an EMT to treat—" He looked at Joe with a questioning glance.

"Blisters," Joe said ruefully.

"Second-degree burns on hands and forearms." Delancey turned to Joe again. "Anywhere else?"

Joe shook his head.

Marcie allowed herself to be irritated and impatient with the detective, who seemed far more concerned about Joe's burned hands than he did about her child. She caught his sleeve. "I want to see my baby now!" she said. "Where is he?"

Detective Delancey sent her an odd look. He glanced sidelong at Joe then back at her. "I'm sorry, Mrs. Powers, but the child is being questioned by a representative from the Department of Children and Family Services right now."

"You're sorry? You're *sorry?*" she said loudly. "That is *my* child in there—" she gestured vaguely "—and I want to see him right this minute. I have not seen him in two years. That is twenty-four months, sir."

A female police officer stepped up. Marcie didn't know where the woman had come from but she looked grim and determined, with one hand in her pocket and the other hand reaching for Marcie's arm. Marcie glared at her.

"Ma'am, why don't you come with me and we'll get a cup of coffee," the officer said, pausing just shy of touching Marcie's arm.

"I don't *want* a cup of coffee," Marcie snapped. "I want my child."

"Marcie, hon, they're going to help you," Joe said, stepping close to her and bending his head to speak quietly. "But first they have to follow the law. Everything's going to be fine, if you'll just—"

"Everything is *not* going to be fine. Just leave me alone," she said, her voice breaking. "Go get your hands fixed."

At that moment an EMT came through the glass doors with a medical kit in his hand. He stopped when he saw Joe. "Hi there," he said. "You must be my patient."

"Ethan," Joe said to the detective. "I really don't want to leave her."

Marcie sniffed. "Leave me, please," she said archly. Deep inside her she knew she was being irrational and mean, but she was afraid if she didn't hold on to this tremendous anger she felt toward Joe right now, she'd break down and start sobbing. She wasn't sure which would be worse in the critical eyes of Child Services as they ruled whether she could take care of her child. *Her child.* And right now she didn't care. She was doing the only thing she could do to stay in control. Anger was all she had right now.

As Joe went off with the EMT to get his hands treated, Detective Delancey laid a hand on Marcie's arm. She flinched, but quelled her initial urge to pull away. That would probably be resisting arrest, she thought with a wry, inward chuckle.

Delancey looked at her oddly for an instant, then composed his face. "Mrs. Powers, if you'll go with Officer Hatcher, I'll check with the official from Child Services and see what we can do about letting you see your son."

Suddenly, she was at a loss for words. She couldn't speak, could barely think. Had he really said she could see her son? Or she might be able to see her son? Mo-

mentarily confused, she allowed the officer to guide
her to a kitchen and pour her a cup of coffee.

"It's fairly fresh," the officer said kindly.

Marcie burst into tears.

Chapter Fourteen

Joe walked up to the house that he and Marcie had bought together when they'd found out they were pregnant. He stood there looking at the doorbell as the past two weeks slid through his head.

Joshua had gone home with Marcie two days after Rhoda was arrested trying to leave the state with him. And Joe had gone back to his apartment. The psychologist assigned to them by Child Services had quickly seen that Joshua would be better off with Marcie than with a foster family.

The three of them were attending twice-weekly counseling sessions. In addition, a social worker visited the house once a week to ensure a smooth transition for Joshua back into his mother's life.

Joe was here this evening because Marcie had called and invited him to spend the evening with her and Joshua. From her nervous and slightly scattered phone call, he figured the invitation was an assignment from the psychologist or the social worker. But that was okay. That day in the police station, when his wife refused his help or comfort, it was painfully obvious that the

two of them would never get back together. So when it
came to his son, he would take anything he could get.
Even an awkward, therapist-assigned evening with his
estranged wife.

He rang the doorbell and took a long, calming breath
as he waited for her to answer. From somewhere inside
the house, he heard a sound that made him smile. It
was Marcie, laughing. He peered through the sidelight
at the foyer. After a couple of seconds, he saw her. She
had on a sleeveless dress that drifted around her legs
and she was barefoot. She came skipping through the
foyer with a beautiful smile on her face, and quickly
unlocked the door.

"Hi," she said brightly. "I didn't realize it was locked.
Sorry." She beamed at him, then turned around and
headed back the way she'd come. "We're in the kitchen,"
she called over her shoulder.

He followed, watching the hem of her dress float
around her calves. It seemed to him that she left all the
scents and freshness of spring in her wake. It made his
heart ache to see her so happy. It hadn't been that long
ago that he'd been convinced that neither one of them
would ever smile again.

When he got to the kitchen, Joshua was sitting at the
little table Marcie had bought for him, trying to fit plastic cubes and balls and pyramids into the same shaped
holes of a brightly colored toy.

"Joshua, look. It's Daddy," Marcie said.

The toddler held up a ball. "Daddeee!" he cried, then
dropped the ball into the round hole. "I'n a good boy!"

Joe crouched down beside him and brushed his hand

over his silky hair that was just like Marcie's. "You're a smart boy. Look what you did."

Joshua picked up the cube. "I'n a smar' boy," he repeated, then tried to push the cube into the triangular hole. When it wouldn't go, he banged it down a couple of times and started whimpering.

"Oh," Marcie muttered and started for him, but Joe held up a hand.

"I've got it," he said, "if that's okay."

"It's great," she replied. "I've still got to feed him. He's sleepy. That's why he's cranky."

Joe took the cube from Joshua's fingers.

"No!" Joshua snapped. "Mine."

"Hey, buddy, I know it's yours, but you don't bang it."

"Bang it. Bang it."

"Here." Joe gave the cube back to Joshua. "Let's put it right here." He pointed to the square hole.

"No," Joshua said, banging the cube against the triangular hole again.

Joe wrapped his hand around Joshua's tiny one. "No banging it. Okay?"

Joshua looked at Marcie, then back at Joe. "No bang it?"

"No bang it," Joe said, trying not to laugh. Behind him, Marcie's sweet laugh rang out like a bell.

"He didn't get a nap today because the social worker came by right when I was getting him into his crib," she said.

Joe guided Joshua's hand to the square hole. The cube dropped right in. "Yay," Joe said.

Joshua clapped his hands together and looked at Marcie. "Mama, look! I'n a good—I'n a smar' boy."

"Yes, you are," she said, sidling past Joe to bend down and plant a kiss on Joshua's cheek. "Mmm. You're a sweet boy, too."

"Swee' boy," he repeated.

Joe couldn't stop the stinging behind his eyelids any more than he could wipe away the grin that spread across his face. Marcie's gaze met his over Joshua's head and her eyes sparkled like they had when they were first married, and while she was pregnant, and every day after Joshua was born until—

"Joe?" Marcie interrupted his thoughts. "Would you mind feeding him while I finish getting dinner ready?"

"Sure. I'll feed him." He was amazed and delighted by his son. He hadn't gotten to spend much time with him at all. Several new cases had recently come into the NCMEC, so that by the time he'd gotten to the house on the few occasions when Marcie had invited him, Joshua had already been in bed or was just about to go. "What does he eat these days?"

"Anything he can get his hands on. Here," she said, handing Joe a bowl with cut-up pasta and cream sauce. "And here's his spoon. You don't really have to do anything but watch him to be sure he's eating and don't let him choke."

"Okay, buddy," Joe said. "How about some spaghetti? What is this anyway?" he asked Marcie. "It smells terrific." He stuck a finger into the pasta to test the temperature, then licked off the sauce. "It *is* terrific."

"It's fettuccini Alfredo with chicken," she said. "He hasn't had it before."

Joe set the bowl down in front of Joshua and handed him his spoon. It took about ten minutes for Joshua to finish the pasta and drink some juice from a sippy cup, after which Marcie cleaned his hands and face and took him upstairs to bed. Joe walked up the stairs with them and watched as she got him settled in his crib and patted him while she sang a short lullaby.

The homey scene that played out in front of Joe almost choked him up. He'd never cried, even as a kid. He'd learned early that Kit, his mother, didn't have any sympathy or time for a crying child and so he'd learned to lock those feelings up inside him. He'd cried more since his son was born than he'd ever cried as a child. He'd shed tears of joy the night his son was born, tears of anguish when Joshua was stolen, and he'd had to accept that his child would never be found. And for some reason, he kept having to fight the stinging in his eyes tonight.

It was probably because it was the first chance he'd gotten to see how smart and adorable Joshua was, and how happy Marcie was, now that she had her baby back. He leaned against the door facing of the nursery and let himself soak in the poignant, precious scene before him.

Just as Marcie's lullaby was over and she'd slowed down on patting Joshua, he stirred and whimpered. He opened his eyes and looked at Marcie, then he started crying and wailing.

"Gram-m-ma," he sobbed. "Where Gramma?" His

crying got louder and louder. Marcie kept on patting his tummy as she tried to reassure him.

"Joshua, it's Mama, baby. It's Mama. You're okay, Shh, shh, baby."

With a squeezing in his chest that threatened to cut off his breath, Joe backed out of the room and went downstairs. He sat at the dining room table and picked up the glass of white wine he hadn't finished.

He swirled the liquid around, following the reflection of the chandelier, but soon he set the glass down. He didn't want more wine. Instead, he got up and took the plates to the kitchen, where he rinsed them and put them into the dishwasher. He put the leftover pasta into the refrigerator and wiped down the stove and counters.

Then he stepped out through the French doors onto the patio. It was pleasantly warm and he could smell the gardenias that Marcie loved so much. He stood looking up at the sky through damp, hazy eyes.

It was so easy for the therapists to talk about reintegration of the kidnapped child back into the family unit, about time frames and usual patterns. He couldn't count how many times he'd sat in his office listening to a psychologist or a social worker giving him progress reports on reunited families. But all of that had very little to do with reality. Reality was a scared little boy who had twice been yanked away from the people who loved him.

He'd only been nine months old when Rhoda had stolen him. It was doubtful that Joshua would ever have a conscious memory of those first months with Marcie and him. Then, twenty months later, he'd been ripped from the arms of the only parent he remembered. His *Gramma.* There was no question that Joshua was better off away from Howard, but would he ever fully recover from the loss of his Gramma? Would he learn to think of Marcie as his mother? And would he get the chance to know Joe, in his role of estranged husband and weekend dad?

Marcie opened the French doors and stepped out onto the patio. She closed the doors behind her and hooked the baby monitor onto her belt.

Joe's head angled slightly when he heard her but he didn't turn around. She stepped up beside him.

Still without looking at her, Joe asked, "So did you get him back to sleep?"

"Yes. It took a while. I've got the baby monitor in case he wakes up again."

"Does that happen often?"

Marcie gave a short, wry laugh. "In my vast experience of twelve days with my son? Yes. It happens every night."

Joe cleared his throat. "He'll get over it. He already calls you Mama."

"And you *Daddeee!*" she said, mimicking Joshua's enthusiastic inflection.

Joe nodded.

Marcie frowned, studying him. The way he wasn't looking at her. The slight hoarseness in his voice. "Is something wrong?" she asked. Then an awful thought hit her, right under her breastbone. "Has Child Services contacted you? Is it something about Joshua?"

He shook his head.

"Then what?" she asked, laying a hand on his arm.

He turned his head, looking down at her hand, then lifted his gaze to hers. "I'm just—" He shrugged and cleared his throat again. When he spoke, his voice was odd, as if he were fighting some strong emotion. "It's one of those days, I guess. Seeing him playing and eating and…"

"I know. It's a miracle, isn't it? That we have him back? Sometimes I just look at him and I start crying. He's so perfect. So beautiful." She took a shaky breath. "And then I get this awful, terrified feeling right here." She pressed her palm to the center of her chest. "And I cry some more, because I'm afraid they're going to take him away from me—" She stopped. "From us."

Joe drew in a swift breath, then whirled and walked away to the other edge of the patio. "You had it right the first time. *From you.*"

"I didn't mean that, Joe," she said quickly, moving to stand beside him again. "He's your son. I would never take that away from you."

He rubbed his forehead. "What would you do, Marcie? When can I expect you to start enforcing your never-want-to-see-you-again policy? Because right now I feel like I'm in a particularly hellish limbo. My son is back in my life—on alternate Tuesdays when you decide that it's a convenient night for me to drop by in time to see him falling asleep. Thanks, by the way, for the half hour of playtime and feeding tonight."

His voice was so bitter, so angry, it took Marcie aback, and she realized that she had been so caught up in the all-day, every-day life of a mom and the miracle of having her child back, even if he didn't quite know who she was yet, that she'd completely neglected and ignored Joe's feelings.

She also realized that the question she'd been planning to ask him tonight wasn't going to happen. Her plan—her fantasy—had been that the two of them would come out onto the patio after dinner and have a pleasant, meaningful conversation about where their lives were going from here. They'd talk about being together for their child and Joe might say something about how expensive his apartment was, which would give Marcie the opening to suggest that he move back into the house.

But instead of being excited about how smart Joshua was and how cool it was to watch him feed himself, Joe had become angry.

"I'm sorry, Joe. I've handled all this badly."

He turned to face her. "No, you haven't. You're a wonderful mom. It's obvious Joshua already loves you."

She shook her head. "He loves *Gramma* and he thinks you are the best thing ever, *Daddeee!* To him, I'm just the nanny." To her dismay, her voice broke.

"You don't see it, but I do. He couldn't take his eyes off you while we were putting the square box in the tri-angular hole. He wanted you to see everything."

Marcie felt the breeze cool on her cheeks as it dried her tears. "I nearly went crazy when he was stolen." She chuckled wryly. "I know, understatement of the year. I know I blamed you. I know I was mean to you and I completely ignored that you had lost a child, too. I was

too sad and too broken to realize that I was destroying
the only person who could help me.

"Marcie—"

"Let me finish. I know now that you had to leave or
I would have totally destroyed you. As it is I've said
things that I know you can never forgive. But, Joe, if
you could try. If you could possibly forgive me—"

"Okay, that's enough," Joe snapped. "What is this?
Did the social worker tell you it's time to mend fences?
Well, it's not going to work. You forget that in my job
I hear all this. The psychologists and social workers
report to me, so I know that this is just about the time
in the reintegration process where the parent is told to
make amends."

"That's not—"

"Come on, Marc—"

"I love you!" Marcie shouted because that was the
only way she could think of to stop him. "I love you and
I want you here, with Joshua and me. Is that *amends*
enough for you?"

For a second, Joe stared at her with his mouth open.
In his eyes she could see a faint spark of hope. But in the
next second he'd thrown up that armor he'd developed
as a child growing up in strip clubs and never knowing who was going to be taking care of him. "Don't,
Marcie. Just don—"

She propelled herself at him and hit her target—his
mouth with her lips. It looked like the only way she was
going to knock him out of his cynical, disbelieving atti-
tude, was to kiss it out of him. And if that didn't work,

if she couldn't seduce her own husband, then she'd have to admit defeat.

At first, his lips didn't move. But he was affected. It didn't take her long to notice that he was becoming turned on. She kept on kissing him, using her tongue as she tried to tease his lips apart. She felt like a victorious warrior when he relented and she was able to explore the inside of his mouth. But then he lifted his head to look down at her and she felt her stomach drop to her toes. Was he going to stop her?

He didn't. What he did was pull her up against him and bend her head back and kiss her until she felt faint. Then he kissed her some more. Hard and deep and sensual. This was a promise and a threat, an awakening and an ending. It was overtly sexual and by the time it ended, Marcie's lungs were heaving with reaction and her body, all the way down to its core, was screaming for release.

Joe stopped suddenly, his own chest heaving, and eyed her as if she were some alien siren. "What are you doing?" he gasped.

"Trying to shut you up," she responded breathily.

"Shut me up?"

She nodded, feeling the tears begin to gather in her eyes. "Oh, I am so tired of crying," she muttered. "I was trying to say something, but you kept interrupting me."

He pressed his lips together. "Okay. Say what you wanted to say."

"Joe, I love you. I always have. Can you please forgive me? If not for me, for the sake of our baby? Joshua needs you, and not just on the days I can work up enough nerve to ask you to come over. He needs you every day, and so do I. I promise you that I will earn your trust again." She'd done it. She'd said her piece as simply and clearly as she could. Now it was up to him.

He didn't find it easy to trust, she knew. Especially women. His mother had seen to that. Marcie had fought for years to prove he could trust her, and then, after Joshua was taken, she'd proven to him that he couldn't. Now she had to start over.

As she watched, his mouth relaxed and the frown lines between his brows smoothed out. Her pulse pounded as she waited to hear what he was going to say.

"Marcie, I—" He took a breath. "You have my trust. And my heart. I want us to be a family again. I want us to be three again."

"Oh," Marcie said, noticing that tears were streaming down her cheeks again. "Hold me, Joe, and never, ever let me go."

Joe pulled her close and she tucked her head into her favorite place, the little hollow between his shoulder and head. He pressed his cheek against her hair. They stood that way for a long time. Finally, Joe took Marcie's hand and led her into the house and up the stairs to their bedroom.

Quite a while later, the two of them lay languid and satiated, on the bed in the master bedroom. Joe tightened his arm around Marcie and kissed the top of her head. "I love you, Marcie," he whispered.

She nodded. "I love you, too," she said in a small voice. "I never thought we'd be together again. I thought I'd lost my baby and my husband."

"Well, you haven't," Joe said. He pushed up in the bed and leaned back against the headboard, pulling Marcie with him. "And you never will again. Joshua and I are right here and we always will be. We're a family," he said. "We are three."

Marcie looked up at her husband. "You know what I'd like?" she asked.

He smiled down at her. "Tell me," he said.

"I'd like it if we were four."

Joe's smile widened into a huge grin. "You would?"

She bit her lip as she nodded. Her eyes sparkled like diamonds. "Want to start now?"

Joe bent his head and caught her mouth in a long, deep kiss. "Absolutely," he muttered.

* * * * *

A sneaky peek at next month…

INTRIGUE…

BREATHTAKING ROMANTIC SUSPENSE

My wish list for next month's titles…

In stores from 17th January 2014:

❏ Undercover Captor – Cynthia Eden

& Rocky Mountain Revenge – Cindi Myers

❏ Blood on Copperhead Trail – Paula Graves

& Rancher Rescue – Barb Han

❏ Tennessee Takedown – Lena Diaz

& Raven's Hollow – Jenna Ryan

Romantic Suspense

❏ Cavanaugh Hero – Marie Ferrarella

Available at WHSmith, Tesco, Asda, Eason, Amazon and Apple

Just can't wait?

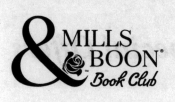

Discover more romance at

www.millsandboon.co.uk

- ❤ WIN great prizes in our exclusive competitions

- ❤ BUY new titles before they hit the shops

- ❤ BROWSE new books and REVIEW your favourites

- ❤ SAVE on new books with the Mills & Boon® Bookclub™

- ❤ DISCOVER new authors

PLUS, to chat about your favourite reads, get the latest news and find special offers:

- 🔲 Find us on facebook.com/millsandboon

- 🔹 Follow us on twitter.com/millsandboonuk

- ❤ Sign up to our newsletter at millsandboon.co.uk

The World of Mills & Boon®

There's a Mills & Boon® series that's perfect for you. We publish ten series and, with new titles every month, you never have to wait long for your favourite to come along.

Blaze.
Scorching hot, sexy reads
4 new stories every month

By Request
Relive the romance with the best of the best
9 new stories every month

Cherish™
Romance to melt the heart every time
12 new stories every month

Desire™
Passionate and dramatic love stories
8 new stories every month